Belcarron

Belcarron

Anna Macklan

PIATKUS

First published in Great Britain in 1994 by
Judy Piatkus (Publishers) Ltd of
5 Windmill Street, London W1P 1HF

**The moral right of the author
has been asserted**

*A catalogue record for this book is available
from the British Library*

ISBN 0–7499–0266–3

Set in 11/12 pt Times by
Datix International Limited, Bungay, Suffolk
Printed and bound in Great Britain by
Butler & Tanner Ltd, Frome and London

Prologue

Wintour People

The first Belcarron went up in flames in 1751. A servant girl's dropped candle, it was said; it might just as well have been a lighted torch from the village. Those times, like most times in Ireland, were troubled. No one knew the truth of it.

John Wintour, a yeoman farmer from Dorsetshire, had built the house in Cromwell's time. After service to the Lord Protector in the Civil War, he had been rewarded with Fitzallan land, which he had been lucky enough to keep after the restoration of Charles II to the throne. Not all the Irish land confiscated by Cromwell was returned, and in any case Padraig Fitzallan was dead of the plague in Spain by 1660 and left no descendants. So John kept his house and kept his land and it was his grandson, Richard, who lost Belcarron to the fire a century later. He began at once on plans for another.

Six years later, the new house rose from the ashes, a Georgian phoenix of lime-washed walls and straight-sashed windows, standing foursquare at the end of the village of Carron, overlooking the sea. By that time, Richard was dead and it was another John who, after many delays, saw the house completed and took possession. When his wife Kate first saw him walking on his lawn above the Atlantic, she burst out laughing and said he looked like a peacock. At which he flung back his yellow hair and said it was true, he felt as proud. He was fourth-generation gentry and had a house that matched his state; he had reason to be proud.

Just so had that first John, the Dorset yeoman, felt proud, when he started his family on the road to quality in their new life in Ireland. He too had a yellow head, which he did not trouble with the rights and wrongs of the Irish question. He would simply do his best for his tenants and his religion, ride to hounds, keep a good table, bring up his children to be God-fearing and marry well. What more could a Protestant gentleman do? For by then, of course, John saw himself as a gentleman and his wife Anne as a lady, and every night on his knees he thanked God that He had disposed things so, while dark-haired Anne lay in bed with her hands clasped, waiting her husband's pleasure.

There was never any formal entail on the Belcarron estate. Eldest son inherited from eldest son through the will of the father alone, with younger sons entering the professions and daughters marrying as well as possible. The old Dorset branch of the family died out but in 1853 a Matthew Wintour took Anglican holy orders and returned to the village of his forebears, first as curate, then as vicar. He no longer wanted to live in Ireland, he said, he had been too much affected by the sufferings of the people during the years of the great famines; in fact, he was not alone in that. It was true that the Wintours were Protestants, members of the ruling class, the Ascendancy as it came to be called, and so on a different side from the peasants. But in hunger they saw there could be no sides. They did what they could.

'It must have been God's will,' Richard, Matthew's father, said to his wife Maria. 'But should it have been allowed to happen, all the same?'

''Tis not for us to question,' Maria answered, but she thought of the children dying, the parents following, she thought of the great burial mounds at Skibbereen, and she wondered.

Matthew's elder brother, John, was the conventional one of the family. Apart from a mild interest in horse racing which he had developed at university in Dublin, he was content to spend his time helping to run the estate. This was of some consolation to his parents when in 1854 his sister, a green-eyed devil of a girl, took herself off to see the world and married a Catholic rancher of Spanish descent in the Argentine. For a time, Belcarron rocked. Then it righted itself. As they had all seen in the famine years, God moved in

4

a mysterious way, and no doubt if there was a pattern in what He did, it would be revealed. Beatrice was forgiven and when her father died in 1860 it was with no regrets. He told John in his last illness he believed he had always done his duty, shown Christian forbearance where necessary and looked after his tenants. He charged John to do the same, to take care of his mother and of Belcarron, and John, newly married to the former Miss Ernestine Wills, promised that he would.

Four children were born to John and Ernestine at Belcarron. Two boys, John and Matthew, and two girls, Alice and Charlotte. For a time as a family they were idyllically happy. Then in 1868 measles took the lives of both boys. Ernestine became a little strange, she had no more children, and as the years went by John came to realise that there was to be no male heir for Belcarron.

In the summer of 1885, Richard, Matthew's son, asked if he and his sisters, Hester and Marianne, might come on a long visit from Dorset. John showed the letter to his wife.

'Oh certainly!' Ernestine cried, attacking her latest canvas with energy (painting had been her only interest for some years). 'They will be most welcome.'

'Most welcome,' John agreed. He thought of his elder daughter, who was dark, and of his younger daughter, who was fair, and it occurred to him to wonder, 'Which one is Richard after?'

Part I
1885

One

When their English cousins came to Belcarron in June 1885, Alice Wintour was twenty years old and her sister, Charlotte, two years younger. Alice was usually considered the prettier, with the straight Wintour nose and her mother's rich dark hair, but it was Charlotte of the yellow mane and bumpy nose whose card was always filled first at dances and who might receive the first 'offers', too, which would be humiliating in the extreme for Alice. Of course, if it were to be known she was to inherit Belcarron, things would be different, but she did not know if she was to inherit Belcarron, her father had never said. Sometimes she thought he might be considering leaving it to Richard and at that she felt mysteriously excited, not aggrieved, and her heart would bound and her pulse race, which was of course absurd. She had not seen him since she was fifteen when she had been so shy she could scarcely look at him and he had been three years older, tall and gangling and still rather spotty. His hair, she remembered, was as yellow as Charlotte's and he had a trick of flinging it back the way Charlotte did, when hers was not 'up', but no one could say he looked in any other way like Charlotte, he was much, much better-looking. His nose, for instance, was the Wintour nose, as straight as Alice's own.

It was Alice who had prepared the house for the visitors. At least, to the best of her ability she had instructed the maids, Nora Ryan and Philomena Donovan, what to do, and Mrs Heenan what to cook, for there was no housekeeper these days and Ernestine Wintour was quite useless when it came to matters not concerning her paints and sketching blocks. Everywhere one went in the house one met brushes soaking in jars of water and paint rags lying on the floor and canvases stacked and sliding, so that one never knew where to put one's feet.

'I declare, Mama seems to live only in a world of paint,' Alice remarked to her sister. Charlotte only gave a lazy smile and said that if she found that pleasanter than the real world, why should they complain?

Both sisters knew, having been told by their Aunt Clara, now dead, that their mother had never been the 'same' since the death of their young brothers.

'The same as what?' Charlotte had asked.

'As she used to be, of course. As herself.'

'It's a long time not to be oneself, isn't it?'

'It was the shock of losing them both, you see, it was more than she could stand.'

'She still had us.'

'And God knows, my dear, you've been her comfort, of course you have.'

'But not enough of a comfort,' Alice had said sadly, knowing that she was putting into words something she should have kept secret.

'More than enough!' Aunt Clara had loyally cried. 'More than enough, my dears!'

They had known it was not true.

If their mother was of no practical help to them, their father was not a great deal better. Of late, he had become very despondent, talking continually of difficulties with the rents, of Gladstone's Land Act, of Charles Stewart Parnell. Things were not what they were, would never be again, he could no longer afford to go racing and all he had in his stable was two second-rate hunters and a pony for the trap – and how long he would be able to keep even the second-rate hunters, he did not know. If he had been a drinking man, he might have sought solace in whiskey, but John Wintour had never been a drinking man and found solace in nothing. Alice said she worried about Papa.

'All he needs is money,' said Charlotte. 'We can't do much about that. Unless, of course, we were to make good marriages.'

Something in her sister's tone made Alice look at her sharply. 'You've met someone?'

'Where should I have met anyone?'

'You were visiting at Castle Morry recently.'

'The Morry family hasn't a bean. You should have seen what Kitty and Edie were wearing. It was the same when we were at school, they were always dressed like scarecrows.'

'I'll bet you played up to their brother, all the same,' Alice said curtly, and Charlotte laughed.

'Cavan? He talked of no one but you, Alice – no, I promise you, it's true.'

'Oh, tush!' Alice bit her lip. Only a little time ago, she would have been excited by Charlotte's gossip, would have been buoyed up at the thought of an admirer, but now with the coming of Richard so near, she could take no interest. They should get on, she muttered, if they wanted Belcarron to look its best for the visitors.

'For Richard, you mean. He's not coming to see Belcarron, he's coming to see you.'

'Last time, I seem to remember he was very taken with you.'

'When I was thirteen? How absurd. I had to spend all my time with bluestocking Hester and boring Marianne, while you went riding with Richard all on your own. I was so envious!'

As Charlotte sat retying the dark-blue ribbon in her yellow hair, Alice studied her, wondering again at her sister's seeming attraction for others – for men. She wasn't particularly pretty and her figure was no better than Alice's, if as good. So what was it men saw? Perhaps it was something they felt rather than saw, something to do with – Alice hesitated before shaping the word in her mind – love. Love, or love-making. Yes, she was sure she was right, for Charlotte had always been so forward in those matters, for ever questioning the maids in corners, although what they had whispered sounded so ridiculous to Alice that she had at first refused to believe it.

But could it be, she wondered now, that Charlotte had within her the possible character of a 'fast' woman? It had been said that Aunt Beatrice, who had married a papist in

11

the Argentine, had had leanings that way and Charlotte was her niece. But then so am I, thought Alice, and smiled and tried to clear her mind as Charlotte yawned and stretched and asked if it wasn't typical Marianne should get herself engaged to Uncle Matthew's curate.

'Why, who says she is engaged?'

'Papa told me there was talk of it in a letter he'd had. The possibility of an offer, anyway, and I suppose Marianne will accept. She is not likely to get a better, is she?'

'But Hester is the elder,' Alice said, worriedly. 'Marianne should not marry before Hester, you know.'

'You must be sure to accept Richard, then, so that I don't have to wait for *you*,' Charlotte replied, with a sweet smile. Alice flushing, swept back her bustled skirts and sailed out of the room.

Philomena Donovan, always known as Mena and the younger of the two Belcarron maids, was everyone's idea of a pretty Irish colleen. She had the blue eyes 'put in with a sooty finger', the black hair, the pink cheeks, and was also, Alice found, willing. Unlike Nora, the ginger-haired parlourmaid, who was known not to be too fond of work.

'Will you look at me hands, Miss Alice?' she wailed now. 'Red as a boiled lobster with all this scrubbing.' Which she claimed was not her job either, seeing as she was the one who did the waiting on, and wasn't she thinking Miss Alice should be calling in them Donovans from the village to do all this rough, instead of a proper parlourmaid such as herself, then?

'Who are you calling *them* Donovans?' Mena cried spiritedly. 'If it's me ma you're meaning, Nora Ryan, it's me hand you'll be feeling, red or not, am I not telling you?'

'And isn't it a Donovan your ma is, then?' Nora shouted back. 'And isn't it the cleaning she does, then? So where's the harm in saying?'

'Please be quiet, both of you!' Alice shook her finger at them. 'You know I won't have this kind of bickering. Nora, perhaps you're right, I should have tried to find some extra help. Mena, could your mother come in, do you think?'

Mena sniffed, her face still scarlet, her blue eyes snapping.

'I can be asking me Auntie Bridget, Miss Alice, if it's what you're wanting, but Ma's got enough to do cleaning for Father O'Mara, so she has, without coming here to be insulted by the likes of Nora Ryan!'

At which Nora turned and stamped away, saying over her shoulder she would be sorting out the linen if Miss Alice wanted her.

'As though the beds is not already made up!' Mena cried after her, then asked Alice softly if she wouldn't like to see the rooms made ready for the young English quality.

As Alice led the way up the graceful staircase, she felt the atmosphere of the house soothing her, as it always could, for there was between her and Belcarron a special rapport that was hers and no one else's. One day she might have to leave it, she knew, but she could not imagine any reason for doing so, unless – the thought persisted – it should become Richard's.

She paused at the long landing window to look down on the lawns at the back of the house and the ragged trees and wild fuchsias of the cliff path bending in the wind. The pale line of the sea was scarcely visible today in the hazy summer light, yet sometimes she had stood here and watched great rollers beating in and heard the gales roaring and tearing and had felt no fear, only joy that this was her home and she was part of it. So why did the idea of Richard's taking it from her not fill her full of dread? Belcarron should be hers, morally and legally, but if it were Richard's, it would be – the word trembled on her lips –

'Ours,' she whispered, and smiled, as Mena behind her shifted from one foot to the other, impatient to get on and show the mistress what she had done.

All the principal rooms at Belcarron faced the back of the house and the sea, but the guest rooms, the two small parlours and the hall faced the grounds at the front and the drive that led to the road and the village. Alice would have willingly sacrificed her own room so that Richard might have her splendid view of the sea, but of course that would not have been seemly. The English cousins had therefore all been given rooms at the front of the house. Pleasant enough rooms, in any case, with fine plasterworked chimneypieces

13

(which, thank God, they would not need in June, for they smoked like the devil) and four-poster beds made up with the best linen sheets, lavender-scented, and mahogany dressing chests where on the day of arrival Alice planned to put flowers.

'Why, Mena,' she exclaimed, walking soft-footedly round the room that was to be Richard's, 'it's beautiful! You've done well, really well.'

Mena blushed and looked down. 'Nora was after doin' the young ladies' rooms, but I did this one meself. And isn't it the best, Miss Alice, though I says so?'

She watched from lowered lashes as Alice moved to the bed and trailed her fingers across the white pillows, plumping and straightening, still half smiling.

'You don't remember Mr Richard, do you, Mena?' Alice murmured, not looking at her. 'You were too young to be here when he came before.'

'I've never seen him, Miss Alice, but cook says he's fine and handsome and his hair's as yellow as Miss Charlotte's.'

Alice at once stood up from the bed. 'That colour of hair is in the family,' she said coldly. 'There is no real likeness between Mr Richard and Miss Charlotte.'

'Oh, no, Miss Alice,' Mena agreed eagerly. 'And sure I never said so!'

After that, Alice briefly looked in at the rooms prepared by Nora for Hester and Marianne, but neither she nor Mena felt the same interest.

'I must get on,' Alice said. 'I still have a great many things to see to. In only three days' time, my cousins will be here.'

She closed the doors of the waiting guest rooms and went downstairs again, her skirt trailing behind her, step by step.

14

Two

They had been travelling so long, they felt as weary as though they had crossed India. Hinton Borne – Yeovil – Bristol – Fishguard – Rosslare – Cork – pony trap – train – steamer – hotel – train again . . . Were they never to arrive? This last little stopping train to Kilvane, the nearest station to Belcarron, seemed slowest of all and the second-class carriage occupied only by the three of them was the hottest and dustiest and perhaps the reason India had come to their minds. But at least when they looked out of the windows, they could see green.

Hester Wintour, who had unpinned her hat and even let down her pale brown hair, sat gazing out at the passing landscape of small fields and distant hills with a thoughtful, almost sombre expression. She was twenty-one years old, not pretty – her face would always be considered too long for that – but her fine dark eyes were intelligent and her mouth generous and sweet. Occasionally, as she gazed, she fanned herself with dark-blue gloves that matched her creased travelling dress and pressed a handkerchief soaked in cologne to her brow.

'I do think, Hester,' her sister Marianne remarked after a time, 'that you should put up your hair. Supposing someone gets in at the next station?'

'Well? Supposing they do?'

Marianne, whose face was also a little long but whose eyes were an innocent blue, looked shocked. 'Why, whatever would they think, to see a grown woman with her hair down?'

'They might think she was hot and tired and in need of a rest. The last thing I expected to find in Ireland was a heat wave.'

'Don't worry,' said Richard Wintour, from the opposite seat. 'It'll probably be raining tomorrow.'

'Rain would be more appropriate.' Hester moved her head wearily and touched her brow again with her handkerchief. 'Oh, don't you feel depressed in this country? I seem to remember feeling it when I came before – other people's misery – it was like a load pressing one down.'

'I can't say I ever felt that,' said Richard.

'Nor I,' said Marianne. 'And poor people are miserable everywhere, Hester, not just in Ireland.'

'I'm not talking about poverty. What one feels here – I can't really explain it – goes much deeper ... ' Hester suddenly sat up and began to wind and twist her hair back into place on her neck and with skilful fingers pinned it into a knot. 'There, Marianne, I'm respectable again. I think perhaps we may soon be arriving.'

'One more station,' said Richard. 'I say, Hester, you're not sorry you came, are you? I mean, you wanted to see Belcarron again, didn't you?'

'Of course.' She gave a sharp, quick smile. 'But you didn't really need Marianne and me, did you? To propose to Alice?'

Richard, sitting back against the dusty railway upholstery, laughed aloud. He too had taken off his hat and the afternoon sunlight streaming into the carriage had turned his hair and moustache to gold. Not for the first time, his sisters (even Hester, who did not care overmuch about appearances) were moved to note with envy his almost extravagant good looks, for if they were not bad-looking themselves, not bad is not good, either, and it did seem hard that their brother should have been given all the beauty. Hester looked back at the landscape, letting a little frown settle between her brows, while Marianne sighed and thought of Everard Lister, her father's curate, who had almost proposed, then fell to wondering if Alice and Charlotte would be much changed. Alice would probably be enchantingly pretty by now and Charlotte would still be flaunting her yellow hair and playing her usual tricks. Eighteen was different from thirteen, but Marianne

16

had no illusions. Charlotte might not now make apple-pie beds but she would have found other ways to tease, her sort always did –

'What makes you think I am going to propose to Alice?' Richard asked lazily. 'Have I ever said so?' ·

'You don't need to,' Hester replied. 'It's quite obvious what is in your mind. Alice is to inherit Belcarron, she's the nearest thing to an heiress you'll ever find, and you've decided to marry her quickly before someone else does. If she'll have you.'

'It's true, I'm no catch. A poor vicar's son, an Oxford man without prospects.' Richard shrugged, but there was a strangely amused glint in his eye. 'What hope have I got except Alice?'

'I wonder.' Hester studied him suspiciously. 'Something seems to be making you smile. What's the joke?'

'He looks as though he has a secret,' Marianne observed. 'We know that look, don't we, Hester?'

'No secret, I assure you. I'm just teasing you, that's all. I like to, don't I? That's something else you know.'

'If you do propose to Alice,' Hester said, after a pause, 'I know it's what Papa would like.'

'We are first cousins, remember.'

'So? There are no illnesses in the family. Cousins often marry cousins. And Uncle John is not very fit, Papa thinks. He may be worrying about the estate, he may be wanting to see things settled.'

'With all this Land Act business, the estate may not be worth as much as we think. The tenants have taken to not paying their rents. They go by this fellow Parnell, and he's obviously set to make trouble.'

'Whatever happens, Belcarron will still be Belcarron.'

'But is Alice definitely to inherit? I don't believe it's ever been made plain.'

'And isn't that why you're coming over? To find out?'

Richard took out his watch. 'One more station and then Kilvane. Perhaps we should be getting our bags together.'

John Wintour had ridden over to meet them and to escort the trap, driven by his groom, Daniel Molloy, back to

17

Belcarron. As they alighted at the little platform of Kilvane, smoothing down their creased clothes, trying to collect themselves, he came up to greet them, kissing his nieces, shaking Richard's hand, exclaiming on the changes in their looks since they had last met.

'Why, Hester, Marianne – you've become fine ladies! Where are those little girls I used to know? And Richard, you're the image of your father. I can see my brother Matt, standing in your shoes!'

Richard said: 'You're looking very well yourself, Uncle.'

That was not in fact true. John Wintour looked thin and grey, older than his fifty-eight years. As he led the way out to the trap, he admitted he had worries. Ireland wasn't what it had been, might never be again the country the Wintours loved, at least if Gladstone had his way. As for Charles Stewart Parnell – they had heard of Parnell? So-called champion of the people? Words could not express the damage he had done, and he a Protestant and a landowner himself, could they believe it?

Daniel Molloy, a tall, heavy-shouldered young man with thick black hair and strong fleshy features, stood impassively by as his master declaimed on the Irish political scene, but Hester thought she detected something in his hard blue eyes that made her shrink from his hand when he helped her into the trap. On the slightest of evidence – that fleeting expression – she found herself wondering if he might be a Fenian, one of the Irish Republican Brotherhood committed to getting the English out of Ireland. As she watched him stowing away their luggage, she tried to tell herself that such ideas were absurd, her uncle would never employ such a man. But then, how would her uncle necessarily know?

'Richard,' she heard Marianne plaintively asking, 'what *is* the Land Act?'

'Marianne, Marianne, don't you ever read the newspapers?' Richard clicked his tongue in reproof. 'You should try to be more like Hester. She reads the papers, she likes to be well informed. Ask Hester about the Land Act.'

'It was passed in 1881,' Hester said sharply, irritated by his patronising tone. 'Marianne was still with Miss Venables then.'

18

'So? An English governess might just possibly have taught her something of what was happening in Ireland. Especially a law that would take away the power of English landlords.'

Hester, with some anxiety, watched Molloy take up the reins and set the pony on the way; she wondered if he could hear them and thought surely he could.

'It does not take away the power of the landlords,' she said clearly. 'Only gives certain safeguards to the tenants, which you must admit they should have.'

'The three F's?' asked Richard. 'Depends how far they go.'

'Fair rents, fixity of tenure, free sale.' Hester was still keeping her eyes on Molloy. 'I don't think those demands are unreasonable, if you look at things from the tenants' point of view.'

Richard laughed. He said, as a possible future landlord, he did not feel disposed to look at things from the tenants' point of view.

The back of Molloy's neck went red.

'But surely, Richard, you would be fair!' Marianne cried.

'Of course. We Wintours have always been fair. I'm sure Uncle John's tenants would be the first to agree.'

For no obvious reason, the pony, which had been stepping quietly through the narrow lanes lined with encroaching fuchsia and honeysuckle, suddenly quickened pace and began to draw the trap forward at an alarming rate. Marianne cried out and Hester closed her eyes.

'Here, steady on!' Richard cried. 'You – what's your name, Molloy? – slow down, will you? You're frightening the ladies!'

'Sorry, sir,' the groom answered, without turning his head, and within minutes the pony was quiet again and the trap back to normal speed.

'What happened?' asked Marianne, trembling. 'Did something frighten the pony?'

'I believe he did,' Richard whispered. 'I believe he whipped her up, I don't know why. Did you see, Hester?'

'No, I didn't see anything. But I don't think he used the whip.'

Her heart was beating fast, her face very pale. Although Molloy had not used the whip, he had in some way communi-

19

cated his anger to the pony, which had responded in fear. He had done it deliberately to frighten them, because they were English and he hated the English, yes, she could tell, he hated them, the three of them in his trap. She could feel his hatred flowing towards them from the back of his black head like a blast from a furnace, and she shivered in its heat.

'Where is Uncle John?' Marianne cried shrilly. 'He was supposed to be escorting us, he should be with us!'

'He's ahead.' Richard screwed up his eyes in the sunlight. 'I can see him, he's waiting at the bend of the road. We must be almost at the village.'

They were very close to the sea now, could smell the salt wind and see the gulls wheeling; the light was piercingly clear. When they caught up with John Wintour at the turn of the road, the village of Carron lay ahead.

'Remember it?' he asked, bending from his horse. 'Hasn't changed much. Drive slowly, Daniel, let the visitors see Carron again.'

There was not a great deal to see. A dusty street, lined on one side with grey-white cottages, on the other, a sea wall. Old men leaning against the wall, looking out at a little harbour, a jetty, a few fishing boats too decrepit now to go out. Two public houses, closed; a tiny shop, open; barefoot children playing, women gossiping, an atmosphere of quiet but not of peace.

The arrival of the trap and the sight of John Wintour on his horse caused some slight interest. One or two of the women bobbed a curtsy, an old man waved to Daniel Molloy, and children began to run by the wheels of the trap until John threw a handful of pennies and they scattered.

'I can't really remember it at all,' said Marianne. 'Can you, Hester?'

Not looking at the back of the groom's head, Hester answered carefully: 'I don't remember its being so poor.'

'Well, Hinton Borne is not so well-to-do,' Richard muttered, pulling uneasily on his moustache. 'A bit more colourful, perhaps.'

'Yes, I agree, that's what's wrong. Look at the fields beyond the cottages – they're so green, and the sea is so blue. But the villages here – the people – are grey, aren't they?'

20

'I dare say Uncle John does his best for them, but what can he do if he can't get his rents?'

They were silent as the trap followed John Wintour out of the village. He turned back, pointing with his whip to a large, Gothic-style church.

'That's St John's, where we worship,' he called. 'It's Church of Ireland.'

'Where is the Catholic church?' asked Hester, but John was riding on and did not hear.

'Two miles back,' Molloy said suddenly, over his shoulder.

'Two miles back?'

'Is what I'm tellin' you. Two miles the Catholics walk to Mass and two miles back.' He laughed. 'And St John's is empty.'

'Perhaps we could move on to Belcarron?' Richard asked, tight-lipped, and the groom nodded.

'There it is, then, sir, there's your Belcarron.'

Their Belcarron. So it was. Another world, their world, and desirable. Only a square white Georgian house set against a background of sky and sea, but they could not wait to reach it, and leave the village behind.

Alice and Charlotte in light dresses were waiting to greet them as the trap halted at the central portico. Molloy, after some hesitation, got down and began carrying their luggage into the hall. He left it to Richard to give his hand to his sisters, for which Hester at least was truly grateful.

21

Three

As Marianne had guessed, Alice, even in plain white muslin, was enchanting, but she seemed shy, even nervous, as she greeted them, and when Richard stooped to brush her cheek with his lips, she blushed like a schoolgirl. Charlotte, by contrast, was quite at her ease, her narrow eyes sliding over them, taking in, her cousins felt, every crease, every travel stain, and when Richard kissed her, she flung back her yellow hair (which she had not troubled to put up) and kissed him back.

'How lovely to have a handsome cousin around again!' she said teasingly. 'I'm sorry to advise you, girls, that the men around this part of the world absolutely do not measure up to your brother.'

'Charlotte,' her father said irritably, 'don't be playing the fool now. Help your sister show your cousins their rooms. Daniel, take my horse, will you?'

'If you please, sir, I've the trap to be seein' to, first,' the groom answered. Although what he said was true, Hester felt his delight at being able to refuse her uncle a service and was sure again that she was right to be afraid. As soon as she had an opportunity, she decided, she would mention his behaviour on the drive; she would let it be known what sort of man was in her uncle's employ.

'Where is Aunt Ernestine?' she asked Alice, as they entered the elegant hall and stood looking up at the high plaster ceiling and the curving staircase.

'Mama is resting,' Alice said quickly. 'But she will be down directly, she's so looking forward to seeing you again.

23

Come, let me show you your rooms. We thought, as it's so fine, we might have tea in the garden – usually the wind is too strong. But do say if you'd rather rest.'

The cousins said they would not rest, they no longer felt tired and would adore to have tea in the garden, once they had washed and changed.

'The maids will bring hot water, then, as soon as they have taken up your things.'

Hester found her room quite charming and said so.

'See, you've even put flowers on my table – how kind, Alice! I can't tell you how glad we are to be here at last.'

'Was the journey too awful?' Alice was edging a little towards the door. She could hear Richard's voice outside and knew that Charlotte was with him. 'Will you excuse me, Hester? I must just instruct the maids . . . '

'Of course.' Hester was unbuttoning her short jacket. 'But could I first ask you, Alice, I promise I won't keep you, but that groom of yours – Molloy, is it? Daniel Molloy?'

'Daniel, yes, what of him?'

'Do you trust him?'

'Trust him? In what way?'

'Well, I mean, is he loyal? He seemed so odd, so rough, and let the trap go at such a rate at one point, we thought we should all be thrown out. I wondered if he might be – you know – a Fenian?'

'A Fenian?' Alice burst into laughter. 'Daniel? Of course he's not, Hester, what a notion! You've been reading too many English papers. The Irish are not all rebels and murderers, you know.'

'I think I know a little bit about the Irish question, Alice,' Hester replied stiffly. 'Fenians are Irish Republicans, that's all; they want Home Rule, they want the English out. From your groom's attitude towards us, I should say he could easily qualify.'

'I'm sorry if he was rude to you, Hester. I'll speak to Papa at once, that sort of thing must not be tolerated – '

'No, it's all right, please don't say anything.' Hester turned as Mena came staggering in with a brass can of hot water. 'I shouldn't like to get him into trouble or anything. I just thought I'd ask, that's all, if you were sure – '

24

'We are quite sure. I dare say it was only his manner. Now, if there's anything else you need, you must just ask Mena here.'

At last, Alice was able to escape and see to Richard. It would not be improper, would it, to knock on his door and enter his room on this first occasion when she was by way of being hostess? Really, this should all have been Mama's duty but, as she had still not appeared, surely it would be all right if . . .

Very gently, Alice knocked at the door of the room she had given Richard and called to him: 'May I come in? Richard, have you everything you need?'

'Oh, I think so,' Charlotte answered, appearing in the doorway. 'I think he has all he needs – probably more.'

'But I can't get her to unpack for me.' Richard, behind her, dropped his hands lightly to her shoulders and left them there for what seemed to Alice an eternity, then lifted them and gave her a little push away from him. 'What a hard-hearted girl she is, is she not, Alice? But she's been taking care of me very well.'

'And Marianne?' Alice asked coldly. 'Have you been taking care of her, too, Charlotte?'

'No, she's been neglecting poor Marianne for me, I'm afraid,' said Richard. 'So, off you go, Charlotte – I want to talk to your big sister.'

'Don't talk too long,' she called over her shoulder, as she drifted languidly away. 'We shall be waiting tea for you.'

'That's true,' Alice murmured. 'You will want to change, Richard, I mustn't delay you – '

'Oh, come, we must have a moment to greet each other.' He drew her quietly over the threshold of his room. 'I want to tell you how glad I am to see you again, Alice. I've thought of you, you know, so much.'

'Have you? You did say you would write.' She laughed nervously. 'But that was five years ago, of course – we were only children then.'

'Children? I seem to remember I was going up to the 'varsity. And didn't you say you would write to me?'

'You knew I could not write first.'

'My fault, then. I'm sorry.' His eyes searched her face.

'You've changed,' he said softly. 'If you were a child five years ago, you are not a child now.'

He bent his head. His face was very close and she could almost feel his mouth seeking hers, but she moved instantly away, feeling for the handle of the door behind her and opening it.

'We have all changed,' she said breathlessly. 'I must go, Richard. Mama has not been well . . . I have to see to the maids . . . '

'Of course, please forgive me. I had no idea Aunt Ernestine was ill. If there's anything I can do – '

'It's not that she is actually ill . . . Oh, look, I'll see you at tea, Richard . . . '

'Alice, I'll look forward to it.'

In order to avoid meeting anyone, Alice ran swiftly down the back stairs that led to the kitchen regions. She felt strange, foolish, as though she had been offered something she wanted and had dashed it away. He would have kissed me in there, she thought wildly. In his room, I'm sure of it, he wanted to – so he must be going to propose. Dear Lord, I can't believe it! Richard loves me . . . And I love him, I know that now, I've loved him since I was a child. She put her hand to her breast to feel her heart's thumping, and thought of her parents and their pleasure, for Richard was a Wintour, she would be marrying a Wintour, they would look after Belcarron together . . .

Her whole body was trembling now, her face as hot and stretched as though she had a fever. As she stood in the flagged passage that led to the outer door, she could hear the clink of china from the kitchen and the murmur of voices: Nora's and Mrs Heenan's, and the deeper sound of Daniel Molloy – the Fenian. Oh, what a joke! But what should she do now? She couldn't let the servants see her like this, for she felt as vulnerable as though she were naked, as though her love for Richard were written all over her for everyone to read, and it was private, private, just for a while, for herself alone. If only she had some water to cool her face, she might achieve some sort of command . . .

Suddenly the heavy door of the kitchen opened and Daniel Molloy stood in front of her. The passageway was shadowy, she could not see his face clearly, but he seemed unsurprised at finding her there, seemed to notice nothing unusual, and after he had stepped aside to let her pass, she took courage and walked into the kitchen, confident now that no one would see anything they were not expecting to see.

'Is everything ready for tea, Mrs Heenan?'

'Yes, Miss Alice.' The cook's heavy, soft-featured face was scarlet as she turned out a batch of soda scones on to a tea towel. 'Hasn't Nora the cucumber samiches already on the table and the pound cake and the jam?'

'Mena's taking the chairs an' all,' Nora said. 'So it's only the kettle to boil and a grand tea ye'll be having.'

'Thank you, that's fine, really fine. Has . . . has anyone seen the mistress?'

'She's given up the painting, Miss Alice, she's ready and waiting out on the lawn.'

'I'd better join her, then. Serve tea as soon as the guests are down, will you, Nora?'

'Yes, Miss Alice.' The maid's small, hazel eyes flickered over Alice's face. 'Is it the heat you're feeling?' she asked, without interest. 'Is it a glass o' water you're wanting? You're terrible red in your face.'

The late afternoon was warm on the lawn and uncannily still. Such days were rare at Belcarron, John Wintour told his guests at the tea table, they must make the most of it. Tomorrow might bring a howling gale when they would all have to run for cover. On the other hand, of course, such weather as this was no good for fishing, but no doubt Richard would be wanting to take a boat out as soon as possible. He could take his pick what he went for, around here there was everything; plaice, sole, turbot, mackerel – the locals went mainly for the mackerel – then, of course, they also had their lobster –

'Oh, we'll be going boating, Papa,' Charlotte interrupted, 'but not just for fish. We mustn't just think of Richard, you know. Hester and Marianne must be entertained, too.'

'Entertained?' Marianne echoed. 'We don't expect to be entertained, Charlotte. We are perfectly happy just to be here with you.'

27

'How graceful, Marianne, but we've already arranged all kinds of things for you, haven't we, Alice? From picnics to croquet to a grand ball. Well, we didn't exactly arrange that, we were invited by the Fitzmirrans, who said you must come too.'

A ball . . . Hester and Marianne exchanged glances.

'I'm not sure we shall have anything suitable to wear,' Hester said, after a pause. 'Naturally, we have our evening clothes, but if it's to be a very smart affair – '

'They will do perfectly, don't worry about it. You're not in London now.'

'We never are,' said Marianne. 'But surely Anglo-Irish society can be very smart, Charlotte? Surely some of the families are titled? And great landowners?'

'Irish titles, Irish land.' Charlotte shrugged. 'Oh, I suppose there's still grandeur in Dublin, but we don't see much of it. Do you know, we haven't even been presented? It's too bad, isn't it, for we should have been. Aunt Clara was to have arranged it, of course, Mama couldn't do anything, but then Aunt Clara died, so here we are, unpresented. No hope of good marriages for us, I'm afraid.'

'Charlotte, please,' her father muttered. 'You are embarrassing us all.'

'As you so often do,' Alice murmured. She dared not look at Richard, had scarcely looked at him at all since he had come down for tea, and now she was too ashamed. Really Charlotte was too bad, the worst of it being one never knew if she was being serious or not.

'Would anyone mind if I excused myself to do a little sketching?' Ernestine Wintour said into the silence. 'The sea, you know, so calm today, as one rarely sees it, and the light so pearly – I am sure I could do something quite remarkable.'

As she rose slowly to her feet, a good-looking woman still with rich dark hair only touched with grey and a smooth, delicate skin, Richard leaped up to help her with her shawl and John took her arm and walked with her back to the house. At the glass door to the drawing room, he turned and called back to Richard not to go away, he wanted to talk to him, he would be back directly. Richard gave a slightly apprehensive smile.

'He wants to ask your intentions, I expect,' Charlotte said cheerfully.

'I beg your pardon?'

'Sorry, I've put it badly. Wants to know why you've come over, I should have said.'

'Do I need a reason to visit Belcarron?'

'No, but I can't understand how you come to be free, though. Shouldn't you be in some stuffy office somewhere? Or getting crammed for Sandhurst, or something?'

As the four young women fixed their eyes on him, Richard seemed to lose his ease of manner. He hesitated, then shrugged and laughed.

'All right, Charlotte, you win, you've found me out. I'm a lazy idle good-for-nothing. I did have a position in the City, but I chucked it just before we came here.'

'Chucked it!' cried Hester. 'Richard, you never said. Does Papa know?'

'Actually, yes. Oh, look, I'd better tell you the truth. I chucked the job because I'm going abroad. You might say that I've come to Ireland to say goodbye.'

There was a long, heavy silence during which the moist air seemed to hold the four girls in suspension, totally immobile. Alice had gone quite white, Hester and Marianne rather red, and if Charlotte had not changed colour, she was certainly for once at a loss for words. In the end, though, it was she who spoke first.

'Well, Richard, you old dark horse, you! Abroad where?'

'Yes, where?' Hester asked tightly. 'Perhaps a mere sister may be told?'

'I said he had a secret, didn't I?' cried Marianne. 'Did I not say he looked as if he had a secret?'

'Yes, and he denied it. Lied, in fact. What possessed you to lie to your own sisters, Richard? What have we ever done to you that you should lie to us?'

He tried to reach over and take Hester's hand, but she snatched it away before he could touch it, nor would Marianne let him take hers.

'Look, I'm sorry , I'm really sorry. I should have told you, of course I should, and I would have done, very soon. It was just that I wanted a little longer to think about it all, you see,

29

before we all began talking and discussing. That's all it was, I promise you.'

'Richard,' Alice said, slowly and distinctly, 'where are you going?'

'The Argentine,' he replied.

Four

'This has something to do with Aunt Beatrice,' said Hester.

It was a statement, not a question, and Richard inclined his head. 'True. She wrote to Papa some time ago.'

'Asking you to go on a visit?'

'Rather more than that. She's a widow now, living in Buenos Aires, doesn't spend much time on the *estancia* – the ranch – and would like me to help for a while. It would be a way of seeing a bit of the world.' He laughed nervously. 'Before I settle down.'

'She wrote to Papa and he never said a word either,' Hester commented sharply. 'Why the silence?'

'I asked him to keep it to himself until it was arranged, that's all. Is that a crime?'

Charlotte rose. 'Maybe not, but you're still in disgrace, Richard. You're obviously going to have to do penance before Hester forgives you. Look, it's a lovely evening, why don't we go down to the shore and put all this out of our minds?'

Marianne readily agreed but Alice said she must find Nora, who had forgotten to clear the tea things, then check all was going well with the preparations for dinner. Mama was not up to it.

'I'm sorry,' Hester said quickly. 'So much comes on you, Alice. Is there anything I can do to help?'

'Thank you, Hester, no. I shouldn't have said anything. I'm sorry. It's just that Irish maids are not like English maids, they have ideas of their own.'

'Which are sometimes better than ours,' said Charlotte,

pulling Marianne up from her chair. 'Oh, go along, Alice, we all know your one aim in life is to be the most efficient housekeeper in the world. We'll go walking and see you later. Richard can stay and talk to Papa.'

'Not before he talks to me,' Hester said grimly. 'I'll follow you in a moment, Charlotte.'

As Alice moved slowly back to the house, a graceful figure in her white dress, and Charlotte began to guide Marianne down the path to the shore, Hester put her arm into Richard's and made him walk with her across the lawn.

'I wish you'd stop treating me like a criminal,' he grumbled. 'I know I should have told you my plans, but it's not the worst thing a fellow could do, and anyone would think it was.' As she did not at first reply, he added truculently; 'You've always had your knife into me, haven't you, Hester? Because I was able to go to Oxford and you were not. Is it my fault that women haven't got the same rights as men? We have to live in the world as it is.'

'Or try to change it.' She withdrew her arm from his. 'Not that I would expect you to. But we're straying from the point.'

'The point being what?'

'Alice.'

'Alice?' He was surprised. 'What has she to do with this?'

'Everything. Do you think I don't know why you didn't want to tell people about the Argentine? Do you think I couldn't work it out for myself? You wanted Alice to accept you first, didn't you? In case she wouldn't accept you at all if it meant leaving Belcarron for a time. You wanted to make sure of both, Alice and Belcarron, before you went off to see what Aunt Beatrice has to offer.'

'That's not true, Hester. If it were, I'd still be keeping quiet, wouldn't I?'

'I must admit,' she said thoughtfully, 'I can't understand why you came out with it so easily.'

He was keeping his face averted from her, but she reached up and turned it so that she could look into his eyes.

'Ah, I see . . . She loves you already, is that it? You've made sure?'

32

He removed her hand. 'I see Uncle John looking for me. Will you excuse me, Hester?'

'Are you going to ask for her now?'

He made no reply but strode away from her across the grass, leaving her to turn towards the path to the sea, her face troubled and unsure.

'Come into the house, my boy.' John Wintour took Richard's arm. 'Let me give you a whiskey before dinner. I want to ask you about your father.'

'He's well, sir.' Richard followed his uncle into his study, a square, book-lined room furnished with a massive partner's desk and shabby wing chairs. 'He and Mother send all their best wishes to you, of course, and to Aunt Ernestine.'

At the mention of his wife's name, John's face took on a look of weary patience and he busied himself setting out a handsome Waterford decanter and a couple of tumblers. He told Richard to take a chair, undo his Norfolk jacket, make himself comfortable. 'No women in here, you know, this is where I do as I like. Irish whiskey be all right for you? And how about a cigar?'

'Irish whiskey would be very welcome, Uncle, but I'll not smoke at the moment, thanks all the same.'

'Very wise, but I might have one later. Just for once, I'll join you with a whiskey, but I'm not much of a drinking man these days. There we are – there's soda if you wish. Let me propose your good health, Richard.'

'And yours, Uncle.'

'You're sure Matthew is well? That dicky heart is not playing him up?'

'Not at all. In fact, he's more worried about you than himself. Thinks you might be keeping something from him.'

'Not about my health. I'm all right, not good, but not bad. If there's anything wrong with me, it's worry. As I was telling you, worry about the way things are going, the tenants, the rents – I don't know, maybe some of the farmers didn't get a fair deal before, although we've always done our best for 'em and that's the truth, I swear. But now the pendulum's swung too far. They want more from us than we can give, or ought to give, come to that.' John set down his glass. 'They

33

don't just want the three F's now, Richard, they want full land ownership for the tenant farmer, they want the landlords *out*.'

'They can't really believe that could ever happen, surely? I mean, the Wintours, for instance, have been landowners for a couple of centuries. Are they hoping to undo all that?'

'What else is Home Rule, Richard? It's everybody like ourselves out. It's not just the landowners, it's the government, the viceroy, Dublin Castle, everything – and Irish Paddies running the country without so much as a scrap of experience among 'em. It's a plan for certain chaos.'

'The north would never stand for it.'

'Of course they wouldn't. There'd be civil war. Which is what some people want, you see. Full-blown war and then Ireland free of England for ever. Parnell wants that, Gladstone, too, for all I know. There's to be an election this year and if the Liberals get back' – John wiped his brow – 'there'll be a Home Rule bill before the House as sure as I see you sitting there. Now tell me, Richard, how can I hand on Belcarron, in these circumstances, to a woman?'

Richard drained his glass and set it down, his hand very slightly trembling.

'You're talking about Alice, sir?'

'Of course I'm talking about Alice. She's my elder daughter, she's expecting to get Belcarron when I go, naturally, seeing as my boys are dead.' John was silent for a moment. 'Both of 'em, Richard, both of 'em. It was hard, wasn't it?'

'Very hard, sir.'

'But God's will, we have to bow to it. I've tried, I've tried to come to terms with it, but when I look at poor Alice, I can't take the risk, you see. It'd be too much for her. You see my point?'

'She's young,' Richard answered carefully. 'Young now, but by the time she came to inherit she'd surely be more experienced?'

'But still a woman, Richard, and Belcarron needs a man.' John took Richard's glass and, without asking him, splashed in more whiskey. 'What I'm asking is this: would you be willing to be that man?'

Richard took out his handkerchief and wiped his brow. He had gone very pale.

'You would make me your heir, Uncle?'

'If you were willing.'

'And where would that leave Alice?'

'I've never promised anything to her and I think she knows my anxieties. She'd accept my decision.'

Richard drank a little whiskey as his uncle watched him with a close, apprehensive gaze.

'Would this be ... conditional?' Richard asked at last, with some effort.

'Conditional? On what?'

'On my marrying Alice?'

There was a long silence, broken by the sound of the sea birds calling over the scraps and crumbs on the lawn. From the study window, Richard could see one of the maids – the ginger-haired girl – bearing away the tea things piled on a tray.

Finally, his uncle gave a crooked smile. 'I see you've followed my thinking well, Richard – maybe it wasn't difficult. Alice is very fond of you, I believe you are fond of her. Yes, all right, I'd like to see you married.'

'That doesn't really answer my question, sir.'

'Is my offer conditional? Well, then, I'd say no. No, it's not. You're my brother's son, you're a Wintour, if any man should have Belcarron, it's you. And a man should have it. I've made that clear.'

'So, even if I were to marry someone else, you'd still leave it to me?'

John twisted in his chair, his hand to his mouth. He seemed loath to speak. Richard, still very pale, drained his glass again and waited.

'Yes, all right, I'd leave it to you.' John was sweating as he met Richard's eyes and he put his hand to his brow. 'God knows, I don't want to disinherit my own daughter, but if she doesn't marry you, she'll marry somebody, some fool, maybe, who'll come into Belcarron when she does – and then what? At least, if I leave it to you, I'll know the man who's taking it on. So, if you want to bring some English girl across, that'll be your privilege.'

35

'I'm not interested in any English girls, sir.'

'Who, then? There's someone in your mind, I can tell.'

'There is, sir.' Richard took a long breath. 'It's Charlotte.'

'Oh, my God!' John stood up and took a box of cigars from his desk, selected one and clipped it. 'I don't know why, but I was afraid of this. Just had a feeling, the way you used to look at her sometimes, when you were here before ... But she 's nothing like as pretty as Alice, I never really thought ... ' He took a deep pull on his cigar and, as its pungent smell began to fill the room, moved to sit down again near Richard. 'Listen, my boy, Charlotte is my daughter and I love her but I have to tell you she is in no way ready to be anyone's wife. In some ways she's older than her years, or likes to think she is, pretends she's a woman of the world, knows it all, but she's still only eighteen. She hasn't a thought in her head beyond dancing and riding and who's going to be at the next ball. Whereas Alice, now, she's serious-minded and practical, she runs the whole house, runs everything – '

'I happen to believe that Charlotte is very intelligent, Uncle. She's very young, but she's clever.'

'You want to marry her because she's clever?'

At the faint sneer in John's tone, Richard flushed and lowered his eyes.

'I'm in love with her,' he said quietly. 'And have been, I think, for five years.'

'You realise Alice thinks you are hers?'

'Has she said so?' Richard looked up in alarm. 'I have never given her the impression, I've never spoken – '

'Oh, no, and neither has she, but there's a light comes into her eyes when she hears your name the cat couldn't mistake if it was looking the other way. She's going to be very unhappy for a while. If Charlotte takes you.'

Richard bit his lip. 'I'm sorry if that's the case, but there is something else, something I haven't told you that might make Alice see me differently. I've been asked by Aunt Beatrice to go out to the Argentine for a time. Alice probably would not want to leave Ireland.'

'I was wondering when you were going to tell me about that offer,' John said evenly, and Richard stared.

'You mean you know? Father told you?'

'As soon as he heard from Beatrice. He had an idea what I had in mind for you here, so, naturally, he wanted to tell me about the Argentine suggestion.' John laughed shortly. 'That wild sister of ours, thinking up a scheme like this – I mean, what in damnation do you know about cattle, Richard?'

'It's only to be temporary,' Richard answered, rather desperately. 'It's not intended that I should stay out there.'

'And you would rather be here?'

'In every way.'

They exchanged a long, steady glance from their similar blue eyes, then John drew a last puff on his cigar and stood up.

'It remains to be seen where Charlotte would rather be,' he said. 'Does it not, my boy?'

Five

Alice was bewildered. She had been so sure that first day when Richard arrived that he loved her. Over and over again in the days that followed, she acted out the little scene in his room when he had drawn her through the door, had held her hands, gazed into her face. He had said so little, but she had felt the warmth of his body so close to hers, had sensed the kiss ready on his lips. 'You've changed,' he had murmured. 'If you were a child five years ago, you are not a child now . . .'

Not a child now. No, a woman. A woman who wanted to be courted and won, who had that right. If he did not care for her, why had he talked so? Looked at her so? But of course he did care, she knew he did. Something must have happened, then, to delay his proposal.

Something to do with the journey he must make to the Argentine? Alice liked to comfort herself with the thought that he was afraid to ask her to go with him, in case she should say no. He knew how much she loved Belcarron, how she would dread leaving. That must be it.

But in the night hours when she could not sleep and stood staring out at the grey sky and ghostly sea, she knew it wasn't true. Because if it were, Richard would still be looking at her, his eyes would be telling her that he loved her – and since that first day of arrival he had scarcely looked at her at all. Worse, if he had let his eyes meet hers, he had withdrawn his gaze immediately; it was as though in her presence he were only embarrassed, even ashamed.

'Oh, but why should he be ashamed?' she would cry,

soundlessly, and fold her arms over her breasts and shiver in her full white nightdress, although the nights were as humid as the days, then trail back to bed and lie, eyes wide, until the light crept over her ceiling and there was another day to face.

Sometimes, she thought of tackling Papa. He had spoken to Richard on that first evening, and quite possibly he had said something to put him off. Perhaps refused his permission for marriage on the grounds of cousinship, or because of the trip to the Argentine. Perhaps had refused him Belcarron and Richard had been disappointed. But then he had only to marry her and it would be his, too, maybe not in law, but because she would want him to share it with her. He knew that, he must know it – so why did he not *speak*?

She wasn't sure how she did it, but somehow she managed to keep outwardly calm and even (with Charlotte's languid assistance) worked through the programme of social events and pursuits they had planned for the visitors. Not that any of them appeared enthusiastic. Hester seemed preoccupied, Marianne was always reading letters from her curate or writing letters back, Richard only wanted to go fishing, preferably with his uncle, just the two of them, two men without women.

Once or twice, though, Charlotte went with them. Whether she had been invited or not, Alice did not know, but she would not ask to go herself and suffered torments until they returned. When they set out, she could follow them with her father's telescope and would watch the two yellow heads and the dark cap that represented John Wintour until their boat rounded the point and could be seen no more. Then she would have to wait until the small dot came bobbing back and of course that would be hours later, during which she would have to do other things, and even when they had returned and brought in their catch, whatever it was, the ordeal was not over for she still could not know what Richard had said to Charlotte and what she had said to him.

I will speak to Papa, she determined. I will find out what happened between him and Richard.

But her father, she noticed, seemed to be avoiding her,

too, and she did not after all raise the subject. Perhaps it would be better not to know.

It was beginning to get more and more difficult to organise the household, feeling as tired as she did and in such low spirits, especially as for much of the time Mena was missing. Ernestine Wintour had suddenly decided at this most inopportune time to paint the young girl's portrait, which involved lengthy sittings with giggling from Mena and complaints from Nora, who said she was doing double work and not being given double pay.

'Oh, pay her and be done with it,' Charlotte exclaimed. 'If painting Mena's portrait is keeping Mama happy, isn't it worth every penny?'

And Alice was inclined to agree with her, for certainly Mama did seem happy and was even doing rather a good job of catching a likeness.

'And isn't it Mena to the life, then?' cried Mrs Heenan, invited to see progress while the mistress was resting. 'Will you look at the little baggage's eyes? And her smile? Now you'll be caught for all time, Mena, pinned up on the wall for all to see for ever and ever!'

'And why her and not me is what I am asking?' Nora sniffed. 'Sure the mistress must be light in the head if she wants to paint a Donovan.'

At which Mena threatened to box her ears and had to be held back by Daniel Molloy, who told her not to be such a little devil, then, even if Nora was at fault for not keeping a civil tongue in her head. He was laughing as he lightly held the struggling Mena, his dark brows for once untwisted, his face relaxed, unaware, it seemed, that Alice and Hester were listening and watching from the doorway. When his eye caught them, his laughter died. He released Mena and stood stiff as a post until the young ladies had come into the room, when he excused himself and left.

When Mrs Heenan and the maids had also melted away, Alice asked Hester with a smile if she didn't think her Fenian was harmless enough, after all?

'He seemed happy,' Hester replied, 'until he saw us.'

'That was just a natural reaction. Servants are not at their ease when we intrude.'

41

'I suppose not.' Hester stood back, studying Mena's portrait. 'Does he live here, at Belcarron?'

'Yes, at the stables. He has a sister in Skibbereen and goes there on his day off. By carrier, if he can find one, or else walks.'

'Skibbereen suffered badly in the famine, didn't it?'

'I'm afraid it was one of the worst affected towns in the whole of Ireland. Papa could tell you terrible tales. So could Uncle Matthew, I expect.'

'He never speaks of it. Even after all these years, he says it is too upsetting. How vivid it must still be in the minds of the people here, Alice!'

'I don't like to think of it myself, but what's done is done, it can't be undone.'

'At least we can see such a thing never happens again.'

'Of course, we're all agreed on that.' Alice took Hester's arm and suggested they should walk down to the shore. 'It's terrible, I know,' she went on, 'to think about all the suffering, but I do feel that things are improving, in spite of what Papa says. If the people are getting something of what they want, they must surely be happier.'

'As long as they don't want violence.'

'Not still worrying about Fenians?'

'Well, not about Daniel Molloy.' Hester smiled. 'Is he perhaps Mena's sweetheart?'

'Mena's?' Alice laughed. 'Of course not. She's far too young for Daniel. He must be at least twenty-six and she's not yet sixteen.'

'But I thought Irish men were marrying later these days and were often much older than their wives.'

'Since the famine, I believe that's true. There are far fewer young people around to get married, anyway. But Mena would never be interested in a dull stick like Daniel. He's one to keep himself to himself, not her sort at all.'

The two girls scrambled down the steep incline, holding up their skirts from the thickly growing fuchsias and brambles, until they reached the soft pale sand of the beach that was regarded as Belcarron's own. It was not possible to reach the village shore and jetty from there, which was, Alice said, its principal attraction, it was so beautifully private.

42

'We could bathe, then?' asked Hester.

Alice seemed astonished. No one ever thought of bathing from Belcarron – why, they had no bathing machines. 'This is not Brighton!' she cried.

Hester laughed and began to toss pebbles into the sea. 'It looks warm, Alice. Don't you think it would be pleasant to take off all one's clothes and just go in? Feel the water against one's skin?'

'You talk like Charlotte, she says things like that.'

'And of course you don't approve?'

'Well, Papa worries about her. In case she becomes – you know – wild.'

'You mean like Aunt Beatrice?'

The colour rose to Alice's face and she looked away from Hester's intelligent gaze.

'Tell me what's happening,' Hester said softly. 'Has Richard spoken to you yet?'

'You know I should have told you.'

'If he asked you, would you go with him to the Argentine?'

'Wherever he went,' Alice replied, after a pause, 'I'd go with him.'

'Even if it meant leaving Belcarron?'

'Even if it meant leaving Belcarron.'

Alice glanced at the little gold watch pinned to her dress and said they must go back, they were due to play croquet with the family of the rector of St Stephen's, Kilvane, the same Reverend Arthur Barnes who said services at Carron, St John's being too small a parish to have clergy of its own.

'We're always going somewhere,' Hester observed. 'You entertain us very well, Alice.'

'Tea and croquet at the rectory?' Alice smiled. 'We should have given you a dance, only Papa is in rather difficult financial circumstances at present.'

'Thanks to Parnell's policies, I believe. Some of the tenants are getting what they want by not paying their rents. Of course, what they really want is Home Rule.'

'That they will never have.' Alice turned to begin the climb back up from the sea. 'At least, I hope not. I shouldn't want to run Belcarron if it were in a foreign country.'

43

'You believe one day you will run Belcarron? Uncle John will leave it to you?'

'I don't know. I don't know anything, Hester. Where I'm to live, if I'm to marry ... Sometimes I almost feel I don't know who I am.'

'That's because you are a woman. Women have to be appended to a man to have an identity, the way things are.'

Alice did not reply but stood for a moment looking at the house above. Her face was flushed from the warm, moist air and the climb, her dark hair was loosening from its knot, and Hester thought how beautiful she was and wondered what possible reason Richard could have for not seeming to want her. But even as she asked herself the question, Hester decided she could answer it. Alice loved him too much, so he would be as contrary as people were and want a girl who didn't love him at all, that would be the way of it; that was the way of the world. On the other hand, though, Alice had Belcarron. Or had she? A light began to shine as Hester remembered her brother's talk with her uncle on the day they arrived. John Wintour must have promised it to him, which meant that Alice – might end up with nothing at all.

Impulsively, Hester took her cousin's hand in hers.

'If you should ever want to talk to me, Alice, I shall want to listen. Sometimes it's easier to talk to someone you don't know so well than, say, a sister.'

'Especially if your sister is someone like Charlotte.' Alice tried to smile. 'Thank you, Hester, I shall remember that.'

In the continuing warm weather, the Wintours played their games of croquet and lawn tennis, rode and walked, went to luncheon parties, even gave one at Belcarron – which was a nightmare of organisation for Alice, but went off well in the end, though her mother only put in one appearance and that was to show off her newly finished portrait of Mena, evoking Mena's blushes and cries of praise from the young people at table.

These young people, Hester noted, were not unlike those she knew at home; indeed, in dress and manner it might have been hard to tell them apart. Yet there were subtle differences. The Anglo-Irish, while seemingly sure of themselves, certain they were entitled to everything they had, were still not as totally at ease as a similar English group might have been. Maybe they were only subconsciously aware that their class ruled as conquerors in a land that had not accepted conquest, but they were aware of it all the same, were at times afraid perhaps of what stirred beneath their very pleasant lifestyle.

Hester noted, too, and was amused to see it, that Richard was singled out for particular attention wherever they went, at least by young women. It was not surprising, of course; men were always in demand and here was a new man, handsome as a legend and eligible, too, for if no one knew exactly what his prospects were, he was a Wintour and planning to go to the Argentine, where everyone knew fortunes could be made. But was he engaged to Alice or not? The whispers circulated, but who could say? Certainly not Hester, who would not betray the little she knew, which was that Richard had not 'spoken'. She was in fact biding her time to do some speaking herself, when she intended to ask Richard what he meant by his treatment of Alice. Until then, she watched and waited.

At least, as she discovered, Alice did have one other admirer. Cavan Morry, who came for a Friday to Monday with his sisters, spent all his time following Alice with his eyes. How aggravating it was, then, that she scarcely seemed to notice him. Charlotte, of course, had admirers everywhere, sometimes deigning to acknowledge them, sometimes not. On a picnic they took to Oyster Island, an enchanted place of white sand and sea pinks, a stout, pale young man with smooth brown hair and a drooping moustache paid quite obvious court. Charlotte, tossing her yellow hair even more than usual, allowed him to accompany her as she sauntered over the beach looking for shells.

'Who is that with Charlotte?' Hester asked Edie Morry, a tall, gawky girl who looked better in the saddle than off.

'Don't you know, then? That's Dudley Sarn, Lord Penning's younger son. He's from Dublin, staying with the Bridleys; I rather think Charlotte met him when he was staying with us.'

'She seems willing to spend some time with him.'

'My dear, he's a catch!' cried Edie. 'There's money, too.

Plenty, I believe, though they do say that Dudley is rather wild and gets through it pretty well.'

'Really? He doesn't look very wild.'

'And not very handsome, either, I expect you're thinking.' Edie narrowed her eyes at the distant figure of Richard, walking with her sister Kitty and two other young men. 'Not nearly as handsome as your brother, now. Goodness, he's like an angel, isn't he?'

'Isn't he, though?' Hester replied, nodding and smiling, there being not much else she could do.

After a splendid lunch of lobster and wine, followed by strawberries, the party explored the island's ruined chapel, the relic of St Columba, Kitty said, or it might have been Columbanus, she wasn't sure – someone very holy, anyway, and very old.

'Very old,' said Cavan, 'I hope I'm never that. I should like to stay the age I am now for ever. How about you, Miss Alice?'

'I don't know,' she answered, giving him her attention for the first time. 'Things might be better when one is older.'

'I agree,' said Marianne. 'I'm looking forward to being older. Well, a little older, anyway.'

'Just enough to be married and have lots of children, I suppose?' Charlotte sneered. 'What a future! I don't want to be older and I don't want to be married, either. Not for years and years.'

'Of course you don't mean that,' Dudley Sarn drawled. 'All gels want to be married, every fella knows that.'

'Every fella is wrong, then.' Charlotte, moving across to Richard, suddenly took his arm. 'Richard, I've scarcely seen you today. Why don't you walk back to the boats with me? I'm sure we should be returning soon, it looks to me as though there might be a storm brewing.'

The devil, thought Hester. She knows where the storm is brewing.

Dudley Sarn's face was as dark as the gathering clouds, Richard's mottled and strained as he bent his head and walked slowly away with Charlotte on his arm.

'See their hair,' someone murmured. 'It's the same colour.

They might be brother and sister.'

'But they're not,' Alice cried, in a high voice that seemed ready to crack, 'are they?'

Six

Throughout the evening after the picnic, the air was so oppressive they could scarcely breathe, yet still the storm did not break.

'It will come tonight,' Marianne said fearfully at dinner. 'I know it will, and I do so hate electrical storms at night – or any time. Hester is frightfully brave, she doesn't mind them at all.'

'I don't mind them because I'm not afraid, there's no bravery about it,' Hester said.

'Nor am I afraid,' said Charlotte. 'In fact, I think I rather enjoy a good storm.'

'So I've noticed,' Richard snapped, and John sent an enquiring glance down the table at him.

Alice kept her eyes on her plate and said nothing. She was looking striking in a low-cut, dark-blue dress, but was making no effort to play hostess, and Cavan Morry on her right was having a disappointing time of it. In fact, only the Morry girls, describing their picnic to Ernestine, were their normal selves, for there was a feverish glitter in Charlotte's eye and her chatter seemed unusually loud. It was a relief when the meal ended and they could move to the drawing room where the long windows showed a black sky and a motionless sea, waiting for the activity to come. No one felt like cards or music; they sat around, breathing hard, the ladies fanning themselves, the men running their fingers round their collars and wiping their brows.

Suddenly, Ernestine clapped her hands and cried: 'Candles! Let's all say goodnight!'

It seemed a very good idea.

'Goodnight, Alice,' Cavan murmured, his melting gaze on her meeting a look so blank it might have been a marble statue's. 'You know I leave tomorrow.'

'Do you? Oh, yes, of course. Well, I do hope it has been pleasant for you.'

'First rate. I was wondering, you know, if we might meet again soon. There's the Fitzmirrans' ball, for instance – '

'Oh, yes, I'm sure we shall meet somewhere,' she replied carelessly, and moved away to kiss her mother goodnight, her eyes over her mother's shoulder on Richard, who was stiffly saying goodnight to Charlotte.

'Splendid picnic, wasn't it?' she was asking him, smiling up into his face. 'I do so love Oyster Island, don't you? So typical of the Irish to call it that, when there are no oysters, isn't it?'

His face in the shadows had taken on that same mottled look it had worn earlier in the day, a look which Charlotte did not recognise but which Hester knew meant that her brother was feeling thwarted. It did not do to go too far with him in this mood, he could be quick to retaliate. Now he made no reply to Charlotte, but, taking his candle from Nora, made a general goodnight and marched slowly upstairs, tossing his hair back as he went.

'He seems upset,' Charlotte murmured to Marianne, her green eyes sparkling. 'I wonder why?'

But Marianne wasn't listening. She was standing very still, her eyes above her candle dark pools of fear.

'I hear the thunder!' she cried. 'It's beginning! Oh, Hester, may I sleep in your room tonight?'

Charlotte burst into scornful laughter. 'What a good job you're hoping to become engaged, Marianne! You'd better fix the date quickly, then you'll always have someone to protect you from the storms.'

'I hate Charlotte, don't you?' Marianne muttered later, from Hester's bed. 'She is so indelicate and so spiteful. I don't know why, because she seems to get everything she wants.'

'You mean the Honourable Dudley?' asked Hester from the window, where she was brushing her hair.

50

'Not just him. Everything, everyone. I believe she could have Richard too, if she wanted him, and I declare, I'd die if he married Charlotte. I thought it was all arranged he should marry Alice.'

As Hester made no reply, Marianne shivered and pulled the bedclothes up to her chin.

'Do put out the candle and come to bed, Hester. I saw the lightning just then and you know how it affects me!'

Hester did put out the candle but she did not go to bed. She told her sister to cover her head, she wanted to watch the storm.

Like Charlotte, Hester enjoyed it. There was something exhilarating, she found, in seeing the elements untrammelled, unconstrained, free as she could never be, and while Marianne moaned under the sheets, Hester laughed as the thunder drums sounded around and the lightning snaked in ribbons across the sky. Even from her room which faced the drive, the sight was impressive; from the rooms facing the sea, it must have been truly magnificent, and she was toying with the idea of slipping into Alice's room to watch from there when the heavens parted and the rains came. Stream upon stream of water fell past her window, boiling, hissing, striking the ground with such force that no one surely could have remained upright under them. Yet, even as she was praying: 'Dear God, I hope there is no one without shelter tonight', she saw the horse on the drive and the man leading it.

'Hester!' cried Marianne. 'Come to bed!'

'Coming,' Hester answered. 'I'm just watching the rain. It's so strong, it's a deluge . . .'

And Daniel Molloy was out in it, with one of his master's horses, battling round the house towards the stables, furtively, as though he had something to hide.

Hester woke early, having slept only fitfully, and slipped out of bed without a sound so as not to wake Marianne. The day was fresh and cool, everything she could see from her window washed clean by the storm, the grass weighed down still with water, the leaves under their drops glittering in the new sun. She would have liked to pull up the sash and lean out to take deep breaths of the pure air, but she knew she dared not; she must move softly like a cat, find her clothes (if only there weren't so many), dress and get out before Marianne sat up and asked her what she was doing. It would not be possible to wash, of course, but at least she could use the one water closet at Belcarron downstairs off the hall and need not worry about struggling with an embarrassing chamber pot while Marianne was still in her room.

She was soon ready, dressed in a blue serge skirt and white muslin blouse, with her smooth brown hair neatly coiled in its knot. There was just one anxious moment when she was crossing the hall and saw Mena in the distance, carrying a mop and bucket, but she was able to move into the doorway of the dining room and was certain the maid had not seen her. What if she had? What should Miss Hester be doing but taking an early morning stroll? No need to feel guilty. She felt guilty.

Outside the house, she moved quickly, stepping high through the wet grass, holding up her skirt with one hand, covering her hair with the other. How saturated everything was – trees, bushes, path – she was herself already quite damp. If anyone were to notice at breakfast, what should she say? Not, she decided, with a wild little smile, that she had been to the stables to see Daniel Molloy. It was so strange that she should be doing this, so completely out of character, she really did not know why she was so driven. If it had been Charlotte, or even Marianne, it might just have been conceivable, but that it was she – no, it wasn't possible. So, she must be dreaming. But she wasn't dreaming.

The stable block, built to the right of the house away from the sea, had once been quite grand, always kept up, the stalls full of horses, two grooms and a boy kept working full time. So Alice had told her, but of course it was not like that now. Now there were only the two old hunters and the pony for the trap, now there was only Molloy. The few times Hester had come over to borrow Mayfly or Boy, she had thought the stables depressing; this was, of course, the first time she had come alone.

At first she could not see the groom and thought he was not yet up. Where, after all, did he sleep? Alice had said over the stables. Was that in a loft or a room or what? The thought of finding him sleeping made a hard, hot blush rise to her face. She had almost decided to turn and go back when she saw him. Not asleep, thank God, but sitting on a deal chair inside the open door of the stable, wearing a collarless shirt and dark trousers, and reading.

Reading? It was the last thing she had expected. What should a groom be reading, then?

She hesitated in the doorway, brushing drops of moisture from her hair, certain that he must have heard her approach, but if he had, he gave no sign.

'Good morning,' she said at last, trying to sound crisp and authoritative, and failing.

Daniel Molloy slowly raised his eyes. For a long moment he held her in their steely gaze, then he got to his feet.

'Good morning, miss.'

'What a storm it was last night, wasn't it? I thought the roof might come down at one point.' Rubbing her arms, which were cold and damp. Hester ventured further into the stable. It was warm there, and she could hear the horses moving in their stalls. After a little while, Molloy offered her his chair.

'Thank you, but I won't sit down. I just thought I'd see if it was all right to ride today. I mean, Mayfly is quite fit?'

'She's fine,' he replied, leaning against the door. 'Why should she not be?'

'Well, I saw her last night – ' She looked him bravely in the face. 'I saw you, too. In the rain. At least, I think it was Mayfly, but it might have been Boy – it was definitely you.'

He was silent, his face expressionless.

'You must have been soaked,' she went on, desperately. 'I thought you must surely take a chill, the horse, too – '

'I told you, miss, the horse is fine. So am I.'

'That's all right, then. I . . . I suppose you'd been over to Skibbereen? To see your family?'

'I have no family. Only the one sister, Theresa.'

'But you had been to Skibbereen?' Hester pressed. 'Such a way, in such weather, and on Mr Wintour's horse. I was told you usually went by carrier.'

'You were asking?'

'No, of course not. My cousin said you visited Skibbereen,

53

she did not say you took one of the horses. Does my uncle know?'

'He does not. Is it you who'll be telling him?'

Hester looked away. 'No, I wouldn't do that. I – well, I'd better get back to the house. I'm sorry if I interrupted your reading.'

He said with sudden fierceness: 'This part of the morning is me own. I've a right to read if I want – or would you be taking that away if you could? Would you be thinking a man like me should not be reading a book on law, is that what would be in your mind, then?'

'Law?' She turned the book in his hand so that she could read the title. '*Principles of English Law* . . . I should say it was no more surprising for you to be reading such a book than for me as a woman to want to read it.'

He gave a slow smile. 'Are you meaning we have something in common, miss? What gentlemen think of us?'

'What men think of us,' she corrected sharply, and his smile became a laugh.

'Is it a man you'd like to be? No point in wishing for things you cannot change.'

'What about things you can change? Don't you want to work for those?'

'I'm not understanding you, miss,' he answered, his face darkening.

'Why, you are changing things for yourself, aren't you? Becoming educated? Isn't that the point of your reading?'

He relaxed visibly. 'Yes, miss, you're right. 'Tis educated I plan to be and I'm not the first in the family to want that. Me da was a reader, taught himself the letters, he did. If he'd had some schooling . . .' Molloy shrugged his heavy shoulders and was silent.

'Would you like me to lend you some books?' Hester asked. 'I have several with me, works of history, mainly, but there are one or two on politics – '

'Seems you're already what I want to be, miss, 'tis educated you are.'

'No, I'm not. Women are scarcely ever properly educated, that's my point – I'm trying to educate myself, just like you. When shall I bring them, then? The books?'

54

'Any time you find convenient. It's here you'll find me.'

'I might bring one or two this evening, then.'

'And Mayfly'll be ready and waiting whenever you want her.'

'Mayfly?'

'Was it not Mayfly you were wanting to ride? Wasn't it the horse you were asking about?'

Although his face was perfectly serious, she knew he was laughing at her and she flushed with anger and embarrassment. Without considering her words, she said quickly: 'I see you think I had some other reason for coming. You were right. I came to find out if you were a Fenian.'

The words out, she was afraid and for a moment dared not look at him, but she could tell from his voice as he answered that he did not seem to mind her charge, perhaps was even smiling.

'A Fenian, is it? And were you finding out, then, miss?'

'No, but I don't think, even if you are, that you would . . . harm us.'

'Because of me reading?' She raised her eyes and saw that his smile had become a sneer. 'You think reading a book makes me a man for peace?'

'Since I've talked to you, I believe . . .'

'What?'

'That I can trust you.'

There was a silence between them. Then Molloy said, quietly: 'Be bringing me the books, Miss Wintour, if you can, and don't be worrying – what I am.'

When she slipped quietly into the dining room, Hester found no breakfast laid and only her aunt present, who said she really did not see why they were not to have so much as a cup of tea, just because everyone seemed to be wanting to run around with buckets catching water from the roof. As for the cottages awash in the village, did it need the whole household to take down supplies?

'I didn't know, I didn't realise!' Hester cried, in confusion. 'Of course, the storm last night was so terrible, the damage must be awful – '

'My dear, where have you been?' Ernestine narrowed her

fine eyes at her. 'Wherever it was, you're looking very well. I think I shall paint you directly after breakfast, if we ever have any. Ring the bell again, my dear, someone must answer.'

Obediently ringing the bell, Hester said she must herself try to help, perhaps tell the groom. He should be helping, shouldn't he?

'My dear,' Ernestine asked, limpidly, 'how do you know he is not?'

Seven

After two weeks of repairs to Belcarron and the village, John Wintour's face was a study in anxiety.

'That damned storm,' he muttered to Richard, 'it's nearly finished me. The roof, the plastering – tiles, timber, masonry – those Skibbereen fellas are milking me dry, I swear it. And then the cottages – roofs right off. God in heaven, what's a man to do? They'll practically have to be rebuilt – and all estate property, my boy, and who's to say they'll ever pay their rents, and me scarcely daring to look the bank manager in the face? There's some, you know, wouldn't do what I'm doing. Plenty would let 'em fend for themselves, say it's God's will, God's judgement, something of that sort, but we Wintours have never been like that. We care, you see, and the thanks we get is nothing at all, that's the way of the world.'

'Oh, come, Uncle, things are not as bad as all that,' Richard answered, trying to sound cheerful. 'Some rents are coming in and the people do appreciate what you're doing, I've heard them say so myself. They'll pay their dues if they can.'

He hoped that was true but there were times, he had to admit, when he wondered how the tenants managed to pay anything at all. He was beginning to understand that owning an estate like Belcarron was not the passport to a land of milk and honey he'd always thought it. On the other hand, he still wanted it; with every day he spent there, he wanted it more.

'About Charlotte,' his uncle said suddenly, 'you haven't approached her yet?'

'No, sir, not yet.' Richard's mouth set in a grim line. 'I haven't found the opportunity.'

'Better make it soon, my boy, before – '

'Sarn asks her first?'

'I was going to say, before you leave for England. What do you mean, Dudley Sarn might ask her first? Nobody told me Penning's boy was courting my daughter.'

'I'm not sure that he is, sir. I may have made a mistake.'

'Well, if you haven't, just goes to prove the truth of what I say. Get things settled, no sense in hanging around.'

'I thought, perhaps, at the ball tomorrow night – '

'Good idea. Girls appreciate proposals at balls, makes 'em feel successful. Rather think I may have proposed to your aunt at somebody's ball.' The familiar shadow crossed John's face as he spoke of Ernestine and he sighed and said he would take a turn on the shore with his cigar. Richard should remember what he had said, ask quickly, get things settled – that was the way.

Richard, his hands in his pockets, paced slowly into the garden from the side door. He felt depressed and irritated by the thought of Dudley Sarn and by his uncle's reminder that time was running out. Of course he should have settled things with Charlotte by now, got an answer from her one way or another, but the thought of possible rejection was not pleasant and for the past two weeks she had led him such a dance, he really had no idea at all of what was in her mind. Was it possible she could be so dazzled by a title that she would tie herself to such a donkey as Sarn? He supposed it was. Girls were such idiots, after all.

He paused, seeing ahead of him in the shrubbery one girl who was no sort of idiot and thought again, as he had been vaguely thinking for days, that his sister Hester was looking remarkably attractive.

He called her name and saw her stop and stiffen a little. She had not yet changed for dinner and was, as usual, carrying a book.

'Same old bluestocking, Hester. Where are you off to, then? For a secret read before dinner?'

'Don't be ridiculous!' Her dark eyes flashed. 'And I wish

58

you would not call me a bluestocking. I don't make fun of you if you want to read.'

'You've been doing an uncommon amount of reading lately, now I come to think of it, always seem to be dashing off somewhere with a book under your arm – what is it this time, then?'

'Political history, nothing that would interest you.'

'*Irish* political history, I see. That's of interest to you?'

'Always has been. Now, will you kindly go where you're going and leave me alone?'

'With pleasure, but don't forget the dressing bell, will you, dear Hester?'

'When have I ever been late for dinner?'

'Once or twice you've cut it pretty fine.'

'You've found the time to take your eyes off Charlotte, then?' she asked acidly, and took an unworthy pleasure in seeing his expression change and the uneasy flush return to his lean face.

'I'm in no mood for one of your lectures,' he said curtly.

'You might just tell me what you think you are doing to Alice.'

'I'm sorry if she's unhappy. I never gave her cause to think I loved her.'

Hester's eyes searched his. 'Has Uncle John promised Belcarron to you?'

'I think that's my business. Mine and his.'

'I think it is Alice's. It seems she's to be deprived of her inheritance simply because she is a woman.'

'Uncle John is afraid of the future. He thinks Alice could not control the estate if there are to be more changes.'

'He wouldn't question her ability if she were a man. Oh, it makes me so angry – '

A bell rang suddenly from inside the house and Hester looked in consternation at the watch pinned to her blouse.

'Oh, see! Now I shall be late. You shouldn't have detained me, Richard – '

'Late for what?' he asked curiously, but she only said;

'For dinner, of course. I must go and change. Excuse me, Richard.'

He watched her hurrying back to the house and wondered

idly at the changes in her, but they did not hold his interest long away from Charlotte, who always moved into the centre of his thoughts as soon as he was alone.

Alice was looking weary at dinner, Hester thought. Several times she noticed her cousin's eyes following Richard's gaze where it rested on Charlotte and then the desolate droop of her mouth as she stared down again at her plate. This while Charlotte, in high spirits, teased her father and flirted so openly with Richard that even her mother noticed, opened her eyes wide and stared at her as though she were a stranger.

Any moment now she will offer to paint her, Hester thought, relieved no one at the table was paying any attention to herself. Directly the meal was over, she excused herself, saying she had a headache and would go to her room.

'You look quite well,' Charlotte observed. 'I suspect you only want to escape my singing.'

'Not at all – I enjoy your singing, Charlotte. I shall look forward to it another evening.'

'You're safe to say that, of course, now that you have so few evenings left.'

So few evenings left.

'How sad!' cried Ernestine.

'I can't bear to think of it,' said Hester, and the truth of it was like a knife in her heart.

As soon as she left the drawing room, she ran swiftly to her room, where she changed into a dark skirt and blouse and threw a light shawl round her shoulders. Then she left the house and made again for the stables.

For the past two weeks she had been visiting the stables every day to see Daniel Molloy, sometimes with books as an excuse, sometimes without any excuse at all. When they met, they talked – of Ireland, of themselves, what they wanted – Hester freely, Daniel with reserve. She had no idea still how strongly he was committed to violence but it did not matter to her how little she knew. All she wanted was to be with him. She was aware, of course, what would be thought of her if their meetings were ever discovered; in fact, she had always herself despised women of her own class who formed associations with servants. But her relationship with Daniel was not of the usual kind. He had never behaved towards her with anything but scrupulous correctness; they were friends, that was all.

Was that what she wanted? Of course. There could be nothing more between her and him. But the strange knife pain persisted in her heart when she thought of saying goodbye.

He was at work in the harness room, polishing a saddle. When she touched his arm, he looked up and smiled.

'I couldn't come earlier,' she said quickly. 'I was detained. Now I've forgotten the book I had for you.'

He said it didn't matter, he still had the others she had lent him, his problem was time –

'Take as long as you like. I don't want them back.'

''Tis not in England you'll be needing them?'

'No, they're for you.'

He took up his cloth and began rubbing the saddle again. He said he was very grateful. Hester watched impatiently.

'I suppose you hate that name,' she said after a time, her voice rather high. 'I mean, England.'

It was a silly remark to make, she knew. They had discussed England and her role in Ireland many times, the long history of domination, the battles, the risings and reprisals, the Penal Laws, even the lack of aid during the famines, which Daniel claimed was the English answer to the Irish question. She knew very well what his views on England were. Now he looked at her in surprise and said nothing.

'Perhaps you hate me too,' she asked, 'as I am English?' She leaned forward and snatched the polishing cloth from his hand. 'Daniel, I am asking you a question. Do you hate me?'

'I do not, then.'

'Why not, if I am English?'

'You know why not, Miss Wintour.'

'Tell me, then, tell me why not. Is it because we've become good friends, these last two weeks? We have become friends, haven't we?'

'Very good friends, miss.'

For a long moment she looked into his face, then she took

61

off her shawl and began to pace up and down the saddle room.

'Do you realise that in a very few days I shall have to go home? Back to England?'

'I knew it must be soon,' he muttered.

'Will you miss me? Miss our talks?'

''Tis leaving I am meself,' he answered obliquely, and she caught her breath.

'Leaving? Leaving Belcarron? Why, where are you going?'

'Dublin.'

Dublin! She stopped her pacing and stood very still, her eyes alight. 'Daniel, that's wonderful! We can meet. We can meet again in Dublin.'

He said he did not understand her. What could she be talking of? She had no place in Dublin.

'I might have.' She was trembling with excitement as she faced him. 'I've been thinking for some time I might stay on in Ireland. There's nothing for me at home, no career, no life of my own. If I don't marry, I shall spend my life paying social calls and visiting the sick. But if I stay here, I shall have a purpose: I shall work for Ireland, make reparation for what my people have done.'

He only stared at her, his face hard and unyielding.

'Don't look so amazed, Daniel! I can do it if I want to. I have a hundred and fifty pounds a year from my godmother which my parents cannot touch, I could manage very well. If necessary, I could also give lessons – '

''Tis rubbish you're talking!' he shouted. 'What could you do for Ireland? You're an English Protestant, your da is a clergyman, your uncle's a landowner!'

'And isn't Charles Stewart Parnell a Protestant? Isn't he a landowner? Do you say he can do nothing for Ireland? If anyone gets you Home Rule it will be Parnell.'

'He's a politician, he's a – '

'Man?' Hester's eyes glittered. 'It's because I'm a woman you think I can do nothing, then? Well, let me tell you something else. I may become a Catholic.'

The words were like a match to tinder. Daniel's face suffused with blood; he stood over her, large, suddenly menacing, and grasped her wrist so hard she cried out.

62

'Are you playing with me?' he asked hoarsely. 'I've heard about ladies teasing – if it's teasing me you are, Miss Wintour –'

'I'm not teasing you!' she cried, as he let go of her and stood back, his face pale now and stern. 'How can you think that of me?'

'Why would you ever want to be a Catholic?'

'Because I love you,' she wanted to scream. 'Because I'd do anything for you, make any sacrifice. Because ever since I came here tonight, it's as though some stranger has been telling me what to say, what to think. Because I've lost myself in you!'

But she said nothing, because she was not too frightened to know that if she did, she would lose him. He would not be able to accept the sort of passion she was offering from someone like her – from any woman, perhaps. She busied herself putting on her shawl again and would not look at him.

'Hester,' he said quietly, and her head shot up at his use of her name. 'You would really have it we should meet in Dublin? It's your meaning?'

'Yes, I've said so.'

'When is it you will go?'

'I'm not sure. It must be before the return to England, which is three days from now. I shan't be able to tell anyone at Belcarron what I am planning, they would prevent me.'

'It's the first train you should take, then, the first out in the morning.'

'I could leave the morning after the ball, then. Would you come with me?'

'No, I could not. 'Twould not do at all, the two of us mustn't be seen.'

He's ashamed of me, she thought. He's ashamed to be seen with an English Protestant. And she could have laughed, hysterically, at the topsy-turvy world she seemed to find herself in, but, with a spirit that surprised, she held on to her control.

'When will you come, then? When shall I see you?'

He said he should by rights give a week's notice to John Wintour, but if he did not –

'Surely you will not!' she cried. 'What does it matter about notice? You must come soon, I know no one in Dublin, you must help me.'

His heavy features were so full of doubt she could have screamed again. It was not that he was unwilling, he muttered, but what could he do? He had friends, but she could not stay with them –

'You must know some hotel where I could stay,' she said eagerly. 'Some good, respectable place? Not the largest, in case they come looking. But I cannot go at all without an address.'

'Mantle's, then, 'tis fair and reasonable. Be taking a cab and wait for me there.'

'I shall leave the day after tomorrow. When will you be able to join me?'

'I shall not be after joining you,' he said quickly, and her face flamed.

'See me, I meant. Surely you understand?'

'Wait for me,' he said, deliberately. 'Trust me.'

'Oh, God, do you think I don't? Daniel, forgive me, do you have money?'

'Enough. And if it was starving I was for a crust, I wouldn't be taking money from a woman.'

'Very well, then, it's arranged. But you still haven't told me why you are going to Dublin.'

'I'm wanted.'

'To work with your friends?'

'To work for Ireland.' His blue eyes flashed. 'What you say you have the fancy to be doing.'

'It's true, I swear it.' She began to move away, still looking at him, her eyes seeming large and dark in the pallor of her face. 'You needn't have told me to trust you, Daniel. Don't you remember what I said to you the first day we talked?'

'Every word.'

'I said then, didn't I, that I trusted you. Now more than ever I mean it.'

He looked at her steadily. 'Don't be worrying, if it is sure you are.'

'It is, it is.' She reached the door, still looking back, then a sob shook her and she ran back and took his hands. 'I am

64

sure, but I can't believe it is happening. Tell me it's true, we are to meet in Dublin.'

He bent his head and kissed her on the mouth. 'There's a whole world between us, but 'tis true, we shall meet in Dublin. Now, you leave me, Hester, before 'tis missed you are.'

No one had missed her. It seemed incredible, but when Hester let herself into the house and went up to her room, she could still hear someone playing the piano in the drawing room. The eternity she had spent with Daniel had been no more than an hour. Did it take so little time to change one's destiny?

She lay on her bed, fully dressed, her hands pressed to her lips as though she could hold the sensations of Daniel's kiss for ever. No one had ever kissed her on the mouth before. She was totally unprepared for what she was feeling now and could have laughed when she compared his kiss with the pecks and brushes silly young men had sometimes attempted in country-house gardens or ballroom conservatories. This was what it was all about, then? Love, sex, marriage, children . . . things she had never let herself think about before, now unrolled before her like the promise of her own future to come. All on the strength of this one hard kiss . . .

'Oh, dear God, what am I thinking of?'

The evening light was fading, there were voices on the stairs. She sprang up and turned the key in her door in case Marianne should look in, then stood, trembling, in the middle of the room.

She had let Daniel Molloy kiss her, she had said she would go to Dublin, see him there, had asked him to see her there – and she didn't even know that he loved her. Did he love her? He had kissed her, he had said he would see her in Dublin, but had made it plain he would not be 'joining' her. Not joining, no, of course not, she had never asked him to, had he really for one moment thought she had meant – She began to blush again, a deep, hard, painful red that rose from her throat to her brow and made her undress quickly and stand at her wash bowl, splashing her face and breasts and towelling herself dry in an effort to shut out her thoughts.

But when she was in her nightgown and lying in bed, the thoughts came crowding back. She had said she would go to Dublin, she had said she would throw her whole life aside, her family, her religion, her position, for that was what going to Dublin might mean, she could not deny it, and all for a man who had not even told her he loved her. A groom. A Catholic. She was mad. Crazy. She tossed in her sheets in agony, crying: 'I won't go, I needn't, I won't go.'

She knew she would go and put her fingers to her lips again. She had no choice.

Eight

Even though she was not looking forward to the Fitzmirran ball (quite the reverse, she was dreading it), Alice dressed for it with particular care. Whatever happened, she must look her best; so much, she decided, she owed herself. The hope that Richard might propose to her was distinctly forlorn, but still he might, and if he did, all eyes would be upon her and she must be ready to meet them. If he did not propose, if he proposed to – she skated over Charlotte's name – someone else, then it was even more imperative that she should be beautiful. Even more eyes, she thought cynically, would be on her then.

Mena helped her to dress, sighing and exclaiming over Alice's smooth skin, her glossy hair, her perfect complexion. First, there was the bathing in the hip bath and the drying in soft towels, then the items of clothing presented by Mena with the manner of a high priestess and draped over Alice as over a goddess. White, lace-edged linen drawers, a lace-edged bust bodice, white stockings, whalebone stays with a metal busk to flatten Alice's already flat stomach and a wire 'camel's hump' to provide the shelf of the bustle effect, then a full-length lace-edged petticoat, followed by a second petticoat with a frill, and finally the ball gown itself, of rose-pink silk with low-cut neckline, three-quarter sleeves trimmed with bows, a ruched apron skirt and a great wave of flounces at the back that fell from the bustle and swept the floor. Then Alice was ready – except for her long white leather gloves, fastened with tiny buttons, her fan of pink feathers, and her mother's seed pearls, borrowed for the occasion and fastened now with reverent care by Mena's small fingers.

'Now,' she breathed over Alice's shoulder, 'there's just yer roses for yer hair ... Oh, Miss Alice, if you could just *see* yourself!'

'Well, of course I can,' Alice said.

She moved slowly to the cheval glass in the corner of her room and studied herself in it. I am beautiful, she thought. No one can deny it, yet what does it signify? Nothing, it seems.

Her eyes moved to the reflection of Mena standing behind her, awed and excited, a little pathetic. Poor child! Life was so unfair. People said there was a pattern, but who knew what it was? The thought came into her mind that if by any chance Richard did take her to the Argentine, she might ask Mena to go with her. It would be a wonderful chance for her, a new life, an exciting life, away from the poverty of Ireland, and at the same time a reminder of home for Alice. A perfect plan. Alice sighed. For a moment she had felt they were already on their way, she and Mena ...

Charlotte came in, sensuously gliding, her yellow hair carelessly arranged, her dress not even properly pressed.

'Really, Charlotte, whatever will the Fitzmirrans think of you?' Alice exclaimed. 'Couldn't you have taken a little more care?'

'Why blame me? You know Nora is about as much good with a flat iron as Mayfly and you kept Mena for yourself.' Charlotte ran her cool gaze over her sister. 'Anyway, never in this world could I ever look like you, Alice. Why am I not pale green with envy, I wonder?'

'You have your own attractions, as you very well know.'

Alice gave Mena a coin or two from her dressing table and told her she had done very well. Perhaps she would run down now to see if the hired carriage had arrived from Skibbereen? They should soon be making a start for Mirran House.

Charlotte suggested they should see if the others were ready. Hester was so much of a dreamer, she was probably still reading a book, and Marianne wasn't even certain she should be going to the ball, what would dear Everard say?

But Hester and Marianne were both ready, Hester in

68

oyster satin, Marianne in pale blue, both with cream roses in their hair and looking rather pale.

'Nerves,' Marianne whispered. 'Before a ball I always get terrible butterflies in my – you know – inside.'

'I'm sure Hester doesn't,' said Charlotte, taking her cousin's arm as they approached the staircase. 'I'm sure she has better things to think about than butterflies.'

'Why, what should I be thinking about?' Hester asked quickly.

'Your old books, of course – Somebody's *Constitutional Law*, Somebody Else's *History of Something or Other* – don't you prefer them to dancing?'

'Not necessarily.' Hester withdrew her arm from Charlotte's. 'Sometimes I enjoy a ball.'

'And I always do. Let's see if the carriage is come.'

John Wintour was waiting for them in the hall, wearing formal evening clothes, for he was to accompany them; Ernestine, who was not, was wrapped in an Indian shawl and giving Nora orders to bring up a dish of tea directly everyone had left.

'Beautiful as you all look,' she declared, 'I shall be much happier with my work and my tea than sitting on a nasty little chair with all the other chaperones.'

'Why, Mama, you may dance if you wish,' Alice said, with concern. 'Papa is here to escort you.'

'No, no, my dancing days are over.' Ernestine sighed heavily. 'Your father proposed to me at a ball, you know – do you remember, John? It was at the Loders', as I recall. I wore a white crinoline and white roses in my hair, which was just as dark as yours, Alice.' As her eyes rested on her elder daughter, she exclaimed: 'My dear, I must paint you the way you look tonight. You must put on your gown and sit for me tomorrow, for you will never remember, you know, when you are old, how you used to look.'

'Oh, tush, Mama, who is going to be old?' asked Charlotte. 'Thank heavens, here comes Richard. Is the carriage ready, Richard?'

'Ready and waiting.'

He looked well in his dark evening tails, a white stock at his throat, his blond hair smoothed straight, but he was

69

plainly not at his ease. Perhaps the sight of the four girls in their glad rags unnerved him, thought John, who sometimes felt there were too many women about himself, or perhaps it was just that he knew he had to propose to Charlotte that evening and was getting cold feet. John felt he wouldn't blame him, if that were the case. Charlotte was attractive enough, but so flighty, so willing to laugh at a fellow, so willing to laugh at everything, in fact, it was as though nothing in life deserved her respect. In some ways, she reminded John of his sister Beatrice, but then Beatrice had settled down in the end, if with a papist foreigner, and, to be fair, had more depths to her character than Charlotte. All the same, if Richard was planning to share his life with Charlotte *and* Beatrice, John couldn't say he envied him, not in the least.

He consulted his gold watch and said they should be making a start, didn't want to be late for the Fitzmirrans. He kissed Ernestine on the cheek and told her not to wait up.

The maids looked on as the ladies were tucked into the carriage, John taking his place between Alice and Charlotte, Richard his on the box beside the driver. Hester's gaze, covertly searching the shrubbery that led to the stables, fell at last on her gloved hands. Of Daniel Molloy, there was no sign.

Mirran House, built at the same time as the second Belcarron, was far more imposing, a country seat rather than a country house, and owned by a family who had the resources to maintain it. The money came from James Fitzmirran's wife Anna, the daughter of a wealthy Viennese banking family, and if there were those who were inclined to look down on such a source, there were others in the gentry who envied its advantages, especially at a time when income from land was becoming increasingly shaky. Certainly John Wintour would have given a great deal for the chequebook power of James Fitzmirran, and Richard, coming into contact with its evidence for the first time, was impressed.

As their carriage bowled smoothly up the long drive through the landscaped park and halted at the portico of the great house, Charlotte said in a loud whisper:

'Now, girls, just watch Richard make a play for Geraldine Fitzmirran. Every man from here to Dublin will be doing the same. What a shame there's no young Mr Fitzmirran for us poor girls!'

'Charlotte, I have warned you about your tongue,' her father said and sighed. 'Kindly control it.'

'Just my joke,' she said sweetly. 'You don't mind a little joke, do you, Richard?'

He gave her his hand to help her down from the carriage. He said harshly: 'Everything is a joke to you, Charlotte.'

'Well, this house isn't. Have you ever seen such a solemn pile?'

'I think it most impressive,' Marianne murmured. 'But it makes me feel more nervous than ever.'

'No need, you'll have lots of partners. There are always loads of young men here for Geraldine and they can't all dance with her – some will just have to ask us!'

'Charlotte,' Richard whispered urgently, as the ladies were being wafted to leave their wraps in the upper regions. 'Will you promise me the supper dance? I have something I should like to say to you.'

'That sounds so intriguing – but I'm sorry, Richard, I have already promised it to someone else.'

'That's impossible, you have only just received your card.'

'I was asked some time ago. On Oyster Island, as a matter of fact, the day of the picnic.'

'By Dudley Sarn?'

'The same. He knew, of course, that we should both be here tonight.'

'Then perhaps you will do me the honour of offering me some other dance?'

'Of course, but ask me when I come down, Richard. People are looking at us and Papa is wanting to present you to the Fitzmirrans. Don't you see Geraldine putting her eyes through you? She's heard all about my handsome cousin from England – I shouldn't be a bit surprised if she were to give you the supper dance, just to give everyone a fright.'

The stately, cold-eyed daughter of the house would not have appealed to Richard even if he had been able to see her properly, but his eyes were unable to focus on anyone tonight

71

except Charlotte. He behaved with perfect correctness, of course, as his uncle presented him to his hosts, but it did not worry him that their eyes slid over him, taking in his good looks and wondering just how eligible he might be, and he did not ask Miss Fitzmirran if he might add his name to her card. As Charlotte had predicted, it was, in any case, pretty full.

The first dance of the evening Richard gave, as protocol demanded, to Alice, the elder of his cousins. They made an extraordinarily attractive pair as they took the floor for the waltz, he so blond, she so dark, and heads turned to follow as he guided her skilfully down the ballroom.

'You are looking particularly lovely tonight, Alice,' he managed to get out, as his eyes raked the other dancers for the sight of a yellow head. Alice made a murmur of acknowledgement, but did not smile; he could feel her hand trembling in his.

'This is a really splendid ball,' he went on. 'I don't believe I've been to anything so grand in England. Of course, I'm not exactly in society.' He laughed. 'As I expect Miss Fitzmirran surmised. She made me feel I should have a label round my neck: son of a Poor English Clergyman.'

'Who may inherit Belcarron,' Alice said quietly.

The rhythm of their dancing was checked as Richard made an error, corrected himself, then smoothly continued.

'Perhaps we shouldn't discuss that,' he murmured. 'Nothing is settled.'

'If it embarrasses you, of course we will not, but I rather think it is settled, is it not?'

'Has your father said anything to you?'

'Not a word. That is how I know it's settled. He has been avoiding being alone with me ever since your arrival. Of course' – Alice's eyes flickered over her sister, moving by in the arms of Dudley Sarn – 'he may have other reasons for that.'

They finished the dance in silence. Richard handed Alice over to Cavan Morry and went through the dutiful motions of dancing with his sisters. Marianne was radiant; whatever dear Everard would have thought, she was having a wonderful time. Many young men had asked for her card, and she had even been booked for the supper dance by a quite exalted being from Dublin. As for Hester – through the mists of his preoccupation, Richard perceived that something was different about Hester. Normally, at a function like this, she would have been firing off volleys of amusing attacks on the absurd rituals of the marriage market, which was how she usually described balls, but tonight all that was absent. She looked elegant, she appeared to be in demand, but dancing with her was like dancing with someone – he tried to describe it to himself – who wasn't there.

'Are you all right?' he asked her. 'Not feeling the heat, or anything?'

'Do I look ill?'

'No. Only different.'

'I'm surprised you know how anyone looks who isn't Charlotte. Has she spared you a dance yet?'

'Of course.'

'But not the supper dance, I'll hazard a guess – that will be for Dudley Sarn.'

Again, Richard finished a dance in silence.

The evening was warm and the glass doors of the ballroom were open to the terrace which ran the full length of the rear of the house; beyond were lawns and a sunken rose garden where some guests were choosing to stroll or sit out. Richard, coming to claim Charlotte, asked her if she would walk there with him. It was not yet quite dusk, it would be quite proper and the scented air was pleasant after the heat of the ballroom.

'Proper? Oh, goodness, we're cousins, aren't we? Practically brother and sister. Of course I'll walk with you, Richard.'

'You think of me as a brother?' he asked stiffly.

'You're the nearest I shall ever have.'

'I believe you know I want to be something more than a brother to you, Charlotte.'

She gave him a sidelong glance and put her hand on his arm. 'Come, let's walk, then, before my next partner comes looking for me.'

'Dudley Sarn?' Richard's face twisted. 'You've been enjoying yourself lately, playing the flirt with him, haven't you?'

73

'One can hardly play the flirt with one's fiancé, Richard.'

He stood very still and put her hand away from his arm. 'I don't understand you, Charlotte. Are you saying Sarn has proposed marriage to you?'

'On Oyster Island.' Her eyes shone. 'I'm afraid he asked for more than the supper dance.'

'I seem to remember your saying that day you didn't want to marry for years.'

'Smokescreen, Richard. We didn't want anyone to know until I'd met Dudley's people – I am to make a visit next month to their place near Dublin. Then Dudley will formally speak to Papa.'

'I see.' Richard stood looking down at her, his eyes glittering in his mottled face. 'It seems I am the one you've been playing with, then. You knew I was in love with you, you knew I planned to ask you to be my wife, yet you deliberately held this information from me, you chose to lead me on, flaunting yourself, making me want you . . . I think you're no better than' – his voice thickened, stumbled – 'no better than a – '

'Be careful,' she interrupted coolly. 'Do not forget that you are a gentleman, Richard.'

'I know I am a gentleman,' he whispered furiously. 'But what are you? What are you, Charlotte? I wish Dudley Sarn joy of his bargain, and I only hope for my uncle's sake that he does not regret it and send you packing when he learns what kind of woman you really are!'

'If you're concerned for my father, please keep your voice down, Richard, and try to stop behaving like a madman. I never led you on, I never promised you anything, you never asked me for anything. If Dudley and I want to keep our betrothal a secret, that is entirely our affair, nothing at all to do with you.'

'Nothing at all to do with me? For God's sake, Charlotte, don't you understand anything of what I've been saying to you? I love you, I want you – in spite of everything, that's still true. I want to take you to the Argentine with me, make a life, have children by you. Look.' He snatched at her hand. 'I'm sorry for the way I spoke to you just then, it was unforgivable, I don't know what happened. I just wanted to

74

hurt you, I suppose, for the way you'd hurt me – please say you forgive me?'

'Of course I forgive you,' she said indifferently. 'But it doesn't change anything. I can't marry you, Richard, and you must accept that. I have given my word to Dudley and I am going to keep it.'

'Tell me if you love him, then, tell me.'

'I'm quite fond of him.'

'Fond? You're only eighteen years old and that's all you want, Charlotte, to marry someone you're *fond* of?'

She was silent for a time, then turned back towards the house. 'It's getting dark,' she said, over her shoulder. 'Look, they're lighting the lanterns. Let's go in.'

At the glass doors to the ballroom, they hesitated, even Charlotte seeming a little subdued.

'We should never have been happy, Richard, we're far too much alike. Alice will make you a far better wife than I ever could, and you were always intended for her, weren't you?'

'I don't love Alice,' he said, in a low voice, 'I love you.'

'But you want Belcarron and Alice goes with Belcarron.'

'No. Your father has promised Belcarron to me.'

He had the satisfaction of seeing real surprise on her features, before her eyes sparkled and her lips curved into one of her cynical smiles.

'Well, well, my poor old sister ... Oh, but don't you see, Richard, Papa only intends for you to marry her, he'd never leave you Belcarron if you were to marry me!'

'That is not what he told me.'

'I don't care what he told you. If you and I had actually married, he'd have changed his will back to Alice the minute we signed the register, he'd never have left her with no husband and no home. Why, I should say you've been very lucky indeed, Richard, that I turned you down!'

The Wintours spoke little on the drive home. John slept most of the way, his head gradually falling towards Alice's shoulder, then jerking upright, then gradually falling again, as she twisted beneath its weight and stared into space. Marianne hummed a waltz tune to herself, then wondered if it would be improper, perhaps, to write how much she had enjoyed herself in her diary, for she and Everard had always said they would have no secrets from each other and if he were to read her diary, what would he think? Should she discuss it with Hester? Not now, for Hester seemed in a world of her own and Charlotte, smiling secret smiles, would overhear. Tomorrow would do. Up on the box beside O'Dowd, Richard was a being apart.

Mena had waited up for them and came running with candles and offers of tea. Was it a good time they'd been having, then? Everything at Belcarron was as quiet as the grave, so it was, but maybe one day she would be getting to a dance then, and why not?

'One day you will, Mena, I'm sure,' said Alice. 'But don't worry now about tea. We're all too tired, we're just going straight upstairs.'

As she took her candle, Hester suddenly called her name. From the foot of the staircase, Alice looked back.

'Yes, Hester, what is it?'

'I – why, nothing.' Hester glanced away. 'I just wanted to say goodnight.'

'Goodnight, then. I do hope you enjoyed the evening.'

Alice went on up the stairs and one by one the others followed, Marianne and Hester last, after John Wintour had shouted down to Mena to be sure to lock up.

'Hester,' whispered Marianne, 'do you think it was proper of me to have enjoyed the ball?'

'Of course it was! It was right that you should.'

'I'm so glad you think so, I've been worrying.'

'Don't always go by what I say, Marianne. I'm not the wisest person in the world.'

'Why, Hester, of course you are!'

Hester kissed her swiftly on the cheek. 'Goodnight, Marianne, take care.'

'Goodnight, Hester.'

In the morning it was Marianne who found the letters Hester had written, one to her parents in Dorset, the other to 'All my family at Belcarron'. Of Hester herself, there was no sign.

Nine

There was no sense in it, Richard declared, Hester's letter to her family made no sense at all. He read it aloud over the breakfast table with Nora standing at the door, ready to clear, and they all agreed, it made no sense at all.

By the time you read this, [Hester had written] I shall be travelling to Dublin, where I intend to make something of a new life for myself. I have arranged with O'Dowd to send over a driver and trap to take me to Kilvane for the first train out and shall be staying in a small hotel until I can find private lodgings of my own. Please do not try to find me. I shall send an address and write more as soon as I can, but please do try to understand that I know what I am doing and that I believe I can be happy. I send my love to you all,
> Hester.

There was a postscript for Marianne in which Hester said she might not be able to attend her wedding but wished her every happiness, and would she please give Hester's other letter to their parents and assure them that there was no need to worry.

'It's the most extraordinary thing I've ever heard in my life,' John Wintour exclaimed, fixing on his pince-nez in order to read Hester's letter for himself. 'We had no inkling, none of us had any inkling, how could she have planned all this without a word? What can she have been thinking of?' He put down the letter, took off his pince-nez and rubbed his eyes. 'If it had been anyone but Hester, anyone but her, I could have understood – '

'No, Papa, you would not have understood,' said Charlotte. 'The problem now is, what do we tell people?'

'Why should we tell them anything? Richard and his sisters were due to leave in a couple of days anyway.'

'So no one need know that Hester has run away to Dublin?'

'Run away?' Alice repeated. 'She has not run away, she has simply left to find her independence. If it had been Richard who had gone, no one would have thought it strange.'

'But Hester is not Richard,' Marianne wailed. 'And Everard will never understand.'

'Will Dudley Sarn?' Richard asked Charlotte, at which she shook her head angrily and glanced at her father, but he was not listening.

'Hester is a young lady on her own,' he muttered. 'She has gone to a city where she has no friends or connections. What am I to tell her parents? They will be distracted. And she was in my care.'

Richard, pushing back his chair, began to walk about the dining room.

'Perhaps I should try to find her, Uncle. I don't know how we can return without her, it would be absurd. I had better go after her and bring her to her senses.'

Ernestine, buttering a last piece of toast, said: 'My dears, I really shouldn't try to do anything. Hester is over twenty-one, she has money of her own, she has a right to do as she wishes. If you were to follow her and find her, I am sure it would only be very embarrassing. She has almost certainly gone off with Daniel Molloy.'

'Oh, Ernestine, Ernestine!' John groaned. 'Please do not make matters any worse than they are.'

But Richard's face had taken on its familiar mottling. 'My God, the books!' he cried. 'Now I know where she was always disappearing to: she was taking books to Molloy. Now her letter makes sense, doesn't it? A new life, indeed – this is the old story, this is love, this is sex – '

'Richard, remember the ladies,' John said sharply.

'Anyway, we can easily find out the truth. Nora, ask Molloy to come here at once.'

'If you please, sir,' Nora answered, without expression, 'Molloy is gone.'

Marianne gave a cry; the others were silent.

'He left a letter with Mrs Heenan, sir,' Nora went on. ''Twas his notice, he was saying.'

'Did he say he was going to Dublin? Was he taking the first train?'

'Not the first, sir, sure he wouldn't have had the time. Wasn't he walking to Kilvane?'

'But he was going to Dublin?'

'Yes, sir, he was after saying he was wanted there.'

'Wanted? What did he mean?'

'I couldn't be telling you, sir, 'twas no more than that he was saying. Shall I be clearing away now?'

John looked across at the grandfather clock in the corner of the dining room and leaped to his feet, his eyes alight.

'Richard, my boy, why are we sitting around here? We have only to take the trap to catch up with Molloy and give him the hiding of his life. He'll be in no state to go to Dublin when we've finished with him – '

'Papa!' Alice cried. 'We don't even know that he is planning to meet Hester. This is all surmise.'

'Of course it is,' Richard agreed coldly, 'or so he would say. What proof have we that he and Hester have exchanged more than a couple of words? They've been too clever for us, travelling separately this way. They've tied our hands, we can do nothing.'

'Then we shall go to Dublin and fetch Hester back, anyway. If Molloy is wanted there, there let him stay, but she must be brought home.'

'No,' said Richard, 'I will not bring her back.'

'What do you mean?' cried John, his face working. 'You must! She's your sister. You're not trying to tell me that you are refusing to save your sister?'

'What sister?' asked Richard. 'My sister Marianne is here. I have no other sister.'

That evening, after a dinner no one could eat, Richard took

79

Alice walking in the grounds. Among the trees, out of sight of the house, he asked her to marry him. He made it plain that he did not love her, but after what Hester had done in the name of love, that did not signify. Alice would be all the happier if he offered her instead his care, his consideration and his honour. If she would settle for these things, they could be married and leave for the Argentine as soon as possible.

Her face as white as the shawl she had put round her shoulders, Alice said: 'Yesterday, you asked my sister to marry you. Did you think she would not have told me?'

'I knew she would tell you.'

'And today you ask me. What am I to make of that? One sister is as good as another, is that it?'

'No. I'll be frank, I want there to be no secrets between us. I am still in love with Charlotte, I can't be free as easily as that.'

'So, how can you speak of marriage to me?' Alice cried fiercely. 'How dare you, Richard?'

'Because I want no more part of that kind of destructive love, because I've seen today what it can do.'

'You're speaking of Hester, yet you don't know – '

'I do know. She has ruined her whole life for a man's body. Yes – don't look so shocked – it's true. I've been saved from making that kind of mistake, I still have a chance of something better. If you will take me, Alice.'

'You must see,' she said, painfully, 'how difficult it is for me.'

'I know and I shouldn't ask so soon, if we had time, but we have not. I have to go to the Argentine and I would rather not go alone.' As she still hesitated, he said softly, 'I am very fond of you, Alice, genuinely fond. We have much in common, including a love for Belcarron. Isn't that more important than anything else? Even than us?'

'Yes, that is true.'

'Then, will you accept me? And in due course we can look after it together?'

'That was all I wanted,' she said, wearily, 'a long time ago.'

'And still want, don't you?'

'I don't know, I don't know.'

'I think you do.'

He passed his arm gently around her waist and drew her towards him. As she did not resist, he kissed her on the cheek, then moved his mouth to her lips, which after a moment of hesitation responded so willingly that the kiss became long and passionate. As they at last parted, both breathing hard, Richard said:

'I believe you have given me your answer, Alice, haven't you?'

When they returned to the house, it was to tell John and Ernestine that they were engaged.

'Thank God,' said John, simply.

'How lovely!' said Ernestine. 'I must prepare a canvas for the wedding.'

Marianne, her eyelids still swollen with weeping, came up at once to embrace Alice. Charlotte cried: 'Congratulations!' and kissed first Alice and then Richard. They both had the feeling she would have laughed in their faces, except that after the blow Hester had dealt, even Charlotte did not feel like laughing.

As they were temporarily without a groom, John said he would himself drive Richard and Marianne to Kilvane for the start of their long journey home. On the morning of departure, Richard and Alice said goodbye at the top of the path to the sea.

'I used to watch you setting off to fish from here,' Alice said. 'Your boat would come round from the village and then I'd watch it out of sight.'

'I never knew that.'

'Today I shall have to watch you going much farther away and for longer.'

'I'll be back in September for the wedding, with the parents.'

'Will they . . . ' Alice hesitated. 'Will they want to go to Dublin, do you think?'

'I shall dissuade them.'

Alice stared down at the sea, dark blue today and calm. 'Richard, would you mind if I took Mena with us to the Argentine?'

'Mena? Whatever for?'

'As my personal maid. It would be a wonderful opportunity for her to lead a new life, and she would remind me of Belcarron.'

'Have you asked her if she'd like to go?'

Alice looked a little shamefaced. 'I have, as a matter of fact. Also her mother, who asked Father O'Mara; you know how they always like to ask the priest's advice.'

'And they were all in favour?'

'Very much so, especially as the Argentine is a Catholic country. There might be someone there for her to marry, whereas there's no one here.'

'Seems you didn't need my permission at all,' Richard commented coldly, and Alice was full of contrition.

'I'm sorry, I was sure you'd agree, but of course if you have anything against it, we need go no further. I know we'd have to pay her fare – '

'Oh, by all means, take her if you want her. I dare say she will be a help to you in the early days. But now, give me your hand, Alice, let's discuss something more important. Does this fit?'

He placed on the third finger of her left hand a handsome, old-fashioned ring of diamonds and pearls. Alice caught her breath.

'Grandmother Maria's ring,' she whispered. 'It fits perfectly.'

'You know it was left to me, as the only remaining son, to give to my bride. So now I give it to you.'

Alice looked at it for a moment, watching the sunlight catch the stones, then burst into tears.

'I know I shouldn't be, with all that's happened, Richard, but I'm so happy – '

'Ssh, you've every right to be happy, every right.' He bent to whisper: 'Don't cry any more, Charlotte is coming.'

She came swaying across the lawn towards them, her yellow hair glinting, and said she was so sorry, Papa was waiting, Richard must go if he wanted to catch the train. Her eye fell on the ring on Alice's finger and she caught at her sister's hand to take a closer look.

'Grandmother Maria's ring? Of course, she left it to you, didn't she, Richard? How lucky that it fits Alice so well! I'm sure I should never have been able to keep it on.'

Ten

The wedding was held in St John's Church, Carron, on the second Saturday in September, a fine, warm, golden day. Charlotte and Marianne in pale-blue silk were bridesmaids, an old schoolfriend of Richard's was best man and a depressed-looking Cavan Morry was usher. The service was taken by the Reverend Arthur Barnes, assisted by Matthew Wintour and Everard Lister, Marianne's serious, narrow-faced fiancé. Richard in morning dress looked almost unbelievably handsome; Alice in cream satin, carrying pink roses, unbelievably beautiful. All the guests, most of the Protestant gentry of the district, agreed it was one of the most perfect weddings possible and the reception afterwards at Belcarron quite superb. How John Wintour had managed to pay for it was a matter for conjecture, but if he had indeed bankrupted himself, it had surely been worth it.

Alice, as brides do, alternated between looking radiant and bursting into tears. (It was said she had spent her wedding morning going round every room in the house to say goodbye and had had to be hauled up from the beach almost by force.) Yet there was no doubt she was totally in love with her bridegroom, could scarcely take her eyes off him, and if his gaze did not follow her so often, no doubt he was still recovering from his bachelor party at Kilvane, where it was said champagne had flowed like water and Richard had not been unwilling to go with the tide.

Probably he was beginning to feel better by the time he had to get into the going-away carriage. Even so, he left it to Alice to do most of the final embracing, which she did over

85

and over again. Several times she left the carriage to kiss her parents yet again and to remind the weeping Mena she would see her tomorrow in Cork, she had nothing to cry about. Then it was time to throw the bouquet and, though Alice aimed for Marianne, it was Charlotte who threw up her hand and caught it, sending a triumphant smile to the bridegroom as she did so.

'Write!' cried John and Ernestine. 'Write!' cried Constance, Richard's solemn-faced mother.

'We will,' cried Alice. 'We will!'

Then Philip O'Dowd flicked the reins over the horse and the carriage began to move, the younger guests running alongside, throwing rice and laughing, before they had to fall back and Alice and Richard were drawn away from sight.

It was a great relief to all concerned that no one at any time had mentioned Richard's sister Hester.

The newlyweds were to spend their first night in Cork, their second in Dublin, from where they were to cross to Liverpool to board the steamship for Buenos Aires. In their reserved compartment on the train carrying them to Cork, both were silent; the strain and euphoria of the wedding over, they were exhausted. Alice's gaze from the window was fixed on the landscape with particular intensity.

'See the fields, Richard? It's true what is said, you know, they are greener in Ireland than anywhere else.'

'Greener and smaller,' he replied.

'Because fathers try to give every son a piece. Papa calls it economic folly.'

'What a phrase for you!' Richard gave an indulgent smile. 'Ah, well, everyone knows the Irish are crazy about land. Can't blame them, I suppose, for trying to make it go further. What would they make of the Argentine pampas, I wonder? They say it's so vast, you can't imagine it, you have to see it to comprehend it.'

'All I comprehend is that we're seeing the last of Ireland,' Alice muttered, with a catch in her voice. 'That is enough for me.'

'Why do you talk like that? You know we're not going for ever.'

'Who knows how long we're going for? We may die there – may never see Ireland again.'

He leaned forward and took her hand. 'This is morbid talk, Alice, not like you. You're overtired. When you've had some rest, you'll see things differently.'

The thought crossed their minds that honeymoon nights were not supposed to be restful. Alice, colouring faintly, said she would read her book for a while and Richard said he would look at his paper.

'When we get to Dublin,' Alice said, after a pause, 'do you think it is possible we might see Hester?'

Richard reluctantly raised his eyes. 'You know my views on Hester, Alice. I do not wish to discuss her.'

'But we don't even know for sure that she is with Molloy.'

'I've said I don't want to discuss her.' Richard looked down at his newspaper again. 'Anyway, it's most unlikely in a city the size of Dublin we'd be able to find her. Papa tried, you know, in spite of all I said, and he drew a blank. So let's forget her.'

'I should just have liked to say goodbye to her.'

'She has said goodbye to us,' Richard said coldly. 'For ever.'

Their hotel in Cork turned out to be quite grand and their room luxurious; it had its own bathroom attached, with a huge mahogany-surrounded bath and vast WC. Alice said she had never seen anything like it and was concerned about the cost. Richard said if they couldn't do themselves proud on their honeymoon, when could they? Anyway, he had come into a little family money on his marriage, most of which they would need in the Argentine, but he had felt quite justified in spending the rest on cabin-class passages on the steamship (except for Mena, of course) and good hotels. There was also the possibility that Aunt Beatrice would cough up something – after all, it was she who had asked him to go in the first place.

'Oh, but she didn't ask me,' Alice said, in sudden consternation. 'I've never thought of that before. What will she say when I arrive, do you think?'

'Don't worry, I wrote to her as soon as we became engaged. She'll be expecting you.'

'Thank heavens for that. A married couple is quite different, after all, from a handsome, unattached young man . . .'

'Why, Alice,' Richard asked, laughing, 'where did you learn to be so cynical, then?'

'From Charlotte, of course,' she replied, and saw his brow darken.

They dined in the restaurant, where Alice worried in case the other guests should see any grains of rice still attached to her elegant dark-red going-away outfit. Richard said even without rice she would still look like a bride, there was nothing she could do about it.

'But everyone is looking at us, Richard.'

'That's because you're so lovely. You should be proud.'

'I believe they're looking at you, too.'

'Ah, with me, you see, it's just the rice.'

Back in their room, Richard said they had had a very tiring day and would have another tomorrow, travelling to Dublin; perhaps they should have an early night? Alice slowly looked from him to the great double bed with its brass-knobbed ends and mountainous pillows and quilts. He cleared his throat.

'We needn't . . . you know.' He paused. 'If you liked, we could just sleep tonight – as you're tired.'

'I'm not tired'. She unbuttoned her jacket and laid it on a chair. 'Are you?'

'No. No, I'm not tired.'

'It is our first night, isn't it? And I do know what that means, Richard.'

He gave a long sigh and ran his hands through his yellow hair. 'I was wondering, I must admit. I didn't see Aunt Ernestine, somehow – '

'Mama?' Alice gave a ringing laugh. 'Mama didn't tell me, Richard, it was Mena.'

'Mena? You're not serious – she's only fifteen!'

'If you live in a cabin with your parents and nine children, you know the facts of life, Richard.' Alice blushed a little. 'I have to tell you, I didn't believe it when she first told us – told Charlotte and me. It sounded so . . . ludicrous.'

'I know. I couldn't connect it with my parents at all, when I first heard.'

'Who told you?'

'Someone at school.'

'I suppose it would have been.' Alice took her nightgown from her dressing case. 'I'll run my bath, shall I? I'm so looking forward to using that beautiful bathroom.'

'All right,' said Richard. 'I'll wait here.'

He took off his clothes, looked at his nightshirt, decided against it and put on his dressing gown. He thought of Mena explaining sex to Alice and Charlotte, of Charlotte listening, and covered his eyes with his hand as though he would shut her image from his mind.

The door of the bathroom opened and Alice appeared, wearing a thin lawn nightdress, her hair loose on her shoulders. Richard, looking up, realised he had never seen her with her hair down before. It made her look different. As she crossed the room to hang up her clothes in the hotel's ornate wardrobe, he watched her body moving beneath the fine lawn; it was amazing. So obviously desirable, so obviously ready for love, he could not associate it with Alice at all. Suddenly, he wanted her.

'I'll turn down the gas,' he said hoarsely.

She moved to the side of the bed. 'Shall I take off my nightdress?' she asked.

'If . . . if you want to.'

'Is it usual, though?'

'Good God, Alice, I don't know what's usual.'

He took off his dressing gown and Alice, after a moment's hesitation, pulled her nightdress over her head. They looked at each other in the shadows cast by the low gas flame, then, under the vast feather-filled quilt, their bodies met. Richard had meant to be very gentle, very considerate, but it wasn't possible, she excited him too much and he took her too quickly and heard her cry out. 'I'm sorry, I'm sorry,' he murmured against her. 'The first time, it has to be this way – '

'I know, I know, I don't care, I don't care at all.'

As he lay away from her, sweating and gasping, he was astonished to find her over him, her long hair damp on his skin.

'I want you again,' she whispered. 'Please, Richard.'

He laughed. 'It's not possible, Alice. You don't understand. I can't – not yet – '

She moved her mouth across his face. 'I want you, though. I want you again.'

'It's not that I don't want you, my dearest, but I've already hurt you once tonight – '

'I've told you, that doesn't matter. Take me, Richard, please.'

It was better the second time. He could feel her pleasure to be almost as intense as his own, but, even as they reached their climax, he was mystified. This he had expected from Charlotte, but from Alice? It was a bonus he could not understand.

As they lay together, spent after passion, he covered her face with soft kisses and told her it was wonderful she wanted him the way she did, he had never in the world expected it.

'I shall always want you this way,' she answered, returning his kisses. 'I know, when you are with me like this, you cannot be thinking of her.'

He was silent for so long that she became afraid and asked what she had done.

'Nothing, Alice.'

'Yes, I have. I've spoiled things. Or she has. As she always does. She has come between us, hasn't she? Even here?'

Charlotte's green eyes danced before him, he could see her, laughing, throwing back her yellow hair, and his mouth filled with dust. He turned on his side and lay staring ahead at the flickering little blue head of the gas.

'Richard!' She tried to turn him back towards her, but her hands slipped on his glistening skin and she had to let go.

'Try to sleep,' he said, over his shoulder. 'We'll feel better in the morning.'

He heard her get up and guessed that she had gone to wash herself, wash herself free of him and his love, and he lay rigid, waiting for her to come back, but he must have drifted into sleep for he did not hear her return. In the morning, when he gradually came awake, he saw that she was already up and dressed and arranging her hair.

'Alice!'

At the sound of her name, she turned and faced him. He was stricken to see how pale she looked and how far she seemed from the radiant bride of yesterday.

'You should take your bath,' she said calmly. 'We must go down for breakfast.'

As she put the last pin into her hair, he left the bed, pulling his dressing gown around him. 'About last night – ' he began, but she cut him short.

'I don't think we should discuss last night, Richard. We both made mistakes. Let's forget it.'

Her gaze fell on the turned-back sheets and she gave an exclamation of distaste. 'Spots of blood – what will the chambermaid say?'

It should have been easier, having Mena as a third person with them when they moved on to Dublin, except that Richard could not look the girl in the face after what Alice had told him. Besides, there was the possibility that her sharp eyes would see something amiss between Alice and himself and that she might be stupid enough to remark on it; fortunately, whether she saw anything or not, she said nothing.

On reaching their new hotel, Alice insisted on going up with Mena to the room they had booked for her, then staying with her and talking to her until she had 'settled'. 'She is so homesick, I must do what I can,' Alice told Richard, who asked, if Mena was homesick in Dublin, what was she going to feel in the Argentine? She must be given time, Alice replied, setting her mouth in an obstinate line. The transition would be better for her in the long run.

Richard sat alone in the hotel lobby and read his newspaper, which was full of the coming autumn election, until the words Gladstone, Parnell, and Home Rule made no more sense at all. He then took a walk on the Dublin streets, hoping he would not encounter Hester, until it was time for a frosty dinner in the restaurant with Alice. Waiting for them upstairs was another brass-ended double bed where they would have to endure the ordeal of lying together with no hope tonight of love. The thought gave them little appetite for the meal, yet they both ate heartily, as though they needed the comfort of food.

'I think I will read a little,' Alice said, from the bed, when Richard came back from the bathroom, which this time was not attached to their room but on the hotel landing. He noticed that she had chosen to wear a high-necked nightdress of thick, frilled cotton and had tied her hair in a plait, the statement being as obvious as though she had worn a placard: 'Touch me if you dare.' Well, that was quite in order; he was himself wearing a nightshirt and had brought a book along too, *The History of the Argentine Republic*.

For some time, they both read in silence, then Richard closed first his book, then Alice's, and placed them on the bedside table. Then he took Alice in his arms.

'You are my wife, Alice, we are on our honeymoon, this is absurd.'

'Is it?' She wrenched herself free. 'When Charlotte shares our marriage bed? You promised me your honour. Where is your honour when you would rather it was my sister who was with you now?'

'I told you I no longer wanted your sister, I no longer wanted to be a part of destructive love. I told you I wanted to be married to you and we are married. What we have now is what marriage means, isn't it?'

'I don't know, I don't know, Richard.'

'Sharing one bed, becoming one flesh,' he said, deliberately. 'Children.'

'Children?' She caught her breath.

'Our children. Have you forgotten the marriage service already?' He took off his nightshirt. 'Now you see me naked – your husband. Will you come to me again, Alice?'

She made no protest as he drew her nightdress away and undid the heavy braid of her hair, and when they made love, which they did smoothly and easily, she responded. But the rapture he had aroused in her on their first night, the rapture that had so delighted him, was not this time present. He wondered if it would ever come again.

They took breakfast next morning in the hotel dining room and were on friendly terms, even smiling together over their

92

coffee, when suddenly Richard froze. Hester, rather thin and pale in her blue walking dress, was weaving her way between the tables towards them.

'What is it?' cried Alice, her own face changing, then, recognising Hester, laughed and held out her hands. 'Hester! How wonderful!'

Richard rose to his feet. Keeping his face resolutely averted from his sister's, he gave Alice a slight bow and asked her to excuse him. Then he walked out of the dining room.

'Alice,' Hester said, thickly, 'Alice, I can't believe it – he wouldn't speak to me! He wouldn't even look at me! My own brother!'

'Oh, my dear! Sit down, let me order you some coffee, something to eat – '

'No, thank you, I have already breakfasted.' Hester sank into a chair. 'I only came to say goodbye. I couldn't let you go so far away and not try to see you.'

'But how did you find us?'

'I saw a notice of your wedding in the newspaper, it gave the date of your sailing to the Argentine. I guessed you'd go to Liverpool from Dublin, asked at the good hotels – hey presto, I found you.' She tried to smile. 'And now Richard will not even acknowledge me. Does he begrudge me the right to my own life?'

'It's not that, Hester.' Alice looked down at her plate. 'I'm afraid it's Daniel Molloy.'

Hester's face burned scarlet. 'You know about Daniel?'

'He left on the same day. It seemed obvious.'

'I had hoped no one would guess.'

'Is it true, then? He is with you?'

'No, it is not. He is in Dublin but not with me. Not in the way you mean.'

'Then I don't understand. Is there nothing between you?'

Hester put her hands to her cheeks as though she would cool them. 'Alice, I want to tell you first I'm taking instruction in the Catholic faith. No, don't say anything. I am not alone in thinking it may be the true church. You know of the Oxford Movement, you know of Cardinal Newman? There is a case, you know, for believing there should never have been a Protestant church founded.'

'Hester, you cannot mean it, you cannot mean you are going over to Rome! It is not possible, that church is corrupt, it owes allegiance to the Pope. What are you thinking of, Hester, what can you be thinking of?'

'Daniel Molloy,' Hester answered steadily. 'I plan to marry him. He could never marry outside his faith and if I can believe his faith is the true one, then I must change.'

Alice, very pale, drank her cold coffee. 'My father's groom,' she whispered. 'A Catholic. Oh, my dear, how can you?'

'He is not your father's groom now and will be no one else's. He has a very good mind, Alice, and great strength of character. All he lacks is education and that he is obtaining now. It will not be long before – '

'Before what?'

'Before he can be of service to his country.'

'Dear God, he is a Fenian?' Alice whispered. 'Just as you said, and I laughed, I remember.'

'I don't say he is, I don't say anything, but he intends to work for the liberation of Ireland and so do I.' Hester's flush had faded, leaving her looking white and strained; she stretched out her hand and clasped Alice's. 'I have always cared for Ireland, I do truly believe the Irish should be free, but that doesn't change me, Alice. I am still the same person I always was, I still love my family and my country.'

'I am going a long way from home,' Alice said, after a pause, 'But you are going much farther. Hester, I think you are leaving us altogether.'

'I'm not, I'm not! Oh, please don't look at me like that, as though I were a lost soul! Please try to understand.'

'All I want is for you to be happy. Are you?'

'Yes. Or I will be, once everything is settled. And you, Alice? Are you happy?'

Alice's gaze fell. She removed her hand from Hester's. 'I should be, shouldn't I? I got what I wanted.'

Hester's dark eyes softened. 'Richard can be selfish,' she murmured, drawing on her gloves. 'I suppose, as the only son – the only boy in the whole family – he's used to getting his own way. But there's no harm in him, Alice, he will never want to hurt you.'

94

'He has hurt you this very day.'

'That's his pride for the family. He sees Daniel as a groom and nothing else. One day he will understand. Until then, I shall have to wait.'

They talked a little longer, about Hester's parents, Marianne and Charlotte, and Hester promised she would tell her father where she was, so that he might see her if he wished. She knew he would be grieving; she was his favourite.

'And you, Alice, you will write to me? Wait, let me give you my address, I have it here.' Hester pressed a scrap of paper into Alice's hand. 'Will you write as soon as you get to Buenos Aires?'

'I will.' Alice's gaze faltered, her lip trembled. 'Oh, Hester, what can I say? That things should be like this for us – so much to face . . .'

'Walk with me to the door,' said Hester.

In the hotel lobby, they kissed and clung to each other for a moment, weeping as much for what lay ahead as for parting.

'Bon voyage,' Hester whispered. 'Think of me. Talk of me to Richard sometimes, don't let him forget me.'

Without waiting for Alice's reply, she walked quickly through the swing doors and melted into the crowds on the Dublin street.

When Alice returned to their room, Richard was standing by the window. The look he turned on her was chill.

'All this time you have been talking to Hester, Alice?'

'Yes, indeed. Why not?'

'You know why not. It was against my wishes.'

'Your wishes?'

'I thought when I left the breakfast table, I had made them very clear.'

'You made it clear what you wanted to do. I was not aware that I had to do the same.'

He raised his eyebrows. 'Perhaps I'd better say, then, that I want you to promise me never to see Hester again, never to speak of her or write to her or have anything to do with her in any way.'

Alice moved to the dressing table and began composedly to put small items into her overnight case.

'I shall not promise you any of those things, Richard. Hester does not deserve that sort of treatment. She has done nothing wrong.'

'Nothing wrong?' His face darkened with blood. 'How can you say that, Alice? You know what she has done.'

'She is living in Dublin on her own. Is that a sin?'

'You're telling me she's not with Molloy? Not seeing him?'

'She is seeing him but is not with him.' Alice hesitated. 'There is to be a proper marriage.'

'To a groom and a papist!'

'Aunt Beatrice married a papist, Richard.'

'That was different. Her husband was a man of breeding, of standing.'

'Hester says Molloy has a very good mind and will do well.'

'A very good mind! Your father's groom!' Richard gave a scornful smile. 'She is besotted. I forbid you to have any contact with her again. You promised to obey me and so you shall.'

'Not in this,' Alice replied calmly. 'For you are in the wrong. Now, if you will excuse me, Richard, I have to prepare for our crossing to Liverpool if you have not.'

He stared at her speechlessly, his mouth slightly open. This was not a side of her he had seen before and he did not like it. Wives were meant to yield, so he had understood, but Alice's beautiful body that had yielded to him the night before was masked now by clothes, the long dark hair he had unloosed firmly coiled and pinned to her graceful neck. This was day, he slowly realised, and day in marriage was very different from night; Alice, it seemed, had already learned that lesson very well.

'Richard,' she called politely, 'would you mind ringing the bell to have our luggage taken down? Mena will be waiting for us in the lobby.'

They sailed next evening from Liverpool, standing pressed against the other passengers on the deck of the SS *Olympus*, waving and calling, until the lights grew smaller and the expanse of sea wider between them and land, when they fell silent.

Alice who had been quite remarkably composed, suddenly burst into hard, dry sobs, and Mena, who was to have been the comforted one, put her arms around her and held her until Richard parted them and said they should go below. Alice said she would watch the lights a little longer.

'You can't,' he said gently. 'They've gone.'

'Ah,' she whispered. 'So they have.'

Part II
1889–1890

Eleven

Alice woke to darkness. Richard was already up, moving round their room in the house on the *estancia*, dressing without the candle so as not to disturb her.

'Darling,' she called, 'I'm awake, I'm getting up.'

'No need,' he whispered. 'You stay where you are.'

'I'll be quick, I promise, I'll take my bath later.' She pushed back the bedclothes. 'You know I always like to watch you go off to *rodeo*.'

'All right, I'll light the candle, but I have to leave before dawn.' Richard peered out of the small lattice window. 'That won't be long.'

For four years he had been running the Estancia Sentos on the pampas and running it well. Beatrice Sentos, his aunt, the widow of Enriques, was pleased with him, had given him every freedom, but so far no hint of anything more. She might, of course, be remembering his commitment to Belcarron; he didn't know, he had never discussed his future with her. Alice said he must and he agreed he would. Maybe this very day when he returned from *rodeo*, the cattle round-up. Now he continued to look out at the dark sky and waited impatiently for Alice to finish dressing.

'Ready!' She flung a shawl round her shoulders. Even in November, almost summer in that part of the world, it was cold before the sun came up. 'Didn't keep you, did I?'

Her hand on his arm, they moved through the long, low passages of the old house, not talking, in case they woke up the children or their aunt who was visiting from Buenos Aires. Lucio, the *estancia* manager, was waiting for them in

101

the vestibule with Paola, his wife, Alice's housekeeper, who had brought a dish of *empanadas*, pastries filled with minced meat, and the coffee Richard preferred in the mornings to *mate* tea.

'All well, Lucio?' Richard asked in Spanish, which he now spoke fairly fluently, though Lucio himself liked to practise his English.

Lucio, a grave handsome man in his thirties, bowed and said everything was ready, the capataz and the gauchos were only waiting for Don Ricardo.

Richard nodded, gulped down his coffee and shrugged himself into a poncho. With muttered thanks to Paola, he put on the dark hat she handed him and clapped Lucio on the arm. *'Vámonos!'*

'Take care!' cried Alice, and he blew her a kiss as he went with Lucio into the slowly lightening darkness.

Alice, at the door, could just see the gauchos, sunk into the saddles of their short-legged, thick-bodied criollo horses which were snorting and stamping as they waited in the dew. They were so unlike the hunters back home that they might have belonged to a different species, as their riders seemed unlike any other men. Strange beings. Half Indian, half horse, the joke went, and it was true that to see a gaucho without his horse was to see a fish out of water. But their horsemanship, as Richard said, was magnificent. He did not mind if they found his own conventional style of riding amusing; over the years, he had in fact modified it.

'If ever I find myself hunting at home again, I shall probably be laughed off the field,' he told Alice, 'I've grown too used to gaucho style.'

'And when will you hunt at home again?' Alice had quietly asked.

García, the *capataz* of the gauchos, walked his horse forward and muttered something to Lucio, then both looked at Richard, who nodded and mounted his horse smoothly, all in one movement. Lucio followed and for a moment they hesitated, two dark figures on straining horses, poised to go. Then Richard raised his hand, García cried, *'Vamos!'* and men and horses moved off in a body, first at the trot, then at the gallop, and in a cloud of dust disappeared from sight.

Alice turned back into the house.

'*Muchas gracias,*' she murmured to Paola and smiled, but the tall, heavy-breasted young woman did not smile back. She made no secret of the fact she did not like Alice, for reasons Alice could not see but which Beatrice said were clear as day. Paola, she said, was jealous of Mena and Mena was Alice's protégée. It was as simple as that.

'Mena?' Alice exclaimed. 'Why ever should Paola be jealous of Mena? The poor girl is a widow, she has nothing.'

'Ah, but Lucio may have shown her sympathy. That would have been enough for Paola. You know how Latin Americans fight like wildcats over such things. Then you make matters worse by indulging the girl.'

'I do not indulge Mena, Aunt. I only try to look out for her. It was my idea to bring her here, I've always felt responsible for what happens to her.'

'You could scarcely feel responsible for poor Liam's death, Alice.'

'No,' Alice agreed, as a shadow crossed her face. 'Not for that.'

It was two years since Liam Flynn, the young Irishman Mena had met on the voyage out, had died of consumption six weeks after their wedding. Only eighteen at the time, Mena had changed from a girl to a woman, old beyond her years. The idea that she could inflame jealousy in Paola's heart would have been laughable, if it had not been so tragic.

'If only I could tell Paola to pack her box and go,' Alice brooded. But it was impossible. Lucio was Richard's right-hand man, and while he stayed, Paola stayed. Two red spots burned in Alice's face as she met the housekeeper's insolent stare, then with a swish of her skirts she left her.

Mena was already up and about in the nursery, where a young wet nurse was feeding the baby, Beatrice Ernestine, born in September of that year, 1889. Alice, who had been unable to nurse any of her children, always felt guilty in the presence of the tragic Maria. It must be so terrible to lose a child as she had done, as Alice's own mother had done. And child mortality was so common, so much a fact of life, it could happen to anyone. Aunt Beatrice had lost all three of

103

her sons, one at birth, two with fever. Alice, averting her eyes from Maria's tears, could not bear to think about it.

There was something else that had upset her. Mena had told her Maria's husband, a worker on the *estancia*, had allowed their dead child to be used as an *angelito*. It was the custom in rural areas for a dance to be held at a local inn where family and neighbours could come to say farewell to the *angelito* on the last journey to heaven. Innkeepers paid well for the use of such a child and no one seemed to mind. Alice had been horrified but Beatrice said, when you were as poor as the poor of the Argentine, you had to think of the living as well as the dead. Anyway, the ceremony was regarded as an honour, something special, not just a commercial transaction. Did Maria see it that way? Alice asked herself.

'*Buenos días,*' she murmured awkwardly, and to Mena said she would just look in on the boys.

''Tis fine they are, Miss Alice, still sleeping, good as gold.'

So like Richard, Alice thought, looking down at three-year-old Victor and two-year-old Jack – yet strangely quite unlike each other. Baby Tina was different again. Was there a hint of Richard's mother in her soft little features? Alice brushed the idea aside. Aunt Constance had many fine qualities but had never been known as a beauty, whereas Tina in Alice's eyes was beautiful already.

'Wasn't I saying, then?' asked Mena, looking fondly down on the boys. 'Good as gold, the pair of them.'

'Now, perhaps, when they're asleep.' Alice, smiling, slipped away. She had meals to order, stores to check. Later she might have time to tend her garden.

After a tiring session of weeding and watering, she rested under the shade trees and looked back at the house, the *casco*, the heart of the *estancia*. It had been built of brick and thatch by the family of Beatrice's late husband, Enriques Sentos. They were criollos, people of Spanish blood born in the Argentine, descendants of the colonists who had come to the 'Land of the Silver River'. So they had named their new country, perhaps after the great Plata, perhaps because they expected to find silver themselves, or riches anyway. Poor things, thought Alice, they had found only hardship and violence.

Violence had always been the story of the Argentine. The new settlers had had to fight Indians and invaders. When they wanted independence, they had had to fight Spain. Spain was powerful, even at a distance, establishing a vice-regency, hanging on to profits from trade, keeping down rebellion. Independence came at last, however, and in 1816 the Argentine Republic was born. After that, the Argentines fought one another.

Buenos Aires fought the provinces, dictators rose who fought everybody, power was kicked backwards and forwards like a ball, until, around 1880, a certain stability was reached. By then the dictatorships were over, Buenos Aires had accepted its position as federal capital and prosperity beckoned.

'How lucky you are, my dears,' Beatrice told the Wintours on their arrival. 'This is boom time!'

In fact, the Sentos family had always been prosperous. Not powerful, they were not caudillos who ruled thousands of acres like feudal lords, simply cattle owners who lived well. In the early years, they had no house in the capital; they kept to the *estancia*, working the stock with wandering gauchos, driving the beasts to Buenos Aires to be slaughtered for hides, not beef. As time went on, they replaced their first rough home with the present low, rambling building and covered the pretty rose-pink brick with nasturtium and mimosa. They extended the barns and corrals, they built a bakehouse and a dairy, they planted willows and poplars for shade and orchards for peaches, they grew flowers and vegetables and even laid down a lawn. They were of course self-sufficient.

In their isolated position on the vast, empty pampas, they had to be. The *pulpería*, the inn that doubled as store in San Vicente, stocked all manner of things, from guns to flour, but San Vicente was fifteen miles away and the Estancia Sentos kept itself going on the work of its half-breed servants, the mestizos, and the peons, or casual labourers. As for the gauchos, they worked strictly with the herds.

They rode to *rodeo*, they carried out the branding and

castration, the selection of animals for the *saladero*, the butchering required for the household. Sometimes they would kill a beast on the pampas and joint it on the spot, sometimes at a certain place behind their quarters, from where Alice and even Richard kept away. That was where the bones and offal were thrown and there the rats flourished. In a small way, it represented the horror of the *saladero* in Buenos Aires, where slaughtering took place daily, although Richard tried to pretend such a view was sentimental. 'It's best not to think about it,' Beatrice advised.

The time came when the Sentos family, following other *estancieros*, bought a house in the city. Everyone who was anyone lived in Buenos Aires, BA *was* the Argentine, according to the *porteños*, the residents. Beatrice, when she married Don Enriques, agreed.

As she told Alice, she was not one for country life. Travelling, yes, that was different. With Enriques, she had journeyed the length and not very great breadth of her new country, from the sugar canes and orange groves of the north to the chill of Patagonia in the south, taking in the magnificent spine of the Andes on the way. But to be a *campesina*, to live with grass and cattle and call a trip to the *pulpería* the height of excitement – no thank you, for her it was the city every time. Enriques had visited the *estancia*, of course – had in fact met his death in a riding accident on the pampas – but more and more had left the running of things to indifferent managers. After his death, it showed.

'You can imagine my position,' Beatrice exclaimed. 'Everything collapsing on the *estancia* at the same time as the cattle trade was exploding into something new. You have no idea how fast things moved. One day, we had a hide trade, the next it was beef. Beef, beef, still more beef. In the old days, only slaves would eat the salt beef we used to export, then somebody invents refrigeration and suddenly all the world wants Argentine beef.'

'Sounds a wonderful opportunity to make money,' Richard had observed.

'Except the cattle were all wrong,' Beatrice replied. They had been bred for hides, not meat. So there had to be new breeds introduced, new methods of feeding because the pampas grass would no longer do, all the *estancieros* had to go back to school to learn how to run their *estancias* on the new lines. Beatrice's green eyes had sparkled.

'All too much for me, of course – so, my dear Richard, I sent for you.'

And four years later, Alice thought, he is still here.

He had done well. He had learned all that Beatrice could not or would not learn; he had appointed a new manager, Lucio Castillo, who was his greatest asset; and gradually he had pulled the *estancia* into the prosperity of the 1880s.

Now he was chafing at the bit, anxious to know what his future held. Alice was anxious too, but for different reasons. When she urged him to speak to their aunt, get something settled, it was Belcarron that was in the forefront of her mind. He must make it clear that his first allegiance lay there. But would he?

Naturally, he had once said, they wanted John Wintour to live for years yet.

'Beatrice, too,' Alice had pointedly said.

'Of course, but the difference is, Belcarron could never support us all, whereas here there is enough for everyone.'

'What are you saying?' she had asked him outright, but he had refused to be drawn.

'I have worked hard,' was all he would say. 'I deserve something.'

What that might be, he could not explain.

Alice, remembering this conversation, looked beyond the lush plantation to the pampas, already showing the yellowing that November brought. She thought of the miles of it stretching on and on without change, so vast that Belcarron and all its patchwork fields would be swallowed to nothingness in a tiny part of it. Yet she would trade the lot for a sight of the old house on the cliff over the sea.

'I'll go back,' she decided, 'even just for a holiday. Next year. That's a promise.'

Her eyes moved to Beatrice coming out of the house, putting up her parasol, and she stood up and waved.

'Oh, my dear, don't leave the shade!' her aunt cried. 'Think of your complexion! Anyway, I am coming to join you. Mena is bringing us tea.'

As they settled themselves under the willows, sipping their fragrant tea, Beatrice smiled and said comfortably: 'Alice, isn't this pleasant?'

'It is, Aunt,' Alice replied. 'Very pleasant.'

Twelve

Every time he rode out with the men, Richard felt free. Not only from his *estancia* paperwork of accounts and payrolls, breeding charts, alfalfa costs, but from the house and feminine company. He loved Alice, of course, but a man's interests were not a woman's, or damned well ought not to be, and living on the *estancia*, away from city concerns, he found he did miss his sport and his clubs and being with other fellows. Small compensation, perhaps, to ride with gauchos, whose Spanish he did not always understand and who could sometimes fill him with primitive fear when they looked at him with narrow eyes and fingered their small knives.

But he was happy to be on his horse in the open air, galloping alongside Lucio as they followed the *capataz* to the clearing where the cattle would be brought. They would wait there until the herds appeared from their various points, shepherded by the gauchos with such cutting and crisscrossing and artistry of horsemanship, Richard's eyes would glaze with admiration and he would pull at his moustache in envy.

The heat was rising now as the sun rode up the sky. Everything as the three men waited was still, except for the movement of the plovers, wheeling overhead. Then the cattle came pounding across the plain, there was noise like thunder and the dust rose, the plovers scattered, and the whooping gauchos, hair flying, scarves fluttering, delivered their charges precisely to their appointed places.

'Amazing,' Richard murmured, and Lucio glanced at him and smiled.

'Is born in them, Don Ricardo, they learn with their mothers' milk.'

'Ah, but it was easier in the old days, Lucio.'

'True, Don Ricardo. Once, all beasts eat grass, now – ' Lucio shrugged. 'Some eat this, some eat that – '

'And we are more than ever dependent on the gauchos not to mix them up.' Richard mopped his brow. 'I suppose times of change are never easy.'

And there were more changes on the way, he added to himself. There was talk of fencing off parts of the pampas, creating sheep runs, even areas for crops. Could anyone see a gaucho herding sheep? Growing potatoes? He would probably rather hang up his boots and cut his throat. Gauchos were wild things, as wild as the criollo horses still roaming the pampas. Yet the changes were coming and every ship landing at BA brought the immigrants to handle them – Italian, Irish, Welsh – all pouring into the Argentine, looking for work and land.

We shall end up like Ireland, Richard thought, with a pack of tenant farmers all wanting to be owners. God forbid.

Then he bit his lip. It was not for him to say whether or not he wanted tenant farmers. Perhaps his aunt might. It was her say, not his, her land, not his. He always came back to that.

'Come, Don Ricardo,' Lucio murmured. 'We rest under the *ombú* trees, yes? And drink *mate* tea.'

The herd inspection that morning had presented no special problems. A few beasts with injuries had been attended to, but that was routine, stock was money, it had to be kept at peak. Richard was relieved there had been no necessity for on-the-spot butchery; as at branding and castration, he rather drew the line at that. There were limits to a fellow's participation, after all, though he never lost face by admitting such. Blood and suffering, death, even their own, meant nothing to the gauchos; they held the lot cheap and kept themselves aloof from human frailty, as long as they had horses to ride and a few pesos for cigars. Now they had come straggling back from the grazing lands and were lying a little apart, waiting for the kettle to boil.

Everyone in the Argentine drank *mate* tea, made from the

110

dried leaves of the Paraguayan ilex. In the gaucho version, it was infused in a gourd which was passed from man to man with no wiping of the filter, the *bombilla*, which would have been considered a great insult. Richard took his turn now, drinking long of the refreshing liquid before handing the gourd to Lucio, as the gauchos looked on with rare, approving smiles.

Talk turned to horses and gaucho skills. Miraculous feats during stampedes when mistakes could mean death under the hooves of the herd, tricks with the *lazo* or bolas, two-horse racing and betting, fighting with knives . . . Richard, lying under the trees, his hat over his eyes, listened, understanding what he could and grinning, until gradually the men fell silent and began to drift away, their break over. The *capataz*, waving his hand in farewell to Richard and Lucio, asked if he would see them later for a drink at the *pulpería*. Lucio shrugged.

'*Quizás, amigo* –' He turned to Richard. 'What you say, Don Ricardo? You wish?'

'No, I don't think so, Lucio.' Richard flattened his hat to his head and stood up. 'I'd better get back.'

'You look worry. Is something wrong?'

'No. I'm just thinking – wondering about my plans.'

'For the *estancia*?'

'For myself.'

They stood together, their eyes on the horizon where the clear sky was broken now by a few clouds. Cattle were moving slowly across the plain, whose yellowing surface waved and rolled like a great sea as the birds dipped over it, singing again freely now that the *rodeo* was over. There was a great sense of peace.

'You no happy?' Lucio asked quietly.

'I'm very happy.' Richard walked towards his horse, tossing its head where it was tethered in the shade. 'I suppose that is the trouble.'

Thirteen

It was the hour before dinner and already growing dark. Alice and Beatrice had been sewing in the *sala*, the parlour, but put their work aside to greet Richard. Freshly bathed and changed into evening clothes, he came in declaring he was starving.

'Not long to dinner now,' said Alice, as a mestiza maid brought in the lamps and withdrew. 'Let us take a little sherry.'

Although its Spanish furnishings were heavy, the *sala* by lamplight was welcoming and Alice had made it more her own by the addition of Wintour family photographs and bowls of spring flowers from her garden. She was looking particularly lovely in a dress of her favourite dark blue, while Beatrice in green silk was charming. For a woman in her fifties, she was well preserved, her hair still yellow, her skin only a little lined. In the early days she had reminded Alice of Charlotte, her green eyes teasing in Charlotte's way, but she had different, finer qualities. Alice was fond of her.

'Had a good day?' Beatrice asked Richard now, as she accepted her sherry.

'Much as usual, thanks, Aunt. No disasters, anyway.'

'Yet you seem a little down.'

'Just weary. It's a long day when a fellow starts at dawn.' Richard flung himself into a chair and looked to Alice. 'Didn't you tell me there was post from home?'

'Oh, of course. I have it here.' Alice sprang up and passed the letters to him.

'Anything interesting?'

'Mainly business, I think, but there's one from Hester and one from Charlotte.'

'Indeed?' Excusing himself to his aunt, Richard glanced through the envelopes, pausing first at Hester's.

It was some time now since he had been persuaded to make his peace with his sister. Just before the birth of her son, when Alice had said it would be a terrible thing if Hester were to die and go to her grave without his forgiveness. So he had written to her and she had replied with so much love and relief that his heart had been full of contrition. Yet he could not bring himself to accept Daniel Molloy as his brother-in-law, even if he were no longer a groom but, as it appeared, some sort of journalist. The fact remained he was a Catholic and an anarchist and if he thought it would achieve Home Rule for Ireland would probably blow them all to kingdom come. How could he be expected to accept a fellow like that? Fortunately, no one had asked him to, not even Alice, so honour was satisfied and he had his sister back again in his affections.

'Seems Hester is going to Skibbereen for Christmas,' he muttered. 'God help her, she always hated it; so full of ghosts, she used to say.'

'But they're to stay with Daniel's sister, who is not too badly off,' Alice remarked. 'She runs a boarding house.'

Richard shrugged and returned to his letters, picking out Charlotte's.

'I see her handwriting is as bad as ever,' he murmured, aware of Alice's watchful gaze. She still harboured unease, he knew, where Charlotte was concerned, though he had told her long ago his old love for her sister was dead.

Now she said carefully: 'She and Dudley are to spend Christmas at Belcarron.'

There was a silence. Richard could feel his face mottling in its familiar, angry way.

'I thought they were in London,' he said stiffly.

'You can read what she says. They were doing very well, then Dudley made some mistakes on the stock exchange –'

'I'll bet he did. That idiot doesn't know the first thing about stocks and shares!'

114

'So they decided to go back to Ireland. As they have no house at present, they are to stay with Papa.' Alice cleared her throat. 'In fact, Charlotte seems to think Dudley could be quite useful.'

'Useful?' Richard's tone was icy.

'Well, you know Papa has continual problems getting his rents, and things have got worse since the Plan of Campaign –'

'Plan of Campaign?' Beatrice repeated. 'Should I have heard of that?'

'It's just a fancy way of saying the tenants needn't pay what the landlord asks.' Richard was contemptuous. 'The agitators persuade them to make a lower offer and if it's not accepted, they put it into a fund for evicted tenants and don't pay a bean.' He laughed grimly. 'No wonder Irish estates are falling apart.'

'It's only tried on with a few landlords now,' Alice murmured. 'But Papa is one and he's getting very tired.'

'And Charlotte thinks her fool of a husband can do something about it?' asked Richard. 'The idea is absurd.'

'I agree,' said Alice. 'I think we should –'

She stopped, as Beatrice stared at her.

'Should what?' asked Beatrice.

Alice still hesitated. She looked towards Richard but he said nothing.

'Go home?' asked Beatrice, her green eyes steady. 'Is that what you think you should do?'

'We have been here quite some time, Aunt.'

'That is true.'

'And, as I say, Papa is getting tired. I feel I should consider him.'

'Of course you should.' Beatrice slid her gaze to Richard. 'And you, Richard? Do you want to go home too?'

He set down his empty glass. 'It's not so much a question of what I want, Aunt. I suppose I really should be thinking of my future. It's been a wonderful experience for me to be here, to have learned all I've learned, but I can't stay for ever. Especially if I am needed at Belcarron.'

'John does have Charlotte and her husband.' At the look on his face, Beatrice shrugged. 'Or is that what's wrong? Oh,

115

I do understand, you know. The trouble is, I don't think I could manage without you.'

Richard was silent, not looking at Alice, who was sitting very straight in her chair, staring at her tightly folded hands.

'Look, would you give me another year?' Beatrice asked suddenly. 'That's not so long, is it? People go to India or Africa for much longer than the time you've spent with me, don't they? It's not so unusual. The thing is, I have some travelling to do myself. I should be so much happier if I could leave the *estancia* in your hands, Richard. Come, what do you say?'

He pulled at his moustache. 'Travelling?' he repeated.

'It's just business. To Tucuman, in the north.'

'That's sugar country. What have you to do with sugar, Aunt?'

'Nothing, but I have things to see to there.' She leaned forward, smiling, her green eyes wheedling. 'Look, all I'm asking is another year, to have you both with me – it isn't a great deal, is it? Then I promise we'll discuss everything again.'

'I'd been so looking forward to going home on a visit next year,' Alice murmured. 'To show the children, you know – '

'Well, you won't be much delayed,' Beatrice said eagerly. 'And it would be easier if the children were a little older, wouldn't it? Oh, you're so young, you have so much time – you can spare me a few months, surely?'

Richard heaved a long sigh. 'All right, Aunt, a year it is, if Alice is agreeable.'

'Are you?' Beatrice asked. 'Are you agreeable, Alice?'

She nodded slowly. 'At least now I have a date to plan for.'

'Of course you have.' Beatrice rose, sweeping the train of her dress behind her. She took their hands in hers. 'Thank you, my dears, thank you both. I can't tell you how much better I feel, now that you're to stay on. Shall we go in to dinner? I'm sure they are ready for us now.'

Undressing for bed, Alice said coldly: 'You didn't say a word, did you, Richard? Not a word about having some recognition for all you've done?'

116

He pulled off his cravat and tossed it to a chair. 'I hinted enough, the Lord knows.'

'Well, Aunt Beatrice didn't take your hints, did she? All she could offer was another year. Then what? I should like to know where we stand.'

Richard sat on the edge of the bed, unbuttoning his shirt. 'I have the feeling,' he said slowly, 'that Aunt B would like me to have the *estancia*, if she could.'

'You mean – make you her heir?'

'Yes.'

Alice turned away. She began to unhook her stays. 'Is that what you want?'

'As we've said before, it's not something that would happen for years yet, but it would give me status, wouldn't it? I'd know where I was going.'

'I thought we were going to Belcarron.'

'Dear God!' Richard ran his hands through his hair. 'I suppose I want that too . . .'

'Why should Beatrice not make you her heir?' Alice asked after a pause. 'The property is hers to do as she likes with, isn't it?'

'Something is holding her back. Don't ask me what and don't ask me why she is going to Tucuman. You know how difficult it is to get her to say what is in her mind.'

'All I know is she has asked for a year and a year she shall have. Then I go home.'

'Without me?'

'Only for a holiday. You could come too.'

'I'd have to, I couldn't bear to be without you so long.'

Her eyes sparkled in the candlelight. 'You mean that? You'd really come with me? Oh, Richard!'

They clung together, laughing and kissing, then Alice said she must have her nightgown and Richard said why should she need a nightgown? Even after three children, her body was as beautiful as ever.

'Look at you,' he muttered, 'just look at you . . .'

'Three children,' she repeated. 'And I'm not sure I want four – at least, not yet.'

'We don't have a baby every time we make love.' He blew out the candle and drew her close. 'Come, don't tease me, darling.'

117

'I'd never do that.' She twined herself around him and as the familiar joy consumed her, forgot as she always did what her worry had been.

Later, though, as they lay gazing contentedly into the darkness, she was surprised to hear Richard mutter:

'Dudley Sarn ... to think of him at Belcarron. I can't stomach it.'

'Whatever makes you want to talk of him now?'

'I don't know. I suppose I'm worried what he might be up to.'

'You needn't worry. Papa would never change his will for Dudley Sarn.'

'What about Charlotte?'

'Not for Charlotte, either.'

Alice's tone was definite but at the thought of Charlotte at Belcarron for Christmas, her contentment faded. It was some time before she fell asleep.

Fourteen

It was not quite Christmas at Belcarron. One o'clock on the morning of 23 December, cold, with a sharp wind and no moon. No lights in the house.

Suddenly, a sharp crack broke the silence, followed by the sound of splintering glass, and John Wintour leaped out of bed. For some moments he stood listening, braving the chill, before pulling on his old flannel dressing gown and lighting a candle.

'What is it, John?' came Ernestine's voice from the bed.

'Nothing, my dear. A noise downstairs. Go back to sleep.'

'If a noise downstairs is nothing, why are you up?'

He put his finger to his lips. 'Ernestine, do keep your voice down, we don't want to wake the household.'

She sat up, putting back her plait of dark hair, and smiled. 'My dear, they are already awake. I can hear Nora shrieking from here and that's Charlotte at the door now.'

'Papa, Papa!' came Charlotte's voice. 'Something's happened downstairs! We heard a noise!'

'All right, all right, it's only a window. They've been broken before, they'll be broken again – '

He flung open the door to find Charlotte in a white robe, her yellow hair loose on her shoulders, her eyes in his candle's light glistening with excitement. Anything for a thrill, he thought sourly. If the house were to burn down around her, she'd probably think it fun. Behind her, Mrs Heenan and Nora were hugging each other in fear, but Dudley Sarn was already on his way downstairs, shouting he was going for the guns.

119

'Take care, then,' John growled. 'We don't want to kill the scoundrels. Mrs Heenan, you stay with the mistress. Charlotte, Nora, come down and light the lamps – we need to see what has been going on.'

The broken window was in the dining room, one of the long, lovely windows that looked out on the lawns at the front of the house. The night wind was billowing the curtains as the shattered glass lay glittering in the lamplight and among it Nora's eyes spotted the stone.

'Oh, sir, is that the rock they threw, then, the devils? 'Twould be nobody from the village, I swear to the Holy Mother of God, they'd never be doing such a thing!'

John bent to pick up the stone, catching his finger on a shard of glass, and sucked the blood impatiently. 'There's a message round it. Charlotte, hold the lamp.'

'What does it say, Papa?'

'Give me time, am I not trying to read it? Damnation, I haven't my spectacles – '

'Allow me, sir,' said Dudley Sarn, putting aside the two shotguns he had brought from the gun room. He smoothed out the creased paper which had been wrapped round the stone. 'Short and sweet. It says, "Next time the house."'

'Next time, the house?' John repeated. 'What the devil does that mean?'

'I think we might make a good guess.' Dudley's heavy face was slippery with sweat. 'Do you smell something?'

'Burning! It must be – '

'The stables!' Charlotte cried. 'Oh, dear God, the horses!'

'Cavan Morry's hunters,' Dudley spat. 'Quick, I'll take the guns – '

'Wait a minute.' John grabbed his arm. 'Let's show some sense. Charlotte and Nora, you two dress and go down to the village, get anybody you can to come back here to help, they're not all against us. Dudley, you and I will take coats from the hall – no point in catching our deaths, we'll not save the stables now. Where in damnation are my boots?'

'While we stand here worrying about coats and boots, the horses may be dying.' Dudley fretted, but John only threw him a coat.

120

'Those are Irishmen out there, Dudley, they'd never risk horses. Anyway, I'm ready.'

They could smell the acrid stench of burning straw as soon as they left the house and as they made for the stable block they could see flames already rising in the night sky.

'I hope you're right about the horses,' Dudley muttered. 'By God, if I can lay my hands on the fellows who've done this –'

'I see them!' cried John. 'At least, a couple of them.' He swung his lantern towards two dark figures ahead. 'Good God, can you believe it? That's my own groom, there, that's Billie Docherty! And the other one, I do believe, is Daniel Molloy!'

'Where in hell are the horses?' cried Dudley.

John was right, they were not going to save the stables. The flames were licking away at the wooden roof and the old tower, which very shortly would collapse, bringing down the remainder of the beams, then that would be the end of it. The doors were swinging open. The inside was an inferno, but at least there were no signs of living creatures trapped.

'The others must have taken the horses,' John muttered, and he ran towards the two still on the scene. 'Docherty, stay where you are! Molloy, what the devil are you doing back here? Don't move, either of you!'

'Don't move,' Dudley Sarn echoed, levelling his gun. 'Or I shoot.'

The men stood still, coughing in the smoke, as Dudley advanced on them.

'You,' he snapped to Billie Docherty, 'where are the horses?'

Billie, a bony, hollow-cheeked youth, hesitated. ''Tis safe they are,' he muttered. 'Weren't the boys taking them to the old sheds? We were never after killing the horses.'

'Though looks like you've a fancy to kill us.' Daniel Molloy sneered. 'A fine way to dispense justice, I'm thinking.'

'It will be for the Resident Magistrate to dispense justice.' Dudley Sarn, coughing badly, waved his gun in the direction of the house. 'Now, move, you two, we'll talk inside. Move, I say, walk towards the house!'

121

In John Wintour's study, Molloy and Docherty were told to keep standing while John sat down and wiped his streaming eyes and Dudley kept his gun poised and ready.

'You can be putting that thing down,' Daniel told him. 'We'll not be running away.'

'Indeed you will not.' Dudley studied him coldly. 'Daniel Molloy, isn't it? The husband of my wife's cousin. Good God!'

'I might be saying the same to you,' Daniel retorted. 'Husband of my wife's cousin. Good God!'

'That'll be enough of your damned impertinence!' cried Dudley, flushing with anger. 'You'll soon sing a different tune when you find yourself in gaol. Mr Wintour here, your landlord, intends to prosecute you for trespass and felonious damage to property.'

'My landlord? Thank God, he is not, though I'm here for his tenants, with that I'll agree. Isn't it half the county he is threatening with eviction?'

John Wintour looked up. 'I have never actually evicted anyone, Molloy, you know that.'

'I am saying you are threatening, you cannot deny it.'

'All I'm trying to do is get the rents I need to look after my tenants, I've always done my best to do that. Is it too much to ask them to pay what they owe when anything they need they've only to ask for? Speak to any one of them, they'll tell you it's true. And this is the way I am rewarded. My windows broken, my stables burned, my very home put at risk!'

Billie Docherty took a step forward, his blue eyes blazing.

'Your honour, we cannot pay what we owe, because time after time you are setting the rents too high! Time after time, we ask you to take less and never are you listening. What else can we do but come to you tonight to put to you our case?'

'Putting your case means burning the stables, does it?' asked Dudley, but Daniel looked only at John Wintour.

'What we've done this night you've brought on your own head, so be letting us go now, or there'll be an end to patience.'

'Patience?' cried Dudley. 'What patience have you shown,

you scoundrel? What patience has Dillon shown, or O'Brien, or your precious Parnell? Stirring up trouble for people who'd pay their way honestly, if it weren't for you?'

'Leave Mr Parnell out of this, if you please,' Daniel said. 'And Mr Dillon and Mr O'Brien as well. And don't be telling me about these wonderful tenants you know who only want to be paying their rents to a pack of damned English who've no more right to take their money than pickpockets and robbers. Sure we are trespassers here, sure we've burned your stables, but what weapons have we got? It's justice we're fighting for here, for the principle of no evictions when a man cannot be paying through no fault of his own. "In bad times, a tenant cannot be expected to pay as much as in good times." Yes, Mr Sarn, my precious Mr Parnell said that and you can be putting that gun away and remembering it!'

Into an atmosphere so heavy with passionate feeling it was almost tangible came Ernestine Wintour. She stood in the doorway, wearing a blue woollen dressing gown, her plait of dark hair hanging over her shoulder, and looked around at the four men.

'I think you ought perhaps to know, John, that there are some people from the village taking water to the fire in the stables. I should have thought you would be trying to put it out too.'

'No point, it was too far gone, we left it to burn itself out. And we had to see to Molloy and Docherty.'

'Why, Daniel, how nice to see you!' Ernestine exclaimed. 'It seems such an age since you were our groom and went off with Hester. I do hope she is well? Such an intelligent girl, I always thought – '

'Ernestine, can't you see there is trouble here?' John interrupted. 'Dudley and I have to have these men arrested.'

'Why, what have they done?'

'They started the fire, ma'am,' Dudley ground out. 'Will you please excuse us?'

'Started the fire? Well, at least it is only the stables. The Langs of Castleabbey lost a whole wing, you know, before they agreed to reduce the rents. By a quarter, I think it was.' Ernestine put her hand on John's arm. 'Couldn't you arrest

123

Daniel and Billie tomorrow, John? Their families will be so worried if they don't get home tonight.'

John gave a groan. 'Come, my dear, let me take you upstairs. It's very late.'

'Exactly my point! Mrs Docherty will be beside herself and then there's poor Hester to think of – John, we must not forget Hester!' Ernestine turned to Daniel. 'Is she staying with your sister, Daniel? In Skibbereen?'

'She is, ma'am, but you need not be worrying. Thanking you for your interest, but it's fine she'll be with Theresa.'

'It is she who will be worrying, Daniel, you must go home to her now. And Billie Docherty, you must go home, too. There is no reason for you to be detained tonight when you can be arrested in the morning.'

There was a silence in the room as Dudley's face flushed and swelled with anger and Daniel's look was hard as flint. John pulled furiously at his moustache.

'Damnation,' he muttered. 'I'm not sure what to do.'

'You're not thinking of letting them go?' cried Dudley. 'Sir, you can't, they're guilty, they've admitted it, you can't let them go!'

'No, of course not, I'm not talking about setting them free. The thing is, Hester – she's my brother's girl – maybe we should – '

'Should what? Should what, sir?'

'Leave this to the morning. I mean, they won't try to run away. Where would they go?'

'Where indeed?' asked Daniel, his face empty of all expression.

Fifteen

Theresa O'Farrell, six years older than her brother Daniel, had his heavy good looks and fierce blue stare. They were the last of a family of seven, the rest having died from illness or want, their parents too, but Theresa counted herself lucky. She had married a man twenty years her senior and been happy with him, until he dropped down dead in his bar one night and left her the pub in Skibbereen. She had made it into a lodging house, providing clean rooms and plain cooking, and it gave her a living; by Skibbereen standards, a good one. Certainly, she was able to help out her neighbours when debt caught up with them, as it usually did.

Hester had been afraid when she first married Daniel that Theresa would not accept her. In fact, Theresa confessed it had been a relief to have Daniel married and taken off her hands.

'Even by me?' Hester had asked, with a smile, to which Theresa had cried:

'Come now, you know I'm not meaning that! But so many men in this country never marry till late or not at all, wasn't I scared out of my wits I'd be left with Daniel and him the most difficult man in the world?'

So Hester had been welcomed, English though she was, Catholic though she wasn't, and of course she had changed her religion and fitted in well. As for little Paul, Theresa's eyes softened when she thought of him. He'd be a priest, so he would, maybe even a cardinal; a sweeter child she'd never known.

'Theresa, he is not yet three!' Hester protested with a

laugh, but Theresa was serious. It was there, she could tell; the child had a vocation, Hester would see.

'Perhaps,' said Hester. Although she loved her adopted church, she wasn't sure she wanted her son to enter the religious life.

There were no visitors at the lodging house that Christmas and the regulars – a couple of homeless old fishermen, a retired priest, and Sean O'Farrell's unmarried cousin – were all upstairs asleep as Theresa and Hester sat in the kitchen and waited for Daniel to come home.

It was past three – Hester's eyes went constantly to the old clock on the dresser – and still he did not come. He had said last night he was going out to see a friend, perhaps have a drink, wasn't it Christmas? None of it had rung true but she had known better than to question. When Daniel's face took on a certain set expression there was no moving him. She was not surprised now that he had not returned, only desperately, frantically worried, and Theresa was worried too, although Hester was certain she knew something of what was going on.

'Theresa,' she said quietly, 'where is he?'

Theresa rattled the poker in the bars of the old range and moved the blackened kettle over to the heat.

'I'll make some more tea,' she muttered.

'I don't want any more tea, I just want to know where Daniel has gone.'

'You know what he's like, he'd not be telling if he didn't want to.'

'But why doesn't he trust me? When we married we said we'd work together for Ireland and in Dublin we do. I have my bookshop, he helps me when he can, we go to all the meetings, I know all his political friends, but here' – Hester's voice shook – 'he simply shuts me out.'

''Tis different here.' Theresa pushed back her hair with a roughened hand and kept her eyes turned from Hester. ''Tis best not to be asking.'

The kettle began to sing, then to boil, and she made the tea.

'Come, Hester, be drinking this and be easy, he'll be coming to no harm.'

Hester reluctantly sipped the strong tea and put the cup down.

'It's to do with the Plan of Campaign, isn't it? With William O'Brien?'

William O'Brien, ex-Fenian and Member of Parliament, was the editor of Parnell's newspaper *United Ireland*. He had taken Daniel under his wing on his arrival in Dublin, had trained him, given him a job on the paper and frequently called on his aid in the campaign to have tenants' rents reduced. So far it had not involved Daniel in violence, although violence had been used by others, but Hester had made it clear she would not support any use of force; until now, she believed Daniel had not gone against her. Tonight was different. Here there was violence in the air, she sensed it, knew it went with the suffering people had endured. But it made her no longer sure what Daniel might do.

'Isn't that the door I hear now?' Theresa cried, not answering Hester, and they both sprang up as the front door banged and Daniel came in. Hester went to him at once, taking his hands in hers, looking up into his face.

'Daniel, I've been so worried – Theresa, too. How could you worry us so? Where have you been all this time?'

He kissed her briefly but said nothing and she drew back, smelling the smoke on his clothes and his hair.

'Tell me,' she said urgently, 'where you've been.'

He moved to a chair and hung his coat on the back of it. 'Is there a cup of tea in that pot?' he asked Theresa. 'I could be glad of one.'

She shook the kettle and warmed up the tea. 'Now, Daniel,' she snapped, putting a cup before him. 'Tell us.'

He drank quickly, not looking at either of the women. 'I'd better be giving warning,' he muttered. 'They'll be coming for me in the morning.'

'Coming for you?' cried Hester. 'Who will? What do you mean?'

Theresa sat down heavily. She raised her eyes to Hester. 'A fine Christmas we'll be having, my dear. He means he's to be arrested.'

'No, no! That can't be true.' Hester's face was paper white, her dark eyes enormous. She turned on Daniel. 'It's not, is it? Daniel, it's not true?'

He kept his eyes down. 'It is, Hester. Billie Docherty and me, we were taken.'

'Taken? Taken where?'

He began to cough and coughed for some time. 'At your uncle's,' he said at last, wiping his streaming eyes. 'At Belcarron.'

Hester too sat down, as though she could no longer stand.

'Belcarron? You went to Belcarron? Why?'

'It was necessary.'

'To cause trouble? How could you? How could you, when I . . . when I'm –'

'Who you are? Hester, it is not important who you are. In this matter.'

'And it's not important you are married to me?' She flushed.

'It is not. Your uncle is one who will not listen to reason. Hasn't there been trouble with him for years? Hasn't he always kept his rents up when the harvest's been down? Hasn't he even threatened eviction?'

'He has never evicted anyone, you know he hasn't. He cares about his tenants, he always has, but how is he to look after them if he is not given the income to do it?' Hester bowed her head and put her hand over her eyes. 'How could you go there behind my back and –' She stopped, lowered her hand and looked at him in sudden horror. 'Your clothes,' she whispered. 'That smell of smoke. Dear God, Daniel, what did you do at Belcarron?'

Theresa went to her and put her arm around her shoulders, but Hester leaped up, shaking her away.

'Answer me, Daniel, what did you do? Why are they coming to arrest you?'

'It was the stables,' he answered in a low voice. 'It was the stables we burned.'

She swayed so he thought she might faint and put out his hand to her, but she stepped aside and would not let him touch her.

'The stables,' she muttered, 'where we met . . . You burned them? To hurt my uncle? Or to hurt me?'

'Hester!' He tried again to hold her but she only shook her head dazedly and went out of the kitchen.

128

'Hester, take a candle!' Theresa cried, but Hester would not. She closed the door carefully behind her as though putting a partition between herself and them.

'Daniel, 'tis wicked you are,' Theresa whispered angrily. 'To be hurting a good sweet woman like that! Is it the devil that is in you, then, that you must be destroying what's best in your life?'

His face was carved from stone. 'It was not to hurt Hester I did it, Theresa. She's wrong in that.'

'Why, then? Why burn the stables of your own wife's family?'

'John Wintour is one who needs showing his fault. It was decided in Dublin.'

'And suited you fine. Because you are wanting to get back at the Wintours and never mind they are Hester's kin! Were you even remembering her when you lit those stables where you met? Or were you remembering yourself as the groom?'

'Is it not the truth they treated me like the dust under their feet?' he cried passionately. 'As all those Ascendancy folk treat us Irish? But I swear to you, Theresa, it was the tenants I was thinking of, not myself, and I was not forgetting Hester, I was not! Ask Billie Docherty, it was a job we were doing, it was work for justice!'

Theresa sat for some moments in silence, her heavy, handsome face darkly brooding.

'You are understanding how it was?' asked Daniel.

For answer she lit a candle with a taper at the range and handed it to him.

As he made no move, she turned him towards the door.

'Go ask Hester's pardon,' she said quietly. 'Hasn't she enough to be facing tomorrow without you not making peace tonight?'

Hester lay between Theresa's coarse sheets and listened to Daniel's tread on the uncarpeted stairs. She closed her eyes and began to breathe long and deeply as though she were asleep. When he came to the bed and said her name she did not reply.

'Hester, will you answer me?'

She kept silent.

129

'Hester.' He touched her face. 'Love . . .'

She burst into tears.

'Oh, Hester!' He put his arms around her. 'You are thinking of those stables, but they were never to me what they were to you.'

'We met there, we kissed there –'

'And precious they were for that. But it was ashamed I was to be working there. For the Wintours.'

'Ashamed?' She lay against him, still sobbing, then, as Paul stirred in his little bed in the corner of the room, grew quiet. 'Why should you have felt ashamed?' she asked in a whisper. 'You were doing honest work.'

'Honest work? For a family that's battened on Ireland for centuries? Ah, Hester!' He groaned a little. 'You have still not an idea in your head how we Irish feel for people like yours.'

'I only know I came to love you in those stables, Daniel, and you burned them down. I can't forgive you.'

He blew out the candle, which he said might waken Paul, and undressed in the dark, piling his clothes neatly on a chair. His nightshirt was under the pillow but he got into bed without it, shuddering with the cold, and pulled Hester close. For warmth, she hoped, not love, and held herself rigid.

Truth to tell, it was she who usually wanted to make love. Like many of his countrymen who were as happy with a drink or a bet on the horses as with a woman, Daniel was no great lover. For him, Hester knew, her rival was politics. He would go anywhere for a meeting, a procession, a speech by Parnell, while making love to her seemed something she had to ask him to do. Tonight, of course, when she did not want him, he wanted her.

As his cold fingers began to undo the buttons of her nightgown, she jerked herself away.

'Daniel, I told you I can't forgive you. You must leave me alone.'

'It's a stranger you are, Hester, so angry –'

'I'm not angry, I'm sad, I'm hurt.'

'Come, then, let me love you, you'll feel better.'

'Making love will not make me forget what you did at Belcarron tonight.'

He was silent for some time, his hands on her breasts.

'Are you not wanting another baby?' he asked gently.

It had been six months since Hester's miscarriage of a daughter. The pain of loss was not yet healed, perhaps never would be, but it was true, she desperately wanted another child. As Daniel began to kiss and fondle her, she felt herself respond as she always did, but still held back, saying they must not wake Paul.

'We'll not wake Paul,' Daniel murmured. 'Be easy, Hester.'

He never could understand that for her the climax came too soon, that she wanted the joy to last, to go on and on, or at least when it was over that he should stay with her, be gentle, friendly, talk with her in the darkness. She never complained, she knew there was no point, there was no changing him, she must be satisfied with what she had. When he turned from her as usual and slipped immediately into sleep, she kissed his back and his rough black hair, still smelling of smoke, then put on her nightgown and tiptoed over to look at Paul. He was not usually in their room and she worried about him, but he had not woken. She straightened his covers and kissed his brow. The December night was chill and she shivered as she stood looking down at him, wondering if this was the night she had conceived.

'Another sister, Paul?' she whispered. 'Or a brother? Please God, let it be so.'

Then from nowhere came the memory of Daniel's words, sharp as a sword: 'I'd better be giving warning, they'll be coming for me in the morning . . .'

Coming for him, coming for Daniel. He might be sent to prison. She might be carrying a child and its father be in prison. And little Paul – how could she tell him? Her eyes probed the darkness to the bed where Daniel was sleeping and she wondered how they could have made love, how she could have let him make love to her, when this great black stifling cloud was hanging over them. She had been thinking only of what he had done and not of what he must pay, and now the nightmare of what was to come enfolded her and she lay sleepless for the rest of the night.

In the morning, the nightmare continued. Daniel was

131

arrested and removed to the police station to await examination by the Resident Magistrate. Hester was not allowed to go with him but was told she might visit next day, Christmas Day. At which she asked Theresa to look after Paul; she must go at once to hire O'Dowd's pony and trap.

'But where is it you are going?' cried Theresa, holding Paul in her arms, his fair hair glinting in the winter sun.

'To Belcarron,' Hester replied.

Sixteen

Breakfast at Belcarron was late that Christmas Eve. Ernestine did not put in an appearance, but Charlotte and John sat yawning over coffee, as Dudley, puffy-faced and red-eyed, helped himself to bacon. He had been out checking on the stables which were still smouldering but seemed safe enough; also the horses which had been found in a shed in the grounds. They had taken no harm, but he would have to return the hunters he had borrowed to Cavan Morry as soon as possible. Without stables or groom, they could not be kept at Belcarron.

'Which means no more hunting for us this season,' he added sullenly.

'There's still old Mayfly,' John observed, but Dudley grimaced.

'Old is the word, sir. He's due for retirement.'

'Ha! Like me.' John coughed and dabbed at his lips with his handkerchief. 'I doubt I can take any more nights like last night.'

Charlotte and Dudley exchanged glances. Charlotte passed John the toast rack.

'It's very true what you say, Papa. Trouble of that sort is too much for you.'

He shot her a suspicious glance from under his brows. 'And what do you suggest I should do, then?'

'Well, Dudley and I have been thinking . . .'

'Yes? Pass me the butter, would you, my dear?'

'Of course, Papa.' Charlotte with a sweet smile passed the butter. 'Dudley and I have been thinking you really must

133

have some help with the estate. It's years since you had an agent –'

'I can't afford an agent.'

'Yes, but Dudley and I have had this very good idea, you see, that Dudley should be your agent.' Charlotte leaned forward, her eyes alight. 'It would be perfect, Papa, the ideal solution. Dudley could take all your worries from you, he's very experienced –'

'Experienced?' John shot an outraged glance at Dudley, who was looking down at his plate. 'Why, he's never run an estate in his life, Charlotte! He's the younger son and in any case his father is still alive and running Penningfield very well, the last I heard!'

Charlotte's mouth tightened. 'Dudley has studied the matter, Papa, and he's certain he could do an excellent job here. Isn't that so, Dudley?'

'Indeed,' Dudley agreed hastily. 'And from what I saw last night, sir, you are badly in need of help.'

'Professional help, maybe, but without wishing to be rude, Dudley, all you've ever done is gambled on the stock market and ended up losing. Am I not right?'

Dudley went scarlet. 'I may have been unlucky, lost a little –'

'Lost a lot, didn't you? And isn't it true your father said he would pay your debts and not a penny more? Forgive me, Dudley, but I have the right to speak of these things. You are married to my daughter, who is wholly dependent on you. I should know your situation.'

Dudley tossed aside his napkin and stood up. 'At the moment,' he said tightly, 'it is true I am not in funds. Things didn't go well in London and for some reason my father is refusing to see to my future. But I shall certainly have a position again very soon; I've had offers, quite substantial offers.' He cleared his throat. 'Only, in view of the way things are here, Charlotte and I thought I should try to be of help to you.'

John moved his gaze to the boarded-up window that had been shattered the night before and he gave a long, heavy sigh. Charlotte gently touched his hand.

'I know how you are feeling, Papa. Particularly since you have been so let down.'

'Let down? In what way?'

'Well, by Richard and Alice, of course. Staying out there in the Argentine with Aunt Beatrice instead of you.'

John stood up and walked slowly across to the chimney-piece, where he stood looking down into the fire, his face worn and grim. Charlotte followed, slipping her arm into his.

'It's a shame, Papa, they should have decided to stay so far away, but I suppose you can't blame them. Everyone knows those Argentine landowners are frightfully rich. Why ever should Richard want to come back here?' Charlotte turned her head towards Dudley watching her and smiled. 'And to think I might have married Richard and turned him down because he hadn't a bean! So, here I am, married to Dudley, who –'

'Charlotte, please!' Dudley burst out, his eyes beseeching, and she shrugged and was silent.

'The Argentines are not as rich as you think,' John muttered. 'I was reading the other day their currency has practically collapsed, there have been bankruptcies.'

'Not for the landowners, Papa. I read that too. While the currency has gone down, the land has gone up.' Charlotte gave a bitter little laugh. 'Oh, Richard won't be suffering, I am sure, and neither will Alice. Aunt Beatrice will be spoiling them both and Alice will be having a marvellous time, fussing over her house, having a baby every year . . .'

John, looking down at his younger daughter's suddenly plain face, thought, ah, some things don't amuse her, then.

Aloud, he said: 'My dear, it's Beatrice who is the land-owner, not Richard, but if he is doing well and Alice is happy, you mustn't begrudge them their good fortune. You've had your own successes, your London seasons –'

'Yes, but what do I have now, Papa?'

John looked round at Dudley, who had walked away to the far end of the dining room and was standing with his back to them. He gave another long sigh and patted Charlotte's shoulder.

'All right, my dear, if it will make you happy, I'll take Dudley on.'

'Oh, Papa, thank you, that's wonderful!' Charlotte hugged him, smiling radiantly. The pinched, bitter expression had

135

vanished. 'Dudley, Papa says he will take you on as agent! Come and thank him.'

Dudley bowed, his face unsmiling, his colour still high. 'You won't regret it, sir,' he said stiffly. 'I promise I'll take care of the estate to the best of my ability.'

'I can't pay you much, you know, but there'll be something –'

'That's all right, sir, all I want is to be of service to you.'

'Do you think I overdid it?' he asked, up in Charlotte's old room, as he pulled on his riding boots.

Charlotte, changing into her habit, shrugged. 'He accepted it, anyway. And we had to do something to keep a roof over our heads. Where should we have gone, I wonder, if this hadn't come off?'

Dudley brushed his thinning brown hair and straightened the collar of his jacket. 'We're not completely destitute,' he said coldly. 'We should have managed.'

'In a little room in Bath, perhaps? Or Brighton? Where all the half-pay people go because they can't afford to live anywhere else? We certainly could not have stayed in Ireland and have all our friends know how poor we are.'

'Well, we're here now and it will do until something better comes along. I'm sure my father will come round in the end, he always does. He has to think of the family name, after all.'

'I just hope he gives me credit for rescuing it, then. Not that he's likely to, seeing that he doesn't like me and never will.' Charlotte yawned. 'And now we have to take those hunters back to Cavan Morry and beg a lift home in their carriage – such a bore when I could have gone back to bed.'

Dudley hesitated. 'That cousin of yours . . .'

'Yes?'

'Do you regret not taking him?'

Charlotte's eyes gleamed. 'Oh, poor darling, are you jealous?'

'A fellow likes to know where he stands.'

'If I had married Richard I should not have been the Honourable Mrs Dudley Sarn, should I?'

'And that's all that matters?'

136

'No, of course not.' She went to him and kissed him. 'I've no regrets. I never have regrets. And Richard would have expected far too much of me, whereas you don't expect anything at all.'

'Not now, I don't,' he muttered.

A bell pealed suddenly through the house and Charlotte looked interested.

'Callers? Do you suppose someone has come to tell us those ruffians have been arrested?'

'I'll go down,' said Dudley at once.

'So will I,' said Charlotte.

They were at the top of the elegant staircase when they saw the visitor Nora has just admitted and Charlotte gave a cry of astonishment.

'Well, I declare! It's my cousin Hester.'

John Wintour was also astonished when Nora showed Hester into the drawing room.

'Mrs Daniel Molloy,' she announced, on Hester's whispered instruction, and at once retreated with a scarlet face to give Mrs Heenan the unbelievable news that she had had to show Daniel Molloy's wife in to the quality. 'Sure and when I called her Miss Hester isn't she after telling me, "My name is Mrs Daniel Molloy, please to announce me"!'

'Never in this world!' cried Mrs Heenan. ''Tis beyond me to believe it!'

It was beyond John Wintour, too, and Charlotte and Dudley, who were staring at Hester as though they had never seen her before. Only Ernestine, who had been decorating the drawing room with evergreens, put down her bundle of holly and went forward to take her niece's hand.

'My dear girl, how lovely to see you! Come and sit down. Let me order you some coffee.'

Hester, as elegant as she could make herself in a dark-blue skirt and jacket and her best hat, shook her head. 'Thank you, Aunt, I won't take coffee, I am not staying long.' She smiled a little tremulously at Charlotte and bowed to Dudley.

Dudley said, coldly: 'Perhaps that would be as well. May I say, Mrs Molloy, that we are very surprised to see you here this morning?'

'Dudley,' John snapped, 'leave this to me.' He turned to Hester. 'I'm bound to say I agree with my son-in-law, Hester. I consider it quite improper that you should be in this house today.'

'I came to see you, Uncle. Would it be possible to talk in private?'

'If it's to plead for your husband, I'm afraid it won't do any good. You know what he and his cronies did last night? Burned down the stables! Smashed windows! And promised more!' John, breathing quickly, stabbed the air with his hand. 'Threatened that this house would be next, Hester, your own family's home. What sort of man have you married, then?'

'If you please,' she murmured with trembling lips, 'I should just like to speak to you for a moment – for the sake of my father, Uncle John.'

'I should advise against it, sir,' Dudley put in at once. 'Mrs Molloy can have nothing useful to say to you.'

'Mrs Molloy,' Charlotte mimicked. 'Her name is Hester, for heaven's sake, Dudley, still Hester to us, even if she has married a Fenian. Papa, I think you ought to listen to her.'

'How is your dear little boy, Hester?' asked Ernestine, strewing holly along the chimneypiece. 'I should so much like to have seen him. Matthew's grandson, John, remember.'

John bit his lip. 'Very well,' he said, 'I'll see you, Hester. Come into the study.'

In his shabby, book-lined room, he shut the door and told Hester to take one of the wing chairs and himself took the other. She thanked him and sat staring uneasily at her hands folded on her velvet reticule. After a moment, she looked across at John.

'I shall have to admit, Uncle, I have come to plead for my husband. In a way.'

'I meant what I said, Hester. It won't do any good. I can't refuse to press charges against a trespasser and an arsonist. I should be the laughing stock of the county!'

'I do not condone what Daniel did, but he is no criminal, I swear it. All he cares about is Ireland.'

'Yes, just as the men who murdered Lord Frederick Cavendish in Phoenix Park only cared about Ireland,' John replied contemptuously. 'It's an argument that is wholly unacceptable. To kill and burn and damage is to kill and burn and damage, whether it's done in the name of patriotism or anything else you fancy.'

'I have said, Uncle, I do not condone violence. But I can understand why it happens. People are looking for justice.'

'Justice? You think justice can be achieved by burning down my stables?' John shook his head. 'Hester, you may say you understand your husband's motives. All I can say is he must face the consequences of his own actions. He and Docherty must be prosecuted.'

Hester was silent for so long that John guessed she was fighting back tears, but he would not look at her in case he was right. Suddenly she opened her reticule and took out a photograph.

'This is a picture of my son Paul, Uncle John. Would you like to see it?'

He found his reading glasses and looked at it. 'Bless my soul!' he muttered. 'He's the image of Matthew.'

'It is Paul's father who is to be sent to gaol,' Hester said quietly. 'I know I should not plead for Daniel – it is true, he has done wrong, he should pay – but I am really pleading for my son, not him. I am pleading for my father, who is not well. I do not know how this will affect him and I should like . . .' Hester's tears began to fall at last. 'I'd like to spare him from it, if at all possible.'

'Oh, Hester!' John gave a groan. 'You're making this so difficult. You think I don't know how it's going to affect my brother? But you knew what Molloy was like when you married him, didn't you? You knew you'd bring trouble down on us all.'

'The trouble was begun long ago,' she muttered, pressing her handkerchief to her eyes. 'Long ago, Uncle, by our own ancestors.'

'Oh, if you are going to bring history into it –'

'Ireland is history! ' she cried. 'It's why there is trouble now, because of history!' She snatched up the photograph and returned it to her reticule. 'I'm sorry, Uncle, I shouldn't have come. I'm asking you to go against your duty and why should you do that?' She rose blindly to her feet. 'Don't worry, I'll see myself out.'

'Wait.' John got to his feet. 'Hester, I'm a fool. I shouldn't listen to you, but I can't face sending Matthew's son-in-law to gaol. God knows what Dudley will say to me. You realise I'll have to drop charges against Docherty as well?'

She was standing very still, her tear-stained face alight.

'Uncle, I don't know what to say to you, except you've made me feel proud. Proud of my own family.' She laughed weakly. 'Which is something new for me these days. Uncle John, you're a good man, you really are.' She kissed him on the cheek and he held her for a moment.

'What a mess we're all in,' he muttered. 'All of us, aren't we?'

He let her out by the side door so that she need not see Dudley and Charlotte again, but she asked him to give her love to her Aunt Ernestine, who had always been so kind. She hesitated. 'And would you mind if I went to see the stables?'

He looked at her sharply. 'You really want to?'

'Please.'

'I'll take you, then.'

They walked in silence to the remains of the stable block. Smoke still hung in the winter air over the mass of charred wood and rubble; there was the foul smell of things burnt, an atmosphere of bitterness and hopelessness and desolation of the spirit.

'It's terrible,' Hester whispered.

John said nothing. He held her arm.

Tears pricked her eyes but she would not shed them. She wished she might have been alone. Images of Daniel came crowding to her mind as she looked at the place he had destroyed. Daniel reading, talking, kissing. Herself running to him, loving him. All here, here, where he had hurled his lighted torch. In spite of herself, a sob burst from her and John said, 'Come, let's leave, this is no place to be.'

'No place to be,' she echoed.

If they had hoped to avoid Dudley and Charlotte, they were unsuccessful. Both were waiting by O'Dowd's trap.

'There you are!' cried Charlotte. 'You surely weren't going without saying goodbye, Hester?'

'I wasn't sure if you wanted to see me, Charlotte.'

'Of course I wanted to see you! It's a shame we've lost touch. Next time I am in Dublin, I intend to visit you. Promise to send me your address.'

'I should like to.'

Hester shook Charlotte's hand and turned to Dudley, who was staring at his father-in-law with a deep frown.

'You are accompanying Mrs Molloy, sir?' he asked, as John prepared to climb into the trap.

'Yes, I must go to Skibbereen and as you know I've no trap of my own at the moment. That's all right with you, O'Dowd, isn't it?'

The carrier touched his cap. 'It is, your honour.'

'You are to see the RM?' Dudley pressed, and John averted his eyes.

'I've decided to drop charges,' he muttered. 'No, don't look at me like that. It's just too difficult, there's nothing I can do.'

'Drop charges against both of them?' cried Dudley. 'Docherty too?'

'It will have to be both of them. Charlotte, send Nora out with my coat, if you please.'

'Well, I declare, Hester, you are cleverer than I thought,' Charlotte exclaimed, smiling. 'Persuading Papa to do as you want, then. I'm sure he would never have done as much for me.'

'Charlotte, will you fetch my coat?' John shouted, and she ran into the house, followed by Dudley, who stalked in without another word and slammed the door behind him.

141

Seventeen

When Daniel came home late on Christmas Eve, he would not look at Hester. She ran to him, her eyes shining with relief, but he put her aside and went upstairs without a word.

'Will you believe it?' cried Theresa, and went up after him. A few minutes later he came down, his face as dark as a thunder cloud, and, flinging himself into a chair near the range, began to rattle the bars with the poker.

'I told him it was downstairs for him or the street,' Theresa told Hester, breathlessly. 'I said I'd not be after putting up with his tantrums. Hadn't he ever been lucky to be allowed home and not charged and wasn't he spoiling it all with sinful pride, then?'

'Not pride!' Daniel shouted, turning his head to fix her with his violent blue stare. 'Principle! Didn't the two of us want to be caught, then, Billie Docherty and me? Didn't we stay when the rest went so we'd be arrested and able to put our case? Weren't we after getting in the news and where's the good of being in the news if you're let out of gaol on your wife's asking?'

'Daniel, please lower your voice,' Hester said coldly. 'You will wake Paul, and on Christmas Eve, too.' As he still refused to look at her, she went to him and stood over him, forcing him to raise his eyes to her face. 'How can you talk of principle, when you burn down another man's property to get your own way? Where is the principle in violence of that sort?'

'I thought you were understanding what we are trying to do,' he whispered furiously. 'I thought you were with us.'

'I do understand, I am with you, but haven't I said over and over again nothing can be achieved by violence? Oh, Daniel!' Hester turned away from him and stood with her hand over her eyes. 'Aren't you at all glad to be back with me? With Paul?'

'Shame on you, Daniel,' Theresa put in. ''Tis the devil that's in you again and to Mass you'd better be going to pray he's pulled out.' She glanced at the clock. 'Go now, the both of you, to Midnight Mass; I'll watch over Paul.'

'I am not ready for Midnight Mass,' Daniel muttered. 'I cannot be going to Communion.'

'No, for it's a sinner you are, but you can be after praying to God to take away your black thoughts. Hester, here is your cloak. Be off, the pair of you!'

'Come, Daniel,' Hester murmured, wrapping the cloak around her.' Theresa is right. Let us go to church, let us thank God we are together for Christmas.'

'Thank St John Wintour, are you not meaning?' he asked. 'Can you not see how it sticks in my throat to be grateful to him?'

'I thought it was being grateful to me you minded,' she said in a low voice.

He stood up, turning his back to her as he struggled for control. She knew better than to say anything at that point, and so did Theresa. They both stood and waited until at last he made a move, took down his coat and shrugged himself into it, still not looking at either his wife or his sister. Hester opened the door to the street and with a backward glance at Theresa went out. After a moment or two, Daniel followed.

'Please, God,' Theresa muttered, as the door closed on him, 'will you be making that wooden head to see sense? Or it'll be me that knocks it into him.'

Maybe it was the effect of his own prayers, maybe it was Theresa's, but by Christmas morning Daniel's anger had subsided. He agreed that Hester had only done what she thought was right and everyone had to do that, but would she please promise him never to do such a thing again, whatever her reasons? He was a man, he must be taking

144

responsibility for his own actions, he could not hide behind the skirts of a woman.

'I think we should not ask for promises,' Hester answered carefully. 'You know what I would ask of you.'

He hesitated and she trembled inwardly, fearing for their fragile peace, but then he gave one of his rare smiles.

'It's straight you are, Hester, Hester, straight and true. Let's not be seeking promises, then.' He kissed her gently. 'And let's not be hurting each other.'

In the sweetness of his kiss and in the Christmas that might have been so terrible, Hester put the thought of the stables at Belcarron to the back of her mind.

It was a good day. Paul had his small presents and his stocking with raisins and almonds, an apple and an orange and a new penny, while the grown-ups enjoyed a fine dinner of roast goose, boiled plum pudding and Hester's gift of wine. When the lodgers, in cheerful mood, had retired to their rooms and Daniel had carried away the sleeping Paul, Theresa said:

'Sure, I think the Lord was watching over us, to be giving us such a day.'

Hester agreed. She did not add she felt like a skater who has reached the bank only to see the ice cracking up behind her, but the hole of dark water seemed very close even as she sat and looked into Theresa's parlour fire. She had saved Daniel and in his own way he had saved her; they were together on the bank. But for how long?

A visitor called next day when they were sitting in the kitchen after the midday meal. It was Frank O'Keefe, a Skibbereen man, now a political journalist in Dublin. Frank was no great favourite with Daniel, who thought him a gossip and too fond of the bottle, but he said he was just down to see his old da, wouldn't keep them a minute, he had news they should hear. Refusing with thanks Theresa's offer of cold goose, he added with a grin he had brought his own refreshment and put a bottle of whiskey on the table.

'Is it a glass you have there, Daniel? I'm thinking you'll be needing a drink when you're hearing what I'll be telling you. Ladies, will you be joining us?'

145

Hester shook her head but Theresa said she would not be minding a small one, it being Christmas, and Daniel said he wouldn't be taking much either, he wasn't one for drinking at that time of day. So what was this great news Frank had, then, that he couldn't be keeping to himself?

Frank, pouring the whiskey, shook his sandy head. 'It's bad,' he answered simply. 'The worst. Just come over the wire before I left.'

'Don't be keeping us hanging,' Theresa snapped. 'What was coming over the wire?'

Glancing round the watching faces, Frank wet his lips with his tongue. He said: 'Captain O'Shea has served divorce papers on his wife. He has cited Charles Stewart Parnell as co-respondent.'

There was a silence in the warm old kitchen, so deep, so stunned that Paul raised his head from his new jack-in-the-box and ran to his mother, who took him on her knee.

'When was this?' asked Daniel, clearing his throat.

'Christmas Eve.' Frank laughed, a little wildly. 'A fine Christmas present, I'm thinking.'

''Tis not possible, is it?' Theresa whispered. 'Mr Parnell? Parnell, the Chief?'

'The uncrowned King of Ireland,' Frank muttered. 'Well, kings make mistakes. We've all been hearing the rumours.'

'I have not, then,' Daniel said harshly. 'What rumours?'

'Oh, don't be putting on the blinkers,' Frank said easily. 'Has there not been talk for years that the Chief and Mrs O'Shea were – begging your pardon, ladies – living as man and wife in England? Hasn't there even been talk of children?'

'I was never hearing this,' Theresa cried, her blue eyes outraged, 'Hester, you are in Dublin – is it true what Frank is saying?'

Hester, setting Paul down to play again, shook her head. She had heard the rumours but she could not speak of them, not when Daniel was sitting there, his whiskey untouched, his face a mask. She knew his devotion to Parnell, the Protestant landowner and politician who was regarded as the saviour of Ireland, the man who with Gladstone, the Liberal prime minister, was pledged to bring Home Rule and justice at last.

She had met Parnell once and did not like him. His background was the same as her own; it was remarkable that such a man should want to fight for Ireland and she knew she should admire him. Yet she sensed a coldness in him, a desire to bring justice to Ireland for reasons of the mind, not of the heart. That he did have a heart, though, was becoming all too clear. It seemed he had given it to Katharine O'Shea, the wife of a Home Rule MP, a former Hussars officer, who, it was said, had been willing to use Parnell's infatuation for his wife for his own ends. For years he had done nothing to raise scandal while his wife's rich aunt was alive; now that the aunt was dead and Katharine's inheritance contested, he had decided to blacken his wife's reputation and throw Parnell to the wolves. So much Hester had heard, but Daniel had not. Because until now he had stopped his ears.

His face filled suddenly with deep, rich colour. He stood up, knocking over his whiskey, which dripped down on to the scrubbed stone floor.

'It's ashamed of yourself you should be, Frank O'Keefe,' he said thickly, 'taking away the reputation of the finest man to fight for Ireland you will ever know.'

Frank looked down into his glass, his thin, foxy face impassive. 'It will be doing no good, Daniel, to put our heads in the sand over this. If there are facts to be faced, it's us who will be facing them.'

'Facts? Is it not a fact there is always talk about famous men? Was not Richard Pigott telling lies about the Chief and the Phoenix Park murders and wasn't he found out and made to answer? O'Shea will be made to answer, too. You'll see, Frank, I'm right, there cannot be any truth in what you're saying.'

'I'm not swearing to truth.' Frank groaned. 'I can only be telling you the Chief's been cited; it will be a lucky man he is, if he rides out the storm.'

'He is a Protestant,' Theresa said. 'And the Protestants are not having the same views on divorce as our Church. 'Tis possible he'll be excused.'

'By Gladstone?' Frank shook his head. 'I don't think so, the Nonconformists in his party will never let him keep a man who's been dragged through the divorce court. And if Gladstone gives us up, it's a lost cause we are.'

'I'll not be staying, I'll not be listening to this!' Daniel burst out. 'Hester, will you be going up now to pack our things? Tomorrow we go back to Dublin.'

'Tomorrow, is it?' Frank poured himself more whiskey. 'It's me will be taking a day or two more with my da. No need to be hurrying back, Daniel, this story will not be running away.'

'Story, you call it?' Daniel shouted from the stairs. 'Lies, I call it, Frank O'Keefe, and every man in Dublin will be after agreeing with me!'

As Hester rose, shaking her head, Frank caught at her hand.

'Be trying to talk some sense into him, Mrs Molloy. He's blind as a bat where the Chief's concerned, but he'll have to be seeing things now the way they are.'

'You know him,' she murmured. 'He is a man who will find things out for himself, or not at all. But I'll do what I can.' At the foot of the stairs she paused and looked back. 'Do you think it will really come to divorce for the O'Sheas?'

'I do. Willy O'Shea has no love for the Chief and if he can bring him down over this, he will. We shall have to be praying the party does not come down with him.'

As Hester began to move around their room, putting out clothes for packing, Daniel watched her in moody silence, his chest heaving with suppressed feeling.

'I'll not have you talking about this when we are at home,' he said at last. 'There is to be no more gossip.'

'When have you known me gossip?' she asked, stung. 'People talk in the shop, I do not talk with them. In any case, there will be no need for secrets if everything is brought out into the open.'

'Everything? What are you meaning? These bastard children Parnell is supposed to have?'

'The children cannot help existing, Daniel. If the stories are true, it will be pointless to deny them.'

He looked at her with bloodshot eyes. 'The stories are not true. If they were, would I not be the first to agree he is no fit

148

man to lead our party? But they are not, he is not what they are saying, the charges are lies, made up to discredit him. O'Keefe is a fool.'

Hester sat on the edge of the bed and wrapped her shawl around her; the bedroom on that winter afternoon was chill. 'I cannot believe, after all he has done, you could ever cast Parnell aside,' she said slowly.

'Have I not been telling you, I do not believe a word of what they are saying against him?'

'If you did, though, if what they say is true, should you not still support him?'

'Support him?' Daniel appeared bewildered. 'Support a man who has thrown away Ireland for a woman? A woman who is another man's wife? Hester, are you out of your senses?'

'Daniel, he fell in love!' she cried, with sudden passion. 'Do you not know what that means? If the rumours are true, he and Mrs O'Shea love each other as man and wife, they share a true marriage. Is his life's work to be denied him because Mrs O'Shea went through a ceremony with Captain O'Shea first?'

Daniel went white. He looked at Hester as though she were a stranger.

'Mrs O'Shea took her marriage vows at the altar!' he thundered. 'Are you saying marriage is no sacrament? Are you saying those vows taken before God have no meaning? Whom God hath joined, let no man put asunder. Except Charles Stewart Parnell. Is that what you are saying, Hester?'

Daniel gave a harsh laugh. 'I see you are still after being a Protestant in your heart, Hester. Was it not your church that was founded on divorce?'

'Will you stop that shouting, Daniel?' Theresa called up the stairs. 'Or is it the whole of Skibbereen you are wanting to hear you? Hester, come down, I'm making a pot of tea.'

Hester, very pale, moved to the door. 'I hope you will apologise to me for what you have just said, Daniel. You are upset now, but later you will see why you should not have spoken to me that way. Whatever Parnell has done, he must not come between you and me.'

149

'He has done nothing!' Daniel cried. 'Will you be seeing that, Hester? It's a man of honour he is and a true lover of Ireland, not Mrs O'Shea. Her husband will be shown up for the liar he is – and then it will be you who'll be apologising to me!'

Eighteen

It was a relief to Hester to leave Skibbereen. As Richard had
said, it was oppressive to her, the ghosts too real, the suffering
too close. Yet Irish suffering was ongoing. There was nowhere in Ireland she could escape from it, from the guilt it
fostered. Her father had felt the same, of course, which was
why he had run away. And there was the irony, Hester
thought, for she could not run away. She did not want to.

All she wanted was to make amends for the harm done by
her forebears, by the class that was the Protestant Ascendancy, who still ruled Ireland, who thought they always
should. No Home Rule for them, they were fighting it tooth
and nail, while Hester longed passionately to see Ireland free.
But not through violence.

She glanced at Daniel, sitting next to her in the dusty train
taking them home, his handsome head sunk on his chest, his
eyelids half closed over his stern blue eyes. Who was it had
said, 'The Creator called nothing into existence in vain,
dynamite is a blessed agent'? An Irishman. And Daniel, it
seemed, would not have disagreed with him. No doubt he
was thinking now of his hero, Charles Stewart Parnell, so
falsely charged, as Daniel believed.

Please God, Hester thought, may he be right and the rest
of us wrong. For Ireland's sake. For his own.

As she took Paul on her knee and smoothed his soft hair,
she wondered if she might find a letter from Alice waiting
when she arrived home. She always enjoyed reading her
cousin's accounts of life in the Argentine and was usually
keen to reply. Next time, though, she would have to tell of

151

the stable fire at Belcarron and Daniel's part in it. Uncle John would be sure to write about it; she must write too, must admit that wrong had been done and Daniel had done it. But what would Richard say? She had been so happy over their reconciliation. Would this cause another rift? Hester bit her lip and stared out at the wintry landscape. If only they were not so far apart! Yet she knew even if she were to talk to Richard face to face he could not possibly be expected to forgive Daniel for what he had done. It had been hard enough for her to forgive him herself. In fact, the wound still throbbed; it would take a long time to heal.

Better think of other things. Babies, perhaps. Alice had had a third child, a daughter, and as Hester's thoughts moved to daughters, her hand slid to her flat belly beneath Paul's sleeping body and her daydreams became pleasant.

Her bookshop – Irish Books for the Irish – had been bought with her father's help and was on the north side of the river Liffey in a quiet side street. The area was poor but not a slum and Hester had created a comfortable flat from the rooms over the shop, furnishing them with good second-hand pieces and filling window boxes with flowers. Daniel did not take much interest but she did not expect a man to join in homemaking; it was enough that he did not object to her running the shop while her little maid looked after Paul. Daniel would indeed sometimes help, when he had the time.

As far as she could be happy anywhere in Ireland, Hester was happy in Dublin. Through the bookshop she had made good friends and the city itself was an exciting, stimulating place to live. Not as thrilling, perhaps, as Buenos Aires, which Alice described so well, but in some ways not unlike it. Both had elegance and beauty from viceregal connections, both had societies that thought rather well of themselves, and both behind their fine façades had slums and horrors it did not do to dwell on. All cities had their two faces, of course, but sometimes Hester could scarcely believe that the slums she visited were on the same planet as the debutante parties and court levees at Dublin Castle. She did what she could, worked for charities, sat on committees, but it was all drops in the boundless ocean of suffering.

In the days after their return from Skibbereen it was impossible not to sense the excitement that gripped Dublin over the news of the O'Shea divorce case. Everyone had a view, a theory, an argument, but in those January days it did appear that Frank O'Keefe's forecasts had been pessimistic. Parnell's supporters were not hurrying to condemn him. Many were like Daniel in believing the divorce case to be just another English plot against him, while even the Catholic Church seemed to be holding its fire. Daniel was jubilant. He had been vindicated, his idol had no feet of clay. Had Parnell himself not said: 'Gentlemen, could you believe that of me?'

'O'Keefe was scandalmongering, as usual,' Daniel told Hester. 'The Chief's honour is safe.'

'Everyone thinks that?' she asked doubtfully.

'Well, it's true the Chief has enemies, it is natural they are out for him now, but it's nothing they can be doing. Even Michael Davitt is having to accept there is no truth in the charges. "The dishonour will not be on my side," the Chief is after telling him – his very words, Hester, could you be asking anything plainer?'

She shook her head. 'I'm relieved, Daniel. Now we can put this out of our minds and get on with our own lives.'

He looked at her in surprise. 'Why, Hester, what are you saying? You know our lives are mixed with his, we stand or fall with him.'

'That's not true. To think that is to deny our own importance as people. Parnell is your leader, but he does not own you body and soul.'

'He does not. He leaves that to God. But if I am having a purpose on this earth it is to see my country set free and the only man who can be doing it is Parnell.' Daniel took an envelope from his pocket and in suddenly smiling mood handed it to Hester. 'Now did I not pick this up for you on my way upstairs? I'm thinking it is from your cousin.'

Hester's face lit up. 'It is, it is from Alice.' Her eyes quickly scanned the pages. 'About her daughter, Beatrice Ernestine, to be called Tina – oh, how lovely, I'm so happy for her! At last, some good news!'

Daniel kissed her, still smiling. 'It's a funny one you are, my Hester. Have I not just now been giving you the best news there is?'

Nineteen

In her letter to Hester, Alice had given the good news but glossed over the bad. As her father had read, however, the economy of the Argentine was in trouble. World recession had hit markets hard. The government had panicked and created inflation, there were bankruptcies and social unrest. Even the middle classes were marching, signalling their disillusion. It was true that land values had gone up while the currency went down, but Charlotte had been wrong in thinking the *estancieros* could stand immune. They made their incomes from what their land produced. 'No sales, no income,' said Richard. 'It's as simple as that.'

Of course, it was not quite as simple as that. There was still an income for the Estancia Sentos, but there was retrenchment, and the knowledge that there was nothing to be done until things got better. Boom time was over.

Late February brought bad news of a personal nature, when John and Hester wrote of the fire at Belcarron. Richard was furious. Did this not show he had been right all along about Daniel Molloy, who would one day surely burn the family in their beds for the sake of Ireland and had now begun with the stables? Alice could say nothing in return, she was as grieved as he, but she thought of Hester and Hester's child and feared for the future. Daniel had escaped gaol this time; would he be so lucky again? Hester, who had suffered so much, would be sure to suffer more. Clearly, she still loved Daniel as much as ever, in spite of what he had done; it was not in her nature to change. 'Whatever happens, we must support her,' Alice decided. 'Even Papa thinks that.'

155

As the summer waned, preparations for winter began. Alice with Paola and the maids, worked hard, conserving the crops from the orchards, not apples and plums as at home, but apricots, quinces and fat golden peaches. They put down eggs in isinglass, prepared chutneys and pickles, bottled tomatoes, pressed beef . . .

'I declare,' Alice said to Richard,' life would be a great deal easier if we did not have to eat.'

But Richard had his own troubles, trying to get the right price for the stock, seeing no end in sight to the depression.

In April, when the weather was cooler, they paid a visit to Beatrice in Buenos Aires. Richard was able to ride to the train at San Vicente but everyone else had to go by ox cart, jolting along on the cattle trails as the pampas still had no proper roads. When the railways had come to the little towns strung out across the plain, no one, it seemed, had remembered stations needed access.

The train journey itself was boring in the extreme. Beatrice used to say it was more fun in the old days when Indians followed on horseback, shrieking and threatening and providing excitement. They had not survived long. There had always been someone willing to dispose of the natives and they were now to be found only in the cities, on reservations or in remote, isolated places where they had quite given up threatening.

'Weren't you afraid, though?' Alice had asked.

Beatrice had said of course she was. But she could remember the time before the railways when she and Enriques travelled in covered wagons and carried guns. Used them, too – not to kill, just to frighten. 'Good days, those, when one looks back.' Beatrice had sighed. Now one was safe and bored to death.

On the day of departure, when the ox cart was brought round, Lucio, courteous as ever, handed in Mena and a second maid, Margarita, then lifted up the children. Alice followed, already adjusting her veil as a protection against the dust to come. When the peons had stowed away the travel hampers and boxes, Richard on horseback gave the signal to start and the cart slowly lumbered off, a mestizo driving. Alice, looking back, saw Lucio pausing to kiss

Paola's dark face before mounting his horse to accompany them to San Vicente, from where he would return with Richard's horse and his own. He was a wonderful husband, everyone said, always so kind, so considerate, yet Paola was never happy, her present complaint being that she still had no son to give Lucio. Why did the Blessed Virgin not answer her prayers, when the señora had two sons and she none?

It would be a relief, Alice thought, to be back in BA where Carlotta, Beatrice's housekeeper, and Vittoria, her cook, presented no problems. Everyone in the old house by the Riachuelo River seemed happy to be there, bewitched no doubt by Beatrice's yellow hair – the Argentines would do anything for blonds. See how their eyes followed Richard, Victor and Jack too, while little Tina with her dark hair attracted no attention. But she was already so lively, so full of personality, it would not be long before she made her presence felt, even in the man's world of South America.

All three children were excited by the trip, although Victor, who at four already had a cool arrogance, was pretending not to show it, allowing Jack to point at every bird and Tina to jump up and down on Mena's knee, laughing at everything new. Jack, Alice considered, was like Matthew, a good-natured child with a high forehead and steady gaze. Hester had written that Paul too was like Matthew, there was not a sign of Daniel in him. How strange it was, the way inheritance worked, picking out a likeness here, a characteristic there. Would it ever be fathomed? Probably not. Alice's eyes began to close, the children's voices receding from her, until Mena touched her hand and said San Vicente was ahead. Richard was to join them there and they would rest and take refreshment before they had to board the train.

To arrive in Buenos Aires was bliss. Slump or no slump, the federal capital was as vibrant, as beautiful as ever, as different from the pampas as the moon. Yet dependent, of course, on the land, on the cattle. One always had to bear in mind, Beatrice said, that behind the power of BA lay the *saladero*.

To Alice it was a wonderful place to stay; to the *porteños*, of course it was the only place to live. There had been moves lately towards making the *estancias* more like estates in

England and France with fine houses and elaborate gardens, but most people in BA still expressed surprise that Richard and Alice should want to live in the country. Without polo or tennis, without dances or amateur theatricals, how did they pass their time?

'I'm sure we're regarded as eccentric,' Richard once commented to Beatrice. 'They don't seem to realise I earn my living on the pampas, I haven't time for society.'

'You will one day,' Beatrice told him. 'And when you want it, you'll be accepted, you'll be what they call *gente decente*, more so than I am myself.'

She had laughed and shrugged and it was hard to know whether she minded or not, being neither true criolla nor, as a convert Catholic who had been married to an Argentine, a true British expatriate. As usual it was difficult to read her mind, but she seemed gratified to think her niece and nephew would have no difficulty in moving in the best BA society. They were English without complication and BA loved everything English.

'I'm Anglo-Irish, does that count?' Alice asked, teasingly.

Beatrice said everyone knew the Anglo-Irish were simply English dominating a piece of empire. The Argentines had fought to win their own independence from Spain but they still secretly admired empire builders. And no one could deny the English were that.

They drove now through the dark streets of the old quarter to the Avenida Lila; it was late, the children were weary, they must be put to bed as soon as possible. Their aunt's house, built in Spanish style with tiled roof and shutters, was hidden behind a high wall in which was set a wrought-iron gate. To gain admittance one had to pull a heavy jangling bell at the side. The courtyard at the front was filled with shrubs and lemon trees and at the back were two patios facing the river, one for the use of the family, the other for the servants and the drying of laundry. It was a pleasant, comfortable place and the Wintours always enjoyed being there, especially the cosseting they received from Carlotta and Vittoria, even on occasion from their aunt.

They smiled indulgently as the children were greeted now with rapture and swept away to be fed and cooed over and eventually put to bed, while Beatrice, attractive in dark silk, poured *mate* tea and told them to hurry with their baths, dinner was ready.

It was a good dinner; Vittoria was an excellent cook and Beatrice kept a fine cellar. Afterwards, taking coffee in the *sala*, they found the sofa strewn, surprisingly, with old English newspapers.

'Catching up on the news?' Richard asked jovially. 'That's a change for you, Aunt.'

'The Parnell case, dear boy, so fascinating – as good as a novel, isn't it?'

'Depends on the novel. It's not exactly Sir Walter Scott.'

'Much more romantic. To give up a country for a woman, what could be more romantic than that?'

'You think he will? I mean, end his career?'

'I think there is no doubt of it. Win or lose, the scandal will finish him. Gladstone will never work with a man who has been through the divorce courts.'

'Supposing Captain O'Shea does lose?' Alice asked. 'Surely it would not be fair to blame Parnell then?'

'Mud sticks, my dear, and from what I read, the mud is genuine. O'Shea won't lose and Parnell will be out of politics by the end of the year, you'll see.' Beatrice took off her reading glasses and lay back in her chair. 'Ah, but reading about the old country makes me wish I was there, you know. Perhaps I'll join you, Alice, when you go back.'

'I wish you would, Aunt. It has always seemed strange to me' – Alice hesitated – 'that you have never been back at all.'

'Well, I suppose I never wanted to leave Enriques and Enriques never wanted to make the trip to Ireland. Since he died I've just been too idle.'

'And Tucuman?' asked Richard casually. 'Have you been up there yet?'

'Tucuman? Not yet. I shall definitely go, though, just give me time.' Beatrice's green eyes slid away. 'I did say I was idle, didn't I?'

'How can one deal with her?' Richard asked fretfully when they were alone in their room. 'She is as secretive as the Sphinx!'

Alice shook her head. 'Imagine being too lazy to go to Ireland.'

'Or Tucuman,' said Richard. 'When she asked us to stay so that she could go.'

They spent a pleasant three weeks in Buneos Aires, visiting friends, being entertained to dinner, attending a winter ball given by Edward Stonefield, their aunt's banker. Alice also took the opportunity to shop, stocking up with things needed on the *estancia*, and to visit her dressmaker, though assuring Beatrice she was not being extravagant. She knew their financial situation, she would never run Richard into debt.

'As for your financial situation,' Beatrice replied, 'I know it too. I should like you to have this.'

She passed an envelope to Alice, who, opening it, blushed and shook her head.

'Aunt, it's awfully kind of you, but I can't take this, it's too much.'

'Nonsense. You have children, you need money, I don't. Please, no arguments, put that in the bank and use it. Nothing would give me greater pleasure.'

'If you're sure – '

'I am sure.' Beatrice turned a large emerald ring on her finger and studied it. 'Alice,' she said, after a pause, 'would you be willing to come back to see me soon? You and Richard?'

Alice, looking at her in surprise, said: 'Of course, Aunt. Is there something special you would like us to do?'

'Well, it's just a matter of business. You needn't stay long, nor bring the children – poor darlings, the journey is so tiring and Mena is so good with them, isn't she? Supposing I were to write to you, arrange a date – say, some time in July?'

'That would be fine,' Alice answered, mystified. 'I'll tell Richard, shall I?'

'If you would, my dear.'

'Now what the devil does all that mean?' cried Richard. 'Whatever is she playing at? If she has business to discuss, why not now when we are here?'

'It may be she has to go to Tucuman first,' said Alice.

'Tucuman ... we always come back to that.' Richard's eyes were stormy. 'If only I could go to her and ask her straight out what is going on – '

'Why don't you?'

'I don't know. Something always seems to hold me back.'

'Then we must just wait for July. Heavens, how she likes to keep us on pins! These are the times when she reminds me of Charlotte.'

'You think she's teasing?' Richard shook his head. 'No, there's something serious behind all this. I wish to God I knew what it was.'

They could be nothing else but patient, bidding Beatrice an affectionate farewell when they left for the *estancia*, waving from the train until they could no longer see her slim, fashionably dressed figure and raised gloved hand. Speculation on what was in her mind for them was useless, they did not even try it, and back on the pampas there was plenty to do; they could absorb themselves in other things. Until her letter came, as promised, one morning in July. Once again there was the ox cart and train, the long, punishing journey, the arrival in Buenos Aires, now in the depths of winter. Once again they were back in the Avenida Lila, looking up at their aunt's house and wondering why every window was lit.

Twenty

Francisco, Beatrice's coachman, husband to Carlotta, had unlocked the gate for them and carried their boxes into the courtyard but made them no greeting. Now he stood at the door to the house, his leathery face averted, his greying head bent. Alice regarded him with some unease. This was not the Francisco of smiles and bows who normally welcomed them to the Casa Sentos. As she listened to the night wind stirring the branches of the trees, she had the feeling that something was very wrong. She sensed Richard felt it too.

The door ahead suddenly flew open and the stout figure of Carlotta appeared on the threshold. At the sight of them she flung up her hands and burst into a storm of weeping.

'What is it, what is it?' cried Alice.

'Doña Beatriz, Doña Beatriz!' Carlotta rocked to and fro, tears spilling down her creased, swollen face. '*Está muerta*,' she whispered, '*está muerta*, Doña Alicia.'

They were frozen before her, their faces ashen in the shadows that surrounded them.

'That cannot be true,' Alice said, huskily, 'Doña Beatrice cannot be dead. There must be some mistake.'

'I'm so sorry,' an English voice said from the house and Dr Ward, their aunt's physician, came to them and took their hands. He led them into the tiled hall and made them sit down. 'I'm so very, very sorry. I don't know how to tell you. Your aunt died during the night. They found her this morning.'

Hugh Ward, a red-haired Englishman in his forties, was as much a friend as a doctor. He had delivered Alice's babies, had fought to save Mena's Liam, had been the support and consoler of Beatrice after the death of Don Enriques. It seemed fitting he should take them to Beatrice's deathbed now.

Their aunt's room, filled with candles and flowers, seemed strange. They had never seen it before with the shutters closed, they had never before seen Beatrice on her bed. Lying on her chaise longue, perhaps, smoking and reading, sitting at her dressing table, putting up her hair, or scrabbling in her jewel box for some mislaid earring or brooch – she was always careless with her things. Now she lay on her heavy Spanish marriage bed, her hands clasped on her breast, her hair smoothed from her brow, her green eyes closed. Vittoria, who had been watching over her, slipped away at their entrance, leaving them to stand looking down at the one sister of their two fathers, their faces working with emotion but not yet weeping.

It was strange, Beatrice no longer looked like Charlotte, Alice thought, but like John, her brother. Alice had never seen the likeness before.

'How peaceful she seems', she whispered.

Richard muttered: 'Yes, but this is not Aunt Beatrice, I don't want to see her – ' He turned and hastily went out, his handkerchief to his face. Alice looked at Dr Ward.

'It's true, she is our aunt and not our aunt, but that is death, isn't it? Why can't I cry?'

'You will, my dear.' He put his arm around her and as she leaned against him it came to her that he was comforting her because her aunt was dead, it was true, there was no mistake, and at last her tears began to flow. He let her cry for some moments, then gently led her from the room.

Later, when they had changed into black and had been persuaded by Vittoria to eat something, Dr Ward came to them in the *sala*. As he seated himself in the chair Richard placed, solemnly adjusting the skirts of his frock coat, fingering his starched white collar and all the time not looking at them, they both sensed he had something extraordinary to say to them. He was a very experienced doctor, it was clear he knew how to convey messages of import, or prepare the way for such messages, without saying a word.

164

'You have something to tell us?' asked Richard.

'Yes. It is not easy.'

'How our aunt died? She had not been ill – was it a heart attack?'

'Not a heart attack. Actually, your aunt had been ill for some time.'

'For some time?' Alice's eyes were large on the doctor's face. 'Why, she never said a word, we had no idea – '

'She had had her suspicions for months, I believe, but she only came to me a few weeks ago. She asked if she could manage a trip to Tucuman – '

'Tucuman!' Richard caught his breath. Dr Ward glanced at him.

'I told her it was quite out of the question, she was far too ill to go anywhere.'

'Oh, Aunt Beatrice!' Alice put her hand to her eyes. 'Why didn't she tell us? Why didn't she explain – '

'Dr Ward, what was it?' asked Richard sharply. 'What was wrong with her?'

'A lung complaint.'

'Consumption?'

'A form of cancer.'

'Something to do with those damned cigars she used to smoke?'

'There's no link that we know of. Many men smoke without harm.'

'No, but for a woman – ' Richard, who had the remains of a brandy before him, swallowed it. 'You're sure you won't take anything, doctor? Alice?' As they shook their heads, Richard poured himself another. 'I'll have to admit, I feel the need of this myself. There's more, isn't there, Dr Ward? More you have to tell us?'

The doctor hesitated, then took from his pocket a small bottle.

'I have been debating for some time what to do,' he said slowly. 'You see, it is my duty to inform you, your aunt's death was not due to natural causes.'

There was a stunned silence. Alice half rose in her seat, then sank down again. Richard clashed his glass to the table.

165

'What in God's name do you mean?' he whispered.

'I mean, your aunt took laudanum.'

'Laudanum!' Alice and Richard exchanged stricken looks. Richard said, unsteadily:

'You had prescribed it?'

'In small dosages. She was beginning to have pain. Last night it appears she took it all.'

'You are saying – ?'

'No more than that, Richard.'

'It might have been a mistake?'

'It might have been.'

'But you don't think so?'

Dr Ward ran his hands through his thick red hair. 'You know I can't answer that. All I can tell you is your aunt was an intelligent woman, she knew what lay ahead.'

'She needn't have died alone!' Alice cried. 'We would have looked after her, nursed her – '

'I know, I know. It wasn't what she wanted.' The doctor sighed heavily. 'You could say, however it happened, this has spared us all a great deal.'

'Shall you tell the authorities?' Richard asked, after a pause.

'No. I've thought about it, I've decided it would do no good. There'd be an inquiry, it would be very distressing. I shall sign the death certificate.'

'Dr Ward, we can't ask you to do that.'

'You are not asking. It is my decision. It may not be entirely ethical in the strictest sense, but I believe it is the right one. I saw your aunt very recently, I can truthfully say she was suffering from a fatal disease.' Dr Ward replaced the laudanum bottle in his pocket. 'What happened here last night is known only to the three of us. We must keep it that way.'

Richard and Alice slowly lowered their eyes and nodded. Then Dr Ward took his leave.

'Try to get some sleep,' he murmured, as he shook their hands. 'You have much ahead of you.'

'I suppose . . . I suppose she didn't leave a note?' Richard asked, then shook his head. 'No, of course she didn't, you would have given it to us. It just seems so strange that she –

well, she asked us to come, you know. She must have known what we should find. Yet, she went without a word – '

'We don't know the truth of it, Richard. We can never be sure.'

'We know she trusted you,' Alice said quietly, and he bent his head gravely.

'I admired her. I thought her a very great lady.'

'All we can say is thank you. You will come again soon?'

'Tomorrow. I shall call tomorrow to see if there is anything I can do.'

'My poor girl,' Richard murmured. 'How do you feel?'

'I don't know. Stunned, I suppose. Shocked. I think it will hit me harder tomorrow.'

He took her arm and paced with her to the patio. It was cold and dark, no one would want to sit there, but they stood there, leaning together.

'See the lights over the river?' Richard whispered. 'Do you remember watching them with her?'

'Very well. I can see her now, sitting in that basket chair, smoking, laughing – oh, I haven't taken it in yet, Richard, that she has gone . . .'

A little later she said they must think about informing people, see the priest, arrange a requiem, there would be a great deal to do.

'Yes.' Richard moved away, lighting a cigar with shaking fingers. 'You realise things may have changed for us now?'

'Don't let's think about that tonight.'

'I know, I'm sorry.' As quickly as he had lit it, he stubbed out the cigar. 'It's a terrible thing, isn't it, that as soon as someone dies, people begin to wonder what they might have left? I never thought I should be like that, but somehow I can't help myself. I didn't want Aunt Beatrice to die, I loved her – '

'Of course you did, Richard.'

'But it's our future's that's at stake, I can't help but wonder – if there's a will – what's in it. You don't blame me, do you?'

'No, I don't.' Alice wrapped her shawl around her shoulders. 'I understand how you feel. I am worrying myself, but tonight I want to think about her. Shall we . . . shall we go and see her again?'

'No, I don't want to, I don't feel she is there, not the Beatrice we knew. I feel her out here much more – don't you?'

'I think I do.'

They stayed where they were, holding hands, and watched the lights over the Riachuelo together.

Twenty-One

The day of Beatrice's funeral was moist and humid. There was a good turnout. People from many strands of society, most of them strangers to the Wintours, had crowded into the Church of Santa Teresa to pay their last respects, which was gratifying in one way, galling in another. When alive, Beatrice had not always had the entrée to certain houses she should have had; now she was dead, her requiem was packed with many who had not chosen to be her friends. Criollo aristocracy, expatriate British, artists, musicians, hangers-on, they were there, filing past the open coffin, later at the Sentos grave, throwing in their token soil, then chattering with one another under the trees.

Standing aloof from these was a tall man of perhaps forty-two or -three, with a prominent nose and distinctive high cheekbones. He wore his black hair long, brushing his collar, and his eyes, which kept seeking Richard, were sombre and heavy-lidded. Alice had noticed him at the back of the church as they followed the coffin out and had wondered where she might have met him; he seemed familiar.

'Who is that?' she whispered to Richard, but he said he had no idea. He took her arm and said they should go, some of the mourners would be returning to the house, they must be there to greet them.

'I don't feel I want to, I don't believe many were Aunt's true friends.'

'They are the society we have to belong to. There is no point in not making ourselves agreeable.'

As they made their way to the carriage, the stranger

stepped into their path. Holding his black hat in his hand, he bowed and asked in Spanish if he might have the honour of speaking with them for a moment.

'Sir, I do not believe we have met,' Richard answered.

'That is true. I wish to present myself. I am Felipe Sentos, of Tucuman.'

They stood quite still, their blue eyes locked with his dark gaze.

'Tucuman,' Richard repeated, his lips dry on the name. 'Sentos.'

'Felipe Sentos, as I say. And you, sir, I believe are Señor Ricardo Wintour?'

'That is correct. May I present my wife, Doña Alicia?'

'I am honoured. I have long wished to meet you. Perhaps you do not know this?'

'Señor Sentos, we have never before even heard your name.' Richard glanced round at the people watching and hastily bowed. 'This is not the place to talk. Would you be pleased to return with us to my aunt's house on the Avenida Lila?'

'I know the house on the Avenida Lila,' Felipe Sentos answered quietly. 'It is the Sentos home and am I not a Sentos? Don Enriques was my father's cousin.'

Alice gave a start. Now she knew where she had seen Don Felipe's face before. He was the double of the portrait of Don Enriques in the *sala* of the Casa Sentos. Aware of Richard's arm stiffening under her hand, she knew he had seen the likeness too, she knew the same thought must be in his mind that was in her own. So like her husband, this Sentos cousin must surely have meant something very special to Beatrice? The reason for the trip to Tucuman was becoming very clear.

'Don Ricardo, Doña Alicia, I shall be most happy to return with you now,' Don Felipe was saying, as he bowed again. 'My grateful thanks.'

The next few hours were confusion. So many strangers in Beatrice's house, eating, drinking, talking, it was like some nightmare party from which Alice could not escape. And every time she raised her eyes she seemed to see the brooding gaze of Felipe Sentos and apprehension would pierce her,

170

not for herself but for Richard, whose face as he moved through the mourners was so white, whose look seemed so lost. At one point, Edward Stonefield, their aunt's elegant English banker, came up to remind Richard there was to be a meeting the next day at the lawyer's for the reading of the will.

'I'm not likely to forget it,' Richard muttered and swallowing the last of his wine, turned to Felipe Sentos and asked if he might present Señor Stonefield of Stonefield's Bank. Edward intervened; he and Don Felipe were already acquainted.

'Indeed?' Richard frowned. 'Yet you and I have never met, Don Felipe.'

'Doña Beatriz and I had, as you say, lost touch,' Felipe said in English, 'Her decision, alas.'

'I understood it to be yours,' Edward remarked, 'May I ask how you came to be informed of her death?'

'*Naturalmente*, the lawyers tell me. I am to attend the reading of the will.' Felipe's eyes were expressionless. 'Now, if you forgive me, Don Ricardo, I think I take my leave.'

'You will not stay for dinner?' Richard asked with an effort, but Felipe said, politely, he would be dining with friends, *muchas gracias*. He bowed and left them and they saw his tall figure stooping over Alice's hand before departing through the crowd.

Richard grasped Edward's arm. 'For God's sake, will you tell me what's been going on? Why were we never told there was a Sentos around? Why was my aunt planning to go to Tucuman to see him? Because she was, you know.'

'She didn't want you worried by an old family quarrel, that was all. After your uncle died, Felipe had the idea he should have been left a half share. You can imagine the trouble that caused.'

'Surely he had no case?'

'It's complicated. His grandfather had inherited the *estancia* jointly with the father of Don Enriques, they were brothers, you understand. Profits from the land were poor at the time and the two of them came to an arrangement that one would buy the other out – these things can always be managed. Juan, Felipe's grandfather, was the one who moved and he set himself up in the sugar industry in Tucuman. That's how that branch of the family comes to be there.'

'Seems they no longer have any connection with the *estancia*.'

'Juan and his son, Felipe's father, are both dead. It's only Felipe who has suddenly become interested. When Beatrice inherited the land, he said he would contest the will.'

'The devil he did!' Richard pushed back the damp hair from his brow. 'What happened?'

'I advised your aunt to let him see how far he got, but she didn't want any trouble. Enriques had left him money and she offered him more. He settled for it but they never spoke to each other again.'

'I suppose he might have been a help to my aunt,' Richard said after a pause, 'if he had been left a share.'

'If he had been a different man, he might, but Don Enriques would never have trusted him to look after her interests. In his youth he was wild, even today he is difficult.'

'She was still planning to go to Tucuman, though, wasn't she? Was still planning to see him? Looks like she wanted to make it up with him before she died.'

'I have no idea what was in her mind. If you were staying on, maybe she wanted to inform Felipe. Or, maybe she did just want to make her peace.'

'I never knew what she wanted for my future. I still don't know.'

'And I can't help you, my boy.' Edward put his hand on Richard's shoulder. 'I may be the executor, but I haven't seen the will.'

'Try not to worry,' Alice said, tilting her black parasol over her face as the carriage moved slowly through the city streets en route to the lawyer's office. 'I know it's easy to say and I know how you feel, but you must try to relax. It will all be over soon.'

'That's why I'm worrying, Alice. It will all be over and maybe everything I've worked for will be over too.' He ran his handkerchief over his face. 'How can you ask me not to worry? You know how much this will means to me.'

'And to me.'

'But I am responsible for you, for the children, I am the one who has to earn the living.'

'It will not be the end of the world if you do not inherit the estancia.'

'You think not? Why will you not face facts, Alice? The estancia can support us; Belcarron can barely support your parents, never mind another family. Then there's everything I've done to build the place up, make things pay. If I don't inherit, I'll have wasted all these years.'

Alice placed her hand over his. 'I don't think we need worry about Felipe Sentos, Richard. He has no claim now and he is a sugar planter, not an *estanciero*. Aunt Beatrice will have thought of that.'

'We can't know what she thought,' Richard answered, bleakly, 'And he is a Sentos.'

Fernando Morales, *El Doctor Abogado*, the lawyer who dealt with Sentos affairs, was middle aged and balding, with a thin nose and shrewd, narrow eyes. His nephew and junior partner, young and serious, was rather taken with Alice, for whom he deferentially placed a chair; he had been educated partly at Cambridge and was proud of his English. Standing next to Edward Stonefield at the window was Felipe Sentos. As they took their seats, Felipe gave the Wintours a polite bow and a friendly smile.

Does he know something I don't? Richard thought, in an agony of speculation.

Dr Morales opened proceedings by asking if Señor Wintour would permit he spoke in Spanish, his English was small.

'I can translate,' Alberto said, promptly, 'If the Señora does not understand.'

As Alice told him she had a working knowledge of Spanish, Dr Morales rose and handed out documents. Copies of the *testamento*, he explained. Richard and Alice turned pale.

Dr Morales cleared his throat. 'You wish I commence?'

They nodded and he took a sip of water. Richard, staring at his copy of his aunt's will, could feel Don Felipe's presence as though it were a source of heat that would burn if one came too near. If he'd had the courage he would have turned

173

the pages of the will to find the only bequest that mattered but he did not wish to be seen doing that; besides he could not seem to focus his eyes on the spidery foreign hand. He would just have to listen and concentrate. In God's name, it's why I'm here, he thought, feeling the sweat trickling down his body under his heavy black clothes. Why should a fellow's nerves get so much in a fellow's way?

Alice too was trying to listen to the measured tones of the lawyer, but her mind kept drifting to Beatrice. Poor Aunt Beatrice, willing away all her possessions, taking such pains. However she had left things, someone would be unhappy.

The early bequests were straightforward. Sums of money to charity, to the servants, keepsakes to friends, a brooch to Mena. For the nieces and sisters-in-law, more valuable items: an emerald ring for Charlotte, garnets for Hester and Marianne, the Wintour pearls Beatrice had received on her twenty-first birthday for Ernestine, Maria Wintour's gold watch for Richard's mother. Then Alice heard her own name.

'For my dear niece, Alice Melissa Wintour, who has been such a comfort to me, the remainder of my jewellery, excluding only the Sentos pearl necklace which I leave to Christianna, wife of Felipe Sentos.'

As Alice flushed a deep rose red, remembering her aunt's diamonds, presents from Enriques, her ruby ring and many brooches, Richard smiled and Felipe Sentos gave a long, soft sigh, but no one spoke.

The heat was rising in the room, the tension simmering. Dr Morales paused and instructed Alberto to offer wine. Alberto enjoyed himself acting host, lingering especially by Alice, who was quite oblivious of him, already trying to decipher the next passage in Beatrice's will.

Here were bequests of money to the children, hers and Marianne's, Hester's Paul, and the two children of Felipe Sentos, not large sums but generous enough. Again, there came a soft sigh from Felipe, as though he was thinking, that's something for us, then, but Alice drank her wine and did not look at him. Now it would be coming, what they were waiting for. Dr Morales was reading again, she had

174

only to listen, to look down at the paper on her knee, but she could not do it. It meant too much – to her, to Richard . . .

Felipe had also been left money. Through the mists of her nerves, Alice heard the lawyer mention a sum, a large one, another handsome legacy. He had done well, but now there came no sigh from him; he had pushed back his chair, he was rising from it –

Dear God, Alice thought, is he going to cry out? Is he going to ask: Is that all? No *estancia*? No house on the Avenida Lila?

She was frantically trying to read her copy of the will as the lawyer's voice went on and Felipe Sentos collapsed back into his chair, but she could not find the part she wanted and would have cried out, 'Where is it, where is it?', but she looked up and saw Richard's face and he was smiling.

'Gracias a Dios,' he was murmuring. *'Gracias a Dios!'*

He reached over and took Alice's hand.

'It's ours, my darling, the *estancia*. Aunt Beatrice has left it to me.'

When Dr Morales finished the reading of the will and laid it down, a silence fell. Richard and Alice kept their eyes on their clasped hands; the two lawyers and Edward Stonefield exchanged glances. Felipe Sentos, remaining seated, ran his fingers over his moustache, his lips, his chin, then he stood up.

'I shall contest the will,' he announced, and walked quietly from the room.

Dr Morales took off his reading glasses and gave an expressive shrug.

'Exactly what I expected,' he murmured.

'Exactly what he threatened before,' said Edward Stonefield.

'What happens now?' asked Richard.

'He will go to his own lawyers, try to begin proceedings.'

'I hope he isn't expecting me to pay him off, as my aunt did.'

'Of course not! He's already taken a hefty slice of the capital.'

Richard nodded, glumly. 'And now he may slow up probate.'

'Probate will be very slow in any case. It always is.'

'In the meantime, what do I do for cash? I can hardly run the *estancia* on promises.'

'You'd be surprised!' Edward grinned. 'Come to the bank tomorrow and we'll sort something out. Come no need to look so down, my boy, you should be celebrating. I believe Alberto here wishes to open another bottle of wine.'

After prolonged leavetakings, during which Alice's head began to throb, Alberto escorted her and Richard to their carriage, where he stopped short, his eyes going quickly to Richard. Waiting for them, a cigar in his trembling fingers, was Felipe. As Alberto opened his mouth to speak, Richard put him aside.

'Don Felipe, you wish to speak to me?'

Felipe bowed. 'I wish to tell you, I mean what I say,' he said, in rapid Spanish, 'I shall contest the will. You have no right to my family's land.'

'You go too fast,' Richard snapped, 'Speak slowly so that I can understand.'

'I translate?' Alberto asked, eagerly, but Felipe raised his hand.

'Don Ricardo, I speak in English. You no inherit Estancia Sentos, is no for you. Is Sentos land, only Sentos land, understand?'

'No, I do not understand. My aunt was the widow of Don Enriques, she had a right to inherit his property. Now she is dead and there are no children, the property may come to me. I am the legitimate owner of the *estancia*.'

'*Legítimo?*' Felipe laughed. He threw away his cigar. 'We shall see, Don Ricardo. *Buenas tardes!*' He bowed distractedly to Alice, then crammed his hat on and walked rapidly away.

'Don Ricardo, I beg you, do not worry,' Alberto said. 'He can do nothing, I promise you.'

'As he said, we shall see.'

Richard followed Alice into the carriage. She put up her parasol against the wintry sun. They both smiled and thanked Alberto, who stood blushing as they were driven away.

176

'There's absolutely no need to worry,' Richard said, taking Alice's hand. 'That fellow won't get anywhere.'

'I'm thinking about you, not the *estancia*.'

'He's threatening a lawsuit, nothing personal.'

'All the same, he could be violent.'

'I say we don't give him another thought, just give thanks to Aunt Beatrice for doing the right thing.'

Alice looked out at the fine streets of central Buenos Aires, at the well-dressed *porteños*, at the handsome horses and carriages like their own.

'Why do you think she was planning to go to Tucuman, Richard?'

'Maybe to tell him what she had decided to do? To ask him how much he would take not to make trouble? I have no idea.'

'She may just have wanted to see him again, to make sure she was doing the right thing.'

Very slowly, Richard turned his handsome face towards Alice.

'You really wanted Felipe to inherit, didn't you? You'd really rather we were packing our bags and going home to Belcarron, where we'd have nothing at all?'

'All I want is for you to be happy.'

'In Belcarron. But I'm happy here, I'm happy now. So is that all right, or is it not?'

'Let's discuss it later, my head is pounding – '

'No, let's discuss it now. I love Belcarron too, I'd be glad to go back if things were different, but Ireland is in a mess, it's no place for landowners, it's no place to bring up children. Here, we have a real chance to do well. The boom may be over but things are picking up, we can be prosperous again.'

As the carriage turned into the Avenida Lila, Alice clicked down her parasol.

'Perhaps there is more to life than being prosperous,' she murmured. 'Although I know it's true, you are the breadwinner, you have to think of our needs.'

'I do.' He caught at her hand. 'But don't think I don't understand how you feel.'

'I must write to Papa,' she said, after a pause.

'We have told him about Beatrice.'

177

'Now he must know about this.'

'Of course. You don't want to send another cable?'

'No, I must write. Surely you see why?'

'Yes, I see.' They waited as Francisco got down from his box and rang the bell at the gate in the wall. 'It will not be an easy letter to write.'

'No.' She averted her face. 'One of the most difficult of my life.'

Twenty-Two

Throughout the winter at Belcarron, Charlotte had been bored, the problem of course being money. There was no money to do anything, certainly not for the Dublin season which came and went, ending in a grand ball for St Patrick's Day, without the presence of the Honourable Mr and Mrs Dudley Sarn. And since John Wintour was paying Dudley a salary, he maintained he could not afford to rebuild the stables, which meant they could not borrow any decent hunters, either. Dudley went out once on Mayfly and was thrown and Billie Docherty, who was following the hunt, had the impertinence to laugh. Dudley had struck him with his crop, which meant he had more trouble than ever in collecting the rents, the tenants for miles around reacting as he might have guessed they would. He and John were in such bad humour in consequence, Charlotte was quite desperate to get away.

'Why not visit Hester, my dear?' Ernestine asked one summer evening at dinner. 'You might help her in her bookshop?'

'Bookshop?' Dudley echoed, staring at his mother-in-law with outraged eyes. 'Are you suggesting my wife should go into trade?'

'Oh, I am sure it is all very ladylike, very worthy. Hester is a very trustworthy person.'

'And married to a blackguard who has made us the laughing stock of the county.' Dudley glanced at John. 'You will forgive me for saying so, sir, but since you dropped charges against Molloy and Docherty, it has been almost impossible to control the tenants here.'

179

'Let's not discuss Molloy and Docherty,' John grunted. 'Particularly not Docherty. Perhaps you will forgive me for reminding *you*, Dudley, that things have been a great deal worse since you struck him.'

'Dudley meant no harm, Papa.' Charlotte concealed a yawn behind her fan. 'Mama, I'm sorry, I'd be no use to Hester. I know nothing about books and do not care to learn.'

'Very well. I simply thought in her present state of health she would be glad to have help.'

Charlotte's green eyes brightened. 'Her state of health? You mean Hester is having another baby? Why didn't you tell me?'

'Your uncle Matthew has just written,' John muttered. 'The child is due in September.'

'I do so hope all will go well,' Ernestine murmured, her head drooping a little. 'Hester lost a baby, you know, some months ago.'

'Don't fret, Mama, I'm sure this one will be quite all right.' Charlotte patted her mother's hand. 'But perhaps I'll take a trip to Dublin and visit Hester. It wouldn't cost much if I stayed with the Lettons or someone and I should hear all the latest about Parnell and Kitty O'Shea!'

'Isn't it a fact only her enemies call her Kitty?' Dudley asked, lazily. 'But I suppose you'd be one, Charlotte, being a right-minded member of the Ascendancy.'

'No, indeed, Dudley. If Mrs O'Shea brings down Parnell, we'd be her true friends. Without her and her divorce case, I see us moving to Home Rule in no time.'

'God forbid!' John cried. 'But you may be right. That divorce will be the end of Parnell. What a fool the fellow has been!'

'And all for love,' Charlotte sighed, rising with Ernestine from the table. 'I'm so unromantic I can make mistakes without being in love at all. Don't be too long over the port, Dudley.'

'Why, will you miss me?' he sneered, opening the door with a courtly bow. John gave one of his long, troubled sighs.

*

180

Charlotte left for Dublin at the beginning of July. She counted herself fortunate that her old schoolfriend Priscilla Letton was able to offer her hospitality, for she really did not think she could have put up with Hester's books and Hester's coming baby as well as Daniel Molloy all on the same premises. July, of course, was a terrible time to go visiting in the city, but at least she would be out of Belcarron and away from Dudley, who was growing more tiresome with every day that passed. Why had she ever married a younger son? She sighed and then, with the honesty that could always make her laugh at herself, admitted it was because no eldest son had asked her. There had been Richard, of course, an only son, but he had been without prospects and Charlotte was training herself not to think about Richard now. He was well and truly married to Alice, with a perfect family and lots of money in the Argentine; he would have quite forgotten her. If they were ever to meet again, though? Her eyes sparkling, she wondered how much might be the fare to Buenos Aires.

Priscilla Letton, Charlotte's schoolfriend, lived with her wealthy widowed mother in a fine Georgian terraced house on the south side of the city. She was tall and languid with ash-blond hair and pale-blue eyes and had been engaged twice, each time returning the ring. As she confessed to Charlotte, she had no wish to be married at all.

'So degrading,' she murmured, as they sat in the drawing room on Charlotte's arrival. 'I could not submit to it, no, I am sure I could not.'

'Fortunately, you have no need to,' Charlotte dryly remarked. 'You have money of your own.'

'You think women marry only for money?'

'Sometimes just for a roof over their heads, but there are other reasons.' Charlotte laughed.

'As I say, degrading reasons. At least, you have not yet had to have a baby. Now that must be frightful. Mama says she never really recovered from having me. You see, even today, she is unwell, unable to greet you.'

'I'm sorry she's ill, although it means you're still in Dublin.'

'Yes, we should have been in Italy . . .' Priscilla rang the bell for tea. 'Charlotte, my dear, why have you *not* had a baby?'

Charlotte shrugged. 'The will of the Lord? No, there are ways and means, Priscilla, but don't ask me to explain. I'm sure your mother disapproves of me quite enough without my telling you anything of that!'

Priscilla raised her eyebrows. 'You mean, Mama thinks you're fast? I'm afraid she does, a little, but you're my friend and if I wish my friend to stay, well, you stay!'

A parlourmaid brought in a tray of tea things and set a flame to a spirit kettle. As she withdrew, Charlotte said:

'I imagine your mama knows about my cousin, doesn't she? I'm afraid poor Hester's marriage didn't do much to help my family's reputation.'

'Is it true she is living here in Dublin? And married to a groom?'

'She did marry my father's groom, but he's a journalist now, quite the gentleman, which didn't stop him burning down our stables.' As Priscilla's pale eyes widened in horror, Charlotte laughed and helped herself to a cucumber sandwich. 'Don't look so worried. We all survived and my father didn't prosecute him because of Hester, so here they are still in Dublin – and I shall have to visit them some time, if you can't find me anything more interesting to do. I do so hope we shall see somebody some time. I am so desperate for a little company.'

Priscilla made the tea and passed a cup to Charlotte. 'I'm afraid it's frightfully dull at the moment, so many people are away, but I dare say someone will turn up. Why do you stay down in County Cork, my dear, if you do not like it? Is it something to do with poor Dudley's money troubles again?'

'No, no.' Charlotte smiled easily. 'My parents just wanted us to spend time with them, you know how parents are. Later, we may go to the Argentine. You know my sister is out there, Alice, who married my cousin Richard? They have three children now.'

'Three? And she is well? Perhaps childbirth is not as bad as we fear, Charlotte?'

'I don't plan to find out, I'm afraid.'

'Nor I.' Priscilla rose to ring the bell for the maid to clear.

'Now you will want to go to your room to rest before dinner. Mama may be well enough to come down by then. Do let me know when you want to visit your cousin, you could take the carriage.'

'Thank you, Priscilla, I should appreciate that, but I don't expect I shall be calling for a while.'

Charlotte's wish for company was certainly granted in the weeks she spent with the Lettons. Priscilla might have no desire to be married, but she was still willing to entertain the young gentlemen of Dublin society, many of whom soon found themselves attracted to young Mrs Dudley Sarn. There were dinner parties and theatre engagements, riding in the park, even an occasional concert, and Mrs Letton, who could refuse her daughter nothing, had to accept Charlotte's presence with good grace and took refuge in more sick headaches than ever. Then Dudley wrote and asked if Charlotte was ever coming back to Belcarron, and Charlotte sighed and said she supposed she must think about it.

'All good things must come to an end,' she told Priscilla. 'Perhaps I'll make it to the horse show, but then I really should go home. It's been so wonderful here, I can't thank you enough.'

'I've so much enjoyed having you, my dear, such a change from Mama's headaches . . . But you still haven't called on your cousin, have you? Why not write a little note and go tomorrow? Poor thing, she must be dying to see someone civilised. What does she do with herself all day?'

'She runs a bookshop.'

'Oh, how terrible!'

'I know, but she's a frightful bluestocking, thinks all women should be educated.'

'Goodness, we all went to school, didn't we? But shall I arrange for you to go tomorrow?'

'Please, but I don't think I need bother about a note,' Charlotte said, carelessly. 'Poor old Hester is always at home.' Ryan, Mrs Letton's coachman, looked down his heavy nose when Charlotte gave him Hester's address the next afternoon.

' 'Tis over the Liffey, I'm thinking, Ma'am?'

183

'I'm sure I do not know. It is for you to find it.'

Charlotte, dressed in pale blue with a cornflower toque perched on her yellow hair, stepped into the handsome barouche and put up her parasol; the late-July weather was sunny and hot. She was beginning to feel a little foolish, visiting Hester. Supposing Molloy were there? What should she say to him? And it might have been better to have taken a cab, no one would have seen a carriage as grand as this outside a bookshop before.

I do hope Hester has not chosen to settle in some terrible slum, she thought, as the carriage moved over the river separating the north from the south of the city. It would be so like her to try to bring literature to the poor when all they wanted was food. Or was that being just a little unfair? Perhaps. Hester must know very well by now what the poor of Dublin required. But Charlotte's gaze from the carriage was wary.

In fact, the bookshop with its little sign, 'Molloy's Irish Books for the Irish', was a pleasant surprise. In a quiet street, surrounded by buildings in good repair, it was well painted and bright, its door handle polished, the boxes at its upper windows filled with flowers. With a sigh of relief, Charlotte alighted from the carriage and told Ryan to wait, then, closing her parasol, entered the shop. And gave a cry of surprise.

'Good heavens, Uncle Matthew!'

The gentle-faced man in a clerical collar looked up from the book he was reading, at first without recognition, then with a wide smile.

'Charlotte, my dear, how good of you to come! Nothing has happened yet but I am told it may not be long. Meanwhile, I am looking after the shop. No one has bought a book yet but I dare say I could sell one, if necessary.'

'What do you mean, Uncle, nothing has happened yet?' Charlotte had turned pale. 'Is it – is it – ?'

'Hester's baby? Yes, of course.' He beamed on her. 'Wasn't it because of that you came?'

'No, I had no idea. I was simply staying in Dublin, thought I'd call. But surely the baby isn't due until September?'

'Yes, but you see it has decided to come early. Babies do, sometimes. I'm afraid poor Hester hasn't been well, so when Daniel wrote to us, we decided to come, to do what we could.' Matthew added, gently. 'Both of us.'

'Aunt Constance, too? Oh, I'm glad, Hester will be so happy.' Charlotte made a move towards a staircase at the back of the shop. 'Should I – do you think I should go up?'

A sudden low moan from the direction of the upper floor made her start and drop her parasol and she was beginning to back away when a door at the top of the stairs opened and her aunt's angular figure appeared. Holding her hand was a small, fair-haired boy in a sailor suit.

'Constance, my dear, look who's here!' Matthew cried. 'Charlotte has come to call.'

'I can see that,' Constance Wintour snapped, descending the stairs with the child. 'How do you do, Charlotte? Are you not supposed to be at Belcarron these days?'

'I'm visiting a friend,' Charlotte murmured meekly, for even she had few defences against Constance's wintry manner. 'I . . . should I go up to see Hester, do you think, Aunt?'

'Certainly not, you'd only be in the way. You would be far better employed taking Paul for a little walk, he tells me there is a park not far from here. There you are, Paul, go to your cousin, she will look after you.'

'But I don't know anything about children!' Charlotte cried. 'Hasn't he a nursemaid or someone?'

'I've set her to making beef tea for Hester. The poor girl's strength is so low, and that husband of hers appears to know nothing about taking care of her – '

'Yes, where is Daniel?' asked Charlotte, suddenly remembering him. 'Shouldn't he be here?'

'He's like all men, never there when wanted. Matthew, there's a cup of tea ready for you upstairs, you had better come up now.'

'My dear, I really think I'd be happier down here,' Matthew murmured. 'I find it so distressing to hear poor Hester – '

'Nonsense, she is being very brave, scarcely making any noise at all.' Constance paused on the bottom step of the

185

staircase to look back at Charlotte. 'My son-in-law has gone to a meeting in Kildare,' she said shortly. 'Typical behaviour, I am sure.'

'He had no idea when he went that the baby would come today,' Matthew put in. 'One must be fair, Constance.'

'That's as maybe.' Constance moved swiftly up the stairs. 'Goodbye, Paul,' she called from the top. 'Charlotte, take care of him.'

'Goodbye, Grandmama,' the little boy answered in a high sweet treble, and, turning confidently to Charlotte, put his hand in hers.

It occurred to Charlotte when she saw Paul's eyes go at once to the waiting barouche that he might like a little drive. Though he gave only a small, grave smile, she could tell he was delighted when Ryan lifted him inside.

'Back to the house, ma'am?' Ryan asked, showing no surprise at his new passenger, but Charlotte said she had been told there was a park nearby, perhaps he could find it. And if there were any shops that sold currant buns or gingerbread, could he please stop so that she might buy some for Master Paul.

So began one of Charlotte's strangest afternoon outings, the first she had ever spent with a child and one of the most pleasant. Paul was quite different from how she had imagined a child would be – so serious, yet so fascinating. Talking to him was like talking to a being from another world, a world Charlotte must have inhabited once but had quite forgotten.

He told her he was three years old and usually looked after by Mollie, but he didn't mind at all being looked after by her, especially as she had such a nice hat. Had she picked the flowers herself?

'I'm afraid they're not real,' she said, laughing. 'Real flowers wouldn't last long enough for my hat, you see.'

'Oh.' He studied the cornflowers with the serious gaze he had inherited from his mother. 'You could have had some from our window box, if you'd wanted them, but I 'spect you're right, those are better.'

How old-fashioned he is, Charlotte thought, charmed. And how like Hester! I see nothing of his father in him at all, except that he has blue eyes; he doesn't even have an Irish accent. What did Molloy make of him, she wondered, would he mind that Paul seemed so English, or be proud he was so like Hester? That would depend on what he wanted for his son, whether or not he wanted him to follow in his own footsteps, be a Fenian, fight for Home Rule, maybe even go to gaol –

Charlotte shuddered and suddenly held Hester's son close. She called out to Ryan:

'Do stop, please! I see a baker's where we can buy those buns!'

The first thing they heard when they stepped into the bookshop on their return, with Paul sticky and grubby but wonderfully happy, was the unmistakable cry of a newly born child. Both stopped, transfixed, then Charlotte cried:

'Oh, Paul, you have a little brother!'

'Or might be a sister,' he whispered, swallowing hard, and he burst from Charlotte's hand to run up the stairs, shouting: 'I want Mama, I want Mama!'

Charlotte drew back, her mouth twisting, as Constance appeared and beckoned her up.

'It's a girl,' she said quietly. 'Born two hours ago. The doctor was only just in time, but the midwife was quite competent.'

'Is everything all right?'

'Yes, Hester did well and the baby is perfect. Very small, of course, she is six weeks early, but Dr O'Hare is very pleased.' Constance set her mouth grimly. 'Now all we should have is the father and heaven knows where he is. But come along, Charlotte, you are not afraid to see a new baby, are you? Some would say it was time you had one yourself.'

Charlotte slowly tiptoed into a large, light room which seemed to be full of people: her uncle, bending over a crib which held a wailing scrap of a baby; a doctor; a midwife; Paul, large-eyed and anxious; Constance, fussing with Hester's pillows; and Hester herself, so tired, she was almost haggard, yet more radiant than Charlotte had ever seen her.

'Charlotte!' she cried, raising her hands. 'How lovely to see you! How clever of you to know when to call!'

'Oh, Hester, I wish I'd brought some flowers.' Charlotte

approached the bed and touched Hester's hand. 'You look so well, Hester, so happy . . .'

'I am happy, Charlotte, so lucky – she's all right, you see, and I was so worried. Paul, darling, come to Mama again, let me kiss you. Do you like your little sister, now you've seen her?'

'Yes, Mama.' He wound himself against her.

'She's so small and sweet, isn't she? Our little Caitlin . . . So precious, but not more precious than you, you know.'

'What's precious?' he asked.

There was the sound of pounding feet on the stairs and Daniel, looking strange in a formal suit with a cravat, appeared in the doorway. All eyes went to him and Hester cried: 'Daniel, it's all right, don't worry, we have a daughter!' He ran to her, taking her and Paul into his arms together, and one by one the others in the room went quietly out.

'You'll take a little sherry, Charlotte?' Matthew asked, as he poured drinks for Dr O'Hare and Mrs Farrell, the midwife. 'Come, you must join us in our celebration!'

'Thank you, Uncle, but I think I must return to my friends, I've kept the carriage long enough.'

Charlotte felt suddenly ill at ease, as though she were an outsider, looking in on happiness that had nothing to do with her. She pulled on her gloves and picked up her parasol. 'Do tell Hester I will call again soon.'

'And you must see Paul,' Constance called. 'I think you've made quite a conquest there, Charlotte.'

'No, he just liked my hat.' Charlotte laughed and, making her farewells, went out to the barouche.

'Well, I declare, what an exciting day you've had!' Priscilla exclaimed. 'How wonderful that your cousin has had her baby and all is well.'

'Yes.' Charlotte unpinned her hat and sat studying it. 'Do you know, when I talked to my little cousin and saw Hester looking so happy, I almost felt envious. Can you believe it?'

'Oh, but think of all the worries, Charlotte – the feeding and the messes and the croup and the measles. Even with nurses, it must be ghastly bringing up children.'

'You're right. Other people's children are best for me.'

Charlotte yawned and stretched. 'Is anyone interesting coming to dinner this evening?'

'Rupert Fitzsimons is just back from London. He says the talk there is still of Parnell and the O'Sheas. It was believed that Mrs O'Shea would try for a plea of condonation and connivance, but that may not happen.'

'Condonation and connivance? Whatever is all that?'

'Just a way of saying O'Shea knew all about the affair and turned a blind eye.'

'Isn't it true Kitty O'Shea had three children?' Charlotte gave a burst of laughter. 'I should have thought O'Shea would have to be blind in both eyes not to have known about them.'

Changing for dinner, she felt quite her old self again and, when she looked in the handsome cheval mirror in her bedroom, saw that she was attractive enough to be almost beautiful. As she dressed her yellow hair and admired her smooth shoulders and high breasts rising from her gown, the memory of Hester's rapture faded easily from her mind.

Twenty-Three

One afternoon in early September, Hester, dressed in black for Beatrice, was back at work in her bookshop. Her new assistant, Rory Doyle, was out for the day, and the children were upstairs in the care of Mollie. Hester was finding it pleasant to spend time out of the home again – whatever her mother, now in Dorset, would have thought.

The shop was quiet. There was only one customer and he did not look up when the doorbell jangled and a tall, bearded man came in. But Hester, rising, recognised him immediately. All Ireland and most of England would have recognised him too.

'Why, Mr Parnell!' She took a step towards him. 'This is an honour.'

At the sound of the name, the young man in the poetry section turned pale and retreated hastily to the back of the shop, quite overcome, it seemed, at the sight of the great man. Hester would have liked to join him. Once or twice lately Daniel had hinted that the Chief might look in to talk to her, and she had said she very much hoped he wouldn't. Hadn't they things in common, then? Daniel had asked. Wasn't she a Wintour of Belcarron and the Chief a land-owner, though he never took a penny in rents? Didn't they both work for Ireland when they might so easily have done the other?

'It's proud I'd be if you and he were to meet,' Daniel told her. 'Then you'd be seeing why he's the giant he is, why he is holding us in the palm of his hand.'

Hester said she had already met Parnell, she knew what kind of man he was.

'Talking with a man is different, Hester.'

'Listening, you mean.'

Daniel smiled and said it was true, the Chief's strength was to go right to the heart when he spoke. If she had been able to attend the Chief's birthday banquet in July, she would have seen for herself the loyalty and affection his words inspired. Hadn't it been the same at William O'Brien's wedding, with every guest listening, loving and supporting their leader, enough to bring the tears to your eyes?

'Maybe,' answered Hester. 'But I still don't want Mr Parnell coming to the shop. I shouldn't know what to say to him.'

'Have I not been telling you, Hester? It will be the Chief who does the talking.'

So, here he was. She must do the best she could.

As he raised his hat and turned his deep-set, dark eyes on her, her nervousness increased. She felt it was easy to understand the spell he so famously cast, why he was called the King of Ireland. There was indeed something royal about him, not just in the impression he gave of power, but in the hauteur of manner which appeared to come as naturally to him as to princes. No wonder his followers were not worrying about the divorce case; even to think of it in his presence seemed a kind of heresy. Yet, in spite of his assurance, his untroubled brow, he did not look well. He was not happy, something was gnawing at him inside, he had not what he wanted, whatever it was. And at the thought Hester's own happiness died a little, for it depended, as did Daniel's, on this man.

He made some remark about her mourning. She explained it was for an aunt who had died abroad, and he expressed regret.

'Daniel and others have told me often about your shop, Mrs Molloy,' he went on. 'It seems an excellent idea – Irish books for the Irish – and well put into practice. You have filled a gap. I should have come to congratulate you before.'

'It is kind of you to say so, Mr Parnell. May I show you round?'

'Please do.'

As she conducted him round the various sections – literature, art, history, politics – she noticed his gaze going often to herself. At last he said he had been interested in her shop for some time, not only for what it offered but because she had chosen to run it. 'There are not so many of us around in the cause that I should miss furthering our acquaintance, Mrs Molloy.'

'I am not sure I understand you, Mr Parnell.'

'Well, you come from an Ascendancy family, I believe – did not your ancestors come over in Cromwell's time? Mine came over after the Restoration but they had Cromwellian sympathies. Very few working for Irish freedom share our backgrounds, Mrs Molloy.'

'My family has always cared for the Irish,' she returned sharply. 'My own father went to Dorset because he could not bear to be reminded of the suffering of the famines.'

'Indeed?' Parnell raised heavy, dark brows. 'And does your family support Home Rule now?'

She was silent, turning aside to straighten a book with a trembling hand.

'Come, I have embarrassed you, forgive me. It is only that I wished to thank you for your devotion to my cause. You know it is unusual. But then isn't that said of mine?'

As she looked at him again, he gave a charming smile to which she could not help responding. When he took his leave a little later, raising his hat and bowing, she felt like the young man still lurking at the back of the shop, overpowered by a personality so much stronger than her own.

By the time Daniel came home, however, enough of Parnell's mesmerism had faded for Hester to have to act a part to join in his delight over the visit.

'Was I not telling you how it would be if you were talking to him?' Daniel cried. 'Were you not thinking all the time what a wonderful man he is, then?'

She could not tell him she thought Parnell quite one of the coldest people she had ever met.

On 17 September, the happy summer came to an end. William O'Brien and John Dillon, the two who had masterminded the Plan of Campaign to reduce tenants' rents, were arrested

193

on charges of sedition. Daniel was thrown into dark despair. He was devoted to O'Brien, the quick, clever ex-Fenian, who had done so much for him on his arrival in Dublin. He could not bear to think of him in gaol again (for O'Brien was one who had shared Parnell's captivity in Kilmainham in 1881), could not bear to think he had escaped prison himself because of Hester's intervention.

'Dear God,' he groaned. 'Sedition they call it, Hester, when a man is only fighting for the people's right to eat! There he is, locked up, and here am I, free as a bird for doing no less than he. Where is the justice, I am asking, where is the justice?'

'You must do what you can to help the paper run smoothly in his absence,' Hester said soothingly, her heart as heavy as stone to see Daniel's eyes so wild again. 'And it may be that if he is convicted things will not be so bad. He is a political prisoner, after all, not a criminal.'

'Why should they be after locking him up?' cried Daniel fiercely. 'Why him and not me?'

September moved into October. *United Ireland* continued to turn out passionate articles on Ireland's situation under English rule. O'Brien and Dillon remained in gaol, awaiting trial. On the evening of 18 October, after the bookshop had been closed and locked for the night, the outside bell rang sharply through the building.

'A customer, at this hour?' asked Hester.

'It is no customer,' Daniel muttered and ran downstairs. Within a few moments he was back, followed by a man in dark clothes with a hat pulled down over his brow, shielding his face. It was only when he raised this hat to her and the light from the lamp shone on his spectacles that Hester recognised him.

'Mr O'Brien!' She sprang up, instantly aware that this freedom of the editor was no cause for rejoicing. William O'Brien, whose nervous energy was always evident in his manner, his voice and movements, now seemed like a coiled spring ready to be released. The whole room vibrated with his presence.

'Mrs Molloy – Hester.' He touched her hand with his.

'You must forgive me for coming so late. Don't let me be waking your children.'

'It's all right, they won't hear us.' Hester turned anxious eyes on Daniel, who said, huskily:

'Hester, they have let him out on bail.'

'Mr Dillon as well?'

'The both of us.' O'Brien sank into a chair. He unloosed the clasp of his cape with shaking fingers and when Hester asked if she could get him anything – tea, a drink, something to eat – he shook his head, saying he would take nothing.

'The thing is, Dillon and I, we're not for staying. This I am telling you in the strictest confidence – no, no, I am not needing to say that to you. But you understand what I am saying?'

'Is it bail you are breaking?' Daniel whispered, his eyes glittering, his face white.

'It is, Daniel. We have hired ourselves a bit of a yacht, we shall be making for France.'

'When? When do you sail?'

'Tonight. In three hours.' O'Brien pulled a watch from his pocket. 'Yes, three hours. From France, we go to America. There is work to be done there, Daniel, fund raising for the people.' O'Brien's eyes flashed behind his glasses. 'And it is more good I'll be doing there than lying in gaol, would you not agree?'

'In the name of the Lord, I say yes!' cried Daniel. 'The law in this country is no law, it is no wrong you are doing at all to be jumping your bail, it is for Ireland you are doing it!'

'Let's keep the name of the Lord out of it,' O'Brien said, with a weary smile. 'But yes, you're right, I am breaking no law.'

'Mr O'Brien,' Hester said quietly, though she was winding her hands together to keep them still, 'why are you here?'

'You come to the point as always, Mrs Molloy. Daniel, I am here to put the paper in your hands. No, I am not asking you to be editor, that will have to be Matthew Bodkin, but when the time comes he may or may not support Parnell. I want you to promise me, Daniel, as I'll not be here to see it through myself, that you will see the paper stands by the Chief?'

There was a silence in the room. Daniel coloured darkly.

'The paper is the Chief's,' he said slowly. 'How should it not be for him?'

'Daniel, I am thinking of the divorce. The case comes up on 15 November. If O'Shea wins, there will be those who want Parnell to go. Even on his own paper.'

Daniel leaned forward. 'Was it not the Chief who said, "You may rest assured it will be shown the dishonour and discredit are not on my side"?'

'It is true, he said that.'

'Then how can the suit go against him? He has no case to answer, he will be walking from that court as he went in, a man of honour.'

O'Brien got to his feet. 'Whatever happens, he is our only hope,' he said heavily. 'We owe him a debt we can never repay.' He thrust out his hand and grasped Daniel's. 'I am asking you not to forget that, Daniel.'

'I, forget? I shall never forget it to my dying day.'

'Then you will support him?' Behind his spectacles, O'Brien's eyes were steely. 'He is surrounded by men who will not. If the worst happens. I am speaking of Healy and Sexton, Davitt, and you know the others. If I am to leave my country, I must know I am not throwing my leader to the wolves.'

'I do not know why you are even asking,' Daniel cried. 'You know I am one who worships him, how could I ever be turning against him?'

O'Brien gave a long sigh. 'Thank you,' he said in a low voice, and began to fasten his cape. 'When the time comes, be mindful of what we have said. I leave the good name of *United Ireland* to you. We'll not go down in history as men who deserted Charles Stewart Parnell.' He turned to Hester and shook her hand. 'Goodbye, Mrs Molloy, take care of this fellow and of yourself.'

'And you, you take care too. Is there nothing I can do for you?'

'Think of my wife. It's hard on her, what is happening.'

'I'll see you down the stairs,' Daniel said, his voice thickening. 'You are not one for talking of God, but I put you in His hands, all the same. Godspeed, sir, and good luck.'

The two men stared into each other's faces for a long moment, then O'Brien turned and hurried downstairs, Daniel following. Hester heard the outer door bang and then the sound of the bolts being closed.

It seemed a long time before Daniel returned. When he did, his face was set and hard.

'What a terrible thing,' Hester murmured, watching him, 'to think of those two men on the sea tonight.'

Daniel made no answer.

'We had better go to bed,' she went on, after a pause. 'There is nothing we can do.'

'Why should he be talking that way?' Daniel asked suddenly. 'It's like me he is, he worships the Chief – why is he asking me to support him? Why is he thinking the Chief is needing me?'

'You know how the law can twist things, Daniel. The case may go against Mr Parnell for reasons we don't understand. And he has chosen not to be represented, some people think that unwise.'

'He wishes to have nothing to do with it!' cried Daniel. 'Sure, it's as plain as plain, he's above it, can you not be seeing that, Hester?'

'Come to bed,' she murmured, taking his arm. 'As I say, there is nothing we can do.'

Twenty-Four

At Charlotte's insistence, the period of mourning for Beatrice lasted only three months at Belcarron. It should have been longer but, after all, who had known her apart from John? Was it not ridiculous to have to wear black at all for someone who had died so far away and never even returned home for a visit when alive? John, having arranged a small memorial service at St John's where his sister had worshipped as a girl, even if she had turned Catholic later, reluctantly gave in. Apart from Matthew in England, it was true he was the only one who remembered Beatrice. Maybe it was hypocritical to exact mourning from young people like Charlotte and Dudley. All the same, his heart was heavy as he thought of his wild young sister; it seemed wrong she should have been the first to go. He only hoped Alice and Richard in the Argentine were giving her her proper due ... And at the thought of Alice and Richard, he bit his lip. This death could make all the difference to them, to him ... He wished to God they would write and let him know what the difference was to be.

To celebrate putting aside her dark clothes, Charlotte persuaded her parents to give a little luncheon for Cavan Morry and his English bride, Mavis. Cavan's sister Edie, still unmarried and still the best rider to hounds in the county, together with a boring young cousin of Mavis's would make up the numbers. All went well until John, over coffee in the drawing room, began trumpeting over O'Brien and Dillon.

'You see what it says here?' he cried, throwing down his copy of the *Cork Examiner* which he had been covertly reading. 'They have jumped bail! Gone to France in a yacht! What next, I ask you?'

'I don't know what you expect,' Dudley drawled, helping himself to another brandy with his coffee. 'These people are not civilized beings, you know.' He turned a spiteful eye on Charlotte. 'How your cousin ever got herself mixed up with such riff-raff is beyond my understanding.'

There was a moment's embarrassed silence as everyone except Mavis Morry realised that Dudley had intended such embarrassment.

'Your cousin?' repeated Mavis, a pretty, dark-haired girl, not unlike Alice as Charlotte had already contemptuously noticed, and something of an heiress.

Charlotte said lightly: 'My cousin from Dorset is married to an Irishman who works for William O'Brien.'

'And was once groom here,' Dudley put in. 'Of course, he is supposed to be educated now, which no doubt is why he tried to set us all on fire last Christmas.'

'Dudley!' John rapped in a voice of steel.

Dudley, rising, smiled and bowed and said he hoped they would excuse him. His mother-in-law had already retired with a headache; he had a headache, too, possibly he had taken a little too much wine at luncheon, wasn't used to it in these straitened times . . . Holding himself very erect, his face scarlet, he got himself out of the room.

'Oh, dear,' Edie Morry said with a giggle. 'I'm afraid he did have rather a lot of wine with the meal. The Sarns never have had good heads.'

'Edie, you're upsetting Charlotte,' Cavan whispered, but Charlotte laughed and said she was never upset over anything to do with Dudley. She rang the bell and asked Nora to serve more coffee, then wandered away to the window to look out at the driving rain. When George Coxe, Mavis's tall, raw-boned cousin, joined her, she asked him if he didn't find their part of the world very dull after London. Not at all, he told her, he didn't see much of society London, he was a medical student at Guy's, only in County Cork to recuperate after an attack of fever, but from what he'd seen, he thought it beautiful.

'The only talk in London, anyhow, is of Parnell and Mrs

O'Shea,' he added, blushing under Charlotte's green gaze. 'I think we shall all be glad when the wretched case is over.'

'You're right there, provided it goes our way,' Cavan Morry murmured, taking a seat near Charlotte as George joined Mavis. 'Tell me, Charlotte,' he asked, lowering his tone, 'how is Alice?'

'Oh, blissfully happy, you know, doing frightfully well in the Argentine.'

Cavan's face fell. 'So I've heard ... And she has three children now? I expect she makes a wonderful mother. Richard is a lucky man.'

'Well, aren't you a lucky man too? Mavis is charming.'

'She is, isn't she? But I heard you telling George it was so dull here – you don't think she'll be too bored with country life, do you? I've nothing else to offer.'

'My dear Cavan, according to Papa, Dudley and I are the only bored people in the whole of County Cork and it's all our own fault. Will you excuse me? I must see to Mama.'

To Dudley, Cavan thought as she left him. Poor old Charlotte.

She found her husband stretched out on a chaise longue in their bedroom, not asleep but staring glassily into space, his hands clasped behind his head.

'Congratulations,' she snapped. 'The one time I persuade Papa to invite people, you manage to disgrace us all. Couldn't you have kept off the wine until dinner when they'd have gone home?'

'To hell with them,' he muttered. 'Who cares about the Morrys? Haven't as much breeding as their horses.'

'That is quite unworthy of you, Dudley.'

'Oh, am I supposed to be worthy now?' He laughed shakily. 'As for that frightful young thing Cavan has married –'

'Come, you wouldn't have said no to her, she has money.'

'You forget, I married for love.'

'Thank God I did not.' Charlotte poured water into a basin from the jug on the washstand. 'Do wash your face and come down, Dudley. Cavan has been pretty decent, after all, lending us those mounts.'

'I can't be polite,' he grunted, sitting with his head in his

201

hands. 'I feel too bad. Everything I touch goes wrong, doesn't it? The racing stables, the City, this business down here. Even you, Charlotte.'

'Why, what have I done?'

'You admitted just now you don't love me. You never have loved me. How is a fella to get on, if his own wife doesn't love him?'

'Oh, you've reached the maudlin stage,' she muttered in disgust. 'Look, I warn you, Dudley, if you don't put in an appearance downstairs before the Morrys go, we may not have a place to put our heads tomorrow. Papa will probably throw us out.'

'Throw us out? After all I've done for him? Slaved away, collecting those rents –'

'And upsetting the tenants so that one of these days they most likely will burn us in our beds. Have you actually threatened eviction, Dudley?'

'I've had to,' he answered sulkily. 'Can't make bricks without straw, you know. Anyway, what's it matter? O'Brien and Dillon have fled the country, there's no one to stir the tenants now.'

'Isn't there?' Charlotte stared at him, furiously. 'Look, I am going down to see Mama and if you're not in the drawing room when I come back, God help you, Dudley!'

Ernestine had excused herself from the luncheon party with a headache but Charlotte knew she would find her in the old wash house, soaking sheets of watercolour paper in tin baths, and so she did.

'Hello, my dear,' she greeted Charlotte. 'Have the visitors gone?'

'Not yet. And you are naughty, Mama, to steal off like this and leave everything to me.'

'You know you enjoy it, dear, gives you something to do.' Ernestine sat on a battered chair and regarded Charlotte with a sympathetic gaze. 'My poor girl, is it very bad?'

'Is what very bad?'

'Being married to Dudley. I'm afraid you paid too high a price for your Honourable, Charlotte.'

'We'd be all right if we had a little money. I'm afraid I did

make a mistake there, I thought he had more than he had.'
Charlotte paced the stone floor, shivering. 'I suppose you
haven't any, have you, Mama?'

'Any money?' Ernestine laughed. 'If I had, I certainly
should not give it to Dudley.'

'But you could give it to me, couldn't you? Enough to pay
my fare to Buenos Aires would be nice.' Charlotte gave a
charming smile. 'For a holiday, you know.'

'Oh, no, Charlotte, I shall not give you any money to go
to the Argentine.'

'Not even to see Alice, Mama? I haven't seen her for such
a long time, I haven't seen the children at all –'

'And you don't want to see Alice or the children now, do
you?' Ernestine put her hand on Charlotte's arm. 'Richard is
Alice's,' she said softly. 'You had your chance for him and
turned it down. Now you must leave him to her.'

Charlotte snatched her arm away. 'Mama, I'm surprised at
you! How can you accuse me of such ideas? I am married
myself, remember.'

'To Dudley Sarn.' Ernestine turned away, smiling.

Charlotte, flushing, drew her shawl around her and walked
haughtily away.

Why do people say Mama is odd? she wondered bitterly.
She seems to know more than anyone what is going on. I
believe she has made that reputation for herself, so that she
can do as she likes and get away with it. Oh, if only I could
leave, go abroad, go anywhere! But it appeared there was to
be no going away, no travelling to Buenos Aires, turning her
green eyes on Richard again, no finding out what the Argentine had to offer . . .

When she reached the drawing-room door, she stopped
Nora going in with a letter on a salver.

'What's that, Nora?'

''Tis the second post, so it is, Miss Charlotte. From Miss
Alice, I am thinking. Isn't it covered with all them funny
stamps, then?'

Charlotte's heart plunged. 'Take it to the master,' she
murmured, and followed Nora in.

John opened it in his study, Charlotte at his side.

'Well,' she cried, 'what does it say? Papa, tell me!'

He was fiddling with his reading glasses, driving her crazy.

'It says, it says . . .' He snatched off his glasses and turned blank eyes on Charlotte. 'Beatrice has left everything to Richard. He is the *estanciero* now.'

'I see.' She stood very still. 'Everything . . .'

'Well, there's an emerald ring for you, Alice says.'

'An emerald ring?' Charlotte began to laugh. 'Oh, how wonderful!' She laughed so long, John wondered if she would ever stop.

It was late evening. Dinner was over and Ernestine had retired to bed. An autumn wind had risen and was wailing round the house, rattling the woodwork and the suspect tiles on the old roof. John, staring into the fire from his chair in the drawing room, was lost in thought, his face morose. Dudley, now sober, was watching Charlotte, and Charlotte was watching John.

'May I speak to you, Papa?' she ventured.

He looked up. 'If it's about money, I'm afraid I can't help.'

'It's about Belcarron.'

'Rising out of Alice's letter, I presume?'

'You must admit, Papa, it's going to make a difference that Richard has inherited Aunt Beatrice's estate. How can he inherit Belcarron too?'

'Who says he will?'

'Why, you told him yourself he would, you know you did!'

'I asked him if he would be willing to take it on, he said he would. That's all I want to say at the moment.'

Charlotte and Dudley exchanged glances. Charlotte leaned forward.

'So you will hear my case, Papa?'

'Your case? You mean why I should make you my heir?' John raised his eyebrows. 'First I've heard you were even interested.'

'I know I am the younger daughter,' she said eagerly. 'But I am here, I am the one who would stay. And Dudley is already your agent, he knows how the estate should be run.'

'Does he?' John laughed shortly. 'From the complaints I've had, I doubt the tenants would agree with you.'

204

'Naturally they complain!' cried Dudley. 'But I am getting your rents out of them, isn't that what you want?'

'If you were getting the rents, your methods might be thought successful – though not by me – but you're not. The more you bully the people, the less they are willing to pay what they owe. You still have a lot to learn, Dudley.'

'If you are such a wonderful landlord, how is it you were singled out by the Plan of Campaign men?' Dudley retorted. 'Everything you've said about me has been said about you.'

'With this difference,' John snapped, his eyes flashing, 'about you, it is true.'

'Dudley!' Charlotte hissed. 'Please leave this to me.' She turned to her father with a placatory smile. 'Papa, I agree, Dudley has a lot to learn, so have I, but we can learn it and I think we'd run Belcarron very well. It is my home, after all, and you must see how unfair it would be if Alice and Richard were to have two estates and I none at all!'

'Life isn't fair, Charlotte, especially for younger sons and daughters.' John stood up. 'Your Uncle Matthew, for instance, has no share in Belcarron, he has had to make his own way in the world. It's hard, but that's the way things are.'

Her eyes filled with angry tears. 'So you won't even consider me?'

He took her hand. 'My dear, I hate to see you unhappy. I'll admit the situation here is unusual, but what can I say? I haven't had time to think about it yet.'

She looked up, brightening. 'But you will think about it, Papa? From my point of view?'

'From all points of view.' He kissed her cheek. 'Now, if you will excuse me, I think I'll go to my bed. See the girls lock up, Dudley, will you? You never know who is outside these days.'

They watched as he took his candle and padded slowly upstairs, his head bent.

Charlotte whispered: 'He has taken it hard that Richard is to stay in the Argentine.'

'All the better for us.'

'Maybe. Papa wouldn't make any promises, would he? But

205

I don't see why things shouldn't go our way. Richard couldn't possibly run Belcarron from the other side of the world.'

'Damned right, he couldn't.' Dudley yawned. 'I'm for bed, too, it's been a long day. You coming?'

'For bed and only bed, if you don't mind. I'm terribly tired tonight.'

'As usual.' He gave a scornful smile and rang the bell for Nora. 'Let's get the place locked up, then.'

Charlotte, taking her candle, said, thoughtfully: 'Dudley, how much do emeralds fetch?'

'How on earth should I know? You'd better have the ring valued, when you get it.'

'It might be enough to do a little travelling, I suppose?'

'Depends where you want to go, doesn't it?'

Charlotte did not say.

Twenty-Five

The O'Shea divorce suit was set to open in London on 15 November. Daniel, who was to attend as one of the reporters for *United Ireland*, was in confident mood. Carefully dressed in a dark suit, his black hair tamed, he told Hester there was no doubt the Chief would be vindicated. Wasn't it a sign, then, that he was to be accused in the very same court where he had been found not guilty before? Pigott had been shown up then as a liar, as O'Shea would be shown up tomorrow, Hester could mark his words.

She remembered the Pigott affair, of course. Letters in *The Times* had seemed to reveal Parnell's involvement in the Phoenix Park murders of Lord Frederick Cavendish, the Chief Secretary for Ireland, and his Under-Secretary Thomas Burke. At the London hearing the letters had been proved to be Pigott's forgeries; he had later shot himself and Parnell had emerged from the ordeal with flying colours. But only Daniel could have seen Captain O'Shea in the role of Pigott on this occasion.

As Hester helped Daniel into his overcoat, she tried again to make the point that the two cases were very different, he must try to keep an open mind on what he would hear.

'Is it not my job to report the truth?'

'Yes, of course.'

'Then will my mind not be open anyway?'

She brushed his collar, agreeing that it would.

'So what are you meaning, Hester?'

'I don't know, Daniel. Nothing.' She could not tell him his mind seemed to her so closed he would be bound to suffer

207

when it was forced open. From the window she said the cab had arrived, they had better go down.

Daniel had only once been out of Ireland and that was on a visit to the House of Commons with William O'Brien. Hester knew his heart must be hammering with excitement, but he kept a calm front as he kissed her and Paul and was borne away.

'Shall we go in a cab one day, Mama?' Paul asked. 'Shall we go in a cab to Belcarron to see Cousin Charlotte?'

'One day, Paul.'

'You did say we could, Mama.'

'Yes, one day, don't *fuss*.'

At the unusual irritation in her voice, he shrank back. She swept him up and kissed him, full of contrition.

'I'm sorry, darling, I didn't mean to snap, it's just that I am a little worried.'

'About Papa? Because he's going on the sea?'

'Not really, he's only going for a day or two, I am sure he'll be all right. Come, let's go and find you a little cake in the kitchen.'

'I liked the sugar bun Cousin Charlotte gave me. I should like another some day.'

'Then we'll go out and buy one. I think I know the very place to go.'

That night, Hester slept badly, dreaming confusedly of Daniel and Parnell. She rose feeling wretched and must have looked as she felt, for Mollie said it was back to bed she should be going and Caitlin's wet nurse agreed.

'Now is it worrying about Mr Parnell you are?' young Mrs Dwyer asked, sympathetically. ''Tis an awful thing they're accusing him of, and an awful lie. But sure 'twill be all over before you know it, ma'am.'

'The case is to last two days,' Hester muttered. 'Somehow I think it will never be over.'

At ten o'clock she went down to the bookshop, which Rory had already opened, her heart in her mouth as she thought of Daniel taking his place with the rest of the press in the law court. Captain O'Shea would be present with his counsel, Sir Edward Clarke, but Parnell and Mrs O'Shea

208

would be remaining in Brighton where it was said they kept house. Apparently, Mrs O'Shea had instructed her counsel, Sir Frank Lockwood, to hold a watching brief for her, but Parnell had chosen not to be represented in any way.

Why should that be? thought Hester. Why should he not have wanted to offer any defence? The only answer filled her with despair. He wanted the divorce, he wanted to make Mrs O'Shea his legal wife. She could not condemn him, it was the right thing to do, the honourable thing to do, but it would mean the ruin of his political career. What it would mean for Daniel, she refused to let herself think.

Customers began to wander in and she forced herself to respond to their chat. Today was not the dangerous day, today they had no news, but tomorrow they would be full of the case and she would have to escape. To go where? The whole of Dublin would be closed to her if she did not want to talk about Parnell, but she decided to go walking, walking on her own through the streets, whatever the weather, until she had to return home.

On the morning of the 16th, she told Rory Doyle she would be leaving him in charge. He was tall and lean and reminded her in his energy and spirit of William O'Brien, now fund raising in America with Dillon, Harrington, O'Connor and Sullivan. How would they be feeling today, she wondered, away from Parnell in his hour of need?

'You're not looking well, Mrs Molloy,' Rory said with concern. 'Is it the weather for you to be going out? See the fog coming rolling in off the Liffey, then?'

'It's only mist, it will soon clear.' She tried to smile. 'I'll be all right, don't worry. Hope you're not too rushed off your feet.'

He laughed. 'It will be more talking in here than book buying, I'm thinking, Mrs Molloy, with the news from London.'

'There can't be real news,' she said quickly. 'The case is not yet over.'

'They are saying it was as good as over yesterday.'

'But there can have been no verdict.' Hester buttoned her coat with trembling fingers and took up her umbrella.

209

'No verdict,' Rory agreed, as he opened the door for her. 'But we all know what it will be. Take care, Mrs Molloy.'

She had been right about the mist, it was clearing and a red-eyed winter sun was peering through the clouds as she reached O'Connell Bridge. Here she was surrounded by traffic and people, so many people hurrying about their affairs, surely they could not all be thinking about Parnell? Yes, all, she answered herself. Catholic or Protestant, he held their future in his hand. And now his own future lay with the decision of a London court. Looking down at the dark swirling waters below the bridge, Hester thought, Mine and Daniel's, too.

She walked on, turning away from the magnificent Custom House towards the old quays and Georgian buildings that had once been the pride of the north side of the city. Fashions had changed, the quality lived over the river now and their once fine homes were lodging houses, warehouses, even slums. It was a sad, lost world looming through the rags of mist today and suited her mood, though wherever she went she took Parnell and Daniel with her. Once she slipped into a little church and lit a candle but could not put into words what she had lit it for – that God should be kind and let Daniel understand, she supposed. Her hopes were so low it seemed better just to let the candle burn and frame no prayer.

The November cold when she began walking again seemed to pierce her bones. She knew she must go somewhere for warmth and something to eat, though every Dublin coffee room, like every pub, would be full of yesterday. 'As good as over,' Rory had said, which meant the news was out and bad. Perhaps she should just face it. To face it would be to be prepared.

She knew a small restaurant where a lady could dine alone in respectable fashion and made her way there, loosening her coat when she was shown to a table and realising again how chilled she was, how desperate for a break from the cold of her thoughts. Around her, city clerks and women shoppers were buzzing together like a hive of bees and, as she waited for her order to arrive, scraps of their conversation rained upon her ears like blows finding targets.

'He called himself Mr Fox, would you be crediting? Mr Fox, Mr Preston . . . slept at the house over and over again . . . climbed down a fire escape, wasn't the cook after saying . . . a ladder of rope and him swinging like a monkey and her husband coming home . . . then in at the door, as cool as you please. I tell you no lie, 'tis done for he is . . .'

'I'm sorry, I'm sorry – ' Hester distractedly rose to her feet as the waiter brought her soup. She began to pull on her coat. 'I'm sorry, what do I owe you? I can't stay.'

She hurried out into the mist that had risen again as the day began to close in and found a cab. There was nothing else to do, she must go home.

Rory said he had not been busy, it was not to be expected, people had been wanting to talk in the pubs – cry, more like, if they were Parnellites, as so many Dubliners were.

'The case went badly, then?' asked Hester, carefully brushing mud from her skirt.

'The news has been coming over all day, Mrs Molloy, he's done for.' Rory's voice trembled. 'He hasn't a chance, I'm telling you.'

'With the politicians?'

'With the priests. Ah, the stuff that's been coming out – a pack of lies, no less, from the maids, but they are saying it will be believed. Can you picture it, Mrs Molloy, the Chief hanging on a fire escape? And him that frail a puff of wind would blow him away!'

Hester shook her head. 'He has been made to look ridiculous – and he gave no defence.'

'That is the thing, Mrs Molloy, he wasn't there to defend himself, he wouldn't be going to give them the truth.'

'What is the truth?' she asked bitterly. 'He is innocent?'

Rory hesitated. 'There have been lies told,' he muttered. 'But, no, I'm not thinking he is innocent. Why let it look worse than it is, though? I am blaming him for that. He has thrown us to the wolves.'

Daniel did not return home until late on 18 November. By then Hester knew, as the whole world knew, that Captain O'Shea had been granted a divorce from his wife on the grounds of her adultery, with Charles Stewart Parnell. All

Ireland was rocked by the news, and so were Gladstone and those Liberals in England who had fought so long for Irish Home Rule. All Hester cared about on that black November night was what Daniel thought.

The children were asleep, there was a meal waiting in the oven, a fire burning brightly in the sitting room over the shop. Hester, supposedly sewing, had thrown her work aside and was walking the floor, listening and jumping to every sound that might be wheels in the street or a key in the lock. 'Dear God, why doesn't he come?' she wailed. 'Has he given us all up? Has the steamer gone down?'

Then there came the unmistakable noise of real wheels in the street, a real key in the door, and she flew downstairs and into his arms as his dark, damp figure came into the shop.

'Oh, Daniel, you're back, you're back!' She kissed his face over and over again and he kissed her once, before progressing steadily up the stairs.

'My dear, how did it go?' She had to pause to lock and chain the door before hurrying after him. 'Daniel, tell me!'

He took off his coat and hung it up; he put his overnight bag on the floor and sat down, staring into the fire.

'Daniel?'

She went to him, kneeling at his side, trying to make him look at her, but he seemed not even to feel her touch. He never took his eyes off the fire.

'Are you very tired?' she whispered, her heart dying within her. 'Was it a bad crossing? There's some supper waiting – '

'I think I'll be going straight to my bed,' he said, suddenly rising. 'You're right, I am tired. Dog-tired.'

'You'll let me make you some tea? Come, you must have something – '

'Thank you, I am not wanting anything. Only sleep.'

She went around mechanically carrying out her various tasks, taking the supper out of the oven, turning out the lamps, damping down the range, checking on the children. Caitlin was fretful, a tooth was coming, and Hester held her for a while until she fell asleep again, then she quietly prepared for bed. Daniel was lying awake, staring into the darkness, and she put on her heavy nightgown and slipped in beside him.

212

'Daniel, I know what happened,' she murmured, drawing his body close to hers. 'I know how you must be feeling . . . '

He lay cold and unresponsive as marble in the circle of her arm.

'You're shocked,' she went on. 'So is everyone, it will take time to accept – '

'Goodnight, Hester,' he said, without emotion, and pulled himself away from her. It was as though he had put up a barrier between them and, though she sobbed quietly for some time, he did not take it down.

Twenty-Six

Charlotte had better things than Parnell's future to think about. She had asked Peggie O'Sullivan from Skibbereen to come over to do some dressmaking for her, as she had done before. Peggie was a stout young woman with ginger hair and hard, dark eyes; her father, a draper who had once been a tailor, had taught her to sew and she was skilful enough and cheap, which was her attraction to Charlotte.

On a damp November morning when most of Ireland was reeling over the O'Shea divorce verdict, Charlotte was in the morning room at Belcarron, laying out materials she had brought back from Dublin for Peggie's inspection.

'The blue velvet for an evening dress, the green merino for a day dress, the serge for a pelisse – Peggie, are you listening to me?'

'I am not, ma'am,' Peggie replied impudently. 'For 'tis nothing I can do for you till I get my money.'

Charlotte stared at her in astonishment. 'Whatever do you mean, you stupid girl? You've made nothing yet.'

'Sure and I have.' Peggie raised a heavy hand and began to tick off on her fingers: 'One grey walking dress, one black mourning dress, two muslin skirts, two muslin blouses, four lace camisoles, four pairs of drawers – '

'Oh, stop, stop!' Charlotte cried. 'Those things have all been paid for long ago, I remember the bills coming. It's not the slightest use trying to pretend you haven't had your money, Peggie, we keep accounts, you know.'

'So do I keep accounts, ma'am. Doesn't my dad check my books every week, then?' Peggie's dark eyes were cold as stone. 'Not a penny has been coming to me from this house,

215

wouldn't the Blessed Virgin herself agree? You speak to his honour, ma'am, you will be seeing I am telling you no lie.'

Charlotte's colour rose, and she flung down the velvet she had been holding. 'Wait here, Peggie,' she snapped. 'I shall be back in a moment.'

With her yellow head high, Charlotte marched through the house to the room at the back which Dudley had made his estate office. Without waiting for him to answer her rap on the door, she went in to confront him at his desk.

'Charlotte!' He looked up in irritation. 'Can't you see I have Docherty with me?' He waved his hand to the stooped, bony figure of Billie Docherty standing before him.

Charlotte spared him no more than a glance. 'This won't take long, Dudley. I simply want to know why you have not paid Peggie O'Sullivan's bills?'

'Who in God's name is Peggie O'Sullivan?'

'She is my dressmaker and she is refusing to make anything else until she has been paid.'

'Dressmakers are like tailors, they don't expect to be paid. Why, I never paid a tailor before five years, at least. Give her a shilling or two on account, that should satisfy her.'

'No, it will not, but my point is I should know when my bills are being paid and when they are not. Please look them out and give me the money now.'

'I shall give you the money when it is convenient and not before. Tell that to your precious Peggie O'Sullivan.'

Charlotte swung round on Billie. 'Docherty, please wait outside. Mr Sarn and I have things to discuss.'

As Billie, his face scarlet, removed himself, Charlotte ran round Dudley's desk and stood over him. 'How dare you embarrass me in front of one of my father's tenants?'

'Ex-tenants,' Dudley drawled. 'I have just evicted him.'

'Oh!' For a moment she was speechless, her eyes so filled with anger, she could scarcely focus on him. 'Oh, you fool, Dudley, you perfectly idiotic fool! But I haven't got time to explain to you how stupid you are. Just let me have my money now!'

He stood up, walking away from her to the windows that overlooked the shrubbery. 'Charlotte, I can't,' he muttered. 'There's . . . I'm afraid there's nothing in the kitty.'

216

'That can't be true. We always have something.'

'Everything we have is spoken for. I haven't been able to pay the estate bills, I haven't been able to pay ours. There's just not enough coming in.'

'I can't believe it,' Charlotte whispered. 'It's a nightmare.'

'We've had trouble over bills before, but we've managed to pay them. This time we can't, unless I can get the rents out of the people who owe them. You call me a fool because I evicted Docherty, but why should his family not pay their dues? They must be put out, it must be seen I mean what I say.'

'Have you told Papa how bad things are?'

'Over and over again. He does nothing.'

'Have you told him about the eviction?'

'Not yet, but he'll have to see it is the only way. In the meantime, if you want to pay your bills, you'd better see him about them. I can't give you what I haven't got.'

Charlotte went out, her shoulders drooping, her head no longer high. At the door, Billie spoke to her.

'Miss Charlotte – I mean, Mrs Sarn, ma'am – is it his honour you'll be seeing now? Mr Wintour himself?'

'What is it you want, Docherty?'

'If you could just be telling him, it's out we are and nowhere to go, my ma's in a terrible state and Mr Sarn, he'll not be listening. If you could be putting in a word, ma'am – '

'Docherty, kindly do not bother Mrs Sarn with your infernal grumblings!' cried Dudley, suddenly appearing. 'She can do nothing for you. Go find yourself a job and pay your debts as others have to do!'

'As you do, your honour?' asked Billie, his eyes flashing. 'And isn't Peggie O'Sullivan waiting now for her money? Aren't all the shopkeepers in Skibbereen waiting for the sight of a copper coin from Belcarron and won't they be waiting five years or more if you have your way?'

'Why, you impertinent scoundrel!' Dudley roared. 'I'll have you up before the magistrate, I'll have you back in gaol where you should have been since Christmas! You were bound over to keep the peace, if I remember, and it's no peace you've been keeping, is it? Get out of this house before I throw you out!'

217

'Do not be worrying,' Billie replied, bowing contemptuously. 'It's going I am, and gladly. 'Tis no place, this, for an honest man with good Irish blood in his veins.'

He stuffed his cap over his black hair and left, banging the side door behind him, as Dudley, his eyes terrible in his flushed, moist face, turned on Charlotte.

'You see what you get by discussing our affairs before the scum of the Irish peasantry?'

'He had a point, though, didn't he?' she asked, suddenly laughing. 'Oh, Dudley, what a joke, telling him to pay his debts as you do! When we can't even find a few pounds for the dressmaker's bill!'

'If he and his kind paid their dues, we'd be able to pay ours, don't forget that!'

'There's only one flaw in that argument, my dear. As you said to me, they can't pay what they haven't got.'

'God damn them all to hell!' cried Dudley and, returning to his office, slammed the door.

Charlotte, no longer laughing, went slowly upstairs to her room. Long ago, she had learned the wisdom of keeping a few sovereigns hidden and now, from this private store beneath her handkerchiefs, she took out three.

'Peggie will have to be satisfied with these for the time being,' she muttered. 'But, dear God, what a mess! How can I get away? This life is intolerable, intolerable ... ' Tears filled her eyes and she let them flow. 'Richard, what a fool I was, wasn't I? I should have followed my heart.' She sat up, blowing her nose. 'Difficult, when I haven't got one ... '

Peggie, astonished, accepted the sovereigns and said, yes, they would do very well on account and sure she would make the clothes Mrs Sarn wanted. She would take the materials back now with the carrier, so she would.

'Not all the materials,' Charlotte said coldly. 'Take the serge for the pelisse, I'll keep the rest until you need them.'

'Sure, you can be trusting me to make them all up,' Peggie protested. 'I'd not be after keeping the stuff, Mrs Sarn.'

'This way,' Charlotte said smoothly, 'we know where we stand.'

*

Dinner that evening was a dismal meal. Ernestine, suffering from a cold, did not appear. John was morose. Charlotte made no effort at conversation. Dudley drank. When the port appeared, Charlotte rose, but John motioned to her to keep her seat. He had something to say.

'I'll come straight to the point. I want you to go.'

Dudley's jaw dropped. Charlotte's green eyes glittered.

'I beg your pardon, Papa?'

'I think I've made myself plain. This business of Dudley's being my agent, it's not worked out well. I don't need him. I'd like him – you both – to go.'

'You're throwing us out?' cried Dudley. 'After all I've done?'

'What you have done is the cause of the trouble.' John hesitated. 'I'm afraid you are simply not suitable as an agent. You haven't the grasp of what is required and you can't handle people. I'm sorry, you'd better try something else.'

'Papa, you can't mean it,' Charlotte protested. 'You can't mean to turn me out from my own home, your own daughter?'

'You're a married woman now, my dear. Your husband is responsible for you, that is what marriage means.'

Charlotte had gone white. 'But we have nowhere to go, Papa. We have no home of our own, Dudley has no position . . .'

John drank some port and shrugged. 'Then the quicker he finds something, the better. Why not try Dublin? Plenty of jobs there.'

'I have no qualifications,' Dudley muttered. 'I never finished my degree, I've never studied anything in particular –'

'It's never too late, my boy. What about the professions? Oh, I know they are considered middle class, but they provide an income. There's the law, banking – '

'He hasn't the brains, Papa,' Charlotte said irritably. 'It's no use suggesting anything of that sort. And don't say we should try Dudley's father again because we have and got nowhere. So, what do we do? Blow our brains out?'

'Damn you, Charlotte!' cried Dudley and rushed from the room.

Father and daughter exchanged hard, unyielding glances. Both were breathing hard.

'Well, Charlotte,' John said, at last. 'You've made a pretty mess of things, I'm afraid. I'd help you if I could, but I can't. Every penny I have is tied up in this estate, there's nothing I could release for you even if it would do any good, which I doubt. You've married a waster.'

'He's not,' she said, sighing, suddenly appearing to soften. 'He's just a younger son without any talent. He's been brought up to money and now there's none. There seems no place for him.'

'There's the Colonial Service. They're always wanting fellows who will go to Africa, places of that sort.'

'And where would that leave me?'

'You could go with him. Wives do.'

'I'd die in Africa. So would Dudley, probably.' Charlotte hesitated. 'I suppose we might try South America.'

Her father gave her the same shrewd look as her mother had done on a previous occasion. 'Not the Argentine,' he said. 'You leave Alice and Richard alone, Charlotte.'

She stood up, flinging her shawl around her shoulders. 'Then what are we to do, Papa? Please, you must help us!'

'I don't know, Charlotte. You must find a solution for yourselves. All I know is I shall have to work damned hard to undo all that Dudley has done and I want to begin as soon as possible. Say, after Christmas?'

'Christmas?'

'January. Yes, tell Dudley he can have until then. Now, will you ring the bell for Nora to clear?'

Charlotte stood very still. 'And what I asked you about, Papa – have you made any decision?'

'Not yet, my dear.' John drained his port. 'But I'll let you know. Do ring the bell, Charlotte, the girls have to get on.'

Twenty-Seven

In Dublin, things were looking hopeful for Parnell. It was true, there were those who agreed with Gladstone's daughter and cried, 'Blot out his name!' And Archbishop Croke had thrown Parnell's plaster bust out of his house. But these were in the minority. For most people, Parnell had been their leader for so long, they could not think of him as anything else. He had sinned, but then he was not a Catholic so could not be expected to know any better, and wasn't the whole thing Mrs O'Shea's fault? Had she not led him on, tempted him away from duty? Meetings were held so that loyalty could be expressed. Politicians said such things as 'The people of Ireland would never allow Parnell to resign' and 'God forbid he who led us in time of difficulty should be deserted by us in cloudy and dark days'. From all extravagances of this sort, Daniel held aloof.

From the day he returned from London, he never voluntarily spoke Parnell's name again. When Hester tried to get him to talk about what had happened, he said he did not wish to discuss it. When she pressed him, he took out a piece of paper and wrote down the judge's words describing Parnell as one 'who takes advantage of hospitality offered by the husband to debauch the wife'.

'You are wanting me to discuss a man like that?' Daniel asked, his blue eyes hard as flint.

'But it's not true, Daniel!' Hester cried. 'Everyone knows Mrs O'Shea was not debauched and Captain O'Shea was a party to the affair. Parnell and Mrs O'Shea were married in all but name, with a home and children and a life together!'

221

Daniel ignored her. Parnell was a hypocrite and a deceiver, he had denied his adultery, he had told everyone the discredit and dishonour of the case were not on his side. But for years he had been living a lie and now the whole world knew it.

'And I know it, too,' Daniel muttered, and bent his head.

'He said those things because he believed he had been true to his own standards of honour,' Hester argued, desperately. 'He did not actually deny his adultery because he did not see it as adultery, he saw Mrs O'Shea as his wife, not Captain O'Shea's. Oh, it's true he has behaved unlawfully, Daniel, but he is a human being, you must show compassion, forgiveness, or your bitterness will fill your soul!'

'Compassion, is it? Forgiveness?' Daniel leaned forward. 'Hester, I am telling you I shall never forgive him. The hurt he has done me, I am not thinking of, it is the hurt he has done Ireland. He has thrown us to the wolves.'

Rory's words. Hester took them in silence. There seemed nothing else to do.

Another grand loyalty meeting was arranged for 20 November and Hester decided she should attend. The Leinster Hall was packed to the doors; it seemed all Dublin except Daniel had turned out to hear Healy, McCarthy and other party leaders air their views, and Hester had difficulty finding a seat. She had to settle in the end for one squashed at the back next to Frank O'Keefe, whose foxy face lit up when he saw her.

'Daniel not with you, Mrs Molloy? Don't be telling me he is playing nursemaid tonight?'

'He did not care to attend,' she answered coldly.

'And it's right he is. This is no meeting for an anti-Parnell man – and that's your Daniel now. Sure, as soon as he was hearing about the fire escape, that was the end for him. The joke is' – Frank leaned forward, grinning – 'there was no fire escape!'

'I've heard the cook's evidence was fanciful.' Hester fanned herself with her gloves. 'My husband did not judge Mr Parnell on that alone.'

'The thing is, the folk here will not have Parnell judged at all. But how long they'll be thinking that way, who knows?'

'What do you mean, Mr O'Keefe?'

'Early days, Mrs Molloy, early days, is all I'm saying.' He nudged her arm. 'See Matthew Bodkin there? Deputy editor of *United Ireland*? He's the fellow your Daniel is working on to take support from Parnell. And then what'll O'Brien say?'

In spite of the heat of the hall, Hester was pale. 'I don't believe it,' she said quickly. 'Daniel would not do that, he promised – '

'Promised?'

'Promised Mr O'Brien the paper would not desert Mr Parnell.'

'That would be before, Mrs Molloy.' Frank grinned again, showing tobacco-stained teeth. 'Before Daniel saw the light. You know he cannot be held to that promise now.'

She lowered her eyes. 'I suppose not. But then he should leave the paper.'

'Come, Mrs Molloy, why should he?' Frank waved his hand around the waiting crowd. 'Within a week, I'm telling you, all this lot will be agreeing with him.'

As the meeting began, Hester thought, wonderingly, he's wrong, he must be. Listen to them now . . .

A cable was read out from O'Brien and the other fund raisers in America giving wholehearted support to the Chief, and roars of approval echoed through the audience. Then, one by one, the party leaders rose and affirmed their faith in the leader, to further cheers and sobs, and as the emotional temperature soared, Hester found her own sympathy rising with it. She was glad she had come: it was right to feel like this, to show compassion and understanding to a man who had done so much for Ireland's cause, who had risked himself only for the love of a woman. Daniel could not feel that, he would never feel it; he was up there on a pinnacle and he had thought Parnell was there too. Now he knew Parnell was in the valley with the rest of humanity, he could not descend himself – it was pointless to ask him – but, whatever his views, the fight must go on.

As Hester rose at the end of the meeting, buoyed up by the passion of those around her (with the exception of Frank O'Keefe), she pledged herself to work on and to work on with Parnell as leader. He had cleared the first hurdles, he could only go from strength to strength. O'Keefe would be proved resoundingly wrong.

A week later, as O'Keefe had predicted, Parnell fell.

At first, it seemed he had won. On 25 November he was elected chairman of the Irish Political Party, he was leader still. But on 26 November, Gladstone published a letter in *The Times*. If Parnell continued as leader, he, Gladstone, must go. The choice for the Irish politicians was clear. Gladstone and Home Rule, or Parnell and disaster. There was never any contest. 'If you sell me, get my price,' Parnell had once said. Gladstone had stated the price and it was paid.

Not immediately. Meetings were called, negotiations opened; O'Brien sent a cable, begging for more talks. But a new vote overturned Parnell's chairmanship, Justin McCarthy was made leader, and Parnell, the cool, balanced commander, suddenly lost his head. He accused Gladstone of trying to cheat the Irish out of power if Home Rule were achieved, he issued a manifesto to the people written in wild and arrogant terms, he seemed quite unable to understand that from being his party's brightest star, he was now death to their political hopes. Now O'Brien and the other fund raisers in America made this clear. They sent another cable, declaring Parnell's leadership to be impossible, that they could no longer follow him. Yet still he fought on, wriggling on the hook on which he had been pierced.

It seems, thought Hester, following events with a heavy heart, it is Parnell who has been thrown to the wolves.

Twenty-Eight

Daniel was beginning to look ill. Gaunt, large-eyed; his clothes so loose, they might have been another man's. He scarcely slept, never finished a meal, yet still went every day to the offices of *United Ireland*, where, Hester had been told, Parnell was due any time. He was counting on great support from Dublin still, but those at the paper, acting on orders from O'Brien, had already deserted him. No doubt it was his intention to confront them – after all, it was his own paper. Hester, dreading the effect on Daniel of Parnell's presence, dared do nothing but wait.

The news came that Parnell was to arrive on 10 December. A great reception was planned, with enormous crowds expected at the Rotunda where he was to make a speech. Hester told Daniel she planned to go, to which he said she was welcome.

'You will go to the paper as usual?' she asked, on the morning of the 10th.

'I shall.'

'If it were possible, I'd like to come with you.'

'It is not possible, Hester, I am not wanting you there.'

She sighed her acceptance. 'Would you at least eat some breakfast before you go?'

'Isn't it my breakfast I am eating now?'

'Crumbling bread on your plate, wasting porridge . . .' She took up his dish. 'See – every morning, there's this kind of thing to be thrown out. Are you trying to starve yourself to death?'

He swallowed some tea, dragging on his coat, said he would see her later.

'When? When will you see me?'

'Tonight, after work.'

'I'm going to the Rotunda tonight, but I shall leave your supper ready. Promise me you will eat it?'

'Sure, I'll eat it.'

He kissed her and went downstairs, leaving her staring after him with troubled eyes.

'Mollie!' she called. 'I must go out. I hope not to be long.'

Rory had not yet arrived at the bookshop, but she left him a note telling him to take the day off. With Parnell in Dublin, there would be no point in opening up. Everyone would be going where she was going – the offices of *United Ireland*.

There was already a crowd outside the building when she arrived.

'Is he here?' she asked someone. The man said sure, wasn't he inside, sending them devils packing?

'Devils? What devils?'

'Bodkin and Molloy and the rest of the damned turncoats. Isn't it shamed they should be, letting a man down in his hour of need?'

As she moved on, trembling, a man with wild blue eyes and a large drinker's nose caught her by the arm and pushed her across the street. They were going to storm the building, he told her, in alcoholic breath, she'd better get out of the way.

'You are not going to harm anyone? You are not going to harm those men in there?'

'Isn't the Chief himself in there?' he shouted. 'What he is doing, we are doing, you be getting away from here!'

A woman, also smelling strongly of alcohol, pulled her into a doorway, telling her not to worry, there would be no violence, when had the King of Ireland shown violence? ''Tis a man of peace he is,' she crooned, 'thanks be to God . . . '

With her heart in her mouth, Hester watched as the crowd surged forwards through the doors of the newspaper building, shouting, threatening, waving their fists. Then all went quiet.

'What's happening?' Hester asked, frantically, but the women around her were soothing. Sure, nothing would be happening. The Chief would be giving the traitors the sack;

hadn't he the right, then, wasn't it his own paper? If they would not support him, why should they be staying?

''Tis all that devil O'Brien's fault,' one said roughly. 'Over in America he is, and after telling us what to be doing in Dublin, did you ever? Up for the Chief one day, down the next, 'tis wicked he is and a bad end he'll be having, I'm telling you.'

'Daniel!' shrieked Hester, whose eyes were searching only for him and who had seen his tall figure come stumbling from the doorway, together with Matthew Bodkin and other men from the paper. 'Daniel!' she cried again, oblivious of the looks of the women around her, and, pushing through the crowds who were also spilling out from the building, she reached Daniel and threw her arms around him.

'Oh, thank God, thank God, you're safe!'

'Hester.' He put her from him. 'What is it you are thinking of, to be here like this? Was I not telling you to stay away from this place today?'

'I was too worried, Daniel, I couldn't, I had to come, to see you were all right. But what has been happening in there? Tell me – '

'Thrown out we are,' he muttered. 'Sacked.'

'By Parnell? Did you see him?'

Daniel's face flushed an ugly red. He would not answer and, as she tried to make him look at her, Frank O'Keefe came up and told Daniel they were to adjourn to a pub to review the situation. He tipped his hat to Hester and said her best plan was to get home before Parnell came out, for this crowd was crazy for him, there'd be such pandemonium, she might get hurt.

'How was he?' she asked. 'How did he seem?'

'Sick. A sick, mad lion, fighting to the death.' O'Keefe jerked his head at the people thronging the doors, waiting for Parnell to appear. 'But they see him like Our Blessed Lord and for them he'll walk on water. Go home, Mrs Molloy, keep out of it.'

'I shall still go to the Rotunda, I want to see him!'

'Is it like these fools here you are?' Frank whispered, as Daniel stood aside, his strange, large eyes staring over Hester's head.

227

'I don't know,' she said in a low voice. 'I just know I must see him, hear him speak. I was never really for him. Now perhaps I must support him.'

That evening, a great torchlight procession, thousands strong, escorted Parnell to the Rotunda where he was to make his address. There were bands playing; people hung, cheering, from windows; a feeling in the air, so strong it was a force in itself, was carrying the crowds onward.

Hester, aware that only a limited number could get into the Rotunda, had arrived early and been given a seat. She and those packed around her could hear the muted music of the bands and the cries from the outside crowd, then the great roar as Parnell himself appeared on the platform. With the rest, she stood, cheering and applauding, as he waited, accepting their homage, bowing, waving his thin hand, until at last they let him speak.

Frank O'Keefe had said he looked sick, a sick, mad lion, and it was true his tall figure seemed frail, but this reception tonight had clearly filled him with new energy. He was as buoyed up as the people themselves by the feeling they had generated, as strong as they could have wanted, the perfect leader still to take them to freedom. What he said, Hester could never afterwards have reported, but it was a solemn, measured speech and balm to his audience who had been lacerated by the wounds of the divorce case. It seemed to say, 'Trust me, I am with you, if you follow me, I can still lead you where you would go,' and that, which was all they wanted to hear, was received with rapture. The cheers were still rising, the tears still flowing, when suddenly Parnell appeared to be given a message and hurried from the platform.

The whisper ran around the hall. '*United Ireland* has been taken again, the Chief has gone back to his paper.'

Oh, God, no, thought Hester and pushed through the crowd to the street, where she was in time to see Parnell being driven at speed away from the Rotunda, the roars of the people ringing in his ears as they fell back to let him pass. Ashen-faced, she watched the receding trap. Somehow, she too must get to the newspaper offices, must get to Daniel, but for the moment she seemed lost, unable to move. She heard a voice say her name and swung round to find Rory Doyle standing at her side. He took her arm, his face so concerned that she tried to smile and say she was all right. He said he would find her a cab, she should not be in such a crush.

'I do want a cab, Rory, but not to go home. I must get to the newspaper office, my husband will be there.'

'Mrs Molloy, they say Parnell is like a man possessed. It's a fight he'll be wanting, if they've locked him out. Let me see you home – '

'No, no, come with me to the paper. Let's walk, let's run, until we find something. Pray God I'm not too late.'

They ran together down side streets to escape the surging waves of people intent on following Parnell, Rory loping easily, Hester stumbling in her skirts. Her breath was coming in long, burning gasps. Rory spotted a cab returning from taking some other fare and they hailed it and fell inside, Hester almost sobbing in relief.

'*United Ireland*?' the cabman repeated. 'And isn't the whole world going there tonight? Sure, the Chief'll be after throwing out them wicked devils, and may they get their just reward for turning on the poor man!'

'Take no notice, Mrs Molloy,' Rory whispered. 'He is not knowing the facts.'

'Facts?' She gave a weary smile. 'Does anyone care for facts in Dublin tonight?'

'Sure, they are not seeing them,' Rory answered. 'Only him, only the Chief is in their minds. It's how it's always been.'

In the press of traffic, their progress to the newspaper office was slow, but Parnell must also have been delayed, for, when at last they arrived and Hester with trembling hand had paid off the cab, they saw the leader still standing at the door of the building, calling for it to be broken down. Men were running up with axes and a crowbar, as Parnell hammered on the door; then, 'Stand back!' he roared, and someone used the crowbar and others swung the axes at a second entrance at the side. There was the sound of wood splitting, a cry from the watchers, then Parnell and his followers vanished inside.

229

'Oh, Rory, what can I do?' Hester whispered. 'Daniel is in there and the men have axes – '

He grasped her arm firmly in his. 'It's all right, Mrs Molloy, there'll be no violence. The Chief's against violence.'

'Who knows what might happen in there? He's on top of the world tonight and his men have already broken down the doors – '

Suddenly, the crowd gave a great shout and Parnell appeared at an upper window, waving and calling. 'He's won!' they cried. 'The devils are defeated, 'tis his paper again!'

'He's coming down,' Rory predicted. 'He has to get to the station and they will be following him, then we can find Mr Molloy.'

They watched as Parnell emerged, a dishevelled but triumphant figure, and to screams of joy from the people climbed into the pony trap and was driven away.

'See, they're following, they will go all the way with him to the station.' Rory, with Hester hanging on to his arm, was trying to push through the mass that still stood between them and the broken doors of the newspaper building. 'We have only to wait and the men will surely come out – '

'They're coming, I see them!' cried Hester. 'Oh, and I see Daniel! I see him, Rory, he is with someone – please, let us get through, let's catch him, he is moving away . . . '

But it was like a nightmare, they were swimming against the tide, the only ones returning as everyone else was leaving, and as they tried to free themselves from the press, Hester could see Daniel disappearing round the side of the building, with a thin, wraith like figure following him that could only be Billie Docherty. Billie Docherty? In Dublin? Hester's heart gave a lurch and she caught fresh hold of Rory. They must find another cab, she must get home; Daniel would be leaving Dublin, she must get home before him.

'Leaving Dublin?' Rory looked down on her, his face white with fatigue and stress. 'But how do you know, Mrs Molloy? How can you possibly know?'

'I can't tell you, I am only sure I haven't much time. Don't come with me, Rory, you've done enough for me tonight, I shall be for ever grateful. Just find me a cab and let me go home.'

Mollie was nodding over the kitchen range when Hester flew up the stairs and shook her awake.

'Is Mr Molloy here?' she cried, but Mollie, rubbing her eyes , said he was gone.

'Already?' Hester sank into a chair, pulling off her hat and gloves. 'Oh, don't say I'm too late!' For a moment she bowed her head and let despair flow over her, then she sprang up. 'Did he leave a note, Mollie? A note, did he leave a note?'

'He did not, ma'am.' Mollie shook some tea into the brown teapot. 'But he was after telling me he was away to Skibbereen.'

'Skibbereen?'

'Aye, and you were not to be worrying.'

'Not to be worrying ... ' Hester shook her head, half smiling, half crying. 'Mollie, I'm going to ask you to help me. Will you go round to Mrs Dwyer's house and tell her I shall be bringing the baby to her very early tomorrow and leaving her for a couple of days? I shall be going to Skibbereen by the first train out tomorrow and cannot nurse Caitlin myself, I must trust her to Mrs Dwyer.'

'Sure and it's trustworthy she is, too!' cried Mollie. 'And a nice clean house she is having, the baby will be fine, so she will.'

'Then will you go on to your mother's and say I want you to travel with me, so you must collect a few clothes?'

'Me, travel with you to Skibbereen, ma'am?' Mollie's eyes lit up. 'Sure, 'tis never out of Dublin I've been in my life! And it's on the train we'll be going?'

'Yes, but you must go quickly now, then come back and we'll sleep a little. In the morning, we'll take a cab to Mrs Dwyer and then to the station.'

'A cab!' Mollie echoed, in rapture. Throwing on her shawl, she clattered away on her errands, while Hester went into the children's room. Caitlin was asleep and Hester hung over her for a little while, watching and sighing, but Paul was awake; he said his father had woken him, kissing him.

231

'So I've been waiting for you, Mama,' he murmured sleepily. 'I knew you'd be taking us to follow Papa.'

'To Skibbereen, my darling?'

'To Belcarron, Mama.'

Twenty-Nine

'So, you're to spend Christmas with Lord Penning?' Ernestine murmured, as she sat with Charlotte after dinner. It was the evening of 11 December and John and Dudley had not yet appeared from the dining room. 'How nice that he has invited you.'

'Of course he didn't invite us, Mama.' Charlotte poured the coffee Nora had left. 'We invited ourselves. Since Papa is turning us out in January, what choice had we? Dudley's father said we could go for Christmas and stay on a few weeks. Then – who knows?'

'So sad, Papa and Dudley don't get on. I'm afraid it's Dudley's attitude towards the tenants.'

'Yes, I knew he should not have tried eviction.'

'Your father says these days it causes more trouble for the landlord than the tenant.' Ernestine coughed a little and said she would retire early; since her heavy cold, her chest had been painful, all she felt like was a dose of linctus and her bed.

'Very well, Mama.' Charlotte yawned. 'I think I'll go to bed early, too, seeing as there's nothing else to do. At least at Penningfield there might be something going on . . . Not that I wouldn't rather stay with you, of course, if Papa were only good enough to allow it.'

Ernestine shook her head. 'We should so love to have you, my dear, but do not, I pray you, ask us to take any more of Dudley.'

When Ernestine had trailed away, wrapped in thick shawls, for the house was icy away from the fire, Charlotte took her

233

candle and her book, a new novel by Miss Braddon, and sighed heavily.

'Isn't it frightful that I should have to entertain myself with books?' she complained to Dudley, coming in with her father from the dining room. 'Don't be long, my dear.'

Dudley only grunted and, flinging himself into a chair by the fire, lit a cigar.

'This is Mrs Wintour's drawing room,' John said pointedly.

'My dear mama-in-law will not grudge me a smoke,' Dudley retorted. 'Anyway, she won't have to put up with me much longer, will she?'

'Good night,' Charlotte called sweetly from the stairs, then halted. In a different tone, she cried. 'Papa, I think I hear something outside!'

'Damnation, if those fellows are here again!' John shot out of his chair. 'Dudley, we'd better check – '

'They aren't here, why should they be?'

'You evicted the Docherty family, if you remember.'

'O'Brien and Dillon are in America, Molloy is in Dublin, so is Billie Docherty, so who's to organise trouble here?'

'Billie Docherty's in Dublin? How do you know that?'

'I know what goes on in the village,' Dudley answered loftily. 'Seems Molloy's sister gave him the fare.'

'The devil she did.' John's brows met. 'All the same, I'm going to look outside.'

While Dudley continued to sit smoking, John undid the bolt and chain on the front door and cautiously peered out. The moon in the December sky looked down on empty lawns; no one moved in shrubbery or trees. After a moment or two, he closed the door and bolted it again.

'Could you see anyone?' cried Charlotte from the stairs.

'Not a soul. You must have heard the wind in the trees.'

'Heavens, I know what the wind sounds like, Papa. I swear I heard footsteps.'

'All right, I'll check the back. Dudley, come and help me, will you?'

With poor grace, Dudley threw his cigar into the fire and came slowly into the hall.

'I thought the whole point of this Plan of Campaign was

that things were settled without violence,' he muttered. 'But the trouble with the Irish is they like violence, it suits their nature. Give them the choice of a peaceful agreement and starting a fire and they'll take the fire every time.'

'For God's sake, stop rambling, man, and check the back door,' John snapped. 'I'll see to the side.'

'Who's there?' cried Nora, shouting up from the back stairs. 'Oh, sir, is it trouble again?'

'We thought we heard a noise, Nora, we're just checking, don't worry.'

'I tell you, there's no one here!' called Dudley. 'Nora, you can go to bed.'

'I'll tell the staff what they can do, if you please,' John said coldly. 'And I would remind you, Dudley, you have put us in a very vulnerable position. We have to make sure there's no repeat of what happened last Christmas.'

'Oh, sir, is it back they are?' Nora wailed. 'Weren't they after saying before, 'twill be the house next?'

'No, no, Nora, don't worry.' John patted her shoulder. 'They'll not be trying that again – '

'Papa!' screamed Charlotte from the landing window. 'They're here! They have torches! I think the house is surrounded!'

Thirty

All day they travelled, Hester, Mollie and Paul, from first light until evening, finally arriving by carrier at Theresa's lodging house in Skibbereen, where she greeted them with astonishment. First Daniel, now Hester! Oh, but it was wonderful to see her, so it was, and young Paul!

'Where's Daniel?' cried Hester. 'Is he here?'

'He is not, my dear, he's away somewhere with Billie Docherty, and why Billie Docherty is back after me giving him the money for a new life in Dublin, I cannot be telling you. But it's mad as monkeys those Dochertys are, the lot of them.'

'Gone with Billie Docherty, and I know where.' Hester raised dark, desperate eyes. 'Oh, God, what am I to do?'

'Nothing until there's a cup of tea on the table. Hester, you're looking fit to drop.'

As Theresa began bustling round her kitchen, showing Mollie where things were, pausing to embrace Paul, Hester said she would have tea, but she had kept the carrier, she must go at once to Belcarron.

'To Belcarron?' Theresa's look was stricken. 'Oh, Hester, do not be saying it. He was looking so strange, so ill. It's not to be the same as before, is it?'

Hester put her arm around her. 'Don't worry, Theresa. I'm here, I shall warn them. Let's quickly have the tea, then Mollie can put Paul to bed and I'll go, it won't take long.'

'You'll never be in time, 'tis hours ago he left!'

'He won't have gone straight to the house; he'll be gathering people, making the plan. If I go now, I believe I shall have a chance.'

237

'If you go, I go with you.' Theresa's chin went up. 'Yes, Hester, he is my brother, I should be there. There are people here will help Mollie, just say the word, my dear – quickly, let's go!'

'It's true I'd be glad to have you,' Hester admitted, hastily swallowing tea. 'Paul, my darling, Mollie will look after you and Mama won't be long. I know you will be good. Theresa, are you ready? There's no time to spare.'

The two women, well wrapped up against the cold of the winter night, huddled together in the back of the carrier's cart, not speaking, only looking up at the moon that showed them the narrow lines winding ahead. Hester's thoughts went back to the time when Daniel, still her uncle's groom, had driven her and Richard and Marianne along this very road. He had made the horse almost bolt when Richard had said something that annoyed him and she had watched his neck crimsoning and wondered if he were a Fenian. She had fallen in love with him then and had not even known it, and now . . .

'Pray God we are in time,' she muttered, and Theresa grasped her hand.

' 'Tis Docherty who's to blame, Hester. 'Tis mad they are, those Dochertys, I am telling you.'

'It's not Docherty,' Hester answered. 'It's not even Parnell. It's Daniel himself.'

They were in sight of Belcarron now and the moon was high, but suddenly the carrier raised his whip.

'Be looking there, will you?' he cried.

'Holy Mother of God, it's on fire!' shouted Theresa, but Hester, straining her eyes in the darkness, said:

'No, I believe it's torches, people with torches. Let us get on, let's hurry – I think we may yet be in time.'

John, Charlotte and Dudley stood together on the steps of the house, with Nora in the doorway. From an upstairs window, Ernestine and Mrs Heenan could be seen, staring down in horror. Facing the house stood two men, Daniel Molloy and Billie Docherty, while, stretching away from them in a ring of lighted torches that spanned the building, were the tenants of Belcarron. It was a stage set of dark beauty, a picture in which the faces of the principals, lit by the moon and the flickering torches, seemed scarcely real. Then John took a step forward.

'Molloy! Docherty! I hold you both responsible for this intrusion. Get these people off my property, or it will go hard with you, I promise you! You will not escape gaol this time!'

'We mean you no harm!' Daniel shouted back. 'Just agree you'll put back the evicted and we'll leave you in peace. It's for you to decide.'

'You damned scoundrels! How dare you come here delivering threats?' Dudley's eyes were staring in outrage. 'There'll be no tenants reinstated and that is final. Get out before I blast you out!'

From behind his back he drew a shotgun.

A great sigh went up from the watchers and Billie swung round.

'See what the quality are after doing to us? Seeking to murder us where we stand? Isn't this what we were telling you to expect?'

'For God's sake, Dudley, put the gun away.' John groaned. 'How can we talk when you're waving a thing like that at people? I told you, no guns!'

'Talk?' Dudley repeated. 'You mean with them? When they're planning to burn down Belcarron?'

'They're not going to burn down Belcarron, they're going to leave in peace when I have spoken to them. Molloy, if you mean us no harm, why don't you and Docherty come inside and discuss things sensibly, while the rest of you go home?'

A chorus of wild denials met this and Daniel laughed.

'Mr Wintour, you are just such another as Parnell, so you are, promising us the moon and giving us dirt. Nobody is going home, nobody is going into your house, until you are saying in front of us all you will put back the people Mr Sarn' – Daniel jerked his head contemptuously towards Dudley – 'has evicted. Are you willing?'

'Daniel, we haven't discussed rents. Isn't it part of the Plan of Campaign that the tenants offer to pay what they consider a fair rent?'

Billie Docherty started forward. ''Tis nothing at all my da

239

can pay! Wouldn't he be paying if he could? He's out in the street, what's he to do? 'Tis back home he should be!'

''Tis back home,' the crowd shouted, 'back home he should be!'

'I'll see you all in hell first!' cried Dudley. 'Those evicted stay evicted. Mr Wintour will reinstate nobody. I will reinstate nobody. And the rest of you can take note – pay your rents in full, or you'll be out on your necks and good riddance to the lot of you!'

There was a stunned silence for a moment or two; then the people began to howl with rage. John Wintour shouted, desperately, he would handle this, for God's sake, listen, listen; but Daniel, lowering his head like a charging bull, ran at Dudley and tried to knock the gun from his hand. Dudley, laughing, raised it higher; Daniel made a grab and forced it down. The two men grappled together, up the steps and back again, down the drive, rolling together, the barrels of the gun moving with them, glinting in the moonlight, until into the silence that had gripped the watchers there came the sound of a shot. It seemed to hang in the air for a long, long moment, echoing from the walls of the house, striking terror into the hearts of the two women approaching at speed in the carrier's cart. Then one man stood up and one lay still and Charlotte screamed.

As the sound of the horse's hooves and rattling wheels came nearer, Charlotte with John at her side ran to the man on the ground and knelt over him. As Ernestine appeared in the doorway, they looked up.

'He's dead,' said John. 'My son-in-law is dead.'

Ernestine ran to take Charlotte in her arms, Nora and Mrs Heenan burst into sobs, the people groaned and crossed themselves, and Billie Docherty took Daniel's hand. But Daniel did not look at him nor utter a word. He stood where he was like a man of stone and at his feet, its barrels still catching the pale light, lay Dudley's gun.

'Daniel!' Hester came running from the carrier's cart, Theresa following, their faces starkly white, their shawls trailing. 'Oh, Daniel, you are safe, you are safe . . .'

As Billie Docherty stepped away, Hester flung her arms around Daniel, while Theresa, murmuring prayers, stood

240

close. But Daniel again made no response. It was as though he were a dead man. But the dead man lay on the ground.

Hester, suddenly dragging her eyes from Daniel, saw the dark figure lying on the gravel, its face covered now by John Wintour's handkerchief. She gave a cry of anguish.

'Oh, no, no! Oh, Theresa, look there. Oh, my God, who is it, who is it?'

'Dudley,' John answered. 'He had the gun, your husband tackled him, it went off.'

'It wasn't Daniel's fault, then?' cried Theresa. 'It was an accident?'

'Yes ... I don't know – it will be for the magistrate to decide.' John ran a shaking hand across his face and turned on the silent people watching. 'You, all of you, go to your homes. Can't you leave us alone with our dead? Nora, get the carrier there to take you to the magistrate's house, ask him to come here as soon as possible. Docherty, you can go for Dr Down.'

As men and women began to scatter at his command, John slowly mounted the steps of the house. He put his hand on his wife's shoulder, told her to take Charlotte inside, get Mrs Heenan to make tea, then he looked back at Hester.

'Hester, my dear, ask your husband to come inside, will you? I'm afraid he will have to be questioned.'

'You said it was an accident!' Theresa shouted.

'I said it would be for the magistrate to decide the truth of what happened here. Your brother may be charged.'

'With what?' asked Hester quickly. 'Charged with what, Uncle John?'

'Hester, please, just bring him into the house.'

Without speaking, Daniel moved forward. Between his wife and his sister, he ascended the steps and for only the second time in his life entered the front door of Belcarron without carrying other people's luggage.

Thirty-One

Richard and Alice were riding the pampas, watching a troop of wild horses galloping on the horizon. It was a perfect December day, warm but not too hot, the sky clear, no sign of thunder clouds. No need for the *pampero*, the storm that brought coolness after heat.

Alice, still in mourning for Beatrice, was wearing a black riding habit and looked pale behind her veil. In the months since her aunt's death, she had felt oppressed, not only by grief but also by anxiety for what Don Felipe might do. Argentine legal machinery moved so slowly, his plan to contest the will appeared to have made no progress. Supposing he grew impatient, tired of waiting for legal action and decided to take some other kind? When she expressed these fears, Richard always laughed, but it was no laughing matter to her.

There was another problem, one that was hers alone, of how to come to terms with a future that did not include Belcarron. She had not been able to face it yet, she only knew it was there, at the back of her mind, waiting for her. There was no point in discussing it again with Richard, he was too happy.

He tried not to show it, because he was genuinely grieving for Beatrice, but he had had never felt better in his life. He had got what he wanted and it was even sweeter than he had imagined: his own land, his own *estancia*. He need never worry about his future again, never strive to wrest an income from the overworked, overburdened land of Ireland or England; he owned a part of the pampas, the greatest space on earth. He felt exhilarated.

They dismounted and tied up their horses under some *ombú* trees and Richard, taking off his hat, stretched and shook back his yellow hair.

'You know, Alice,' he said, 'when I'm out here, riding, I feel like those horses there, completely free.'

Alice, fearful of snakes, spread a blanket on the ground and sat down, unloosening her veil. 'Poor things,' she replied. 'They're only free until the gauchos take them.'

She was right, of course, Richard thought, unwillingly. All the same, they were there, those tough little descendants of the conquistadores' horses; they were still roaming the pampas, enduring all weathers, living on what they could get. Their freedom might be illusory, so was the gauchos', so was his own, but when he rode out and watched them, he knew it lifted his heart.

'I suppose I could be called sentimental,' he went on, 'but if I had my way, I'd never have them caught or broken. I'm doing as much as anyone for change, I suppose, but I'd still let those horses go free.'

'This from the man who doesn't mind hunting the fox and the rhea?' Alice asked, with a smile.

'Hunting's different, it's a challenge.'

'The gauchos say breaking horses is a challenge.'

'Come, the horse never has a chance. Not like the fox, certainly not like the rhea when I'm after it.' Richard grinned. 'I'm not the world's best with the bolas yet.'

Alice thought of the great ungainly ostriches lumbering out of Richard's way and said he was probably right, he wasn't much of a threat to their freedom. She lay back and looked up at the glossy leaves of the *ombú* tree above her; they were poisonous, of no use to anyone except for shade, but for that on the pampas they were prized.

'We still have heard nothing from Don Felipe's lawyers,' she observed. 'What do you suppose is happening?'

'Nothing, I hope. Our fellows say he will abandon the suit, he really has no hope of winning.'

'In the meantime, it makes things difficult.'

'Very difficult. I'd give a lot to have it settled.'

Alice gave Richard a sideways glance. 'I know you think I am foolish, but I can't help worrying over those threats

Felipe made. He did say you would never inherit Sentos land.'

'Well, I have inherited it. I've told you, he can do nothing.'

'This is the Argentine. He may not wait for the law.'

'Darling, he is a sugar planter, not a bandit.'

'He is concerned about honour, maybe revenge. You cannot know what is in his mind.'

Richard sat up and pulled on his hat. Alice, we've been very, very lucky. Let's enjoy what we have and not worry about things that will never happen.'

I suppose some people would think me ungrateful, Alice thought, as they remounted their horses and turned for home, to be given so much – land, money, houses – but if it is not what one wants, does it matter how much there is?

Mena was waiting for them as they entered the house. At the look on her face, Alice's heart rocked in her breast.

'Mena, what is it? What's happened?'

''Tis a wire, Miss Alice, a cable thing.' Mena, her blue eyes enormous, put it into Alice's hand. 'From Ireland, I'm thinking.'

Alice and Richard exchanged quick looks.

'Let me have it,' said Richard, but Alice shook her head.

'I'll open it – if it's from Ireland, it will be for me.'

'Well?' The three of them were trembling as she tore open the flimsy envelope. She raised her eyes.

'It's Dudley Sarn – he's dead.'

Mena gave a little sigh and turned away. A flash of relief showed in Richard's face as he took the cable and read it for himself.

'DUDLEY SARN DEAD STOP SHOOTING ACCIDENT STOP MOLLOY HELD STOP COME IF POSSIBLE STOP WINTOUR. What in damnation does it mean?'

'Obviously there's been some sort of fight. Maybe Daniel tackled Dudley and Dudley brought out a gun – oh, poor Hester, Richard! And poor Charlotte!'

Richard set his mouth grimly. 'I can't be a hypocrite. Dudley Sarn is no loss.'

'Richard!'

'All right, one shouldn't speak ill of the dead, but Charlotte

245

never loved him, did she? She took him for his title and his money and didn't get what she bargained for.' Richard looked down again at the cable. 'Your father surely isn't serious, though? Wanting us to go home?'

'We are needed, Richard.'

'Why? I am sure Charlotte will survive her loss.'

'And what about Hester? Daniel Molloy is involved.'

'We have to go across the world because Molloy has behaved like a madman?'

'You don't know how he has behaved!' Alice turned quickly to Mena and asked her to bring coffee. 'You heard there's been bad news from home?' she added, in a low voice.

'Yes, Miss Alice. Mr Sarn is dead.' Mena crossed herself. She moved to the door, where she hesitated. 'And Daniel, Miss Alice? Is it trouble he's in over this?'

'I'm afraid so, Mena, but don't worry, my father said Mr Sarn died by accident. No doubt it can all be explained.'

'I hope you're right,' Richard muttered, when Mena had withdrawn. 'We shall just have to wait for more information.'

'You mean you don't intend to go home?' Alice asked swiftly.

'How can I? It means spending months away. Apart from all I have to do on the *estancia*, there's the problem of the lawsuit. I can't be away if that comes off.'

'You said it wouldn't, you said he had no case.'

'Well, we can't be sure, can we? It's possible he might still try to make trouble.' Richard ran his hands through his hair. 'There is no question of my leaving the country for six or eight months, anyway. I'm sorry, darling, but you must see that.'

'It needn't be for as long as that.'

'It would be six months at the very least. I simply can't afford the time.'

'Didn't you once say, if I went back, you would have to go too?'

'Yes, but not for something like this.' He caught at her hand. 'Be reasonable, Alice!'

'If you won't come with me, I shall go alone,' she said,

246

with decision. 'I am needed. Papa would not have asked otherwise. I must go.'

'Darling, it will all be over by the time you get there. What's the point in going when you can do nothing?'

'What will be over?'

'Molloy's trial, I suppose. I presume it's for manslaughter, something of that sort. There will be nothing practical you can do.'

'I can support my family, Richard, and I intend to.'

Richard dropped her hand. 'You've wanted this for so long, haven't you? And here it is, the perfect excuse to go back to Belcarron.'

The colour flooded her face, and her eyes flashed. 'Is that what you think? I'm using my sister's tragedy, my cousin's misery, as an excuse to take a trip home? How can you even suggest it?'

Richard lowered his eyes. 'I'm sorry, Alice, I shouldn't have said a thing like that. I suppose I'm just so . . . floored. One minute, I'm the happiest man in the world, the next, facing something like this.' He pulled her into his arms. 'I don't want you to leave me, that's the truth of it.'

She relaxed against him. 'And I don't want to go, not like this, not alone. But you know I must, don't you? Richard, say you understand.'

'I suppose I do.' He kissed her gently. 'Yes, you must go. We'd better start making arrangements. You'll take Mena with you?'

'Of course. I expect she'll be over the moon at the thought of going back home.'

But, strangely, Mena did not want to go back to Ireland. Alice could not believe it.

'Not go home, Mena? But why? Why should you not want to go?'

'I want to go, Miss Alice,' Mena muttered, her face twisting anxiously. 'Never be thinking any other. 'Tis my soul I'd give to see my ma again and Carron and all.'

'Well, then!'

'But if it was back there I was, if I was to be seeing it all again, I'm thinking I'd never be coming back. And Liam is here.'

247

'Then of course you'd come back,' Alice argued. 'I shall be coming back, you would come with me. I don't understand the problem, Mena.'

Mena began to cry. 'If I was to see my ma again, oh 'tis so torn I'd be. My Liam is here, is all I am thinking. Miss Alice, don't be asking me to leave.'

Alice put her arms around her and told her not to cry, she need not leave Liam. In fact, it might be as well if she stayed and looked after Miss Tina. To take a baby on two long sea voyages would be risky, it would be safer to leave her at home, if Mena were willing.

'Willing? Oh, Miss Alice!' Mena wiped her eyes and gave a watery smile. 'You could not be asking me anything I'd want to do more!'

'That's settled, then,' said Alice, privately wondering how she would ever bring herself to say goodbye, even for a few months, to Richard and her baby. But she would have Victor and Jack and her father had asked for her, she could not let him down. 'Come, Mena, we must begin to pack,' she said, brightly, 'I shall be leaving for Buenos Aires as soon as possible.'

Once again, Alice was on the deck of a steamship, standing with Richard while her two boys hung on to their father's hands. There was the usual scene of confusion, which would sort itself out once they were at sea, but now, with the passengers and crew milling around, relatives sobbing and bags and baskets still going aboard, it seemed as though they would never be ready to leave Buenos Aires.

The time came, though, when the ship's hooters sounded and Richard grasped Alice's hands. 'I must go, my darling. They're wanting us off.' As she burst into tears, he pulled her close. 'Oh, why in God's name are you leaving me?'

'I'm not, I'm not, it's only for a visit, I'm coming back!'

As the boys began to cry with her, Richard held her away from him and searched her face. 'You mean that, Alice?'

'Don't be so foolish, how can you even ask such a thing?' Alice dabbed at her eyes with her handkerchief. 'Promise me, you'll keep yourself safe, you'll never ride out alone, you'll keep away from Felipe Sentos.'

'I promise.'

'And you'll take care of my Tina? I do so wish Mena could have brought her to say goodbye.'

'You know it was better for you to say goodbye to her at home, this port's no place for babies. And of course I'll take care of her, I'll take care of everything until you come back.'

'I don't want to go!' she said, suddenly. 'I needn't, need I? We could come back with you.'

'Now who is being foolish?' Richard shook her gently. 'You must go, you're needed, and it will only be for a few months.'

'I know, I know.' Alice bent down to the boys. 'Come, kiss your Papa goodbye, the ship is leaving now.'

They clung together, all of them, kissing and weeping, until Richard at last pulled himself away and left the ship, his face averted. Alice, with Victor and Jack clinging to her skirts, hung over the side, watching and waving, as the steamship again sounded its sirens and began to move slowly down the waters of the Plata, the silver river, on its way to the open sea.

Part III
1891–1892

Thirty-Two

Parnell was dead. 'Of rheumatism of the heart,' said the doctors. 'Of heartbreak,' said his friends. He had died at Brighton on 6 October 1891, in the arms of his wife, who had been Katharine O'Shea; they had been married only since June. Now, on 11 October, he was making his last journey to Glasnevin Cemetery without her.

The coffin had been brought from Holyhead to Kingstown in the early hours of the soaking wet Sunday and from there, accompanied by huge crowds, was taken by train to St Michan's Church in Dublin and then to City Hall. Among the thousands filing past to pay their respects at the lying in state were Hester Molloy, Charlotte Sarn and Priscilla Letton. All were in mourning, Priscilla for the occasion, Hester and Charlotte for Dudley and also for Ernestine Wintour who had died of pneumonia in April.

Hester and Charlotte had met by accident, much to Hester's embarrassment. Charlotte seemed not to care that Daniel had been involved in Dudley's death, but to Hester the knowledge was extremely painful. To make the situation even more delicate, Daniel, while on bail from charges of breaking the peace and causing an affray, had followed O'Brien's example and fled to America. He was now in New York and doing well, working for an Irish paper and fund raising for Home Rule, a freer, happier man, as he wrote to Hester, than he had ever been in the old country. Although to defy the law went against everything in her nature, she had accepted that what he had done was for the best. Even a short spell in gaol might have been enough to push him further into the terrible apathy he had exhibited after Dudley's death; there had been times when she had feared for his sanity. At least she knew now, even though they were separated by the Atlantic, that he had found himself.

Alice, as soon as she arrived, had been a rock of support, the best person possible to help Hester come to terms with the tragedy that had affected her more than Charlotte. But everyone had leaned on Alice at that time, even Charlotte herself, and after Ernestine's death, John Wintour especially had needed his elder daughter. Hester knew how much it had cost Alice to leave him in the autumn, but what was she to do? Her home was in the Argentine, Richard was there, and baby Tina – she had to return. As she and Hester tearfully kissed at parting, Alice whispered, 'Yes, where Richard is must be my home, but you know I leave a part of myself at Belcarron.'

'You'll come back, Alice, one day you will.'

Alice nodded, her eyes bleak. 'Visit my father, Hester, will you? When you can? Promise?'

'I promise.'

Now Hester was alone in Dublin, running her bookshop, taking comfort in her children. She had watched Parnell's last struggles, his frantic by-election campaigning in all weathers that some said had caused his death, although it was Hester's view that rain and wind did not kill a man who wanted to live. Parnell had had a sickness of the heart that was not physical, the same sort of sickness she had seen in Daniel after the divorce hearing. Had he wanted the gun that killed Dudley to kill him instead? When he had retreated into mental blockage, it had been no surprise to Hester. She knew he had wanted to be finished with consciousness for ever.

'My dears,' Priscilla whispered, when they had joined the crowds outside City Hall, 'did you see the wreath from his wife? "To My True Love, My Husband"? I thought that was so affecting. Just think, she waited ten years to be his wife and then he had to go and die almost as soon as they were married!'

'She's not here today, is she?' Charlotte remarked, her

254

green eyes darting everywhere. 'They say she won't set foot in Ireland. I consider that pretty bad form.'

'I'm sure she is just too shocked to be here,' Hester muttered. 'But it would be an ordeal for any widow, especially for her.'

'The Irish are so crazy, she probably thought they'd mob her. So many blame her, you know, for what happened to him. Her, or the clergy. Did you see that amazing wreath with "Murdered by the Priests" worked in flowers? As though the priests could be blamed! He brought it on himself, I say.'

'You're right,' Hester agreed. 'What we do has to be our own affair.'

She thought of Daniel. The very fact that he could not accept his leader's flaw in a sense revealed his own. Fortune had been on his side – away from the heady atmosphere Parnell had generated and the terrible letdown he had allowed to happen, Daniel was flourishing as he had never flourished before. But Hester thanked God he was not in Dublin that day to see his broken idol worshipped in death even more than in life.

'What are you going to do now?' Charlotte asked her. 'You are surely not planning to go to the cemetery?'

'I think I will, Charlotte, I'll join those on foot.'

'But it will take hours! They're talking in thousands here, you know, thousands from this place, thousands from that, a delegation from everywhere that has so much as a post office.'

Hester said, all the same, she would like to go, and Charlotte and Priscilla said, very well, they would go home, though how they would find a cab, they had no idea, they had not dared to bring the carriage into such crowds.

'But see, the sun has come out,' Priscilla exclaimed. 'We shall not get wet if we go now.'

She put out her hand to shake Hester's and bowed. 'Goodbye, Mrs Molloy, I do hope things go well for you.'

'You are very kind, Miss Letton,' Hester murmured, as Charlotte kissed her and said she would keep in touch, why not? She would certainly call to see Paul again.

'Although I don't suppose he will still love me in this frightful black bonnet!' she cried, with a light laugh. 'You know, I wish poor dear Mama no disrespect but I am so frightfully tired of mourning. It must be ghastly for Alice to have to travel all the way to South America dressed in black.'

'Perhaps she will discard it now she's at sea?' Priscilla suggested. 'I'm sure I should.'

'Oh, not Alice, she likes to do what is right, isn't that so, Hester?'

'She is very loyal,' Hester answered. 'So is Paul. He will always love you, Charlotte, whatever hat you are wearing.'

When Charlotte and Priscilla had moved elegantly away, Hester took her place in the immensely long funeral procession, walking with the thousands of ordinary people who had loved Parnell and now followed his hearse and his horse carrying his riding boots reversed in its stirrups. The occasion was so solemn, so particularly tragic, she wept with the rest as they wound slowly through the streets to Glasnevin Cemetery. The crush was so great, it was not possible to see the actual grave. Nor, because of the tears in her eyes, did she see the meteor which was supposed to have dropped through the sky as Parnell's coffin was lowered to its resting place. A falling star . . . that would have been fitting. She was sorry she could never afterwards say if it had actually appeared.

'I do think your cousin is delightful,' Priscilla told Charlotte, as they made their way home through mourning Dublin. 'Such a lady . . . one can't imagine the life she has led with that man who has run away to America.'

'He's a madman, of course. I dare say he intended to kill Dudley all the time, but of course Papa had to see he wasn't charged, the scandal would have been frightful. As it was, we managed to hush it up as much as possible and when he was on bail for some minor thing, he left the country, thank God. So we can forget all about him.'

'But you lost poor Dudley. What do you think you will do, my dear?'

'For the time being, of course, I must stay with Papa. He is still so terribly shocked by Mama's death, never expected her to go before him. Richard and Alice staying on in the

Argentine, that's been another blow. Alice tries to make out they will come back one day, but of course they won't.'

'Yet your cousin Richard is your father's heir?'

'Perhaps. Perhaps not. Papa will not say.'

Priscilla smiled. 'Why, then, my dear Charlotte, it looks to me as though you might inherit Belcarron yourself.'

Charlotte shrugged and drew her cape around her shoulders. 'Who knows? Alice is still Papa's favourite, I'm afraid. You don't know how fortunate you are, Priscilla, to be an only child.'

'Indeed, I thank God for it every night. But take heart, Charlotte, you're at Belcarron and Alice is on her way back to South America, that must count for something.'

Charlotte, waving to the first empty cab they had seen, gave a brilliant smile.

'You're right. What a comfort you are, Priscilla, to remind me.'

Thirty-Three

The long voyage was over. Alice was back in Buenos Aires, back in Richard's arms, deaf to the rush and clamour of the port as it surged around them like a noisy sea. The boys, though, would not wait for their own welcome and wailed and pulled at their father's jacket until he dragged himself at last from Alice and bent to hug them.

'Did you think I'd forgotten you? Never in this world! Just had to kiss Mama first, you see, that's the rule, isn't it? Mama must come first.'

'We've brought you lots of presents,' Victor announced, importantly. 'They're all surprises.'

'For Mena, too,' said Jack, 'and Tina.'

'Tina!' Alice repeated, looking at passing faces. 'Richard, where is Tina? Where is Mena? I was so sure they'd be here to meet me!'

'You know it's difficult, darling. For a start, we can't all fit into the carriage. They're at home, waiting for you.'

'It's been so long, Richard.'

'I know, I know.' He kissed her again, then took the boys' hands. 'Come on, let's see who can get to the carriage first. Don't worry about the baggage, Alice. Francisco will take your case, the rest will follow.'

'Francisco!' As the coachman came to greet her, his face wreathed in smiles, she felt absurdly touched that he was so pleased to see her. A sudden warmth of feeling swept over her and it seemed to her she had, after all, come home.

Here was the old Sentos house again on the Avenida Lila, with its coloured tile roof and faded shutters, its forecourt

259

with lemon trees and shrubs, its unchanging air of well-being and comfort. The front door was open now, filled with the household waiting to greet her: Carlotta, Vittoria, Maria, and in the background, Mena, holding Tina by the hand.

'Mena!' cried Alice, 'Oh, how good it is to see you! And is this my Tina? Oh, but see how she has grown! Richard, look at her. I declare, she is not a baby any more.'

As Alice folded the child into her arms, Tina set up a loud wail at which the women laughed affectionately, except for Mena, who, after one long penetrating look into Alice's face, suddenly burst into tears and disappeared.

Alice, turning to Richard, looked stricken. 'Why, whatever's the matter? Why has she run off like that? What have I done?'

'Nothing, darling, she's just overcome, been waiting to see you for so long. It's understandable, isn't it?'

'Of course,' Alice said blankly.

But she did not understand it at all.

'You were away so long, so long,' Richard groaned later, failing to keep his hands off Alice as she tried to unpack in their room. 'You don't know what it's been like for me!'

'You think it was easy for me?'

'It's different for women.'

'So men say. But I never stopped thinking of you.'

'And thinking of making love?' He was trembling as he pulled her to him. 'Alice, please, I must have you, I must, it's been too long. Stop that damned unpacking and let me take you to bed.'

'Richard, I'm sorry I was away longer than planned, but with poor Mama dying so unexpectedly there was so much to do, I couldn't leave Papa –'

'I know, I know, I was so sorry, but now you're back and we can forget everything except being together.'

'It's the middle of the afternoon, there are the children – '

'No, no more, not another word. You have nothing to think about except me.'

The lovemaking that followed was quick and violent, leaving both shaken and Alice quite bruised.

'I declare,' she gasped, 'I haven't felt like this since I was a bride.'

'You enjoyed it when you were a bride.' Richard grinned, leaning back against the pillows. 'Don't you remember?'

Alice slid from the bed and looked at herself in the cheval glass.

'See how you've marked me, Richard, I shall look a perfect fright tomorrow!'

'No one will see except me and you'll look beautiful, anyway.' Richard leaped from bed and came to her. 'Oh, I'm sorry, darling, if I was a bit rough. It's what happens when a fellow has to wait, you see.'

'I hope you'll remember next time that I have feelings too. You treated me just then as though I existed only for you.'

'I've said I'm sorry.' He put his hands through her long dark hair. 'But, oh God, it's so good to have you back, Alice!'

'And I'm so glad to be with you again. I was afraid sometimes you might have forgotten me.'

'Forgotten you? I've just been living for your return.'

'Was it very dull, poor Richard?'

'Terrible.' He released her to look at his watch on the dressing table. 'But maybe we'd better dress now. I've just remembered, the Stonefields are coming round at four.'

'The Stonefields? Coming here? Why ever should they?'

'To welcome you home, of course. They've really been very good to me while you were away, Edward and Mrs S and Lucinda.'

'Lucinda?'

'Their daughter. You remember, don't you? Lucinda's the younger one. Georgina's the one who is in England at present. Then there's Arthur – he's been pretty useful, too, introducing me around. I think you'll find we'll be much more sociable in future, darling.'

Alice, brushing her hair, said slowly, 'You haven't forgotten I am still in mourning, Richard?'

'Half mourning, isn't it?' Richard, still naked, was walking round the bedroom, opening drawers, laying out clothes. 'Would you ring for some hot water, darling?' he asked, over his shoulder.

261

'If you put on your dressing gown. Richard, didn't you think I might be tired when I first arrived? Didn't you think I might just want to be with you and Tina on my first day home?'

'I did, but they were so insistent they wanted to see you.' He smiled reassuringly. 'Don't worry, they won't stay long.'

'We've hardly had any time to talk, though. I wanted to tell you about Hester and Daniel – '

'For heaven's sake, Alice, don't mention Molloy to the Stonefields. It would be the end of our being *gente decente* if they found we had a gaolbird in the family!'

'Daniel is not a gaolbird, Richard!'

'He would be if he hadn't skipped bail.' Richard, flinging on his dressing gown, shook his head. 'And to think you once wanted me to welcome him into the family . . . shows I was right, doesn't it? Right about him all along.'

Dressed in grey with black bands and touches of white, Alice betrayed no sign of her feelings when she greeted the Stonefields at four, but she was in fact dismayed at Richard's obvious involvement with them during her absence. Edward Stonefield was courteous and charming, but Venetia, his wife, was cold and snobbish and had brought up her children to be the same. Alice had no wish to be friends with them but for Richard's sake supposed she must be welcoming.

'So sorry to hear about your bereavement, my dear,' Edward murmured. 'What a thing to happen on your holiday, eh? I think Richard was worried at one time in case you never came back.'

'Still played some fine polo,' Arthur drawled, fixing a pale stare on Alice's lovely face.

Alice swung round on Richard. 'Polo? I didn't know you had taken up polo, Richard. You have no ponies, have you?'

'Sort of,' he answered. 'I've . . . well, I've hired a couple.'

'I thought you couldn't spare time from the *estancia*.'

'Oh, my dear, that's true,' Venetia put in quickly. 'We had a very difficult time, making him come into BA to relax a little. After all, you know what they say, all work and no play makes Jack a dull boy!'

'And no one could describe Richard as dull!' Lucinda

exclaimed, laughing. When Alice and Venetia turned their eyes on her, she blushed and looked down.

There was a short, awkward pause before the Stonefields rose for farewells, promising to call again soon, although they understood of course that Mrs Wintour was in mourning.

'Richard only really came into BA on business,' Edward whispered, over Alice's hand. 'Legal matters to do with the estate, Don Felipe's lawsuit, that sort of thing.'

'Has a date been set?' she asked quickly.

'Yes, hasn't he told you? No need to worry, my dear, the hearing is not for months, next June, in fact. The law moves very slowly here.'

Venetia, ignoring Alice's troubled look, swooped on her and kissed her. 'So delightful to have you back, Mrs Wintour. Richard was so lost without you, we really felt we had to entertain him.'

'Thank you so much,' Alice replied smoothly. 'I was quite worried at leaving him for so long.'

'No need, my dear, he was in very good hands, I assure you.'

'So I understand,' said Alice.

'It's not the way it looks,' Richard said when they were alone. 'I don't know what impression you've been given, but I haven't been spending all my time playing polo and having dinner with the Stonefields, I promise you.'

'Really? But Miss Lucinda is a charming girl and calls you by your first name, I notice.'

'That's just because she's not much more than a schoolgirl, no more than seventeen.'

'The age when girls are presented to society.' Alice studied the flowers the Stonefields had brought her. 'And Lucinda has put up her hair, so she is scarcely still in the schoolroom.'

'She's as plain as a pikestaff and exactly like her mother. Would I look at her twice when I am married to you?'

'If I were in Ireland, you might.'

'Oh, for God's sake, Alice! Your first day home and we are talking like this!'

'Because I'm tired!' she cried, dashing down the flowers.

263

'Because I am at home and not at home! Because you invited other people round and I feel I don't belong!'

'Oh, my poor girl!' Richard took her in his arms and held her close, saying he had been selfish and stupid and he just hoped she would forgive him, all he wanted was to have her back and happy, he didn't give a damn for polo or Lucinda Stonefield. Now she must have a quiet dinner and go to bed and rest and in the morning she would feel quite different.

'I suppose you're right,' she murmured. 'I'm sorry, Richard, I really am exhausted. And worried, too. Edward told me about the lawsuit, you know.'

'Don't think about that. It's months away.'

'But it will come, we can't put it out of our minds.'

'You can, for the time being, anyway. Look, I'll ring the bell and tell them to hurry on dinner.'

'I must see the children first. The boys will be wondering where they are and I haven't had any time at all yet with Tina.'

'No need to worry about her, Mena looked after her beautifully.' Richard led Alice to a chair and made her sit down. 'You know, I really felt sorry for Mena when you were away. In fact, I tried to make her go out with the other girls, get to know some people, and I believe she did in the end. After all, she can't mourn all her life for Liam.'

'Why, Richard, that was good of you,' Alice said, warmly. 'You see, you're not the cold fellow you sometimes make yourself out to be.'

'Mena was lost without you, that's all. I knew how she felt.'

'The strange thing is, she doesn't seem pleased to see me back.'

'What nonsense! She was fine when she came to you, wasn't she? When she'd got over her crying? That was just nerves, anyway.'

'Was it? I'm not sure.'

'Well, she was delighted with the presents you'd brought and the things from her mother.'

'Yes, but every time I meet her eyes she looks away. Did anything happen to upset her while I was in Ireland?'

'No, not a thing. I'm sure you're imagining this, Alice. Mena is probably feeling like you, a little overwrought.'

Too tired to argue, Alice said no more, but she knew Richard was wrong. All was not well with Mena and questioning would probably do no good. One day she would come to Alice and tell her about it, whatever it was, and until that happened, however hard she found it, Alice must leave her alone.

Thirty-Four

There had been changes in the Argentine, Richard said, while Alice had been in Ireland. The worst of the slump was over but there were new movements rising which opposed the dominance of the *estancieros*. It would be ironic if, just as Richard had become one, their powers began to wane, but he didn't think it likely. Land was strength in the Argentine and the *estancieros* held the land. No politician would last long if he tried to change that, although life might be made more difficult and for Richard it was difficult enough anyhow. Because of the Sentos lawsuit, he could not get at the funds he needed for the expansion he wanted to make.

'So how are we managing at all?' asked Alice.

Richard grinned. 'Courtesy of the Stonefield Bank. Now do you begin to see into your husband's devious mind?'

'Oh, Richard!' Alice gave a relieved laugh. 'I had forgotten Edward was a banker.'

'I hadn't,' said Richard.

He had been cleverer than she had given him credit for, she realised, but where the Sentos lawsuit was concerned it seemed to her that he was wearing a blindfold. He could not or would not discuss what their future might be if Don Felipe were successful.

'We must face it,' Alice told him. 'We must make some plans.'

'There is no point, he can't win, he has no case.'

'You say that, but you can't be sure. If the courts were to overturn Aunt Beatrice's will, we should have no life here, we should have to leave.'

267

'Don't hope for it,' he said shortly. 'It won't happen.'

'If you think I am hoping for Belcarron, you're forgetting that Charlotte is there. And she is a widow.'

'So?'

'So my father might have to consider her situation.'

Richard's eyes flashed. 'You mean he might cut us out for her? I don't believe it!'

'We have the *estancia*, she has nothing.'

'Uncle John told me he wanted a man to run Belcarron and Dudley Sarn is dead.'

'He'd rather anyone ran it than Dudley Sarn. Charlotte has much more chance of inheriting now she is alone.'

'Did you discuss this with your father?' Richard asked, after a pause. 'Did you tell him about the lawsuit?'

'Yes. It was then he told me had made no decision about how to leave Belcarron.'

'The devil he did! Why, he told me he was making me his heir!'

'But you have since become Aunt Beatrice's heir,' Alice pointed out.

It had been a great joy to Alice to be reunited with Tina. She was not a pretty child but was already showing the personality and strength of will that was to draw others to her – Jack, so gentle, so like Matthew, being one. Victor at five was the handsomest of the three Wintour children, strikingly like his father, but in Alice's view the most difficult. It was not that he was disobedient or wilful, just that he seemed to show a coldness, even hardness, towards those around him. He was her firstborn, she adored him, but sometimes she had the feeling he would never love her, would never perhaps love anyone in the years to come. Where his character might have come from, she had no idea.

Heredity interested her. Without knowing anything of the scientific theories of the time, she liked to note the strands in her own family tapestry, to wonder why one person might have a particular thread, another something quite different. Why should she and Richard both have inherited the straight Wintour nose, yet share no other family characteristics? Why

268

should Charlotte have the yellow hair of the Wintours but the bumpy nose that came from her grandmother's family, the Powells? In the case of her own children, why should Victor and Jack be pure Wintours and Tina pure Reynolds, Richard's mother's family?

She discussed it with Richard one humid November evening when she should have been packing; they were to leave for the *estancia* next day. Richard was smoking a cigar, only half listening to her, she felt sure, although he declared he was interested, yes, indeed . . .

'I've thought about it myself,' he murmured, lying back in his wicker chair on the patio. 'Especially when I look at Tina and see my mother, then look at Jack and see my father. Sometimes, the funny thing is, they give a little turn of the head or a smile, and I see you.'

'How strange, I have never seen myself in Tina at all.'

'I'm afraid she's certainly got my mother's great beak of a nose, poor child.'

'Darling, she's only two years old! She hasn't got a beak of any sort!'

'It'll come.' Richard drew on his cigar. 'But I know someone else who has the Wintour nose.'

'Who?'

'Mena.'

Alice's face slowly flooded scarlet. She caught her breath. 'And what do you mean by that?' she asked sharply.

Richard sat up, colouring himself. 'Well, you know what I mean. There's no need to look like that.'

'I don't know what you're talking about!'

He kept his eyes on his cigar. 'Did Mena's mother ever work at Belcarron?'

'Yes, most of the people from the village worked at Belcarron at one time or another.' Alice was trembling. 'Are you suggesting that my father – Papa – Richard, I can't believe my ears!'

'Look, it happens all the time, doesn't it? I'm sorry I said anything, but I always thought you must have at least suspected.'

'I didn't! I wouldn't! My own father, deceiving my mother in that way!'

'Maybe he didn't deceive her, maybe your mother knew. After all, she went through a bad time, didn't she, after your brothers died? In 1868, wasn't it? And when was Mena born?'

'1869,' Alice said, in a low voice. 'Oh, Richard, it's not true, is it?'

He threw his cigar away and pulled her to his knee. 'Love, I'm sorry, I'm really sorry, but Mena has always had a look of you, you know.'

'I look like my mother, she couldn't look like me!'

'She has the Wintour nose.'

As Alice stared blankly at the morning-glory flowers twisting round the patio, Richard said, gently:

'Does it matter? You've always felt an affinity with Mena, haven't you? Perhaps this is why.'

'Charlotte is my full sister and I have no affinity with her whatsoever. Oh, it does matter, Richard, it does! If it were true, it would be so unfair, wouldn't it, that we should be sisters? When you compare my life and Mena's? I shan't know where to look when I see her again.'

'You must never say anything to her,' he said quickly. 'For your father's sake.'

'For hers,' Alice replied.

Later, when Mena brought in the lamps, Alice, taut as a wire, looked up and smiled.

'Thank you, Mena. Would you – would you help me finish my packing?'

'Sure I will, Miss Alice.' Mena turned to Richard. 'There's a letter for you, sir. Delivered by hand it was, not ten minutes ago.'

'Oh?' He took it from her. 'Did you see who left it?'

'A messenger from Mr Stonefield. Shall I be holding the lamp for you, Mr Richard, while you read it?'

'No, thanks, I can manage.'

As Mena curtsyed and withdrew and Alice watched her, Richard opened the letter and scanned its contents. Then he raised his eyes to Alice and in the lamplight she saw them glitter.

'It's from Edward, Alice. He has just received word that

270

Felipe Sentos is dead. A heart attack, it seems. The lawsuit is to be withdrawn.'

They stood together, too stunned to speak. Alice could feel Richard's arm trembling, sense his heart pounding. At last he said, in a voice thick with emotion:

'It's over, Alice. All the worry. It's over.'

'I'm so happy for you, Richard.' She kissed him and would not think of Mena, her newfound sister, or herself. Exiles both from Belcarron.

Thirty-Five

John Wintour was walking alone in the grounds of Belcarron. It wasn't possible to see much; a soft November mist hung over the trees and the sea and coated the grass so that his footfalls left a silver trail of moisture disturbed. He didn't mind the weather, it was right for this time of year, as Belcarron was right for him at all seasons. If Alice and Richard wanted to live in a land where the sun shone and flowers bloomed in November, that was their choice, not his, but at the thought of them out there in the Argentine, a knifelike pain entered John's heart and he had to walk quickly to the clifftop to put them out of his mind.

Now he could hear the sea crashing below but not see it and he stood for a while by the bushes, smelling the salt air. Soon he would go back to the empty house, work on his accounts in the study by the fire, and try not to think of Alice or Richard or Ernestine. He missed his wife more than he had ever thought possible. Everywhere, he expected to see her, moving dreamily through the house or the garden, clutching her brushes, shaking back her dark hair and calling to somebody to come and be painted.

'She should never have gone first,' he muttered. 'She was younger than me, she didn't have a bad heart or anything – why was she taken?'

Foolish talk, he knew, everyone had to go when their time came, even if those who were left didn't think it the right time. Look at Dudley Sarn, snuffed out before the age of thirty . . . but then he had brought his going on himself and was no loss, even to Charlotte. Perhaps especially not to Charlotte.

At the thought of Charlotte, John heaved a long sigh. She was away at the time, staying with Edie Morry and her new husband, some fellow from the north who'd made a fortune manufacturing thread. Or was it linen? Most of the county had expressed disapproval, anyway, but Edie wasn't the kind to worry what people thought and as long as the bridegroom was prepared to take a house for her hunting every winter, that was all she cared about.

Charlotte said, 'And quite right, too,' but then she was dazzled by money these days, even money from trade. As she had admitted to her father, she was tired of being the Honourable Mrs Dudley Sarn and would be quite happy to be plain Mrs Nobody, as long as there was cash in the bank.

And Belcarron to spend it on? John turned back to the house, wondering. Charlotte was better than no one to have around, he was glad of her company, but he knew she was waiting for him to make her his heir and whether that was right or not he couldn't decide. Certainly, to think of Richard or Alice now was pointless, they would never come back from the Argentine. On the other hand, Charlotte was a widow and might marry again. There was the rub. What sort of fellow might she take on next time? She hadn't made much of a choice first time round . . .

The fire in the study was welcoming after the raw chill of the cliffs and when Nora had taken away his damp coat and hat, John sank into his armchair with a sigh of relief. Often these days he found himself putting off problems in favour of a rest or a cup of coffee or even a nap, but this morning he couldn't relax as usual because Nora was still hovering around.

'What is it, Nora?' he asked finally, and she blushed and looked down at her feet.

'Did you want to speak to me? Is there something wrong?'

'Oh, no, sir, nothing at all. It's just, well, it's married I'm planning to be.'

Married? He couldn't believe it. Marriage and Nora, somehow he'd never associated the two. And yet there was no reason why she shouldn't marry, she was attractive enough and, though not overfond of work, had been well trained and would make a good wife. So few Irishmen seemed to want wives, good or otherwise, he wondered where she had found someone and asked who was the lucky man.

Still scarlet in the face, Nora said his name was Joseph Heenan, he was from Skibbereen where his father was the butcher and he was Mrs Heenan's nephew by marriage, so he was, and wasn't she delighted to be having Nora coming into the family?

'Well, I'm delighted for you too,' John said. 'I couldn't be more pleased for you and wish you every happiness.' But then an unpleasant thought came into his mind. 'Why, I suppose you'll be leaving us, Nora? What on earth shall we do? We shall have to find another parlourmaid.'

'And isn't Maisie, the housemaid, just dying after my job, sir? I was after telling her I'd put in a word.'

'But then we shall have to find a housemaid. Oh, dear, Nora, you'd better see Miss Charlotte about this.'

Nora, sniffing her opinion of Charlotte's ability to find servants, said if he didn't mind another Donovan, wasn't Mrs Donovan looking for a place for her Bridie? Bridie, who was Mena's sister, seventeen years old and working as kitchen-maid for the priest? Sure, she'd not be bad at all, Nora added, magnanimously, for a Donovan.

John sat shading his face from the fire, his thoughts going not to Mena or Bridie but to their mother, Maureen, a pretty woman still, who had been even prettier twenty-two years ago. She had never said the baby was his, sure it could just as well have been her husband's, she had laughed, but he had gone through a bad few months until it was certain the little girl was not going to have his yellow hair. The nose, now, that wasn't so obvious – noses took a long time to take their final form – but he'd paid his dues anyway and when the Wintour nose appeared as plain as plain to him on the girl who was to be his housemaid, well, he'd been glad he'd got off so lightly. He didn't think anyone had ever suspected, people didn't look closely at servants' faces, but when Ernestine had painted Mena's portrait, there'd been a few more bad moments and even now he wasn't sure whether his wife had known or not. Probably she would have forgiven him, anyway. Ernestine was generous in understanding and she had refused him her bed for years after the boys were taken. Strange, though, the way Alice had always shown such affection for Mena, almost as though she had known she was her sister and preferred her to Charlotte. Yet he was certain neither Alice nor Charlotte had any idea of the truth and now that Mena was away in the Argentine he had no need to worry. As for Bridie, if she came to Belcarron he could pass her in the corridors without looking the other way; she, thank God, could not have the Wintour nose.

He told Nora he would be quite happy if young Maisie were promoted to parlourmaid and Bridie Donovan taken on as housemaid, but Belcarron would not be the same without Nora herself, he did not like changes and she would be missed.

'Oh, sir,' Nora murmured delightedly, but added it was to be hoped Mrs Heenan was not after leaving too. It was tired she was, specially with Miss Charlotte in the house, wanting this and that and the moon.

'New dishes for her entertaining,' John grunted. 'Yes, I understand, leave it to me, Nora. I'll have a word with Miss Charlotte when she returns. Now, would you be so good as to get me some coffee?'

But with the coffee came visitors.

'Mrs Daniel Molloy,' Nora announced, with a deep frown, showing in Hester.

'And me!' cried Paul.

'Hester!' John exclaimed, advancing gladly to take her hands. 'How cold you are! Come by the fire. Nora, a cup for Mrs Molloy, please, and a ginger nut for Master Paul.'

Hester, still in black, looked pale and drawn, yet happy enough as she put back her veil and sipped her coffee. Paul, eating his biscuit, was looking round the study with interest, finally asking where Cousin Charlotte might be, he hoped she was not out.

'I'm sorry, my boy, she is away, visiting some friends,' John told him. 'But I'll tell you what, if I ring this bell Nora will come and if you are a good boy, she'll take you to the kitchen and give you another ginger nut. Would you like that?'

276

'Yes, please, Great-Uncle John,' said Paul with a sigh. As Nora led him away, Hester smiled.

'Charlotte's most faithful admirer ... I dare say he will remember her even when we're in America.' At her uncle's look, she nodded and put down her coffee cup. 'It's what I came to tell you, Uncle, we are to join Daniel in New York.'

'Oh, no, Hester, no!'

John stared at her, visibly distressed. Since the tragedy of Dudley Sarn's death, he had come to know and respect his niece, who might have adopted strange ideas but who was a woman of principle, Matthew's daughter to the marrow, someone he felt he could ill afford to lose.

'Why, my dear, sink in your lot with Daniel, when he is so clearly unstable? To say nothing of having a charge over his head in this country which will mean prison if he ever returns.'

'I know it was wrong of him to jump bail at the time, Uncle, but in America he has begun to see things more clearly, more rationally. He has lost the terrible grudge he had against our family, he is even more understanding of Parnell ...' Hester hesitated, raising her dark eyes to John's face. 'He is actually happy, although it seems strange to say so. Happier than he has ever been before. So, he wants us to go to him.'

John poked the fire gloomily. 'Well, I suppose you know what you're doing. But what about your parents? What do they make of it all?'

'They've accepted my decision, they understand I must be with my husband.'

'You'll be going to see them?'

'Yes, we sail in December, I shall go to see them in Dorset before then.' Hester moved to take John's hand. 'Please don't be sad for me, Uncle, I know I'm doing the right thing. We shall have a better life in America than here, because of the circumstances, and we'll still be able to work for Ireland.' She looked down, her voice breaking a little. 'I'm just so sorry for what happened here. But Daniel was not himself that night, he truly wasn't, and he never, I swear, meant any harm to Dudley.'

'I know that, Hester. It was Dudley who would have

277

harmed him, but that was because he thought he meant to do violence.'

'He was ill, Uncle John, quite ill. I blame myself, I should have prevented his coming.'

They had both risen, Hester standing in John's encircling arm, almost in tears, but he kissed her brow and told her it was all in the past, she must put it behind her now and think of her new life and her children.

'It's always the children we must put first,' he reflected. 'They are the future. Your Paul is a fine boy, Hester, just such another as my brother Matthew. So is Alice's Jack, and Victor, he's another Richard. It's strange, though, to think there will be Wintours in the Argentine and New York.'

'There are Wintours still at Belcarron, Uncle.'

He shook his head. 'I haven't much hope of Charlotte's ever having a family. As for me, I'm getting old.'

There was nothing Hester could say. She knew her uncle's burden of grief was not only for her Aunt Ernestine.

Later, John drove her to St John's Church, Carron, where they walked through the hanging mist to the Belcarron gravestones. Here were the monuments for previous Johns and Richards and Matthews, weathered and sinking, for they had never made a family vault. Here was the sad little angel marking the spot where John's young sons had lain since 1868, and next to it the new white marble memorial for Ernestine Anne, Dearly Beloved Wife of John Wintour of Belcarron, Born 19 January, 1840, Died 6 April, 1891.

'There's space on that for me, you see,' said John, pointing with his stick. 'It's a comfort, in a way, to know one's resting place.'

Hester, uttering no platitudes, took his arm and pressed it, and they both turned slowly away.

Back at the house, when she and Paul were ready to leave with the trap from Skibbereen, John kissed them both and asked Hester to write.

'I was hard on you once,' he muttered. 'I'm sorry about it now. You had a right to do what you wanted with your life.'

'I understood, Uncle, I always understood. But people

have been kind, you know. I've had a lot of understanding myself.'

'You'll keep in touch, then?'

'Of course I will. Give my love to Charlotte, tell her I'm so sorry I missed her.'

'And me,' said Paul, as the trap bore them away, 'tell her I was sorry too.'

If only I had capital to settle on people, John thought, sitting again in his study after his solitary dinner. I'd like to leave Hester and her children something – God knows how that rascal will be able to provide for them in America. And then little Mena, I could leave her a hundred pounds but it would set tongues wagging – unless I were to say, 'for services to her mistress', something of that sort. What an odd thing it was he should have two daughters by different mothers and both end up nine thousand miles away from home! Just as well as far as Mena was concerned, maybe, but Alice – oh, God, that was different . . .

The pain of thinking about her held him again as in a vice and he sweated and groaned and reached for his pills.

This is the way I'll go, he thought, as he gradually felt easier. Quietly, in my chair, alone. And in the Argentine, they won't even know.

Thirty-Six

Nine thousand miles away or not, Alice thought constantly of her father. Leaving him without the consolation of her mother had been one of the hardest things she had ever had to do and though the months had gone by, she still could not forget that last look on his face when they parted, his last words; 'Shall we ever meet again?' It was selfish, she knew, to brood, to indulge herself in homesickness, for the Argentine was her home also and she had her own family to consider, but she could not throw off the feeling that she had seen her father for the last time.

It helped to busy herself with the routine of the *estancia*, where at first nothing seemed to have changed, but Richard had the capital now to begin making plans again and change was on the way. He had been talking to other *estancieros* in Buenos Aires and all were agreed; cattle and sheep were fine, essential to the Argentine economy, but the coming thing was wheat production, they'd been crazy not to think of it before.

'Look at America, look at Canada!' Richard urged Alice. 'They've made fortunes out of grain and we have the land to do the same. We'd be fools not to use it!'

Of course, initial outlay would be expensive, there would be new equipment to buy, more men to take on, but the Argentine was already choked with immigrants wanting jobs, labour was no problem, and Rosario, the next largest city to BA, was planning to build huge grain stores. If the export trade could be built up, there was no saying how far the new trade could take prosperity.

'Sounds wonderful,' Alice observed. 'But it's not so long ago you were bemoaning changes on the pampas. What's going to happen to the gauchos if all this comes about?'

'I don't know. I'm hoping we can keep some sort of compromise with the old ways.'

'With your lovely wild horses,' Alice said gently.

'The pampas is pretty big,' he answered, after a pause. 'No one is suggesting it all goes over to agriculture. The thing is, as a country, we can't afford to stand still.'

'And where's the money coming from for all this expansion?'

'Investment. Britain's always invested here, but Edward says other countries are seeing the potential and the money's coming in. It's not boom time again, but things are looking up.'

'I'm glad to hear it.' Alice rose. 'So do you think you could tell the poor threatened gauchos to put that beast they're killing out of its misery? They seem to want to make it bellow as much as possible and it does so upset Jack. He crawls under his bed and howls in sympathy.'

'There has to be butchery, Alice, we do need meat.'

'Yes, but they could kill quickly, couldn't they? Even animals in the wild do that.'

'I'll speak to Lucio,' he muttered, not relishing the look in the gauchos' black eyes when he told them to be less cruel. Less cruel to an animal? They could not have understood it if he had told them to be less cruel to a man. Was it women he wanted them to be? Pain and suffering were part of life and definitely part of death, at least in the Argentine, which was the only world they knew.

The long summer days of December and January were excessively hot. The pampas grass turned yellow and the dead thistles brown. Everything was tinder dry, there was the constant fear of fire and no prospect of rain. Unless the *pampero*, the violent southwest wind, arrived, in which case there could be thunder and lightning and a tempest that drove all before it. But afterwards there would be cool air and grass free from thistles and the pampas would be itself again.

'I pray to the Lord it come soon,' said Vittoria, who had come over from Buenos Aires to replace Paola, occupied with yet another baby girl and keeping to her quarters at the back of the house.

'I, too,' sighed Alice, who had been checking sugar stores in the kitchen. Soon it would be time for the peaches and apricots to ripen and they would be making conserves and jams and bottling for days on end; in heat like this, it would be unbearable. She yawned and stretched and drank thirstily from a glass of fruit juice as Mena came in, moving slowly and fanning herself with her handkerchief. Alice, trying not to think about Richard's revelation but failing as she always did, smiled and asked if Tina had fallen asleep.

'At last, Miss Alice,' Mena murmured and flinging back the shutters, opened the casement window.

'No, no!' cried Victoria, not wanting to let in the outside heat, but Mena said she must have some air, even air that felt like a blast from an oven, it was choking she was. For some moments she stood at the open window, as Alice, leaning back in her kitchen chair, idly watched her and the fiery air unfolded them. Then, as Alice had done, Mena yawned and stretched, raising her arms above her head, revealing as she did so the contours of her body. All the colour drained from Alice's face, leaving it white and cold.

'Oh, Mena,' she whispered. 'Mena – '

Mena swung round, her eyes going straight to Alice's. She put her hand to her lips and swayed, then, before either Vittoria or Alice could catch her, slipped to the floor.

'*Está embarazada, Doña Alicia,*' Vittoria whispered, half lifting Mena and putting her head to her knees. '*Si, si, embarazada!*'

'No, dear God, no!' Alice wailed, but Vittoria was smiling.

'*Si, Doña Alicia, está embarazada, pobrecita.*'

Poor thing, poor little thing. Yes, Mena looked that, lying now on her bed in her small room next to the nursery, her face as white as her coverlet, her blue eyes ringed with black.

'Miss, Alice, 'tis wicked I am,' she said, in a low voice. 'I was not wanting you to know, but – '

'You could not keep this hidden, poor Mena, I had to know sometime. But don't call yourself wicked, it is not

283

wicked to have a child, whatever the situation.' Alice gave a heavy sigh. 'Foolish, perhaps, when you're alone.'

'You are kind, Miss Alice, you are always kind, but what you're saying is not what the Church is saying. 'Tis wicked what I did, yes, I am believing it.' Mena moved her head restlessly against her pillow. ''Twas madness, only madness, and now I am thinking of Liam and if he is looking down at me, and of you, Miss Alice, you were after trusting me and I . . .' She closed her eyes and lay still. 'I am a sinner.'

'Mena, it will do no good to talk like this,' Alice said quietly. 'What's done is done, now we have to think of the future. All I want to do is help you. First you must tell me, when is the baby due?'

'May, I'm thinking, maybe June.'

'Have you seen a doctor?'

'I have not, Miss Alice.' Mena opened her eyes. 'Would I be seeing a doctor and me without a husband?'

'You must see one, all the same. I'll take you back to Buenos Aires and you shall see Dr Ward. He's very good, very understanding. But for now, I want you to try to rest.'

'Miss Alice, 'tis not rest I am needing.' Mena sat up and began to get out of bed. 'Who is to take care of Miss Tina if it's lying here I am?'

'In this heat, I insist you stay where you are.' Alice gently forced her back against the pillows. 'Remember, you must think of your baby now.'

Mena turned her head away without speaking. After a moment or two, Alice said softly:

'Mena, I have no right to ask you this, but I have to try to help. Who . . . who is the father?'

Mena remained silent.

'You know I don't wish to pry, but he must marry you, he must give the child a name.'

'Miss Alice, I cannot be telling you his name.'

'I want to speak to him, I want to make him see that he must stand by you.'

'He cannot, Miss Alice.'

Alice's heart sank. 'He is married already? Oh, Mena, what a muddle! What a terrible state of affairs . . . Where did you meet him? When you went out with the other maids in BA? Some café?'

Mena burst into tears and said she could say nothing, nothing, and Alice, deeply distressed, held her and soothed her until she grew calm.

'We'll say no more just now, Mena, it's too upsetting for you, but if you should ever want to talk to me, remember I'll always be ready to listen, to help.'

'Yes, Miss Alice.'

'Now, try to rest and I'll get one of the girls to bring you some supper later. Don't worry about Miss Tina, there are plenty of people to look after her.'

''Tis good you are, Miss Alice,' Mena muttered. 'Too good to one like me.'

'Don't talk nonsense. I'll look in on you later.'

An almost tangible heat still filled the house as Alice checked that Maria had care of the children and made her way to her own room, where she flung herself on the bed. Richard was out with Lucio but he would be back soon and she wanted a few moments to herself to think about Mena. Such an old, old story, yet always new in the misery it caused. Mena's own mother had been caught in exactly the same trap but had been more fortunate, she had a husband who would accept the child as his own, whereas Mena had no one. Poor, foolish girl . . . Alice, gasping in the heat, pulled off her dress and lay in her chemise and petticoats, wiping her face and arms of the slippery sweat that ran again as soon as it was sponged away.

This would not have happened if I had been here, she brooded, painfully. Or if I had made Mena come back with me to Ireland.

Why had she not come? Perhaps she had already met this man and did not want to leave him? But where could she have met him? She saw so few people. Even going out with the other servants, it was not likely she would have struck up acquaintance then; Argentine men did not approach respectable girls and Mena, with her sad air, her preoccupation with her dead Liam, would surely not have been a target anyway? Besides, the man was married. Where would Mena have met a married man and known him so well she had allowed him to make love to her?

Alice slowly sat up. The sky outside her bedroom window was darkening, even though it was still only afternoon, and birds were flying wildly past, screaming and calling.

'The *pampero*,' she whispered, and lit a candle with a shaking hand so that she might find a dress to put on. Normally, she would have been afraid, the *pampero*'s duration was a frightening experience, but her mind was filled with fear that had nothing to do with the wind.

'A married man,' she kept repeating. 'Where would Mena have met a married man?'

'Here,' she answered herself, 'in her own home'. On the *estancia*, in the house on the Avenida Lila, it did not matter, Richard would have been there.

Great drops of rain were falling now and rolls of thunder were following the jagged lines of lightning that were splitting the dark sky.

I must go to the children, thought Alice, but still stood with the flickering candle in her hand.

Why had Richard suddenly told her of Mena's likeness to the Wintours? He must have seen it long ago and never spoken, no doubt to spare Alice's feelings. Now on her return he had come out with it. Why? To cover himself, to prepare her mind so that if Mena's baby bore a likeness to him, it would only be because of her own Wintour heritage?

'Oh, God!' Alice shrieked as a clap of thunder sounded immediately overhead, making the whole house rock. Her limbs jerked free and she ran from the room to find the children.

All the mestizas were moaning and wailing in the vestibule, Vittoria was wringing her hands and Maria, holding Tina, was trembling from head to foot.

'Where are the boys?' Alice cried. 'Where are the boys?'

'Here, Mama,' called Victor, composedly, and he crawled out from under a table. 'Jack's under his bed where he always goes, but I wanted to see the lightning and I can see from here.'

'There's a good boy, but stay under cover, things can come down and hurt you in a storm like this.'

The great wind itself was now blowing, sending everything outside that was not fastened down turning and tossing through the air, and hailstones hurtled down like missiles being thrown. Birds were falling straight from the sky as though shot and those still alive were squawking and beating their wings. Melons and unripe peaches, bricks, fencing and huge branches of trees went whirling by.

'Vittoria, has anyone seen Don Ricardo?' Alice cried. 'Don Ricardo, Lucio – where are they? Dear God, not still out on the pampas?'

Vittoria had not seen Richard or Lucio, though the gauchos were back and locked with their horses in their own quarters.

'Go to Paola,' Alice ordered. 'She will be terrified and has the baby and the children – oh, Mena, what are you doing? You should have stayed in bed!'

'Miss Tina,' Mena muttered. 'Where is Miss Tina?'

Her eye found Maria and she ran to her and took Tina from her, as Maria collapsed against her, weeping with fear.

Suddenly Vittoria at the window shrieked that she could see Don Ricardo and Lucio, they had their horses and were trying to get to one of the barns. Alice ran and, as a flash of lightning illuminated the sky, saw Richard and Lucio bent double in the wind, hanging on to their terrified, rearing horses as the debris of the storm spun around them.

'Richard!' Alice screamed, though of course he could not hear her and she dared not open the door to go to him. 'Lucio! Oh, they will be hit, they must be, they can't move – oh, see those branches!'

'*Madre de Dios,*' whispered Maria, crossing herself, and everyone watching prayed aloud, whatever prayer came into their heads.

Victor, running to Alice, cried; 'Is it Papa? Is he out in the storm?'

'He is, my darling, but he will be safe; we'll pray to God that he will be safe, Señor Lucio, too. Jack, stay where you are, don't come out, you'll be safer there – '

'I want Papa!' cried Jack. 'I must see Papa!'

'Miss Alice, it's saved they are!' called Mena. 'Inside the barn, the horses and all, thanks be to God!'

'Gracias a Dios,' the women murmured.

'Gracias a Dios,' Alice echoed, and held the boys close.

Gradually, the *pampero* subsided, the sky cleared, and Richard and Lucio came stumbling across the dead birds and wreckage of the storm to the house. Paola had appeared, holding her latest baby, her face as dark as the clouds rolling away, but Lucio enfolded her and kissed her and Alice, in Richard's arms, saw nothing but his beloved face bending over hers.

'You're safe,' she whispered. 'Oh, Richard, you're safe!'

He wiped his streaming face and put back his hair, so wet it appeared dark, and stooped to hold Victor and Jack.

'Yes, thank God, I'm all right,' he muttered. 'But we'll have to wait till morning to see how much we've lost.'

'I suppose the orchards will have been wrecked?'

'Absolutely, you won't be doing too much bottling this year, my love. The vegetables have gone too and your garden flowers – '

'And the birds, the plovers – '

'And the stock. God knows how many animals have been hit out there.' Richard tried to laugh. 'But the thistles are gone, if that's any comfort.'

Alice, turning her head, saw Mena sitting with Tina and her heart plummeted as heavily as the damaged birds outside.

Thirty-Seven

Whatever happened, they still had to eat. As the household gradually returned to normal, breathing freely again in the beautifully cool air, Alice went to the kitchen to speak to Vittoria. Any sort of meal would do, she told her, just something cold perhaps, but Vittoria threw up her hands in horror. Of course there would be a good hot beef dish as usual, with tomatoes and peppers, there would be potatoes, there would be a pudding, *manzanas en miel*, apples in honey, the favourite of Don Ricardo. Never would he or Doña Alicia be asked to eat something cold from her kitchen! There would be a good wine, too, maybe, to celebrate the end of the *pampero*?

'Oh, yes, indeed,' Alice agreed, 'The best wine tonight, please, Vittoria.'

As she was turning away, Vittoria touched her hand and asked after the little Mena. Not too shaken by the storm? Ah, how sorry Vittoria was for her, such a sad little widow, men were the same the world over, yes?

Alice said perhaps they were, although she knew of course that Vittoria went to church whenever she could to pray to the Virgin for a husband, who had not so far appeared as Vittoria had no dowry.

Of course, everyone excused him, Vittoria was continuing. Who would not, knowing the sort of wife he had? Who would blame him if he had allowed his eyes to turn to the pretty little *Irlandesa*?

Alice stood very still. 'Vittoria, are you saying you know the father of Mena's baby?'

289

'*Cómo no!*' Vittoria gave her wide smile. 'Is Lucio!'

A great light seemed to fill the kitchen and Alice, though she felt she could have seized Vittoria and danced with her on the ceiling, had to sit down as her legs would not support her.

'Lucio, Vittoria? Are you sure? I mean, how can you know?'

'I see them when Don Ricardo bring them to BA,' Vittoria answered. 'I see the look Lucio give little Mena when the spying Paola is not there to make his life a misery. I know what I know, Doña Alicia, believe me, Lucio is the one. Maybe he make Mena happy, maybe he make her forget Liam for a little while, but in the end, you see, she pays. Always, always, is the woman who must pay!'

'Vittoria, does anyone suspect this apart from yourself? Does Paola?'

'Paola? If she suspect, Lucio is a dead man, but he is still alive, so she believe what others believe – Mena meet some wicked man in BA. Mena never say no to that.'

'You said everyone excused him, though – excused Lucio?'

Vittoria shrugged. She said, naturally, people wondered, Lucio was certainly fond of Mena, now here was Mena *embarazada* but then it was true, she might have met someone in BA, no one was accusing.

'Then we must pray Paola never finds out the truth, we must keep this absolutely to ourselves, Vittoria.'

'Doña Alicia, you need not tell me,' Vittoria said with dignity. 'Never would I cause trouble between man and wife!'

'Of course not, I am sorry.' Alice pressed her hand. 'You are good, you are loyal, Vittoria, I know that.'

'And you, Doña Alicia, you are good, also. You look after your little maid as though she were your sister.'

Alice started, then hastily recovered herself. 'It is only that I brought her here,' she said smoothly. 'I feel responsible for her. Now, I must go and change out of this terribly sticky dress. How lovely it is to feel cool again!'

Richard was tying his cravat and raised his eyebrows in surprise when Alice flew to him and kissed him passionately on the mouth.

290

'What's that for, my darling?'

'For being safe,' she answered lightly. 'For not letting the storm damage you.'

'Don't talk about damage!' He groaned. 'I don't know when we shall recover.'

'We are all safe, Richard, that's all that matters.'

'I know.' He held her a little away from him. 'So, what's the matter, then?'

She gave a rueful smile. 'I can never hide anything from you, can I? I'm afraid it's Mena.' The smile faded from Alice's face, leaving it pinched and anxious. 'She is to have a child.'

He drew back, his head jerking up a little. 'Mena? No, that can't be true. You must be mistaken.'

'I wish I were. She has told me herself that the baby is due in May or June.'

'Good God!' Richard finished tying his cravat. 'Who is the father? Will he marry her?'

'She wouldn't tell me his name, but she said he was married already.'

'But where one earth did she meet him? She's scarcely ever even out of the house!'

'I thought you had encouraged her to go out, meet people, in BA?'

'Yes, but that was only with the other girls, she wouldn't have met any men that way.' Richard turned troubled eyes on Alice as she began to lay out her clothes for the evening. 'What's to be done?'

'Heavens, you know what has to be done! We support her, we do what we can. After the child is born, well, I suppose it must be brought up on the *estancia*, but it will be awkward.'

'The Argentines adore children, they won't judge Mena too harshly and they'll probably make the child very welcome.'

'Yes, but Vittoria says the father is Lucio.'

'That's absurd,' Richard said, after a pause. 'How could it be Lucio? He is completely wrapped up in his family.'

'Yet I believe Paola has always been jealous of Mena. Maybe because she has sensed Lucio is attracted to her.'

'Who knows what Paola thinks? She is a stupid woman

291

and always has been. But Vittoria should watch her tongue. To take a man's character away, it's wrong, it's dangerous –'

'I suppose you couldn't . . .' Alice hesitated. 'Speak to him about it?'

'Speak to him? Of course I couldn't. The less said about this, the better.'

'But if he is responsible, Richard, he should help, shouldn't he? I mean, help financially?'

'And explain that to Paola?' Richard shook his head. 'We'll just have to do what we can for Mena ourselves. I'm afraid it's all going to be hard on you, Alice, your little protégée . . .'

'I blame myself, anyway. I shouldn't have left her.'

'Oh, that's ridiculous!' Richard began to brush his hair, attacking it fiercely, a hairbrush in each hand. 'She's a grown woman, isn't she? And you're not her nursemaid.'

Alice seemed not to be listening. 'Have you realised,' she asked, quietly, 'the child will be my nephew or my niece?'

Richard swung round from the mirror. 'I shouldn't dwell on that', he said shortly.

Thirty-Eight

On a cold afternoon in late April, Alice was in her room, packing a small case. Tomorrow she was to accompany Mena, not to BA as had first been planned, but to a convent five miles beyond San Vicente where the nuns ran a small hospital for local women and were said to be very kind and efficient. Vittoria had known of it and suggested Mena might be happier to go there rather than travel to the city, no easy matter for one in her condition. In the last few weeks she had grown very large and looked far from well, but no one commented, least of all Lucio, whose eyes those days were permanently cast down. Dr Marco, who attended the clinic at the convent, had pronounced Mena fit. He was sure she would have no problems; after all, bringing children into the world was a natural affair.

'Indeed,' Alice commented to herself. 'So why do so many women die?'

Would he agree to be present at the birth, she had asked, but he had said the nuns were experienced midwives, they would call him in if necessary.

'And the chloroform?'

'*Cloroformo?*' Dr Marco smiled. 'Come, there will be no need of that.'

'I should like it to be available, Dr Marco. Please obtain it.'

'Señora, the nuns would not know how to use it.'

'But you do. Please see that you have it and are present to be able to provide it. You will be well paid.'

With his reluctant promise, Alice had had to be content,

293

but her mind was not at ease. It was not so much Mena's physical condition that worried her, more her attitude towards the coming birth, which she seemed to see as no more than proof of her guilt.

'Come, try to take an interest,' Alice would say, putting sewing or knitting into Mena's hands. 'The child must have a layette, you know.'

And Mena would put in a few stitches or knit for a while, then put the work aside and let her hands fall idle. Alice guessed she was thinking of Liam, going over and over her failure to keep faith, her wickedness in carrying another man's child when Liam was gone. Life, it seemed, held no meaning for her at present, but pregnancy took women in strange ways. As soon as the baby was born, nature would see to it, Alice reasoned, that Mena wanted to live for her child's sake. Even in the poorest circumstances, women would do that, it was all part of the great trap in which they found themselves.

She fastened up her case and looked at her watch. Time for a cup of tea, she was thinking, when frantic knocks sounded on her door and Maria called to her to come at once, she was needed for the *Irlandesa*.

'Too late for the convent now,' thought Alice, running through the house, 'What are we to do?'

Mena's waters had broken and the first stage of her labour had begun. As soon as Alice went to her, she grasped her hand hard, staring up into Alice's face, speechless with fear.

'It's all right, Mena, it's all right, there's nothing to be afraid of. Haven't I had three children myself and weren't you with me every time?' Alice swung round on Maria. 'Please send to Dr Marco at once and tell him to be sure not to forget the chloroform.'

'*Cloroformo!*' cried a voice from the door and Paola strode forward to look contemptuously down on Mena. 'Who need this *cloroformo*? I have children, I need no *cloroformo*, I need no doctor! Why this one need so much?'

'If you would like to be of some use,' Alice said, coldly, 'Perhaps you would help the girls to make up a bed in a room away from the nursery?'

'I?' Paola stared, her face working with emotion.

294

'Please.' Alice, her chin high, returned the stare, but Paola walked away, tossing her black hair.

'Is not my job!' she called back over her shoulder, and Alice shrugged. If she had lost the round, at least she had also got rid of Paola, who would stay out of the way now. Turning back to Mena, she gave a smile of reassurance she did not feel.

The peon who had been sent for Dr Marco returned some hours later, accompanied only by a wizened little woman dressed in black who had ridden her own piebald pony side-saddle from San Vicente. This was Señora Calado, the local midwife, he explained, the doctor had sent her.

'Why has he not come himself?' cried Alice.

It appeared there had been a serious accident on a distant *estancia*, if possible he would come later.

'We are grateful to you for coming, then,' Alice said to the midwife, concealing her dismay, and showed her to the room where Mena lay, gasping as the contractions gripped her but making no sound. When the little woman went to examine her, Alice quickly suggested she might like to wash her hands first.

'*Qué?*'

'Perhaps she does not understand my Spanish,' Alice whispered to Maria. 'Please fetch hot water so that the Señora may wash.'

'*Entiendo!*' the midwife cried and plunged her hands into the basin of hot water, at the same time fixing Alice with a sharp black stare.

Please God, may she know what she is doing, Alice prayed, silently, May Mena pull through.

It was four o'clock the following morning that Mena was at last delivered of a fine boy. She had proved an exemplary patient, scarcely giving a cry until the end when she had clung to Alice's hand and uttered one long shriek as the baby emerged. The old midwife had been efficient and kind, alternately soothing and encouraging Mena in words of soft Spanish, handling her so gently she was not even torn, finally putting the wrapped, washed baby into her arms and shedding a quiet tear.

'Oh, Mena, it's always such a miracle,' Alice whispered, 'And he's so beautiful!'

Radiance had replaced the old apathy in Mena's expression as she looked down at her son.

'Beautiful,' she repeated. ''Tis right, Miss Alice, he is.'

'What shall you call him? Have you thought of a name?'

'Francis. 'Twas my father's name.'

Alice lowered her eyes. 'A fine name,' she murmured. 'You've done well, Mena, you've been very brave, I'm proud of you.'

A look of pain crossed Mena's face. 'Don't be saying that, Miss Alice, please.'

Alice, shaking her head, took the baby and laid him in the crib they had prepared. Mena must rest now before she gave the first feed, Maria would bring her some tea. Smiling, she touched Mena's cheek, then turned to the midwife who was about to leave.

'I can't thank you enough,' she whispered. 'Please take this for your fee.'

The old woman's black eyes lit up with pleasure as she examined the money Alice had given her. She said she was well satisfied and Alice, with a last look at Mena, showed her to the kitchen where Vittoria and Maria were already up, making tea.

'It's all over,' Alice told Richard, who was waiting for her in their room. 'Mena has a beautiful boy.'

'What a relief! It wasn't too bad for her, was it?'

'No, she got through very well and the midwife was excellent. I must admit, I was terribly worried at first, but no need. They're both fine.'

'Come to bed, then, you must be exhausted. Not that there's much of the night left now.'

'No, and I'm too excited to sleep. I think I'll go back to Mena and have some tea.' Alice pressed a lavender-soaked handkerchief to her brow. 'Tomorrow,' she added casually, 'you must tell Lucio the news.'

'As long as I don't have to tell Paola.'

'I'm afraid she'll be furious. A son first time for Mena . . . It's a mercy she does not know the truth.'

'We'll have to hope that the child does not look like Lucio. What colour eyes has he?'

'Blue, but then all babies have blue eyes. So far, if he looks like anyone, I think it's Mena.'

'Thank God for that, then,' said Richard.

Apart from Paola, everyone on the *estancia* liked Mena. They had mourned with her when Liam died and had never blamed her that she had 'fallen'; these things happened and at least she had been lucky enough to bring a man child into the world, who would support her in her old age and become the asset every male was thought to be to the community. In the first two days after the birth of the boy, everyone visited, even Lucio, still with his eyes cast down, even Paola, who had to conceal her chagrin. Silver coins and rosaries were laid on the baby's crib, and Mena looked happy and proud.

On the third day, Alice found her feeling not so well. She was running a fever and had internal pain. Milk fever, Alice thought, but Mena appeared to have no problems with feeding and the baby was particularly content.

'These things usually right themselves,' Alice said, comfortingly. 'But try to rest, Mena, that's most important.'

'Miss Alice, am I not resting? It's never a foot I am putting out of bed, but it's bad I'm feeling, all the same.'

Alice said she would send for Dr Marco.

After he had examined Mena, he smiled and said there was no cause for alarm, but in Alice's sitting room, he shook his head and looked grave.

'What is it?' she asked urgently. 'It's not – it's not childbed fever, is it?'

Puerperal fever. She knew how many lives were lost to that every year, everywhere, and was already gripped by apprehension.

'It is early to be sure, señora, but I have to tell you that is my present diagnosis.'

'But what can have caused it? We were so careful.' Alice's voice was rising. 'I made the midwife wash her hands, I am sure there can have been no infection.'

'There are a number of reasons for this condition, señora. You ask for the chloroform and now I bring it. I will examine the patient again under general anaesthetic.'

At first, Mena cried out in horror at the very idea, but

297

when she was told it would simply mean going to sleep, she submitted. Dr Marco discovered that a part of the placenta had been left behind and was giving rise to the infection. It was nobody's fault, one could not always be sure of these things.

'Have you removed it now?' Richard asked.

'I have, Señor Wintour.'

'Then she will be all right?' Alice's eyes had brightened.

The doctor hesitated. 'She has a better chance.'

'Chance? But if you have removed the cause – '

'The cause, yes, but not the infection. Now the patient must fight that herself.'

'What can be done?'

'If you permit, I should like to stay tonight. Are any of the women capable of nursing?'

'I shall do any nursing that is required,' Alice said, as Richard pressed her hand.

Neither Alice nor the doctor slept more than a snatch or two that night. Mena's fever did not abate and she groaned and tossed, only gaining relief from pain when Alice applied hot cloths to her abdomen. In the small hours, Dr Marco resorted to laudanum, which brought sleep, and as they watched Mena's exhausted face, he told Alice she should try to sleep too. For a little while she dozed as the doctor kept watch, but then the baby woke, crying with hunger, and Mena, struggling through the mists of laudanum had to feed him. Afterwards, her pain returned and her fever grew; Alice applied hot cloths again and so the night passed.

At daybreak when the *estancia* began to come alive, Mena seemed a little easier. Vittoria sat with her while the doctor rode home, promising to return shortly. Alice washed and changed and looked in on the children.

'You must have breakfast,' Richard said solicitously. 'There's no point in your making yourself ill, that would help no one.'

'I know, I know.' Alice drank coffee. 'But I'm so afraid, Richard, I'm really afraid.'

'She'll pull through, I'm sure she will. She's young and strong, there's no reason why she shouldn't.'

298

'The doctor said she must fight the infection herself. I don't know that she wants to.'

'Surely, when she has the baby – I thought you said she was so happy, so proud?'

'Yes, but he is not Liam's baby, is he?'

By the time Dr Marco returned in midafternoon, Mena was again distressed, her temperature very high, her pain acute. The hot cloths appearing to have no effect, Alice begged that she might be given more laudanum. The doctor agreed, but at the look on his face, Alice caught her breath.

'What is it? Doctor, what is it?'

'I am very much afraid – ' he ran a hand over his lined brow – 'that blood poisoning has set in.'

'*Madre de Dios!*' cried Vittoria, wringing her hands. Alice could not speak, only rocked a little on her feet.

'A wet nurse must be found,' the doctor went on. 'The mother is too ill now to feed her baby.'

'A wet nurse?' Alice was dazed. 'Wherever should we find a wet nurse? Someone in San Vicente?'

'No, no, Doña Alicia,' Vittoria put in quickly. 'Paola's little Isabella is only five months old, she is still feeding her and has plenty milk – '

'Paola!' cried Alice. 'You suggest we ask Paola?'

'Yes, yes, we ask her. She will agree, yes, you will see, Doña Alicia, Paola will not let a baby go hungry!'

As Mena drifted into heavy, drugged sleep, Paola appeared, triumphant-eyed.

'You wish me to feed the baby of the *Irlandesa*?' she asked.

'If you please, Paola.' Alice kept her eyes down. 'We should be very grateful. As you see, Mena is not well enough to feed her baby herself.'

Paola's gaze went over Mena, her glistening skin and dark wet hair, her closed, shadowed eyes. 'She will die, that one,' she said carelessly. 'I know. I see many, many like her.'

'Paola!' cried Vittoria, with a quick glance in Alice's direction, but Paola only shrugged.

'Give me the baby,' she said curtly.

As soon as the child was in her arms, her face changed,

softened, became wreathed in smiles, and as she carried him away, she sang.

Can this be Paola? thought Alice in amazement, and was relieved. Whatever Paola's feelings towards his mother, young Francis would not suffer. But of course Paola had no notion who was his father.

Afternoon passed into evening. Mena slept on, moaning and moving her limbs but not waking. Richard came and watched for a while, his face sombre, then asked if the doctor and Alice would like dinner. They said they would have something on a tray, but when it came only the doctor could eat. Alice tried, but her throat seemed to be closed, she could not swallow. Anyway, she was not hungry.

At ten o'clock, there was a change. Mena's fever abated and the doctor, feeling her hands, said they were very cold. She was no longer moaning, but still moving her legs beneath the bedclothes, and when the doctor laid down her hands, she began to pluck at the sheet.

'Doña Alicia,' the doctor said gently, 'I think you should send for the priest.'

Padre Bartolomé came and went, saying nothing of what passed between himself and Mena, except that she had accepted the last rites, thanks be to God. Then Lucio, ashen-faced, led Vittoria, Paola and the rest of the household in a sad pilgrimage to Mena's bedside, but she made no sign that she knew them. They wept and crossed themselves, but she lay perfectly still, even her hands on the sheet motionless, her face yellowish, her fine Wintour nose strangely prominent, her eyes closed. Richard asked Alice if he should wake the boys but she flinched and said not. It was not the custom, she knew, to shield children from family deaths, but she could not bring herself to try to explain Mena's. The boys had been puzzled enough by the death of their grandmother, whom they had scarcely known; to see Mena as she was now could only upset them. Especially Jack.

When she raised her eyes again, she saw that only she and the doctor remained at Mena's bedside.

Only a year ago, she reflected, she had sat like this beside her mother and watched and waited as she waited now. Who could have thought Mena would follow Ernestine so soon? It was difficult to accept that this death could be happening and with one part of her mind Alice knew she was not accepting it. Mena was too young, too strong, she should not be going like this, slipping away so quickly, without even a struggle. Yet the young did die and quietly, too. Liam had gone without a murmur; Alice's small brothers had moved from life to death with so little sign, it was impossible to tell when their breaths had stopped. Being young was no protection against death.

'Doña Alicia,' the doctor whispered, and Alice, ashamed that her eyelids had dropped, sprang up to find Mena's eyes open and resting on her own face.

'Miss Alice?'

'I'm here, Mena.' Alice smoothed the thick dark hair from Mena's brow.

'Miss Alice – '

'Don't speak, don't try to speak,' cried Alice. The breath was gurgling in Mena's throat, and her face, covered in sweat, was twisting in her last concentration.

'Miss Alice . . .' Her eyes seemed to be beseeching, she was longing to speak but no words came. Then the gurgling breaths ceased, the tired young face sagged. Still Mena's eyes remained open and fixed on Alice's face.

The doctor reached across and quietly closed them.

'It's absurd,' Alice told Richard, as she sat rigidly in her room, 'but Mena has gone and Paola is feeding her baby. Can that be right?'

'Hush, darling.' He guided her to the bed. 'Lie down now and try to rest.'

'Try to rest? I used to say that to Mena. She is resting now.'

'She is. She is at peace, Alice, you must remember that. At peace and with Liam.'

Alice, looking into Richard's face that was so dear to her, was grateful for his comfort. Yet somehow she had never felt so alone.

Thirty-Nine

Mena was buried in Liam's grave in Buenos Aires after a requiem mass in the Church of Santa Teresa. 'Sacred to the Memory of Liam Flynn' read his stone and at a later date would be added: 'Also, Philomena Mary, beloved wife of the above, 1869–1892, RIP.'

'Rest in peace,' Alice whispered. 'I am sure they do.'

Back at the house on the Avenida Lila, they sat by the fire and drank the *mate* tea Carlotta had brought them.

'Lucio did not come to the funeral,' Alice observed.

'I suppose he did not dare to show too much interest.'

She stared darkly into the crackling flames. 'I don't think I can ever forgive him, you know.'

'He's only human, Alice, and he couldn't know what would happen.'

'That's true and I don't want to sit in judgement, but all I can see is that he is alive and Mena is dead.'

'I don't suppose he has got off scot-free,' Richard said, after a pause.

'Perhaps not.'

When the tea things had been cleared, they sat on in silence for some time. Richard eventually spoke.

'It would have been difficult for Mena, you know, bringing up a child on her own. As it is, the boy will have a good home and a settled future, at least we can be glad about that.'

'What are you talking about?' Alice asked, staring. 'I don't understand you.'

'I'm sorry, darling, I should have told you before but I

303

didn't want to bring it up before the funeral. Lucio has asked if he might bring up Mena's son as his own. He and Paola want to adopt him.' As Alice seemed unable to speak, Richard added, hastily: 'You know how much they have both wanted a son.'

Her face working with emotion, Alice said at last: 'I can't believe what you're telling me, Richard! You are seriously suggesting Paola should bring up Mena's son without knowing her husband is his father? It would be wrong, it would be immoral. And Francis is my nephew, I intend to bring him up myself.'

'Now it is you who astound me!' Richard cried. 'You know it is quite impossible for you to bring up Mena's son with your own!'

'Why? Why is it impossible? As I say, he is my nephew.'

'But you cannot shame your father by letting any hint of that escape, so how would it look if you tried to make Francis the equal of Victor and Jack?'

'Mena was more than a maid to me, more than a half-sister. She was my very dear friend, she was sweet and loyal and thought more of my family than she did of herself. I won't hear you running her down, Richard!'

'I'm not running her down,' he said, desperately. 'But you must see that it is not practicable for us to bring up her son. Lucio and Paola will give him a good home and he need never know any other. Please be sensible about this, Alice.'

'I feel I owe it to Mena to take her boy,' she answered, worried now. 'She trusted me, you see, she always trusted me.'

'It is what Lucio wants,' Richard countered. 'To take the boy.'

Alice stood up and began to pace the room as the sky outside grew dark and the autumn day died.

'But what of Paola?' she asked. 'Is it right she should love Lucio's son by another woman when she has no idea of the facts?'

'It's not perfect, I agree, but this is a difficult situation for everyone. We can't take him and you wouldn't want Mena's family to take him, would you? Would you want him brought up in an Irish cabin?'

She shook her head.

'Well, then, we should let Lucio give him the best life he can, which is what he wants to do.'

'But if Paola were ever to find out the truth, Richard, what might she do?'

'Nothing to harm Francis. There's one thing about the Argentines, they adore children.'

Next day, Alice returned to the *estancia* alone. Richard had business with the bank and his suppliers but she was anxious not to leave the children too long. The absence of Mena, the sadness of the household, were all mystifying to them, and she felt she must be with them.

To arrive and find no Mena to greet her was piercingly hard, and each day would bring its own memories and burdens. She must just get through until time covered the wound. Of late she had been no stranger to grief, with the deaths of Beatrice and her mother coming only a year apart, but the loss of Mena was different even from these. She had been so close to Alice for so many years, from the time she had helped to dress her for balls and her wedding, to the long hours of childbirth when she had sat with Alice, wiping her brow, holding her hand. When they had sailed for the Argentine, Mena had been with them; when she had wanted to marry Liam, it was Alice she had asked. When Liam had died, it was Alice she had sought for comfort; and when the final papers were signed and the *estancia* was theirs, it was Mena who had opened the champagne.

And now she was gone. I shall never find another like her, Alice thought. I gained more from her than she ever gained from me and I know I shall miss her for the rest of my life.

The children, though, were her comfort, and delighted to see her back. Jack, it seemed, was also relieved.

'He worry you will die, Doña Alicia,' Maria told her.

'I?' cried Alice, sweeping Jack into her arms. 'That is foolishness, Jack, I'm not going to die.'

'Mena died,' he answered solemnly.

'But Mena was ill and I am not ill.'

'She died and was taken away and you went away.'

305

'But only to Buenos Aires with Papa. And you see I'm back now.'

'Papa is not back.'

'Oh, dear!' Alice tried to laugh. 'You're like a little dog, Jack, counting everyone in the family and not happy until everyone is home. People will always be going away, my darling, you mustn't think every time they're going to die.'

'I told him he was silly,' Victor declared. 'I told him and told him but he wouldn't listen.'

'Wouldn't listen,' Tina repeated, climbing on to Alice's knee and slipping a plump hand into hers. 'Jack wouldn't listen, Mama.'

'Well, he will listen to me, as you all will. It is true that some people die but it's only when they are old or very, very ill. Papa and I are not old and we are not ill, so there is no need to worry. Now, you must go with Maria, for I must visit Paola.'

'Paola has Mena's baby,' Victor said, with his important air. 'Somebody had to take it or I expect it would have died.'

'It's not old, so is it ill?' asked Jack.

'Babies need feeding, that's all, Jack, as everyone does,' Alice replied, rising, but Jack caught at her hand.

'Why couldn't we have had it, Mama? We could have fed it and I'm sure it would much rather live with us than Paola. She is so very cross, isn't she?'

'Go with Maria,' Alice whispered. 'Later, we'll all have tea together.'

Lucio and Paola had been given some rooms at the back of the house which they had made into a pleasant apartment, with a patch of grass outside a glass door where the little girls could play when it was fine. Today, though, was cold and wet, and everyone except Lucio was around the fire.

'Buenas tardes,' Alice said politely to Paola. 'How are you?'

Paola, sitting with Isabella, her own baby, on her knees, nodded and said she was well. Anna and Carlotta, the older girls, were playing with dolls at her feet and in the corner, tucked into a small crib, slept Francis Flynn. Alice, giving the girls sweets she had brought from BA, smiled at their ecstatic cries and went to have a peep at Mena's son.

306

'It's so good of you to nurse him, Paola,' she murmured. 'And he looks so well, I congratulate you.'

Paola shrugged and said someone had had to do it. Alice sat down. 'Is it true your husband wishes to adopt him?' she asked hesitantly.

'He wants a son.' Paola's large dark eyes were expressionless. 'And here is one nobody wants.'

'That is not quite true. I might have adopted him myself.'

'You?' Paola laughed, harshly. 'That would be a joke.'

'I beg your pardon?' Alice flushed, darkly. 'I don't understand you, Paola.'

'No?' Paola swung her baby to her shoulder and rocked her to and fro. 'Then I ask you, what woman would agree to bring up her husband's bastard? Not you, I think, Doña Alicia.'

The room swung and Alice with it, then righted itself as the instinct for self-preservation told her this was exactly what she might have expected Paola to say.

'You no understand me?' Paola asked, in English.

'I understand what you say is not true,' Alice answered, clearly.

'Is true. And is your fault. *Es toda su culpa!*' As her words began to flow, quickly and spitefully, Paola reverted to Spanish. 'A woman who leaves her husband has only herself to blame. Don Ricardo is a man, he needs a woman, and who is there, waiting, but your own little Mena? So like you, Doña Alicia! Pretty soft hair, pretty little face, big blue eyes. Oh, yes, is Mena, all ready to replace you. And you are surprised? Never would I have gone away if I had been you!'

'Paola, it isn't true, I know it isn't true!' With a supreme effort, Alice tried to take control. 'I know because the real father is – '

'Yes?' asked Paola mockingly.

'Is someone Mena met in BA. Ask the girls, ask anyone, they will tell you.'

'Those girls? Vittoria? They say anything to suit you. Mena never met any man in BA.' Paola brought her heavy face close to Alice's. 'But I know the truth because my Lucio, he tell it to me.'

'Lucio?' Alice drew back. She was very pale.

307

'My Lucio is a man of honour. Never would he ask me to take the boy without the truth. Don Ricardo, he ask Lucio to help, he say he has got the *Irlandesa* with child and you must never know. So Lucio, he agree to take the boy and I say yes.'

There was a silence in the small, overheated room. Even the children were quiet, staring with huge eyes from Alice to their mother.

'So I have told you,' Paola muttered. 'And God forgive me, for I swore I never would. But I say is right, is always right, to hear the truth.'

'Yes,' Alice replied. 'Yes, Paola, it is right.'

Forty

She crept through the old house, shadowlike, keeping close to the walls as though that way she would not be seen. When she reached her bedroom, she slipped inside and locked the door.

A cheval mirror stood near her dressing table and for a long time she gazed at her own reflection. She remembered looking at herself in the same considering way before the Fitzmirran ball, long ago. She had thought herself beautiful but had feared it meant nothing. And she had been right to be fearful – that was the night Richard had proposed to her sister. He had never really loved her, she decided, not as she loved him. He said he did, perhaps he believed it, but when the test came, he had seduced her maid, the one other person in the world she had trusted as she trusted him.

How quick she had been to believe Vittoria! How gladly she had lapped up the story about Lucio as a cat laps cream! Yet when Mena had first said her lover was married, hadn't she been terrified he might have been Richard? She remembered the night of the *pampero* and the suspicions that racked her because he had suggested Mena was a Wintour, she remembered her fear that he might be harmed in the storm, her relief when he was safe, her joy when Vittoria had said what she had said. Poor Lucio, how happy she had been to malign him, and Richard had let her do it. 'He's only human,' he had said, and no doubt had been thinking of himself. When people were described as 'human', it never meant anything good, only foolish, weak or even wicked. Which of these was Richard? Not wicked, no, she would not say that, but weak. And Mena? Mena had been foolish, very, very foolish. And she had paid with her life. That was because she was a woman, 'daughter of Eve', as the churchmen said. Women must always pay a higher price for love than men.

Very deliberately, Alice took off her black dress and tossed it on the bed. She crossed to the large Spanish wardrobe and picked out a blue dress with a pin-tucked bodice and elegant sleeves and put it on. Naturally, without Mena to help her, she disarranged her hair and had to take it down and brush it and put it up again. Her loss was beginning to sink in as a wound's bleeding soaks and spreads. She felt it as a physical pain and put her hand to her heart. The room was growing dark but she could not bear to light a candle. She sat on alone, facing the death of the Richard she had adored and the new death of Mena, as terrible in its way as her real death five days before.

Gradually it came to her that she must find relief, must staunch this wound that was draining her. She could do nothing about Richard, what he had done could not be undone, but Mena – Mena was different. Alice knew the last thing Mena would have wanted to do was hurt her; therefore the blame for what had happened should not be Mena's. She was young and inexperienced, had never known love, even with Liam, for by the time they were married he was already dying. How could she have known what Richard wanted? Alice remembered his violent lovemaking on her return from Ireland. 'Sorry I was a bit rough,' he had muttered. 'It's what happens when a fellow has to wait, you see . . .' Well, Mena had been there and he had not waited. 'Fellows' were like that, of course . . .

Poor girl, poor Mena, thought Alice. She had no one to turn to, no one to tell. Right until the end, she had had no one to tell. The one person who had always helped her in the past was the one person this time she could never ask.

Alice leaped to her feet and fumbled in the dark to light the candle, then by its light changed from the blue dress back into the black. She had finished once again pinning her hair when a young voice at the door called,

'Mama, Mama, are you there? You said you would come to tea, you *promised*, and you never came!'

'It's all right, Jack, dear, I am coming now.'

She had not shed a tear, she thought she must look well, but when Victor saw her in the lamplight, he asked her if she had been crying.

'No, I have not. Why do you ask?'

'Because you look so strange. I thought you must have been crying for Mena again. You cry a lot for her, don't you?'

'I do,' said Alice.

When Richard returned from BA, Alice, pale and slight in her black dress, was waiting. At the look on her face, he asked at once what was wrong – it wasn't the children?

'It's not the children.'

In their room, they faced each other, Richard still in his outdoor coat. Alice, sounding strange even to herself, said:

'Richard, Paola has told me the truth.'

'The truth? About what?'

'Oh, please.' She shook her head wearily. 'Let's not pretend any more. I know you're the father of Mena's child, you may as well admit it.'

He went quite white, then the familiar mottling suffused his face. Very deliberately, he unbuttoned his coat and hung it up. He turned to Alice.

'You have accepted what Paola told you without even giving me a hearing?' he asked quietly. 'The word of a servant who hates you?'

'Hates me? You think she is telling lies because she hates me?'

'It's obvious. You always spoiled Mena and she was jealous of Mena. Now she has seen her chance to destroy your happiness and protect her own. If she can make you believe I was Mena's lover, she can hurt you and delude herself. Naturally, she has to believe that Lucio is innocent.'

'How easy it is for you to say that,' Alice said bitterly.

'There's nothing easy in this, Alice. There's no way you can ever be sure. You must choose between Paola's word

311

and mine.' Richard looked away. 'After what we've been to each other,' he added, in a low voice, 'I'm surprised you find that difficult.'

Alice sank into a chair and bowed her head. How strange! Somehow, Richard had managed to put her in the wrong. Perhaps she was. She looked up at him, her face so strained, her eyes so lost then he took a step towards her as though he would have taken her in his arms. But she put up her hands against him and he turned aside.

'I want to believe you,' she muttered, 'God knows I do, but I've been through so much these past days, I can't . . . not now . . . I can't. I'm sorry.'

He moved heavily towards the door, where he looked back at her.

'How tired you look,' he whispered. 'You've been putting yourself through hell. Will you try to rest?'

She made no reply and after a long, trembling silence he left her. At once, she sent a message to Lucio, asking him to see her in her sitting room.

'You wished to see me, Doña Alicia?' he asked, his handsome face apprehensive in the lamplight.

'Yes, Lucio, please sit down.'

As he uneasily took a chair, she remarked on the black tie he was wearing for Mena.

'You were fond of her, Lucio?'

He swung his hat in his hands. 'Everyone like Mena, Doña Alicia.'

'But she meant something special to me, Lucio. I feel I must . . . I must know . . .' Alice put her hand to her brow. 'Lucio, you understand me, don't you?'

'Señora?'

'Please, please help me. Please tell me who is the father of her son?'

A dark colour rushed into Lucio's lean face and he stood up, pushing back his chair.

'Doña Alicia, I cannot, you know I cannot answer you.'

She took his hand and looked up into his face, her own so troubled, so beautiful that he lowered his eyes.

'No, no, do not ask me, do not ask me!'

She continued to grip his hand in her own. 'Is it Don

312

Ricardo, Lucio? I demand you answer me. Is it Don Ricardo?'

'No! Not Don Ricardo, not Don Ricardo!'

She released his hand and took a step away. 'Thank you,' she said.

'Doña Alicia, please let us not speak of this. Please let me leave you.'

'Very well, Lucio.'

As he went to the door, she followed. 'You are very loyal. I appreciate it. *Muchas gracias*.'

He wished her goodnight, a hunted look in his eyes, and escaped, while Alice slowly made her way to the dining room, where Richard was already waiting.

'I'm sorry I'm late.' She took her place at the foot of the massive oak table, brought over many years before from Spain by the Sentos family. 'I have been talking to Lucio.'

Richard started, then drew his brows together. 'Are you going to tell me why?'

'Let's wait until coffee.'

'As you please.'

They did not speak again until they were alone in the *sala*, the coffee tray before them. Alice passed Richard a cup, he lit a cigar.

'You don't mind if I smoke?'

'Of course not.'

'I feel I need it.' As she said nothing, he said, savagely: 'For God's sake, tell me what he said!'

'He said you were not the father of the child.'

'You asked him? You actually asked my manager a thing like that?'

'You told me I should choose between Paola's word and yours, but I thought there might be another way of finding the truth.'

Richard, trembling, drew on his cigar. 'So, do you think you've got it?'

'I don't know.'

'You don't know! Lucio tells you the truth and you won't believe it? Because you've already made up your mind not to believe it? Do you understand what you're doing to me, Alice?'

313

'I know what you're doing to me, Richard.'

'I have done nothing – nothing!'

They were staring at each other with anguished eyes, Alice's bright with tears she would not shed.

'Oh, Richard, what is happening to us?' she whispered. 'We are tearing ourselves to pieces.'

'All I know is, I love you, Alice.'

'And I love you.'

'Then for God's sake why are we behaving like this?' He threw his cigar into the fire and knelt on the floor beside her. 'Look, let's put all this out of our minds, be as we were, nothing between us – '

'I can't, Richard, I can't. I want to, but it's no use, I can't – at least, not yet.' She began to sob.

'Very well.' He got to his feet. 'We'll talk in the morning.'

But in the morning a cable was brought over from San Vicente. John Wintour was dead. Belcarron had been left jointly to Alice and Charlotte. Richard had been omitted from the will.

'I can't forgive him,' Richard said harshly. 'He promised he would leave me Belcarron and he has broken his word. I can never forgive him.'

Alice, sorting clothes for packing in her steamer trunk, raised reddened eyes.

'You are speaking of my father who has died, Richard.'

'Your father and my uncle and I loved him. But I never believed he could do a thing like this.'

'Surely you understand why? You have a property and a good living here. Charlotte has nothing.'

'He could have included me the way he included you. After all, how will you two women manage? Neither of you has the faintest idea of how to run an estate.'

'We can learn. As you did.'

'You and Charlotte?' Richard smiled coldly. 'You know what will happen, don't you? You'll collect the rents and she'll spend the money. God help us, your father must have been crazy – '

'Would you excuse me, Richard?' Alice turned aside angrily. 'I have a great deal to do.'

314

He straddled a chair, watching her. 'This has worked out well for you, hasn't it, Alice? You're getting what you've always wanted.'

'At a price.' Her voice shook.

'You mean me?' Richard left the chair and came close to her. 'You are exchanging me for Belcarron?'

'Don't talk like that!'

'But you are intending to stay?'

'I don't know.'

'And what about the children? They're mine, too, you can't separate them from me for ever. Unless you are planning a divorce?'

She flinched, as though he had aimed a blow. 'Divorce? Oh, Richard, we have moved a long way apart if you can think of that!'

'I'm not thinking of it, you know it's the last thing I want. But you're going to Ireland, I must know where I stand. As I say, you're taking the children – '

'You're only thinking about the children?'

'No!' He took her suddenly into his arms. 'No, I am not only thinking of the children.' Their mouths met in a long, desperate kiss, then Richard pulled himself away and groaned. 'Alice, how am I going to get through without you?'

'Come with me! Please, come with me!'

'No, things are critical here.' He hesitated. 'Besides, I don't want to. I have no place at Belcarron now.'

'That's not true. What I have is yours, Richard.'

'To share with Charlotte?' He shook his head. 'No, you must go alone. But if we are to save our marriage, you must come back. You will, won't you? You promise you'll come back?'

'I promise,' she answered, steadily.

Part IV
1893–1894

Forty-One

On a fine September morning in 1893, three boats rowed by young men from the village left Carron jetty for Oyster Island. Alice and Charlotte were taking weekend guests on a picnic.

Alice had been back for more than a year but this little party – for Cavan Morry, Edie and Arthur Hurwood and Arthur's cousin, Bennett – was the first she had arranged. As she had reminded Charlotte on her tour of Belcarron in the late summer of 1892, not only were they in mourning, there was simply not enough money in the bank for them to entertain.

'Oh, rubbish!' Charlotte had retorted. 'We may be in mourning now for poor Papa, but that doesn't mean we should live like hermits. I shall go mad if I don't see somebody and I am sure we can afford it, whatever you say.'

'I looked at the accounts last night, Charlotte. We're breaking even only by not paying our bills.'

'No one in the world pays all their bills, Alice. Do you have to be so terribly middle class? I pay when people get difficult. As poor old Dudley used to say, they're usually quite happy to wait.'

'You think it's all right, then, that we've become a byword in the shops for outstanding debts? The tradesmen depend on us, Charlotte, as we depend on the tenants. We must pay our way.'

Charlotte had said no more as they moved together through the shabby old house, Alice stopping often at remembered views of cliff and sea, but as they descended the fine staircase, she asked casually if Richard could not do something to help them out.

'Richard?' Alice opened the door to their father's study, gazing in at his chair, his desk, his ashtray where his cigars had so often smouldered. 'He has given me a little money towards immediate repairs, otherwise he has nothing to spare. The country has been going through a bad time, people are not as rich as they were.'

'Oh, come, everyone knows the Argentines are rolling in money. Don't pretend you're hard up. Richard got the whole *estancia* from Aunt Beatrice, didn't he? Whereas I got this very nice ring.' Charlotte looked down at the emerald on her finger. 'The *estancia* for Richard, the rest of her jewellery for you, one ring for me. Would you say that was fair?'

'The emerald was her favourite, it's beautiful,' Alice replied, her voice shaking. 'And you have no right to complain. Papa left you a joint share of Belcarron when he had promised it to Richard.'

'So he's in a huff? Actually, I think you're the lucky one, Alice, that Papa included you. Considering you deserted him and I stayed.'

'You know I did not desert Papa, Charlotte! A wife has to go where her husband goes. No doubt you would have gone with Dudley, if – '

'If he had anywhere to go? Say it, Alice, I don't mind. Poor Dudley had nowhere to go except death. I'm afraid he is well out of this world where he could never do anything right.' Charlotte shivered and suddenly leaped up. 'Come, let's go into the drawing room and have coffee.'

Alice stayed for a while, looking round her father's room, then she blew her nose and followed her sister.

It was Bridie who brought the coffee and at the sight of her, Alice felt the familiar stab of grief. So like, yet not like. On the day of her arrival it had been almost too much to see the young, dark-haired girl come running from the house to help with the boxes.

'Who is that?' she had gasped.

'Bridie Donovan, Mena's sister,' Charlotte told her.

'She is so like Mena,' Alice whispered, 'so very like.'

320

'You thought you'd seen a ghost? She's not really so like. She has quite a different nose.'

It was a blessing, Alice reflected later, that Charlotte's eyes were not always so sharp as she liked to think.

Alice had not dared to delay too long before visiting Mena's mother in case she should never find the courage to go at all. The experience had been just as bad as she had feared. The tears and wails, the cries for the lost grandchild taken over by foreigners, the extreme difficulty Alice herself found in looking at Mrs Donovan, so pretty still, yet so ravaged by sorrow and hardship. There had been Mena's few possessions to hand over, including the brooch left her by Beatrice which had brought the one spark of pleasure to Maureen Donovan's eye. This she would treasure to her dying day, so she would, and it was gracious Miss Alice was to bring it all those miles across the sea.

'Ah, but you'll be coming again, Miss Alice,' Maureen had finished, eagerly, 'to be telling me more of my poor foolish girl?'

'Of course I'll come again,' Alice assured her. 'I shan't be returning to the Argentine for some time, I have a great deal to do here.'

Too much, in fact. She had been horrified by the state of not only her old home but also the village houses and the tenants' properties around the county, now owned by herself and Charlotte. Her father's solicitor, Lionel Pearce, a steady and practical man, who had taken her on a tour of inspection, told her bluntly there was nothing she could do. Not without a huge outlay of capital, which she and her sister hadn't got and couldn't afford to borrow. Every landowner was up against the same problem, which might only be solved when tenants were allowed to buy their own land.

'Buy their own holding?' Alice repeated. 'How could they?'

'Oh, it's being worked on, Mrs Wintour, has been since 1886. We shall certainly see more Land Purchase Acts come in as time goes by.'

Alice thought for a moment, then said slowly: 'But that will mean the end, won't it, for the landowners themselves? We could not exist without the income from the land.'

The lawyer nodded his narrow head. 'I'm afraid that is true.'

'So all this talk of Home Rule is unimportant. The change in Ireland will come without it.'

'Economic change, perhaps, not political. But the one might well follow the other.' Pearce lightly touched the reins and the pony trap rattled down another tiny, twisting lane. 'Back to Belcarron, Mrs Wintour?'

'Please,' said Alice.

As they neared the house, the lawyer expressed his concern over the tasks ahead for the sisters. He really did not know how they were to manage, they should have an agent, a factor –

'We can't afford one, Mr Pearce.'

'I know that, Mrs Wintour. That is my worry.'

'But there's no need to worry, really there isn't. We can do what is necessary ourselves, we are quite capable.'

'But with so few resources, Mrs Wintour – '

'My husband has allowed me enough to rebuild the stables and to repair the worst parts of the roof. We shall also be able to buy a decent pony and trap, which means we can visit all the tenants regularly, discover what they need and make them understand we are a sort of partnership. If they pay their way, we can pay ours and provide what is necessary.'

'All sounds a little Utopian,' Pearce observed with a smile, but Alice shook her head.

'I call it practical. If they are happy as tenants, why should they want to own the land?'

'To answer that, I should need to be a true Irishman, which I am not. But you may have a point, Mrs Wintour, and I wish you the very best of luck.'

As the boats progressed steadily towards Oyster Island, Alice, holding Tina close, decided her first year back at Belcarron had been a good year on the whole. She missed her father, she missed Richard, but there had been achievement in the running of the estate and it would be false modesty to pretend it had not been hers alone, for Charlotte had done nothing towards it. She was delighted to be out of mourning at last, to have a little money from the rents Alice had persuaded the tenants to pay, to be able to have transport again and even a respectable horse – and to do her justice, she was always willing to acknowledge it was all Alice's doing. That was gratifying, but did not relieve Alice's worries about the future. One day she must return to the Argentine. The children should not be without their father too long and she should not be without Richard. Whatever the truth about Mena's child, she was prepared now to lay the matter to rest. Mena was dead, but she and Richard were alive and what they had was too precious to throw away. She smiled as she thought of him and bent her head over Tina's soft hair, as Cavan Morry whispered at her side:

'A penny for them, Alice?'

'Not for sale,' she answered, laughing, and held Tina aloft. 'See the lovely island, my darling? That's where we are to have lunch.'

Forty-Two

Charlotte had a new beau. Bennett Hurwood, cousin to Edie's husband and partner in the family's Belfast linen firm, was undoubtedly paying court, which was exactly what Edie had intended. He was a widower without children, a strong-featured, handsome man with a splendid head of bright-red hair.

'Auburn, he calls it,' Edie whispered to Alice, as they watched Charlotte swaying away with Bennett to the edge of the sea. 'But ginger it is, just as my poor Arthur's was before he lost it.'

'Arthur is charming,' Alice murmured tactfully. 'So kind.'

'Isn't he? That's why I decided to marry him.' Edie tossed her head impatiently. 'People say he's trade. I say, what of it? Most of our ancestors were horse stealers or worse, I expect, and at least Arthur makes his money honestly. Sometimes I think the Irish gentry is as crazy as the peasants about owning land.'

'The Argentines are the same.'

'Really? When there is so much?'

'But owned by too few people.'

'The same as here, then. Heavens, Alice, let's talk about something more interesting than men's obsession with acres.'

When Edie had left her to play with the children, Alice turned her gaze again on the fair head and the red head in the distance. She felt some disquiet. Bennett Hurwood was a forceful character, the sort of successful man who could put Belcarron back on its feet. But would he be right for it?

Would he appreciate it? And if he moved in, how much say would he allow Alice in the running of it?

He would expect me to go back to the Argentine and take no interest, Alice thought. In which case he could think again. Then she laughed at herself. What an imagination she had, to picture Charlotte already married and Bennett in charge! Why, they were not even engaged. As she scrambled to her feet to join the others at the rock pools, she felt distinctly more cheerful.

Lunch was over and cleared away. There was that pleasant feeling of tranquility that comes over people in the afternoon when they have eaten well and the sun is shining and duty does not call. Even the maids were at their ease, talking and laughing with the boatmen as they waited for the quality to tire of the delights of Oyster Island and ask to be taken back; it had been a rare treat for them. As Bridie said, she wished Miss Alice was after fixing up a picnic every day.

Edie was at the water's edge, instructing Victor in the art of playing ducks and drakes, watched over indulgently by Arthur, while Jack searched for starfish and Miss Wynne, the nursery governess, carried on one of her many battles with Tina over taking a nap.

'It's a special occasion, Miss Wynne,' Alice called. 'Let her off for once.'

Reluctantly the flushed, solidly built young woman gave in. She was the daughter of a Church of Ireland clergyman, with a strong will of her own, as her sharp chin testified, but already she was finding her struggles with Tina hard going.

'One can scarcely believe the child is so young,' she remarked once to Alice. 'So young to be so strong. From where does she obtain her character, I wonder?'

'From her grandmother,' Alice had replied promptly. 'No question of it, she is a second Constance Wintour. But she will develop qualities of her own, I'm sure.'

'No doubt,' Meg Wynne grunted. 'But as soon as she is old enough, I strongly recommend a good boarding school. Discipline is what Tina requires.'

While the children played, the gulls called and Charlotte and Bennett Hurwood exchanged light banter, Cavan Morry

326

came looking for Alice. Would she care to walk with him to the ruins?

She looked towards the old chapel some distance away and said really she felt too lazy, she would prefer just to sit watching the sea, admiring the wild fuchsias trailing into the sand.

'Then may I join you?' He took a place on the rug beside her, his velvet-brown eyes as full of admiration as ever, in spite of the existence of the young wife he adored, at present visiting her sister in England. 'You know, you've been back nearly a year, Alice, and yet we've hardly met.'

'I've been in mourning, Cavan.'

'I know, I'm sorry ... But now you must tell me how things are with you. I hear you've been doing great things at Belcarron.'

'I don't know about great things. The estate is in a slightly stronger position than it was.'

'You've got rents out of the tenants and at the same time they think you're wonderful. How have you managed it?'

'Oh, come! I've done a few repairs for them, that's all.' Alice laughed, not displeased. 'Who says I'm wonderful?'

'Everyone.' Cavan let a handful of white sand run through his fingers. 'What happens, though, if you go back to South America?'

'Charlotte is part owner. I suppose she will run things.'

'You do have to go back?'

'Oh, yes, I must. Perhaps not to stay, though. I mean, not for ever.'

'It's not my place to speak, but I think you should be here, in Ireland. Belcarron – it's where you belong.'

Alice made no immediate reply. When she did, she changed the subject. 'I'm so sorry Mavis wasn't able to be with us today, Cavan. I like her so much.'

'And she likes you. I've been very fortunate she's taken me on.'

For some time they watched Edie and Arthur, now running races with the children, waved on by Meg Wynne, Edie laughing, Arthur mopping his face and balding head.

'Do you remember that picnic we had here before?' Cavan asked suddenly. 'I mean, when Dudley Sarn and all that crowd came?'

327

'I remember it very well. What of it?'

'It's strange the way things work out, isn't it? If Richard had not been with us that day, maybe you and I – ' He stopped, but took her hand. 'You are happy, aren't you, Alice? Truly happy?'

'There could never be anyone else for me but Richard, Cavan.'

'You don't mind . . . that I asked?'

'We're old friends, of course I don't mind.'

'If ever you need anything, you know Mavis and I . . . you've only to ask.'

She smiled and pressed his hand, then let it go. They both stood up, brushing sand from their clothes, and Alice shook and folded the rug.

'I hate to say it, but I think we should be going back. I don't want to be too late because of the children's bedtime. Miss Wynne gets so cross if they are out of routine.'

'Mustn't upset Miss Wynne,' Cavan agreed and, with his brown eyes cast down, followed Alice to join the others.

Long before they drew near to the mainland, it was possible to see the façade of Belcarron standing out, strong and white, like a sentinel on the cliff. Alice, who had always loved this view of the house from the sea, kept her gaze trained on it as Tina, worn out at last, slept in her arms. The sun was sinking now, its warmth leaving the air, and as the boats moved steadily through the water, people shivered a little and did not talk. Edie, in fact, had fallen asleep, resting her head on her husband's shoulder, while Bennett, next to Charlotte, spent the trip staring into her green eyes, for which she sometimes rewarded him with a slow smile.

Suddenly, Alice stiffened. 'Cavan,' she whispered urgently, 'may I borrow your field glasses, please?'

'Seen something exciting?'

'Someone, perhaps.' With trembling fingers, she adjusted the glasses, as Tina, disturbed, began to cry. 'Hush, my darling, hush – '

'Who is it?' Cavan asked with interest. 'Alice, who is there?'

She put the glasses down and turned to him with starry eyes.

'It's Richard!' she cried. 'Richard has come to Belcarron!'

Forty-Three

Richard was looking well and particularly handsome. He had seen the approach of their boats and by the time they came in, was at the jetty to greet them, sweeping Alice and the children into his arms, as the rest of the party watched from a tactful distance.

'But why didn't you tell me, Richard?' Alice cried. 'Why not tell me you were coming?'

'Letters take forever and I wanted to surprise you. I just wanted to arrive, hold you like this . . .'

'You said you couldn't come, you've always said you couldn't come, and here you are – '

'Because I couldn't stand being without you all any longer. I just booked myself a passage, left everything to Lucio, and came.'

'Oh, darling!'

As the boys clung to him and Tina, puzzled, stared into her father's face, Alice turned to her guests.

'Edie, Cavan – you remember Richard, of course?'

Richard bowed. 'Mr Morry, Miss Morry – '

'Mrs Arthur Hurwood now!' Edie corrected, proudly. 'Richard, it's wonderful to see you. May I introduce my husband, Arthur Hurwood? His cousin, Bennett?'

'And this is Miss Wynne, the children's governess,' Alice put in. 'Miss Wynne, my husband.'

'Has everyone forgotten me? ' asked Charlotte coolly.

She crossed the rough stones of the jetty to take Richard's hand, looking up at him, her green eyes sparkling in the way he remembered so well.

'I haven't,' he answered quietly, and kissed her on the cheek. 'How are you, Charlotte?'

Alice was walking round the bedroom as though she could not keep still. 'I can't believe you're here,' she kept saying. 'Richard, I can't believe you're here, in Belcarron!'

'I'm here, all right,' he said steadily. 'Come to me, Alice.'

She stopped her pacing and looked at him over his half-unpacked cases. He held out his arms.

'Alice, will you come to me?'

Without another word, she went to him.

'We are supposed to be dressing for dinner,' she murmured later, lying in his arms.

'Too tired,' he answered. 'Far too tired. Tell them to send something up on a tray.'

'Darling, we're not in a hotel. I am the hostess.'

As she raised herself on one elbow to look at him, his gaze went over her and he gave a delighted burst of laughter.

'Oh, what a hostess you'd make, Alice, if you went downstairs like that! Wouldn't little Cavan Morry's eyes pop out if he could see you? I'd wager it would be too much for him, he'd collapse – '

'He is married, you know, to a sweet English girl with lots of money.'

'Who doesn't look like you.'

'Who does, rather.' Alice suddenly leaped from the bed and put on her dressing gown. 'Richard, come on, we must dress. Bridie will be waiting to bring our hot water.'

He was in a silk robe, laying out his evening clothes, when Bridie carried in the cans of hot water for their bath. Alice murmured her thanks and he looked up. The colour left his face.

'Oh, God! Mena . . .'

'No, sir,' said Bridie, dropping a curtsey. ''Tis Bridie I am, Bridie Donovan, Mena's sister.'

'I thought I'd seen a ghost,' he muttered to Alice, when they were alone. 'She's so like, isn't she? So very like.'

'Her nose, of course, is different. But didn't you see her down at the jetty?'

'I didn't see anyone except you and the children.' Richard's

332

look was sombre. 'Must have been quite a shock for you when you first saw her here.'

'It was as though I'd stepped into the past. She was Mena as she used to be – that hurt.'

When they were ready and about to go downstairs, he asked, in a low voice: 'Is it over for you now, Alice?'

'I hope so, Richard.'

'You won't let it come between us?'

'Nothing must do that,' she cried, with sudden passion. 'Nothing ever again, Richard!'

'Nothing ever again,' he repeated, and their mouths met as the sound of the dinner gong boomed up from the hall.

When the ladies had retired to the drawing room, leaving the men to sit over their port, talk turned to Ireland. Cavan said since the death of Parnell, the political scene had changed, the spirit had gone out of the nationalists, it was the Ulstermen who had taken command. If Gladstone's second Home Rule Bill had got through, there would have been bloodshed, but thank God it had been defeated in the House of Lords only a couple of weeks before.

'By 419 votes to 41,' Cavan finished. 'I think we may safely breathe again.'

'Bennett and I are Belfast Protestants,' Arthur Hurwood remarked, lighting a cigar. 'You don't need to be told how we'd have felt if that bill had got through.'

'Yet from what I've heard Westminster was to have remained in control,' Richard put in. 'Would the nationalists have accepted that, anyway? I very much doubt it.'

'They can't seem to agree among themselves what they want.' Cavan sent the port on its way. 'But for the future, as far as we can see it, Home Rule is dead, and, as a landowner, I say again, thank God.'

'You've still got plenty to worry about,' Bennett Hurwood said shortly, as he stopped the port and filled his glass. 'What happens when all your tenants end up owning their holdings? That's coming, you know, and then what will the bloody landed gentry do? I don't mind telling you, Arthur and I are damned glad we don't make our money from land!'

'Bennett,' Arthur muttered, flushing, 'you're embarrassing Cavan.'

'Embarrassing Cavan? Not half as much as his kind have tried to embarrass us. Mention trade and you'd think it was leprosy – instead of what makes the world go round.'

'I'm sorry if we appear to have been at fault,' Cavan said stiffly. 'It was never our intention – '

'Forget it.' Bennett drained his port. 'Doesn't matter a damn.' He turned his reddish-brown eyes on Richard. 'You're by way of being in trade yourself, aren't you, Wintour? Selling corned beef to the world, isn't that what you do? And make a damned good living out of it, too, I'll be bound. What a fortunate fellow you are, then, to be out of this godforsaken country.'

Richard, regarding him with distaste, drew on his cigar. 'You can hardly say I am out of this country when my wife owns Belcarron.'

'Half owns it. Charlotte was made joint heir.'

Charlotte ... At Bennett Hurwood's use of Charlotte's first name, Richard's jaw tightened. Who the devil was this fellow? A suitor for Charlotte? She'd never consider him, or would she? Richard, waiting for the port to come back to him, flushed with annoyance, and Bennett, watching, seemed to read his thoughts, for he smiled. It was a smile of triumph.

As Alice handed him his coffee in the drawing room, Richard whispered; 'Who is that fellow Hurwood?'

'You mean Arthur? Or Bennett?'

'You know I mean Bennett. I know he's Edie's cousin – sort of – but why did you invite him here?'

'He was staying with Cavan, I could scarcely exclude him. Besides, Edie was anxious for him to meet Charlotte. She is playing matchmaker, you see.'

'You are joking, of course?'

'Charlotte needs a husband, Richard.'

'Not him, for God's sake!'

Alice raised her eyebrows. 'He's very wealthy.'

'Wealthy?' Richard's gaze went to Charlotte, who was sitting at the piano, sorting out music, as Bennett Hurwood's fiery head bent close to hers. 'She had made one mistake, Alice, we can't let her make another.'

'It is not for us to tell Charlotte what to do,' she retorted. 'But I'm sure she would be gratified by your concern.'

'My concern is a brother's,' he said sharply. 'You know that, Alice.'

'Of course,' Alice murmured, after a pause. 'Of course I know.'

When Bennett Hurwood and the other guests departed next morning, only Richard was relieved. With no one to occupy her, Charlotte rested her eyes on Richard more often than Alice cared to see.

At the beginning of October, Matthew and Constance Wintour came over from Dorset, accompanied by Marianne and her children, Frederick and Cecily. Everard, it appeared, could not be spared from his new parish where he had taken over as rector.

'He has done so well,' Marianne trilled to her cousins. 'Imagine, my Everard a rector and I a rector's wife!'

Plump and self-satisfied, she seemed not to mind that she was already more matronly than either Alice or Charlotte. Marriage suited her, she wished for nothing more than she had and knew she had been lucky to achieve it. In a theatrical whisper, she asked after Hester.

'Still in America with the fugitive? Oh, it's unbearable to think about – my own sister, living in such a way! We pray for her every night, you know, Everard and I,' she confided, 'that she may see the light and return to the true religion.'

'And leave her husband and children, I suppose?' asked Charlotte drily. 'Come, Marianne, accept that Hester is happy and is doing very well. As a matter of fact, she has opened a bookshop again and may open another.'

'A bookshop again!' cried Marianne. 'Oh, this is worse than I thought! I had no idea she was still in trade.'

'And pray what is wrong with trade?' Charlotte's eyes gleamed. 'Trade means money, Marianne, and there is nothing wrong with money.'

'On the contrary,' Marianne snapped, 'St Paul said money is the root of all evil.'

'The love of money,' Charlotte corrected. 'Now I don't love money at all, only what it can buy.'

She laughed and moved away, leaving Marianne to look after her in the same old wounded fashion.

'I see Charlotte hasn't changed,' she muttered to Alice. 'Still the same irritating creature she always was. It seems she has learned nothing from her troubles.'

'Well, I suppose she is over Dudley's death by now,' Alice replied soothingly, as she helped Marianne to hang up her dresses.

'And it didn't take much getting over, did it? No doubt she has her eye on some other man now who will have to jump through her hoop for her attentions. I wonder who he is?'

'A manufacturer from Belfast, very wealthy.'

'Indeed?' Marianne's tone was cold. 'So that is why she is all in favour of trade now. I'm sure I wish her well, then.'

'And so do I,' said Alice.

Matthew, wrapped in a greatcoat with a shawl also draped around his shoulders, was sitting on the clifftop, staring out at the steel-grey sea and sky. There had been rain all morning and clouds were still gathering. Richard said they should perhaps go in.

'No, not just yet.' His father rested his hands on the knob of his cane. 'I want to look at the view a little longer.'

'You're not well, though, are you?' Richard, gazing uneasily at Matthew's pallor, drew the shawl more closely round his shoulders. 'There was no need for you to make this tiring trip, you know. I was intending to come to Dorset.'

'I wanted to make it, I wanted to see Belcarron again.' Matthew put his thin fingers in Richard's. 'Though you know what it means to me to see you again, my boy, you and the family.'

'I'm sorry it's been so long, Father.'

'Not your fault, we all understood.'

For some time, Matthew was silent. 'I miss John,' he said at last. 'Especially here. Ernestine, too, of course, but it's John I see. And Beatrice. We grew up here, you know.'

'I know, father.'

'We'd all go scrambling down those cliffs, Beatrice in the lead. Always liked to be first, always wanted to make sure we

336

knew she was as good as we were. In a way, she was better – had more nerve, anyway.'

'Still had when we knew her,' Richard murmured.

His father smiled. 'Yes, I can imagine it. She'd have been more than a match for anything she ever came up against.'

'Alice used to say she was like Charlotte, but I never thought so.'

'No, no, nothing like at all ... She went quickly at the end, didn't she? Didn't suffer?'

'Didn't suffer at all. Come, Father, it's really too cold for you now, let's go in.'

As Matthew obediently stood up and began to move slowly back to the house, Victor and Jack burst out of the side door and raced across the lawn, followed by Frederick, Cecily and last Miss Wynne, calling to them to come back at once. 'At once!' they heard her cry. 'All of you, come back, I say!'

Matthew, leaning on his stick, laughed and shook his head.

'Nothing changes, does it? Children at Belcarron ... Richard, couldn't you stay?'

'Father, Belcarron isn't mine.'

'I know and I'm sorry John went back on his word, but it was only because you had Beatrice's place and Charlotte had nothing. And he didn't forget Alice, you know.'

'I was grateful for that, but it's made things difficult. For her, I mean – going back.'

Matthew's faded blue eyes widened. 'Why, Alice would never leave you, my boy. Where you goes, she goes, I'm sure.'

'She said that once,' Richard muttered. 'I hope it's still true.'

337

Forty-Four

Some weeks later, on a dark, moist November afternoon, Richard sat in John's study, working on the Belcarron accounts. His parents and Marianne were now home in Dorset after the bittersweet visit of reunion and farewell. He still did not like to think of the last sight of his father in the train at Cork. His mother had shown no emotion when she kissed him goodbye, but he knew this did not mean she felt any less than Marianne, who wept such floods of tears she set her children crying too.

'If only you weren't going so far away!' she had wailed. 'I declare, it's the other end of the world! Who knows when we shall all meet again?'

'In a year or two,' Alice murmured. 'No more, I promise you.'

'Because they want to check up on me.' Charlotte laughed. 'Don't worry, Marianne, they'll be back again before you can say Everard!'

As Marianne frowned and withdrew into the compartment, Matthew leaned out for one last shake of Richard's hand.

'Take care of the family, my boy,' he muttered. 'Take care of yourself.'

'And you, Father, you take care – '

'As though he ever does!' cried Constance, as the guard raised his flag and the train began to move.

'I'm sure he'll be all right, Richard,' Alice whispered, as the train curved away and vanished into the distance. 'Try not to worry.'

'I feel so guilty, going away . . .'

'Children always feel like that, leaving their parents. I expect ours will feel the same one day.'

'Marianne was right, though, wasn't she? Who knows when we'll meet again?'

'We must just hope for the best,' said Charlotte. 'Do let's hurry, or we'll miss the Skibbereen train!'

It was growing too dark to see now in John's study and Richard, at the heavy old desk, laid down his pen. The fire was burning up well and he moved to the chimneypiece to stand looking down into the flames, thinking still of the accounts. They were showing Belcarron's finances to be in surprisingly healthy state. Alice had done a good job; she had a sound business head on her shoulders. No doubt she could even run the *estancia* if he let her, although at the thought of her riding to *rodeo*, he tried to grin. He felt guilty about Alice as well as about his parents, for taking her away as well as going away himself. But thank God she had agreed to leave! What he would have done if she hadn't he could not contemplate.

He pulled out his silver watch and wondered if he should ring for the lamps. Also, tea, or was it too early for tea? As far as he knew he was alone in the house, Alice having taken Miss Wynne and the children to spend the day with the rector's family in Carron and Charlotte out somewhere visiting friends. Instead of bothering about tea, he decided to smoke and, lying back in his uncle's armchair, gave himself the pleasure of drawing on one of his favourite Havanas. His thoughts went to the day long ago when John had first broached the subject of Belcarron, here in this very room. Richard's face darkened as he sat, smoking and remembering. He had told John he wanted to marry Charlotte – what a damn fool he would have been if he had actually done that. Alice had proved a far better wife in every way, beautiful, loyal, an excellent mother, whereas Charlotte – Richard shrugged. Well, it hadn't happened and he hadn't been given Belcarron, either. That still hurt, he had to admit. Even though he had the compensation of the more profitable *estancia*, the loss of Belcarron still stung and probably always would –

340

'Hello, Richard.'

He sat up with a start, peering through the dusk of the room to the slender figure in the doorway.

'Charlotte? I thought you were out visiting?'

'Only for luncheon. It was so frightfully boring, I left early. Heavens, don't you want the lamps?'

'I suppose I do.' Richard, who had leaped to his feet, threw his cigar into the fire. 'I'll ring now, shall I? And for tea?'

'No.' She moved slowly towards him and it seemed to him that there was something different about her. The dark-green dress she was wearing hung loosely, appeared to have no waist, and it came to him with a slight shock that she was not 'laced'. Such a thing was pretty well unheard of; he had hardly seen Alice, even, when dressed, without her stays.

'No?' he repeated uneasily. 'You don't want tea?'

'I don't want tea and I don't want the lamps. Come, sit down again, Richard, and I'll sit near you. It's so nice like this, isn't it? In the firelight?'

Charlotte sat down, not on a chair but on the floor, where he could just make out her smiling face and white throat, the demurely fastened buttons of the softly flowing dress.

'Now we can talk,' she murmured. 'And you must admit you haven't been talking much to me since you came home.'

'You haven't had much time for talking, have you?'

'You mean I've been out a lot? Well, one has to see one's friends.'

'As long as they don't include Bennett Hurwood.'

'You don't like Bennett?'

'Not as a husband for you.'

'My, such authority!' Charlotte laughed, her eyes shining in the firelight. 'I think you take the role of brother-in-law a little too seriously. I have the right to choose my own husband, I believe?'

He leaned forward, staring into her face. 'You wouldn't take him, would you? He's not right for you and he's not right for Belcarron.'

'Ah, I understand. You're worrying about Belcarron, not me. But Bennett would run Belcarron perfectly, just the way he runs his business. He'd have it making money in no time.'

'There's more to life than making money, Charlotte.'

'Is there? Why don't you see what he thinks, then? He's coming over tomorrow.'

'The devil he is!'

'Only for dinner. Naturally, he's staying with the Morrys again.'

'Naturally, he's courting you.' Richard sat back. 'Well, you're right, I have no say in what you do. I can only tell you I think you'd be very unhappy if you married a fellow like Hurwood.'

'And you wouldn't want me to be unhappy? You do care for me a little?' Charlotte rose so that she was kneeling close to him. 'After all these years, you still care for me, Richard?'

'Not in the old way,' he said steadily. 'But yes, of course I care for you.'

'Please don't say as a sister.'

'What else? You are my sister.'

'Oh, no, Richard.' Charlotte took the pins from her yellow hair and let it fall around her shoulders. Then, very deliberately, she undid the top buttons of her dress and, taking his hands, put them round her breasts. 'I am not your sister and you know I am not.'

There was a silence in the room. Drops of sweat formed on Richard's brow and he stared into Charlotte's eyes like a man hypnotised. Charlotte remained perfectly calm.

'This isn't fair,' Richard stammered at last. 'To do this to a fellow, Charlotte! I love Alice. I don't want ... anyone else.'

'Very well. Take your hands away.'

He hesitated only a moment but as soon as he had removed his hands, she caught his face between her own and pressed her mouth to his with such passionate, tonguing force, she left him gasping.

'Still think I am your sister?' she asked mockingly, and as he continued to stare at her, fascinated, she undid the rest of the fastenings of her dress.

'My God, Charlotte, you're not wearing anything underneath,' he muttered stupidly. 'I thought all women wore layers and layers – '

342

'Not always.' Quietly, she shook the dress to her feet and stepped out of it. 'Come, undress, Richard – or must I do it for you?'

'Charlotte, I can't make love to you. It would be wrong – wicked. I love Alice – '

'She won't know anything about it, won't be back for hours. Oh, you know I've always loved you, you can't refuse me now.'

'You've never loved me, Charlotte, you've never loved anyone, have you?'

'Well, perhaps not.' She smiled, quickly undoing his cravat, his waistcoat, the buttons of his shirt. 'No, I don't love you, Richard, but I'm very attracted to you and that's as good, isn't it? Perhaps you don't think women can feel sexual attraction?'

'I know they can.'

She raised her eyebrows, pulling now at the sleeves of his jacket. 'Are you talking of my sister? You surprise me, you really do. But please do get out of these clothes, my darling. We may have plenty of time before Alice returns but we mustn't waste it.'

'I can't, I can't make love to you, Charlotte! It's wrong, I tell you! I can't!'

'Can't you?'

As she stretched out before him on the floor, her body glistening in the firelight, he felt sick with desire for her. It was too much, by God it was, how could a fellow refuse? But he no longer loved her. What he had felt all those years ago had been a young man's love, an infatuation, a dream. It wasn't real, had never been real, because he had known love since and knew the difference. Of course, when he looked at her as she displayed herself now, he wanted her, what man wouldn't? But everything in him was warning him, here was danger, here was disaster –

'Have you forgotten where we are?' he cried. 'Anyone could come in! Supposing the maids bring the lamps? For God's sake, Charlotte, get up, dress yourself – '

'No one will come in,' she answered tranquilly. 'But if you're worried, lock the door.'

'Lock the door? That would look even worse – ' He broke

343

off, turning white. There were sounds in the hall. Footsteps. Voices. One was Alice's. The other, Bennett Hurwood's.

Richard and Charlotte stood transfixed. Then Richard began frantically to try to button his shirt, his waistcoat, to tie his cravat, with fingers that seemed too huge and numb. Sweat rolled down his face and neck and the body he could not seem to cover. Charlotte, meanwhile, had dropped her dress over herself, but her hair was still down, flowing over her shoulders, and she too was having trouble with her fingers as she tried to twist the hair into a knot and could not seem to make the pins stick. The study door opened and Alice appeared, smiling, Bennett Hurwood at her shoulder.

As their eyes went over Charlotte in her strange, loose dress, her hair half up, half down, her face so pale, their expressions froze. Alice's gaze went to Richard, who was by a miracle completely dressed, even to his cravat's being tied, but though he knew his whole future depended on it, he could not speak.

It was Bennett Hurwood who spoke.

'You must excuse us,' he said hoarsely, a dark colour flooding his face from chin to brow beneath his bright hair. 'I am afraid we have interrupted you.'

Charlotte was recovering. She had succeeded in securing her hair into its knot and was a little less pale. 'Whatever do you mean?' she asked lightly. 'Richard was only working on the accounts.'

'The accounts!' Bennett laughed harshly. 'That's a good one – active work for you, my dear, if it brought your hair down.'

'I declare, it's very hard when a lady may not lose a hairpin without causing a gentleman to laugh,' Charlotte replied calmly. 'I have only just returned from the Carltons. As a matter of fact, I had the most shocking headache.'

'I too have been unwell,' Alice said in a low voice, and turned away.

'Unwell?' cried Richard. He took a step towards her, but she moved swiftly to the door.

'A little faintness, nothing more, but I think I shall go to my room. Mr Hurwood, I am sure my sister will give you tea in the drawing room.'

He bowed stiffly. 'Thank you, Mrs Wintour, I shall not require it. I am about to take my leave.'

'Bennett?' Charlotte went to him, two spots of scarlet now staining her cheekbones. 'Please . . .'

He looked at her with a hard, cold emptiness in his reddish eyes. 'I came over today because I couldn't wait to see you until tomorrow. Seems that was a mistake.' The empty gaze travelled to Richard, whose own look wavered and dropped. Then Bennett Hurwood turned and strode out.

When he had heard the front door bang, Richard, without a glance at Charlotte, who was standing quite still, ran from the room and up the stairs to find Alice.

She had taken off her hat and mantle and lit the candles. In the soft yellow light, her face was a stranger's. As Richard went to her, she raised her hand.

'Don't say anything, there's nothing to say.'

'There's everything to say, Alice! What you saw down there – it wasn't what you thought. I know how it must have looked, but the fact is nothing happened between Charlotte and me – nothing! Do you hear me?'

She walked to the window and stood looking out into the darkness; they could both hear the sound of the sea in the distance. This was the room she had wanted to give him years before. Her room. Now his, too. But not for much longer.

'Nothing happened because I returned early,' she said quietly. 'Isn't that so?'

'No, it's not, I swear it! I would never have made love to Charlotte.'

'Richard.' Alice looked at him. 'She was not wearing anything under that dress. Did you think I couldn't tell? Did you think I couldn't see the look on her face? On yours?'

'Alice, she came to me – ' Richard stopped, running his hand across his face. 'Look, she is your sister, I shouldn't – '

'Oh, don't try to save her reputation. I know she came to you and let you see she wanted you and all the old feeling came back, didn't it? And if I hadn't returned early, you'd have taken her.'

'No! Don't you understand? All that old feeling I had, it's

dead, finished. I knew when I looked at her, there was nothing there. Alice, for God's sake, you must believe me!'

'I might have done,' she answered drearily, 'if it had not been for Mena. Now, will you take your things out of here? Tell Bridie to make up a bed in Papa's dressing room. Say I have a bad back, it is better I sleep alone.'

He stared at her, his face working. 'Is this how it's going to be, then, Alice?'

'Until you return to the Argentine, yes.'

'You're not coming with me?'

'Of course I'm not coming with you.'

'And what about the children?'

'We will discuss the children later. Now, we should change for dinner.'

'Keeping up appearances?' He gave an unsteady laugh.

She made no reply.

'And what of Charlotte? What are your plans for her?'

'I intend to buy her out.'

'With what? You haven't any money.'

'I have Aunt Beatrice's jewellery, that should fetch a good sum, and if necessary I can borrow from the bank. Whatever it costs, I shall have her out of Belcarron as soon as she can find somewhere to go.'

'By God, Alice, you're strong, aren't you?' Richard shook his head. 'I think I am only now beginning to know you.'

'But I don't know you at all, do I?' she cried, her wonderful composure beginning to crack. As wild, violent sobs shook her frame, she waved at him to keep away. 'I – I've changed my mind about dinner. Please tell them . . . I shall be staying in my room.'

'And isn't Miss Charlotte after saying the same, then?' cried Bridie, when Richard, grey-faced, gave the message. 'Is it all sick you are, sir? Sure, but you'll be taking something yourself?'

'Brandy,' he said shortly. 'That's all, Bridie.'

Forty-Five

Charlotte took no persuading to accept cash for her share of Belcarron. Who wanted to live in Ireland, anyway? A crazy country going downhill fast. London was the place to be and she would settle herself there as soon as the finances were organised. In the meantime she would stay with the Lettons in Dublin and announced to the air at breakfast one December morning she would be leaving that day. Neither Richard nor Alice made any comment.

'Perhaps you would be good enough to tell me when you're sailing, Richard?' Charlotte asked politely.

'On 29 December,' he replied, without looking at her.

'Then you will celebrate the New Year on board – I believe it is very festive.'

'Is it?' He swallowed some coffee and asked if they would excuse him, he had things to get in Skibbereen.

Alice rose and, putting aside her table napkin, went out.

'Richard, may I speak to you?' Charlotte asked urgently.

'Charlotte, where is the point?'

'No, listen, I've been thinking. London is all very well, but why should I not go with you to the Argentine? I've always wanted to see Buenos Aires, I think it would be just my sort of place. And it would be a new life for me – God knows I've had enough of the old. Richard, what do you say?'

For a moment he seemed unable to say anything. He was staring at her, his blue eyes outraged, his colour rising.

'Go with me to the Argentine?' he cried. 'Are you mad? As what, I wonder? My sister-in-law, while my wife stays here? Or my mistress? Is that what you're hinting?'

'Do you have to put things so crudely? Naturally, I could be anything you want. And you will want someone, you know. Alice is never going to join you.'

Richard was shaking with rage, his hands twisting and clenching as he looked down at her.

'I could strike you,' he muttered. 'Do you know that, Charlotte? I could knock you down now for what you've done to me.'

'And isn't that the typical male answer to everything?' she cried, laughing. 'Poor Dudley was just the same, always threatening – '

'And Bennett Hurwood might have done more than threaten.' Richard, breathing hard, turned aside. 'One of these days you're going to go too far, Charlotte.'

'Perhaps, but it will be with a man who is a man, not a fool and a hypocrite. We could have had a good life in South America, Richard. I could have had my own establishment, I could have made you very happy, but oh no, you must pretend to be so virtuous – '

'You simply don't understand, do you? You have no idea what you have done to Alice and me.' Richard strode to the door and opened it. 'Goodbye, Charlotte.'

'Richard! Is that all you have to say to me? We may never see each other again!'

He hesitated for a moment, holding the door ajar, then he went out and closed it behind him.

He had no hopes that Charlotte's departure would change Alice's attitude towards him and it did not. When others were present, she made polite conversation; when they were alone, which was usually only at mealtimes, she behaved as though he did not exist. All he wanted himself was to make the break she demanded, for it was clear to him now that she was not able to forgive him. The wound had gone too deep. For their marriage, it was mortal. Not until the night before he was due to leave did he even attempt to talk to her, but by then it was necessary, there were practical matters that had to be discussed.

The Christmas tree was still up in the hall at Belcarron, the evergreens the children had gathered were decorating the

348

picture rails and windowsills. Everything looked so cheerful, so festive, it seemed unbelievable that underneath was a flow of bitterness that was eating its way into his very soul. Alice's, too.

'Alice, I'm sorry to disturb you,' he said at dinner, 'but we must talk before I go.'

'You mean about money?'

'And other matters.'

'Very well.' She rose. 'We had better go into the drawing room.'

The drawing room, with its lamps and crackling fire, was welcoming, but they took their own frost wherever they went and, though they stretched out their hands to the blaze, they were still cold.

'Coffee?' Alice asked.

'Please.'

They drank the coffee in silence.

'You had better say what you have to say,' Alice said, setting down her cup and not looking at him.

Suddenly, all the things he had planned to discuss – their future, the future of the children, how much money she would need – went from his mind. He pushed aside the table with the coffee things and grasped her hands roughly in his own.

'For God's sake, Alice, give way, please! We can't part like this, after all we've been to each other. I know I've hurt you, but – '

'Hurt me?' She pulled her hands from his, her eyes sparkling with anger. 'You have destroyed me!'

'That's because you won't see the situation clearly, you won't see that you are being absolutely unfair – '

'After what I saw? You two together? Have you any idea how you looked, the pair of you?'

'I keep telling you, nothing had happened between Charlotte and me!'

'But it would have done. Look, I forgave you Mena, Richard, but my own sister – no, I can't forgive you her!'

Richard returned to his chair. He said quietly: 'You never have believed me about Mena, have you?'

She hesitated. 'No . . . not really. Not deep down. For a

349

while I was happy when Vittoria blamed Lucio, but I was only believing what I wanted to believe. Mena would have been different with me if it had been Lucio.'

'She reminded me of you, Alice. That's how it happened.'

Alice became very still. 'Go on,' she whispered.

'I always wanted to tell you, you know, but I couldn't. Mena begged me not to, she said she would kill herself if you ever found out. I could never make her see it wasn't her fault.'

'I knew it wasn't.'

'There was just the one time,' Richard went on, drearily. 'It was in the house on the Avenida Lila. I'd come back late one evening, she was sitting up for me with the lamps. She'd been crying, thinking of Liam, maybe, or missing you, and I was missing you so much myself. She looked so like you, sitting there and crying, you see, I just put my arms around her and kissed her. And it happened. Afterwards, it was terrible, she was inconsolable and I . . . wanted to shoot myself.'

'Oh, Richard!' Alice murmured.

'I thought it was the worst moment of my life. Then I heard about the child.' Richard took out his handkerchief and wiped his brow. 'Can you imagine what it was like? I had to act the part, I had to pretend it had nothing to do with me, just another case of a servant's getting into trouble. I couldn't talk to Mena, couldn't help her. . . Then Lucio came to my rescue. When Mena died I went through hell, but Lucio said he would take the boy, bring him up as his own, he had always wanted a son and Paola was willing.'

'Because she knew the child was yours.'

'She would never have taken him if he had been Lucio's.'

'Things worked out well for you, then.'

At the bitter note that had returned to Alice's voice, Richard raised his head and looked into her eyes.

'You think so? When Mena died because of me? I'll carry that knowledge for the rest of my life.'

'Madness, she said it was,' Alice said, after a pause. 'Just madness.'

'Well, she paid a high price for it. So did I. But that was the only time I was unfaithful to you, Alice. There were plenty of times when I might have gone to the waterfront, bought myself a woman, the way men do, but I never did. I'm not saying I'm a saint, you know I'm not, I've let you down, I've brought you grief, but the only woman I want to share my life with is you. If you could only believe that – '

'I do believe it, Richard. Don't you see, that only makes things worse? I'm talking about Charlotte, not Mena. I know you don't love Charlotte now, I know you don't want to leave me for her. But when she came to you, you still didn't send her away, did you?'

'I tried, I wanted to – '

'But you didn't. And if I hadn't come home early, you would have made love to her and every time she looked at me afterwards, she would have been able to say, "Alice doesn't know . . ." Do you still ask me to give way, Richard?'

'Yes,' he said, heavily. 'Because it wouldn't have happened that way.'

But she turned aside and after a moment or two left him.

Next morning, he stood on the cliffs for the last time. It was light, but only just, they had had to breakfast by lamplight; now it was scarcely possible to distinguish grey water from grey sea. He thought of his father on this same spot, thinking he might never see Belcarron again. Now it was his turn to think that and he didn't seem able to take it in. In an effort to close his mind from the darkness that gripped him, he walked on to the point that looked down to the strip of sand below. For a moment, as his eyes raked the swirling mist, he knew how men felt who reached out, took that one step into air, into oblivion. His own foot lifted, his hands went forward, he stood trembling on the edge of nothingness –

'Richard!' screamed Alice.

She was at his side, her lovely face framed by the hood of her dark cloak, her hands on his arm.

'Richard, what are you doing?' Her voice was shaking.

'Looking at the sea. For the last time.'

'But you were so close – '

'Did you think I was going over?' He looked down into her eyes. 'Would you have stopped me?'

'I thought I had . . . no, you were only looking at the sea.'

'As I say, for the last time. That's what you want, isn't it? You don't want ever to see me here again, do you?'

'I don't know.'

His heart lurched but he did not move. 'What does that mean?'

'I suppose I need time.'

'Time? Oh, Alice, if I thought you'd ever come back to me, I wouldn't care how long I had to wait! Take all the time you want, all the time in the world.'

She drew her cloak around her and said nothing.

'May I hope? ' he asked, quietly.

'I'll write, Richard, I'll keep in touch. But you must hurry now, the trap is waiting.'

It was more than he had hoped for, it made the leave taking bearable. As he kissed the children waiting to say goodbye to him, he had the feeling he might not have to disappear from their lives for ever.

'Why are we not going with you, Papa?' asked Victor. 'I'm sure Mama said we were all to go on the ship together.'

'I'm going ahead, that's all. Now you must be very good, Victor, and help Mama to look after the others. I'm putting you in charge.'

'He's already in charge,' said Jack, who had been crying. 'But I don't want you to go, Papa, I don't want you to go!'

'I don't!' cried Tina. 'I don't want you to go, Papa!'

Richard crushed them to him, unable to speak, as Miss Wynne blew her nose and Alice stood with her face averted.

'I must go,' Richard muttered and, turning to Kevin Kelly, the groom, asked if everything was in.

'Sure, it's all in, sir.'

'Right, then.' Richard's eyes went to Alice. She put back her hood and offered her cheek, but he turned her face in his hand and kissed her on the mouth.

'You'll write? You promised.'

'I'll write. Goodbye, Richard.'

'Goodbye.'

He looked up at the old white house, wreathed still in December mist, at the servants on the steps, at his family, then he leaped up into the trap and let it carry him away.

Alice, moving slowly into the house, told Miss Wynne she was going to lie down, she did not feel well.

'Oh, I'm sure you don't, Mrs Wintour,' Meg said sympathetically. 'Is there anything I can get you?'

'No, nothing, thank you, it's just a headache.'

But it wasn't a headache. Before climbing the stairs, Alice went into the lavatory off the hall and brought up a thin white phlegm. She leaned back, wiping her lips and brow, and closed her eyes.

'Please God,' she murmured, 'not that, not that.'

It was too late, of course, to make that sort of prayer. Ever since she had come home ill from the rectory that terrible day, she had had her suspicions and now she was certain. By June, there would be another Wintour at Belcarron. And Richard didn't even know.

'Why did I let him leave me?' she whispered, rocking to and fro. 'I can't live without him, I can't, and now there is to be another child . . .' Then Charlotte's green eyes smiled at her and she rose and went to her room, where she lay on her bed.

Time, she had told Richard, she needed, and it was true. Time must obliterate that last sight of Richard and Charlotte together in her father's study. For now, she must face what she had to face and so must he, there was nothing else to be done. She thought of the new child to come and after a while she slept.

Forty-Six

Edward and Venetia Stonefield, with Lucinda in tow, called on Richard as soon as he arrived back in Buenos Aires. He had not even had time to unpack but, as he explained, he was not staying in BA. Next day he planned to return to the *estancia*.

As Lucinda's plump young face fell at this news, Venetia cried: 'But where is Mrs Wintour, Richard, where is dear Alice?'

'Unable to return with me,' he answered smoothly. 'Pressure of business in Ireland, I'm afraid, to do with her father's estate.'

'Oh, poor boy, but you'll be so lonely! Why go straight to the *estancia*? We haven't seen you for months and there is so much going on in BA at the moment. So much more money about, you know, it's quite like the old days!'

'Not quite like the old days,' Edward said cautiously. 'But it's true, Richard, things are looking up. You'd be very welcome if you stayed on for a while.'

'You would indeed,' Lucinda murmured.

'But you know your own business best,' Edward went on, as Carlotta brought in tea and sweet cakes. 'Any *estanciero* worth his salt would want to see how things were if he'd been away. Have a good fellow in charge, though, don't you, Richard?'

'The best,' said Richard, and handed on the mate tea.

The conversation buzzed. He supposed he must take part in it, but his head was banging like cannon fire and all he could think was that he was back in BA and Alice was not with him. The pain was intense.

'Why didn't I make her come?' he groaned inwardly, as Venetia chattered on and Lucinda watched him whenever she thought her mother wasn't looking. 'I could have made her, I could have, I'm sure, she was beginning to waver before I left. A day or two might have done it. Will these people never go?'

They went at last, making him promise to return to BA as soon as possible, when they would see he met people and had a splendid time.

'Just wish you'd brought your dear wife back with you, my boy,' Edward murmured, shaking Richard's hand. 'And I won't be the only one in BA to say that, I can tell you!'

'Indeed, you are both very well thought of,' said Venetia. 'But as Alice is not here, we must make the most of you, Richard. Lucinda, my dear, say goodbye.'

'Goodbye, Richard,' Lucinda said obediently, then blushed. 'I mean, Mr Wintour.'

For some time after the Stonefields had left him, Richard held his throbbing head and fought the ghosts that surrounded him. The long voyage back had not prepared him for the desolation of spirit that held him here in the old house he had shared with Alice. This was where they had first stayed on their arrival from Ireland, where the children had been born, where Beatrice had been so wonderfully alive and then had died, and Mena – he covered his eyes with his hand at the thought of Mena. The past was too cruel, he couldn't face it. But then he couldn't face the future either. Alice was the key. If she came back, his life would have purpose again, would have meaning. If she did not –

He leaped to his feet, went to his aunt's old bureau and began feverishly to write. Words did not usually come easily to him, but now they flowed as though some outside force were directing the pen. Discarding all that had come between them, all that Alice blamed him for, the unfairness he thought she had displayed, he told her he loved her, he could not live without her, everything was empty, an aching void, a sham. Now that he was back in BA, he could see things clearly. Maybe without him in front of her, she was seeing things differently too. She had asked for time and time they had both been given, he hoped it had told her as it had told him,

356

love was all that mattered. Men were supposed to care for other things and he supposed he had put his career in the Argentine before anything that Alice wanted, but if she could find it in her heart to return to him, he would be waiting wherever she wanted him, Belcarron, the Argentine, anywhere, he no longer cared, as long as she and the children were with him and they were a family again. He would await her reply with an impatience she couldn't possibly imagine and he was her most loving husband, Richard.

He felt better when he had written the letter, as though he had actually talked to Alice. He pictured her opening it, being moved by it, perhaps deciding at once to arrange a passage over . . . For a time the daydream was pleasant, but when he lay alone in the big Spanish bed after his solitary dinner, the anguish returned. He lay on his back, staring into the darkness of the stuffy, unused room. Maybe things would be more bearable on the *estancia*. He would have work to do there, and good hard riding across the plain could banish thought from any man's mind. Besides, he would be able to see Julio, whose mother had named him Francis, who was his son.

'My son,' he murmured, and grew calmer. Even if Julio were Lucio's now, there was a part of himself there on the *estancia*, waiting for him, he would not be entirely alone. With this strange comfort sustaining him, he fell asleep.

In the morning, he posted his letter and took the train for the country. The thought of Alice accompanied him all the way but it soothed him to be travelling again.

It was evening when, riding his hired criollo horse, he saw ahead the outline of the plantation poplars and knew he was nearly home. He was covered in dust, so sore after his long break from riding pampas-style that his bones were crying out for rest, but he was back. The long journey was over. He let his horse amble slowly up to the entrance of the house, then dismounted, looking again at the gardens Alice had tended, taking in the mixture of scents, basil, mulberry and drying grass. Then he pulled the bell.

A small mestiza maid looked out, her narrow black eyes suspicious of the stranger, then she let out a squeal of excitement and Lucio appeared, his arms outstretched.

'Don Ricardo!'

'Lucio!'

The two men grasped hands and stared into each other's eyes with deep, shining pleasure. Lucio was the same as ever, handsome, graceful, steady, but after he had drawn Richard into the house, it was plain he was concerned at what he saw.

'So thin, so change!' he cried. 'Don Ricardo, you are ill?'

'No, no, just weary. The long voyage, you understand.'

'*Si, si.*' Lucio's look was still troubled. 'And Doña Alicia? She is in BA, she come later?'

'She is still in Ireland.'

'She no come?'

'Not for a while. She is busy, you see, has her father's estate to run.'

'Ah, yes, is good, the *estancia* for the señora.' Lucio's eyes were filled with sympathy. 'But is lonely for you, Don Ricardo. No wife, no children – '

'Don't worry about me, tell me how things are with you.'

'I do all I can, I think is well, I think you happy.'

'You know I trust you in every way, Lucio, but I wasn't asking about the *estancia*. How is Paola, how are the children?'

'Paola is fine, Don Ricardo, *gracias*, the children also.'

'Julio?'

'Julio . . .' Lucio's grave expression melted into joy. 'Ah, Don Ricardo, already he is so close to me, I feel my heart beat with his. And Paola, she feel the same, she love him like her own.' Lucio touched his lips with his fingers. 'And you no worry, Don Ricardo, she say nothing, I promise you.'

'I say again, Lucio, I trust you in every way.' Richard stood up, stretching his aching body. 'Tomorrow, you must take me on a tour of inspection, but now I think I will wash and rest.' He put his hand on Lucio's shoulder. 'It's good to be back.'

'Is good to see you, Don Ricardo, *bueno, bueno.*'

After the greys and greens of Ireland, the soft mists and rains, Richard could scarcely believe the blueness of the sky next morning, the clarity of the light, the lushness of the plantation, the vastness of the land beyond. Space! He had forgotten, after the months of seeing little lanes, little fields, that there were places like this where there seemed no limit to land.

Now I remember why this country means so much to me, he thought, looking into the far distance as his horse stood waiting. Alice has never felt as I do, Ireland's too much in her blood. So it had always been easier for her to choose where she would live, yet she had chosen to live with him. He had wanted Belcarron, he had wanted the Argentine. Now he only wanted Alice and he no longer knew if she wanted him. The pain was as sharp as ever, there was no antidote but work.

'Lucio!' he called, 'Let's go!'

It was too late to join the gauchos so he gave his horse to a peon and walked round the plantation, beginning with the orchards. Work on the grain development had been left to his return but Lucio told him they were progressing well on the sheep enclosures and he had taken on extra men. Italians, Irish immigrants, a few fellows from Jujuy and Rosario, he hoped that was in order.

'Of course,' Richard answered. 'We're going to need plenty of workers if things move as fast as I hope. Irishmen, did you say? I'll have a talk with them later. It's good to know the country is coming back to prosperity, Lucio. About time, perhaps.'

'Are other problems, Don Ricardo. Political problems. Unrest.' Lucio shrugged. 'Here is always unrest.'

'At least this year we have peaches,' Richard observed, as they walked through the orchard and looked at the trees, heavy with fruit. 'There were times when I thought we would never recover from the pampero, but you see we have.'

'*Por cierto*. See the apricots, also, and the quince.'

But who would make the jams this year? Richard's heart twisted, remembering Alice superintending in the kitchen, her dark hair tied up in muslin, her face flushed, as she tasted and stirred and smiled up at him when he came to find her.

'Vittoria, she make the preserve,' Lucio murmured, reading his thoughts. 'She visit in Rosario but she return soon and Paola picks the fruit now.'

359

'Paola?'

'There is Paola, Don Ricardo.' Lucio pointed to the stout figure of his wife ahead. She was piling the luscious fruit into a basket as a small, dark-haired boy played at her feet. 'And there is Julio. Come, Don Ricardo, see my boy!'

'*Buenos días*, Paola,' Richard greeted her and she smiled, grudgingly, and tossed back her heavy black hair. 'And here is Julio – how he has grown since I last saw him.'

He bent down to look into the child's face and caught his breath. The blue eyes, the nose, the turn of the head – Good God, he was a perfect little Wintour!

The image of me, Richard thought. Do they see it?

Of course they did. Never would anyone believe this boy was Lucio's. Thank God he had told Alice the truth.

'May I hold him?' he asked and swept the boy up to look at the peaches hanging, rosy and creamy, high in the leaves. As he did so, something stirred in his heart. He felt the same as when he had been given the newly born Victor to hold and had looked down and thought, This is mine, this is mine.

But Lucio was looking on, smiling so fondly, Richard knew he must avert his face as he set Julio down. Julio was not his, he had given up all rights to him and had been glad to do so. Now the comfort he had thought he might take in the child was not after all to be his. No consolation there.

They left the orchards, looked in at the bakery, where thin little mestiza girls were making bread and pastry for *empanadas*, and the dairy, where in the heat the vats of cream were yellow and sour. A man outside the gauchos' quarters was nursing an injured leg, sharpening his knife and regarding Richard with a flat, dark stare. They talked to him for a while, then Richard said he would like to ride out to have a look at the sheep, after he had seen the books.

'*Si, si*, Don Ricardo,' Lucio muttered anxiously. 'I hope is all right.'

'Lucio, I'd trust you with my life, never mind my accounts.'

Everything was in perfect order. While Lucio hovered in the background, unable to settle, Richard went through the

360

bills, the receipts, the records. Figures for beasts killed, beasts dispatched to BA, prices paid for bulls, for sheep, sums paid out in wages, repairs –

'Lucio, I don't think this place needs me at all!' he exclaimed, sitting back in his chair. 'I may as well go back to BA and play polo.'

Lucio's brow cleared. 'You are kind, Don Ricardo – '

'Not so, you have worked well and I'll see you are rewarded. I must just say again, I don't know what I'd do without you.'

Riding the pampas again, Richard felt the bittersweetness of his homecoming. The great sea of the waving grass seemed to consume him; the plovers wheeled, the dark clumps of the *ombú* trees beckoned with their shade. He had missed this, even at Belcarron; he knew a part of him was always here and now he had returned to it. But still Belcarron came into his mind and he saw himself on the cliff, searching the sea for Alice's boat, just as she had told him she watched for his boat coming back from fishing. He remembered the elation that had sent him running to the jetty, standing on the slipway, waiting, then calling her name, lifting her off her feet, while the children stared –

'Is all right, Don Ricardo?' asked Lucio. 'Is too much, the heat?'

'No, I'm fine, thank you, Lucio. Let's press on.'

They reached the men working on the fencing for the sheep runs, among them the newly arrived Irishmen. Richard took pleasure in listening to their voices. Sure, they couldn't believe their eyes, they told him, all this sun, all this land. One of these days, see if they did not speak the truth, they would be after having a piece of land for themselves.

The Irishman's dream, Richard thought. And for them it might come true. He wished them luck and went on to speak to the other new workers. They were astonished, it seemed, at the way the pampas was changing. Who would have thought they'd be working with sheep? But sheep were easier than cattle and if the world liked mutton, why kill yourself for beef?

Richard laughed and said there were certainly changes coming and he was all for them, but he still believed beef would reign supreme for the Argentine. Mutton, wheat, whatever else they produced, they would always produce beef.

He had begun to feel so tired, so woefully out of condition that when they left the sheep runs he found it necessary to tell Lucio he must return to the *estancia*. He would visit the herds the next day.

He felt better when he had bathed and changed. Well enough to work on the codicil to his will he had been thinking about ever since seeing Julio again. He asked Lucio to find him two men who could come in after dinner to witness his signature on a document.

'I myself can be witness,' Lucio replied promptly.

'Not this time, Lucio. You are, you understand, *beneficiado*.'

'I?' Lucio's sallow cheek flushed, he lowered his eyes. He said he was embarrassed.

'Why? You work well, I wish to do something for you. Also for Julio.'

'Julio?'

'He is my son. I feel responsible for him.'

'You no take him back, Don Ricardo? Is mine, is my son!'

'Of course he is, Lucio, don't worry. I only wish to remember him, to make some provision for him in the future.'

Visibly relaxing, Lucio said that would be difficult. Maybe people would say, why should Don Ricardo remember Lucio's son?

'I know, I know. I am trying to be discreet. But see if you can find me two men to come in after dinner, will you? Two who can write their names?'

'I do my best, Don Ricardo.' Lucio shrugged. 'Only, riding the horse is one thing, writing the name – ah, that is another.'

Richard enjoyed his dinner; the fresh air had given him an appetite he had not had for weeks. Afterwards, he smoked a cigar and had a brandy, but only one because he wanted to keep his head clear. For some time he worked at his desk, stopping occasionally to listen to the sound of the gauchos' guitars and hoarse singing, usually of unrequited love, which suited his mood. At last he put down his pen and opened his office door to stroll out into the plantation.

He could see the gauchos' fire and the men lying round it, smoking and talking. They asked him to join them for a drink and he did drink with them and talked as best he could in their Spanish, but he knew he would find no witnesses here and eventually moved on.

Lucio came to him from the willows where Paola was sitting, fanning herself.

'Any luck?' asked Richard. 'What about those Irishmen, perhaps?'

'The Irish have gone to San Vicente, Don Ricardo, but one of the men from Jujuy say he can write his name, also one Italian. You wish I send them now?'

'Please. I have the document ready for signing.'

He had lit another cigar when the two young men appeared and he put it down. They watched as he signed his name, then added their own.

'*Muchas gracias.*' He blotted their signatures and gave them a few coins, at which the Italian flashed his teeth and melted back into the darkness, but the other, tall and slender with good features, seemed to want to linger.

'*Gracias,*' Richard said again and smiled his dismissal. The young man moved and Richard sat down, reaching for his cigar. He never saw the knife as it arched and landed. He tasted the blood in his mouth, he felt the pain in his chest, but he could not ask, 'Why? For God's sake, why?' Only his glazing eyes asked that.

The young man, who was not from Jujuy, bent over him. With strange compassion, he whispered:

'Don Ricardo, you should have read my name.'

It was Dr Morales, the lawyer, who read it, scribbled at the foot of Richard's will.

'Antonio Carlos Sentos,' he murmured. 'The son of Don Felipe. Dear God, does he think he has avenged the slight to his father now? When they catch him, he will say his family's honour has been restored. What good will it do him?'

Antonio Sentos was never caught. By the time the authorities found his trail, he had reached the borders of Paraguay.

Forty-Seven

It was the day of the christening, 23 September, 1894. Alice's second daughter, a beautiful fair-haired baby, was named Melissa Hester at a ceremony in St John's attended only by her godparents, Cavan and Mavis Morry; Cavan's sister Kitty; and Hester Molloy from America. In view of the circumstances (everyone was still in mourning for Richard) there could be no real celebration, but champagne was provided at Belcarron and a christening cake which the children enjoyed.

Alice looked so pale, so ghostlike, the Morrys said they would leave early, but she assured them she was feeling better, much better. Really, she was managing very well.

'Thank God you have your cousin,' Kitty murmured. 'Maybe I shouldn't say so, but I really do think it's very bad form Charlotte is not here with you, after all you've been through.'

'She is in London.'

'Well, London's not the moon, I suppose? There are still boats running to Ireland if I am not mistaken? Of course, I know your uncle and aunt are too ill to come over – '

'They've been very hard hit,' Alice said, in a low voice. 'Hester's sister came for a while.'

'Marianne?' Kitty's long face expressed her opinion of Marianne. 'Had to get back to the parish, didn't she? Almost made one think she was the vicar herself. But you, Hester, you've been wonderful, coming all the way from New York, with the children too!'

'Nothing would have kept me away,' Hester insisted. 'Please don't thank me, I wanted to do it.'

'If there's anything we can do, you have only to name it,'

Cavan whispered to Alice as he and his pretty wife made their goodbyes. 'All we want is to be of service to you.'

'I know that.' She took their hands, smiling, trying to dispel the concern she could read in their eyes. 'You have done more than I could ever ask. I am truly grateful.'

But when with Kitty they had driven away, she sank on to the sofa and closed her eyes.

'Oh, Hester, I am so tired!'

'Of course you are, you poor girl. Look, let me help Miss Wynne to get these children to bed. Victor, do you think you should be taking any more of that cake?'

'I don't see why not,' Victor snapped. 'There's plenty left.'

'He's already had two pieces!' cried Tina. 'I know, I saw.'

'Tell-tale-tit, tell-tale-tit,' sang her brother. 'Your tongue shall be slit and every little puppy dog shall have a little bit!'

'No, they shan't, they shan't!' Tina shrieked, covering her mouth with her fingers. 'I won't let them! You horrid, horrid boy!'

'Right, all of you, upstairs now!' cried Meg Wynne, grasping Victor and Tina and ordering Jack to follow, as Paul Molloy looked on, large-eyed, and Caitlin began to whimper.

'Heavens, it's like a bear garden,' Hester commented. 'Has Bridie taken the baby? Alice, we'll get them all out of the way and leave you in peace.'

'No, come back soon, Hester. I want to talk to you.'

The September day had been one of Indian summer warmth, which still lingered as the cousins moved out to the cliffs and looked down at the sea.

'You must be exhausted,' said Hester, noting the shadows under Alice's eyes, the new little lines around her mouth. 'Things have been too hard for you for months.'

'Yes, it's been hard, I won't deny it.' Alice shivered. 'When I first heard about Richard, I wanted to die myself. But of course I did not. I had the baby to think of, I had the children. Somehow, one seems to survive.'

'You've been very brave, Alice.'

'No, I've done what had to be done, that's all. Shall we go down the cliff path a little way? Or is it too late?'

'I think perhaps it's too late this evening. Let's sit on the old bench over there.'

When they had settled themselves, Hester watched Alice's fingers pleating and repleating the folds of her shawl.

'Do you really feel better?'

'Yes. Perhaps Melissa's day has been a turning point. I feel I want to talk.'

'I've often thought there were things you wanted to tell me but were not ready.'

'You were right, I wasn't ready, but now I feel it would help to talk to you, Hester, if you wouldn't mind.'

'Mind? Of course I shouldn't mind. You know I'd do anything to help you, Alice.'

'In one way I have already been helped. God has been good to me. He has helped me to bear something that was destroying me. And now I feel I can talk about it.'

As Hester raised her dark eyes in mute enquiry, Alice looked again at her hands twisting her shawl.

'The thing is, Hester, Richard . . . was the father of Mena's child.'

'Dear God!' Hester snatched at Alice's hands. 'Mena? Mena and Richard? No, I can't believe it!'

'Would you believe me if I told you Mena herself was Papa's love child?' Alice shook her head. 'Another secret, you see, I have kept from you.'

'You have been through more than I realised,' Hester said, after a pause.

'These things happen, I have had to try to understand. I did understand about Richard and Mena. It was just the one time, when I was away. A moment of madness, they called it – and you know the result.'

'Poor Mena,' Hester said softly.

'And poor Richard. He suffered too. I loved them both so much, I let it go. Then something else happened.'

'If this is too painful, my dear, may we not leave it?' Hester asked, as Alice seemed unable to go on.

'No, it's too important to me, I must speak of it. When Richard came over that last time, Charlotte was here. Perhaps you've wondered why she isn't here now?'

'Well, I knew she was in London, I knew you had bought her share of Belcarron.'

367

'But you don't know why. She – forgive me, I don't like telling you this, but I must tell someone or I shall go mad – she tried to seduce Richard. She went to him and offered herself and what I never knew, could never be certain of, was whether he would have taken her. I came home early and surprised them, you see. Richard swore nothing had happened and never would have happened, but you know he was once in love with her, don't you, Hester? You can see how it would have looked to me?'

'Of course, Alice, of course,' Hester cried, her face crimsoning. 'Why, what are you saying?'

'I'm saying I was too hard, too bitter. I knew Charlotte was to blame, but I couldn't stop remembering he'd asked for her before he asked for me. And every time he denied he would ever have made love to her, I thought of Mena.'

'Any woman would have done the same! You mustn't blame yourself, Alice, for thinking that way.'

'I do, though, I do blame myself, because I was thinking more of Charlotte and of how Richard had let her hurt me than of our marriage. It seemed to me she had triumphed, she had come between us. But I was as much to blame as Richard, you see, I let her do it.'

The colour had faded from Hester's long, sweet face. She put her arm around Alice.

'It was natural, it was only natural – '

'Was it? All the time, I knew in my heart how Richard was suffering. I knew he would have to return to the Argentine without me, without the children, I knew how terrible that would be for him. When he said goodbye, I almost gave in. I almost said, "Wait for me, wait for me."' Alice touched her lips with her handkerchief, staring at the darkening cliffs with sightless eyes. 'And if I had, who knows what might have happened?'

'That young man would have killed Richard anyway, Alice, whether you were there or not. He was crazy, a fanatic. Don't torture yourself with thinking things like that.'

'We shall never know, shall we? I didn't go.'

'You said God had been good to you,' Hester prompted gently. 'In what way?'

Alice gave a sudden, radiant smile. 'I give the credit to God, but maybe it's Richard's alone. I don't know, but I got a letter. One day when I had been feeling so terrible, so dead in heart, Bridie brought it in. He must have written it the day he arrived in Buenos Aires.'

'It must have been a terrible shock, Alice.'

'Yes, but it was so beautiful, Hester, the most beautiful letter I've ever received from anyone. I didn't even know Richard could write in such a way, he never cared for writing. But this one – it was like balm, like some wonderful cure for all my hurt. He told me all the things I was longing to hear, how he loved me, how he missed me and the children, how his life was empty without us. He said now he was back in BA, he could see things more clearly and he had come to realise love was all that mattered. He had put his life on the *estancia* before what I wanted, but now if I could return, he would be waiting. Wherever I wanted him to be.' Alice fixed Hester with an intense blue gaze. 'He meant he would give up the Argentine for me, Hester. Just as now, I would give up Belcarron for him.'

'You have always given up Belcarron for him,' Hester said quietly. 'Don't you remember saying, all those years ago on the little beach, "Wherever he went, I'd go with him"? When I asked, "Even if it meant leaving Belcarron?" you said yes. And you have been true to that, haven't you?'

'Until now.'

'But there were reasons, Alice.'

'All the wrong reasons. Whatever Richard did or didn't do, I should have remembered he was only human, people make mistakes. Yes, all right, I am human, too. I couldn't say the words I should have said before he went away, so when I heard he was dead, I thought he would never know how much I loved him, and that I would have gone back to him one day. I thought he had died not knowing and I couldn't bear it, Hester, it was too cruel . . .'

'And then the letter came?' asked Hester, after a pause, during which Alice struggled for control.

'Yes, the letter came, and I realised he did know. He couldn't have written to me like that unless he knew my heart was with his. We had lost our way, but he knew we'd

369

find it. And we have, Hester. We are together again.'

It was now almost completely dark and the air had grown chill.

'Come, my dear,' said Hester, making Alice rise with her. 'We must go in.'

Forty-Eight

After dinner, when they were sewing in the long drawing room, Hester spoke of her life in New York. Her bookshops were doing well, she had just opened another in Albany and there were plans to expand into New England. Most of the people she employed were of Irish origin, but the Irish-American community was fast becoming a force in American politics and American life. Daniel was in his element, running a newspaper now, as well as fund raising and lecturing, there was even talk of his entering politics himself.

'Daniel? In politics?' Alice exclaimed, trying not to show her surprise, but Hester gave a faint smile.

'You are thinking of his jumping bail? I agree, he would have to answer that.' She shook her head over her mending. 'It seems wrong, I know, but that was the best thing that could have happened to us. I'm not speaking only of material success.'

'Though that has come too.'

'It has, but what matters more is we've been able to make our own status over there in a way we never could have done back home. There is not the same class system in America as we have here, that's the difference, you see.'

'Surely, they have their old families?'

'Oh, yes, their old families, their old money, they're very proud of those. But everyone has the chance to do well. No one holds it against Daniel that he began as a groom.'

'I'm glad,' Alice said, quickly, 'I'm glad you're so happy, Hester. But are you saying you'll never come back?'

'Not to live.' Hester picked a sock from her work basket

371

and searched for matching wool. 'If Daniel were to think of standing for Congress, though, he would need to become an American citizen and that would mean coming back to fight the old charge. Nothing is decided yet.' She drew wool through her needle. 'What about you? Shall you ever go back to the Argentine?'

'Oh, yes, I must. There is the question of Richard's estate, you see.'

'Does that come to you?'

'Not entirely, I share it with the children. But you can imagine there is a great deal to do and I am one of the executors, they are waiting for me to return. In the meantime, Edward Stonefield, our banker, is looking after finances for me and Lucio is managing the *estancia*.'

'A lot for you to think about, Alice.'

'Maybe, but I've put off thinking about it for too long. I must soon make arrangements to go back.'

As Alice folded her sewing, Hester rolled up Paul's socks and stuffed them back into her work basket. She gave Alice a quick glance and after a pause, asked delicately, 'Was Richard able to do anything for Mena's son?'

Alice's gaze was unflinching. 'It was one of the last things he did. He left money to Lucio in a codicil. Antonio Sentos witnessed it.'

'Oh, no!'

'Obviously, it was meant for the boy. Richard may have made mistakes but he was always ready to honour his commitments.'

'Of course he was.' Hester reached over to press Alice's hand. 'You look so weary, my dear, why don't you go on up to bed?'

'I think I will.' But Alice lingered, staring down into the fire. 'There's another reason why I want to go back to the Argentine. Richard is buried there.'

'You thought that best?'

'Yes, because he loved his second country, as Aunt Beatrice did. They are near each other, in Buenos Aires, and I must visit them.'

Hester went to her and held her and for some moments they clung together.

'Thank you again, Hester,' Alice said, softly, 'for coming. It's made all the difference to me.'

'After all you did for me when I needed you, do you think I'd have left you here alone?'

'But you have Daniel to consider, you mustn't stay too long.'

'I'll stay until you have to leave for South America. Don't worry about Daniel, he understands.'

When Hester had taken her candle and gone to bed, Alice carried out her nightly duty of checking doors and windows. Bridie appeared from the kitchen, stifling a yawn, and began to put out the lamps. She asked if there was anything else Alice would be wanting but Alice said no, she was just going up to look in on the children. Everything was secure, there was nothing to worry about.

'Good night, then, ma'am.'

'Good night, Bridie.'

All was quiet upstairs in the old house. There was a warmth about the rooms and passages, the residue of the golden September day, and as Alice progressed on her round of inspection, the shadows cast by her candle seemed as welcoming as friends.

One by one, she looked in on the children. Hester's Paul, another Matthew, and Caitlin, a true little Molloy, sleeping with her thumb in her mouth. Victor, stirring, was so like Richard, he brought the quick tears to her eyes. At eight years old he was ready to go away to school but she had not been able to bring herself to send him. Not this September, anyway. Mr Barnes had agreed to give him Latin lessons, so he would not be too far behind if she sent him next year when Jack could go too, although she dreaded to think how the tender hearted Jack would survive school. She would have to be very careful to choose the right place, one where there would be no bullying and not too much caning. Maybe she wouldn't send them away at all, she thought, rebelliously, but guessed she would probably have to conform in the end.

Here was Jack now, sleeping with his stuffed rabbit in his arms, and Tina next door, so still she almost seemed not to be breathing and gave Alice fright until she detected the gentle movement of her chest. Tina, so strong in personality, would she mind having a sister who would almost certainly be prettier? Alice hung over her elder daughter, willing herself not to think of Charlotte. Not all sisters were rivals, some were very good friends, take Kitty and Edie Morry, for instance. Anyway, there was nothing to be done. Children were individuals and must face their own problems, however much their parents might want to face the problems for them.

Finally, Alice crept by Meg Wynne's room and into Melissa's nursery where Monnie Docherty, the wet nurse, was sleeping beside the crib in a truckle bed. She started up at Alice's entrance and Alice apologised for waking her, she just wanted a peep at the baby.

'Don't be after worrying, ma'am,' Monnie whispered, hoarsely, 'Tis fast asleep she is and am I not here to hear her the minute she wakes?'

Alice pressed her arm and glided away down the stairs to the main landing where she stood looking out into the darkness. From here she could catch the sound of the sea and make out the lights of the fishing boats riding the waves.

Belcarron. She was back in the house that had belonged for so many generations to her family and was now hers. She had stood at this very window and thought of marriage and now had come full circle and stood here as a widow. Crossed the world and come back and nothing had changed and everything had changed, but there were Wintours still at Belcarron. Pray God there always would be. But for herself, she knew if she could hold Richard in her arms again, she would leave Belcarron tomorrow.

'You are exchanging me for Belcarron?' he had once asked.

'No!' she cried now into the darkness, 'No, Richard, never!'

No house, even this one, could replace love. But it was her home, she must take what comfort she could from that.

In her room she washed and changed into her nightgown and said her prayers. When she rose from her knees, the light of her candle caught the glass of Mena's portrait, which she had had framed and hung near her dressing table. How well she remembered her mother painting it. Nora had complained and Mrs Heenan had laughed. 'Now you'll be caught for all time, Mena, pinned on a wall for all to see for ever and ever!'

'No, my poor girl,' Alice thought, 'Not all. Only me.'

She had no portrait of Richard, only a few wedding photographs and brown, fading snapshots, showing him on the estancia with Lucio and the children. Tomorrow, she promised herself, she would have those snapshots framed, she would have them near her on the table by her bed, that bed she looked at now where she had lain long ago and dreamed of Richard, where they had lain together and made love and conceived Melissa.

'I have her,' she murmured, 'And Victor and Jack and Tina. I have Hester. And I have Richard.' Oh, yes, he was near, she sensed him. He was not in her arms, she would never hold him again, but as she had told Hester, they were still together. They always would be. The years ahead would be hard, but she would live them, she would bring up the children, she would keep faith. The bitterness had gone, leaving space for her love. It grew and filled her being, it brought remembered joy.

I'm fortunate, really, she thought, as she climbed into bed.

She reached into the drawer of the little bedside table and took out Richard's letter. As the old house creaked in the night wind and the fishing boats rocked, she moved the candle closer and began to read.

You have been reading a novel published by Piatkus Books. We hope you have enjoyed it and that you would like to read more of our titles. Please ask for them in your local library or bookshop.

If you would like to be put on our mailing list to receive details of new publications, please send a large stamped addressed envelope (UK only) to:

Piatkus Books: 5 Windmill Street
London W1P 1HF

PIATKUS